BADKITTY

Goes to
The Vet

NICK BRUEL

SQUARE
FISH

A NEAL PORTER BOOK
ROARING BROOK PRESS
NEW YORK

SQUARE
FISH

An imprint of Macmillan Publishing Group, LLC
175 Fifth Avenue
New York, NY 10010
mackids.com

Our books may be purchased in bulk for promotional, educational, or business use. Please
contact your local bookseller or the Macmillan Corporate and Premium Sales Department at
(800) 221-7945 ext. 5442 or by e-mail at MacmillanSpecialMarkets@macmillan.com.

Library of Congress Cataloging-in-Publication Data

Bruel, Nick.
    Bad kitty goes to the vet / Nick Bruel.
        pages cm. — (Bad kitty)
    "A Neal Porter Book."
    Summary: "Even the best bad kitties can get sick, and when it happens, it means just one
thing: a visit to the vet!"— Provided by publisher.
    ISBN 978-1-250-10380-2 (paperback)
[1. Cats—Fiction. 2. Veterinarians—Fiction. 3. Humorous stories.] I. Title.
    PZ7.B82832Baj 2016
    [E]—dc23
                                                                                2015014997

Special Book Fair Edition ISBN 978-1-62672-580-5

Originally published in the United States by Neal Porter Books/Roaring Brook Press
First Square Fish Edition: 2017
Square Fish logo designed by Filomena Tuosto

3 5 7 9 10 8 6 4

AR: 3.4 / LEXILE: 600L

• CONTENTS •

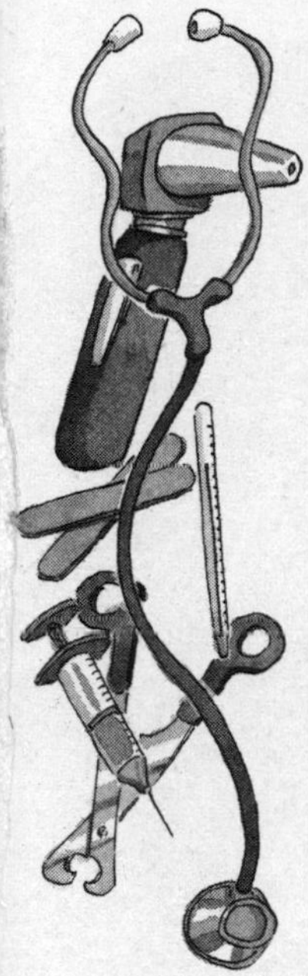

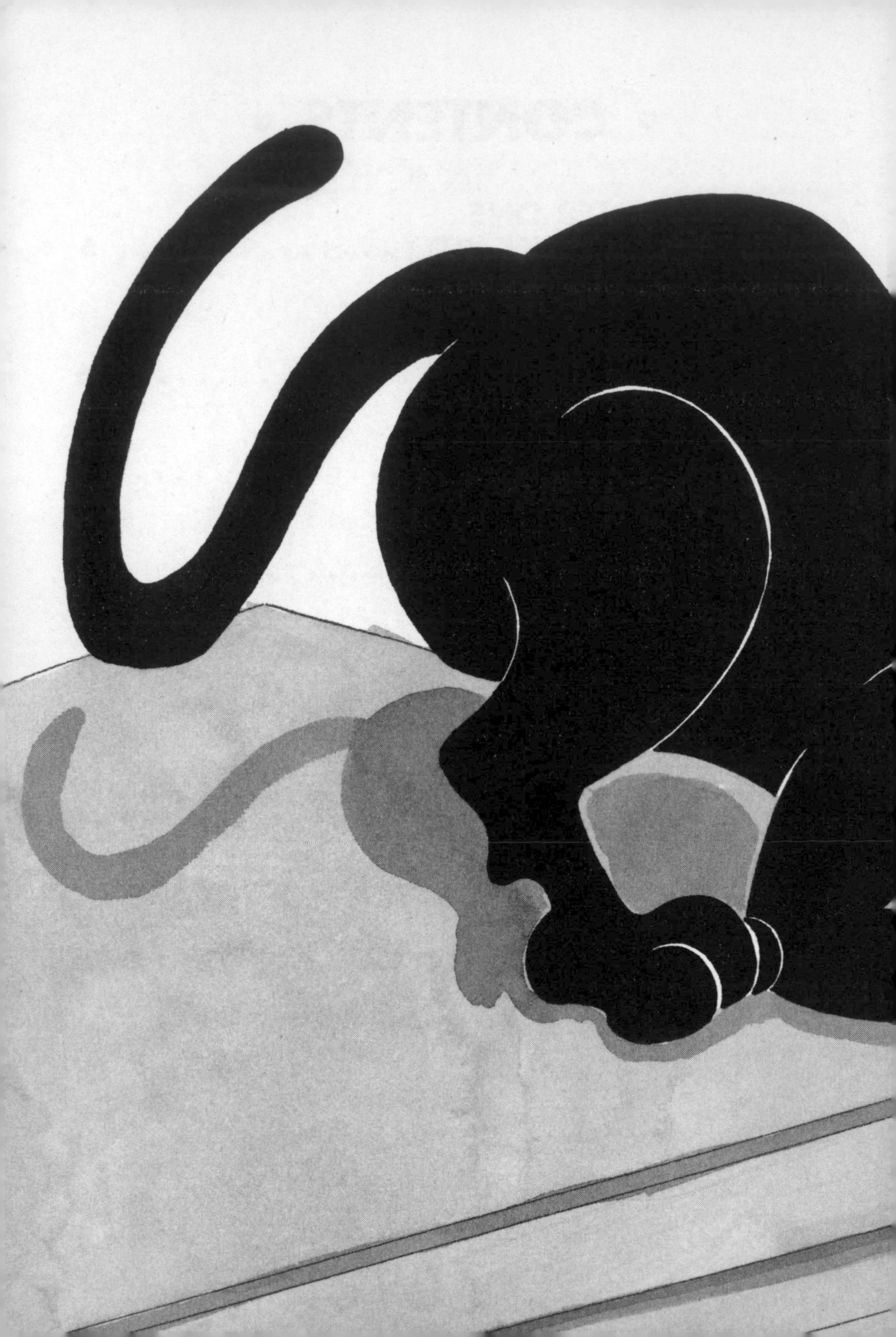

•CHAPTER ONE•

POOR, SICK KITTY

This is what Kitty looks like when she's a happy, healthy pussycat.

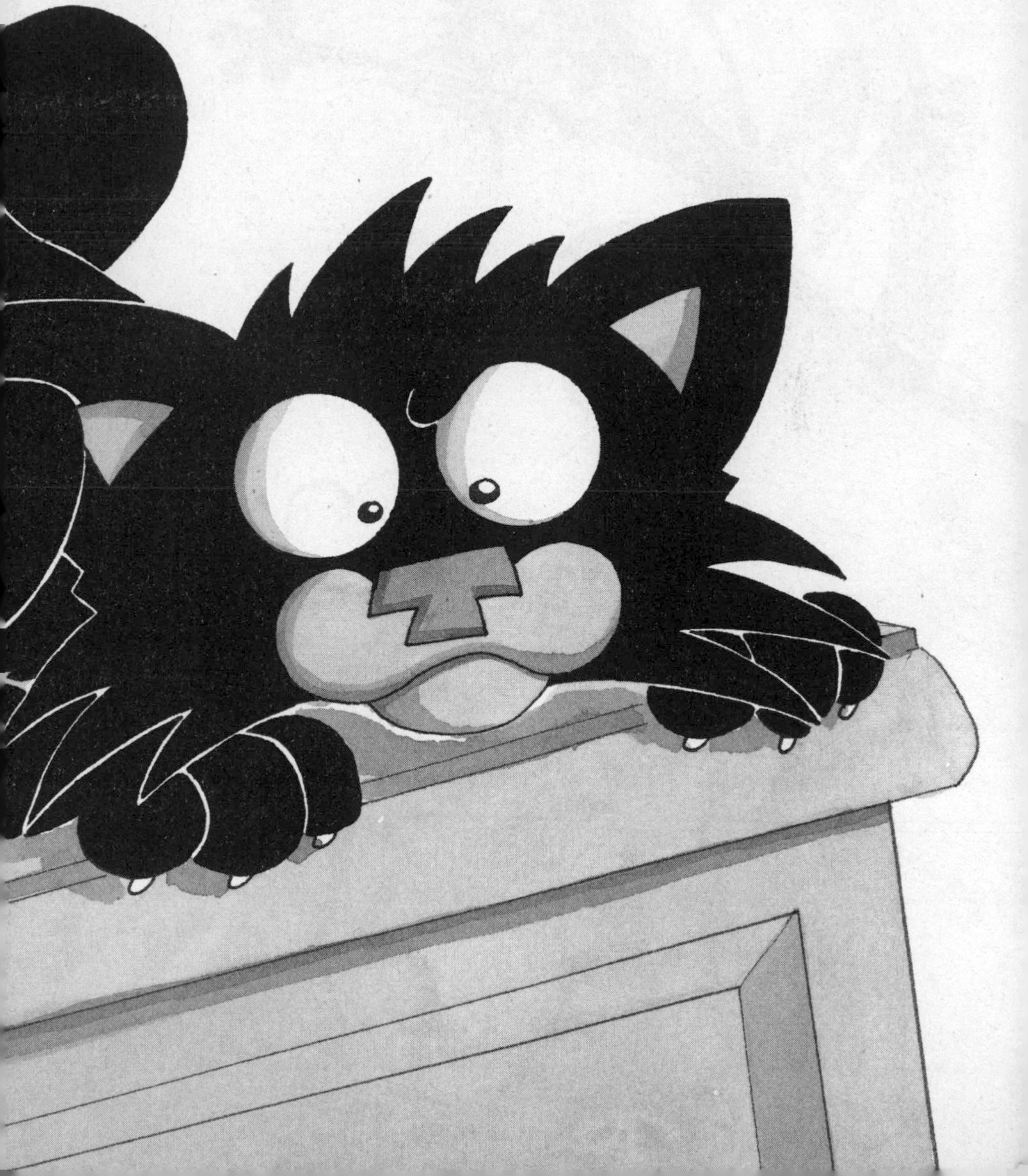

She has lots of energy.

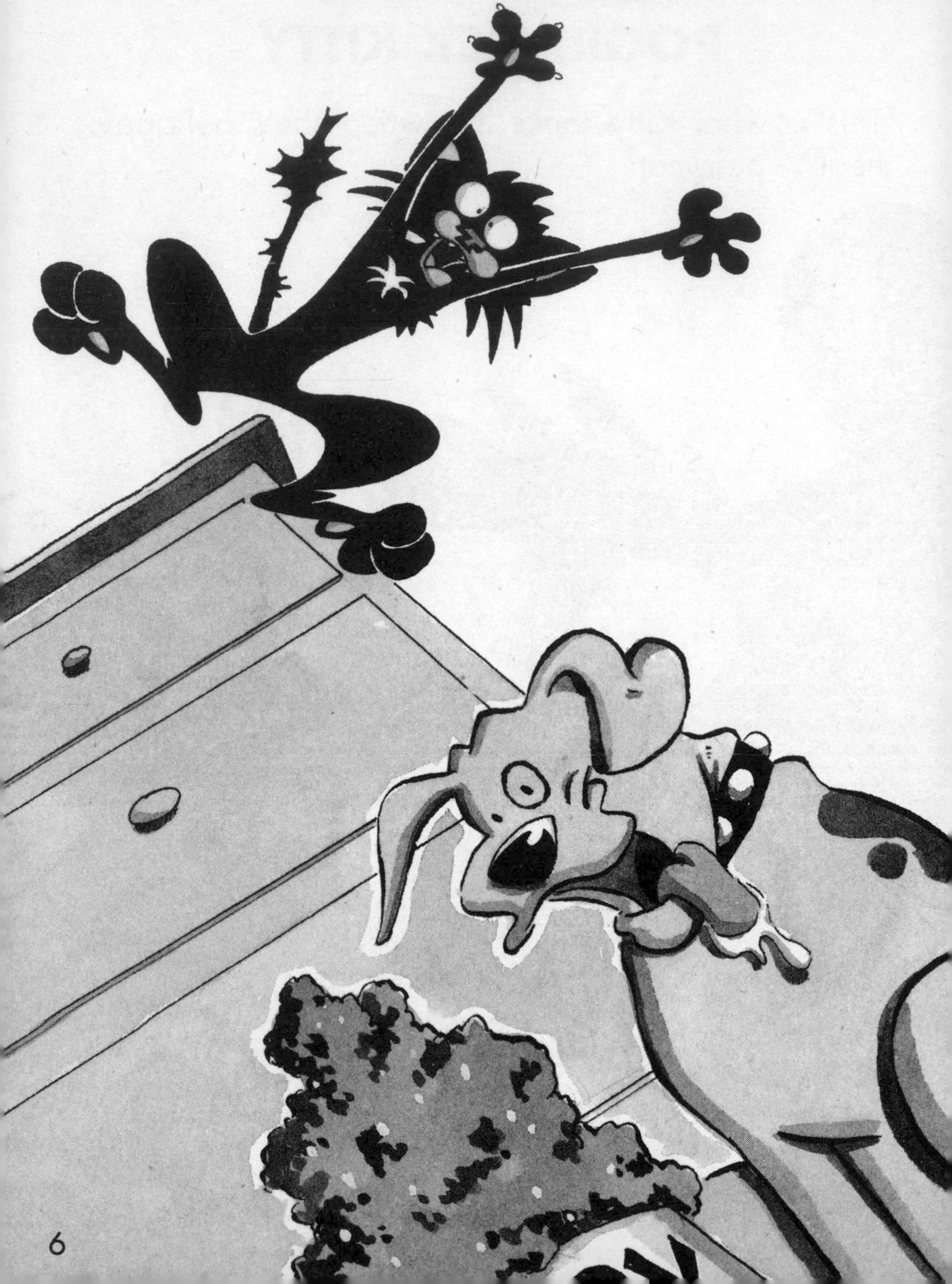

She has a good appetite.

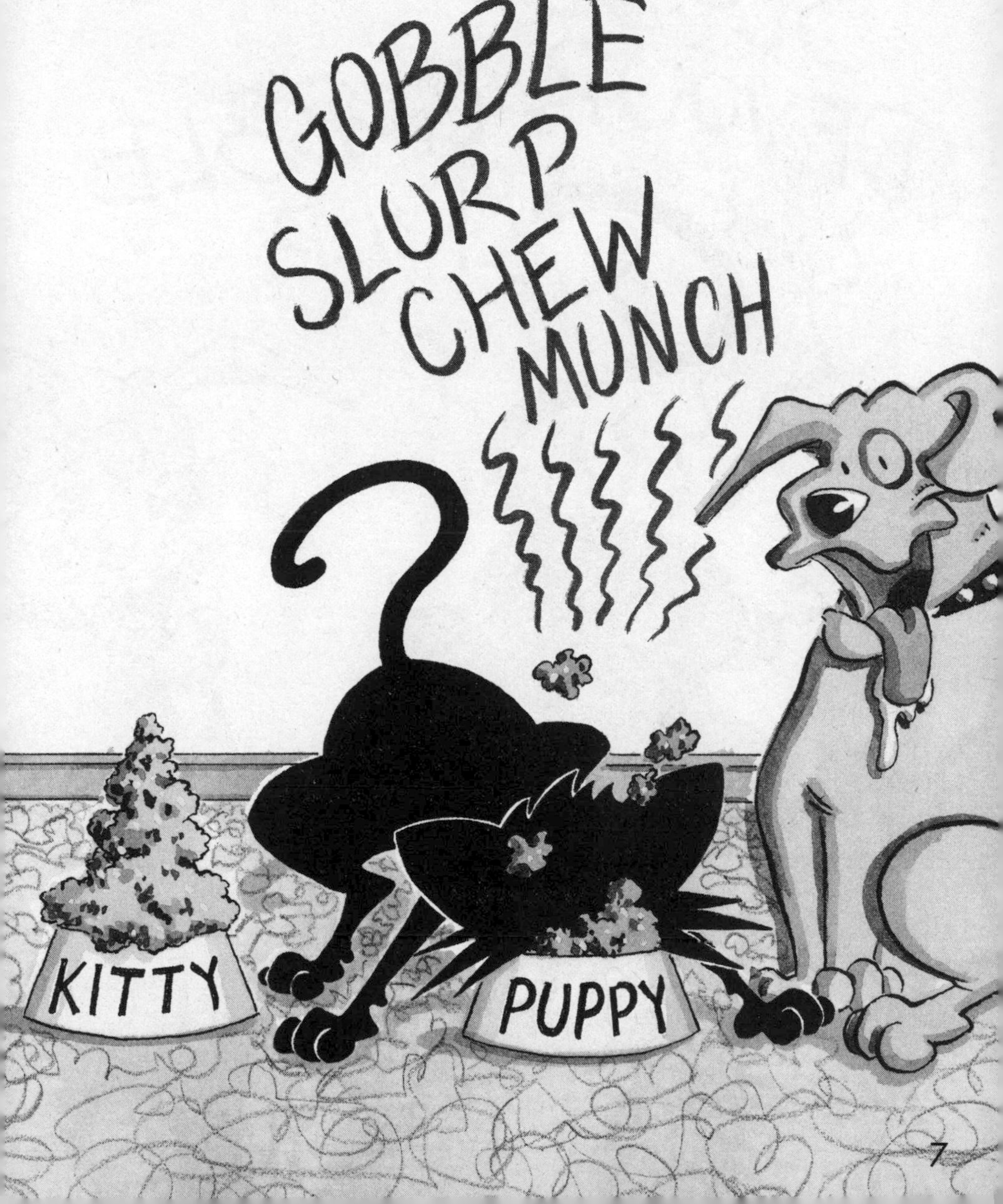
GOBBLE
SLURP
CHEW
MUNCH
KITTY
PUPPY

She has a really, REALLY good appetite.

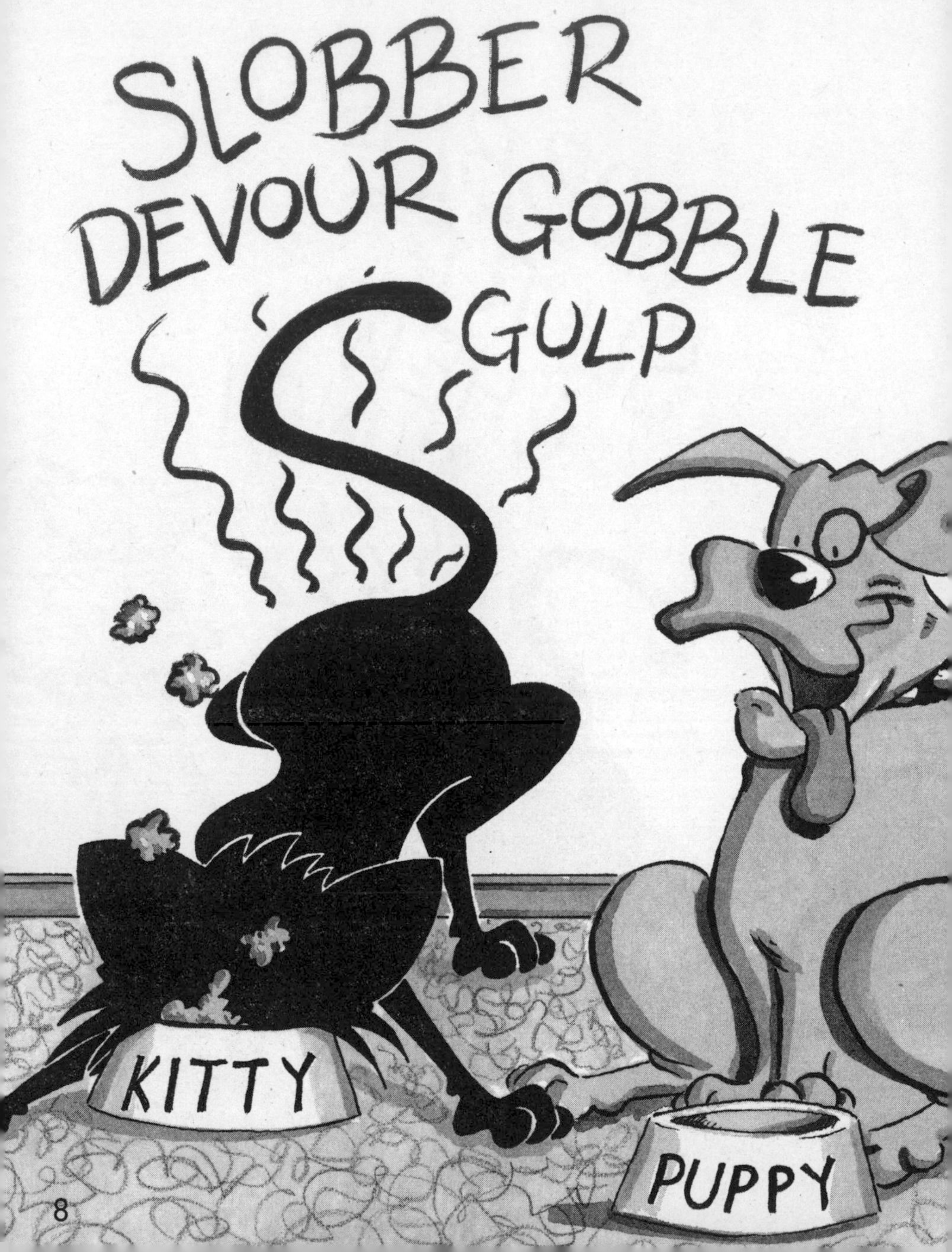
SLOBBER
DEVOUR
GOBBLE
GULP
KITTY
PUPPY

And she keeps herself nice and clean.

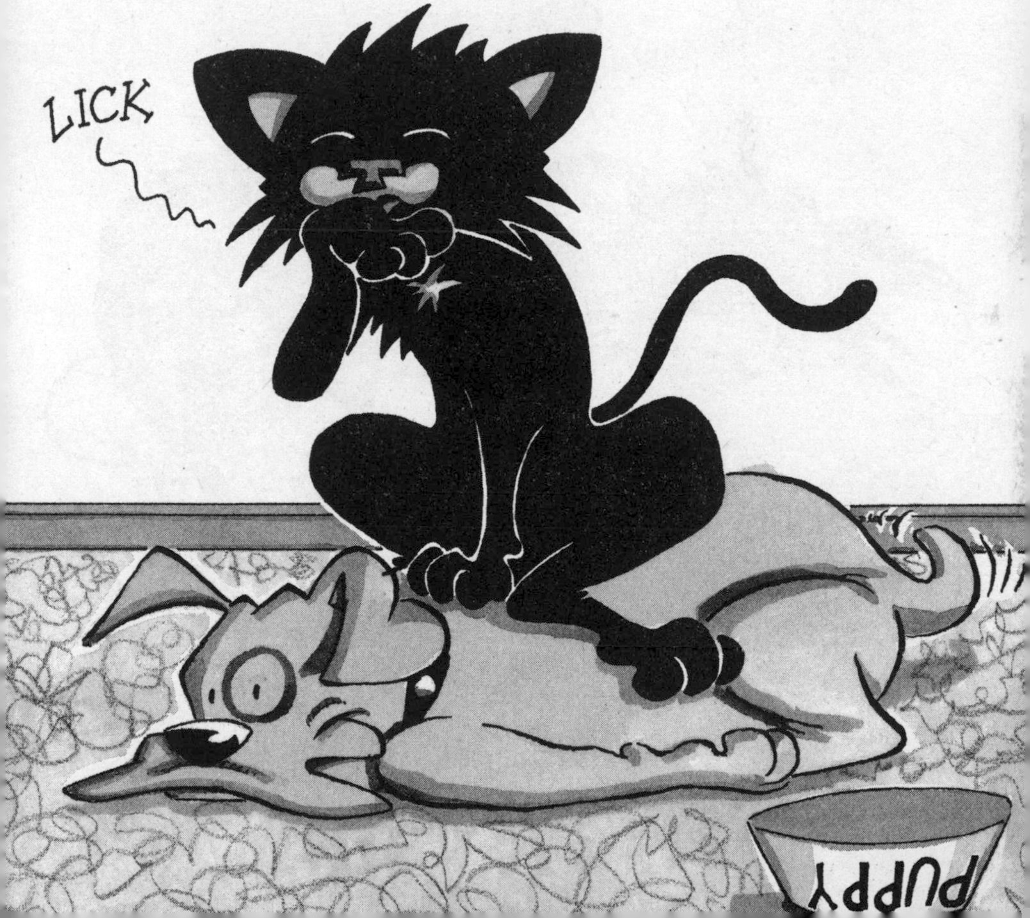
LICK
PUPPY

But that's not how Kitty looks today. She looks terrible. She looks tired. She looks unhappy. She does not look healthy at all.

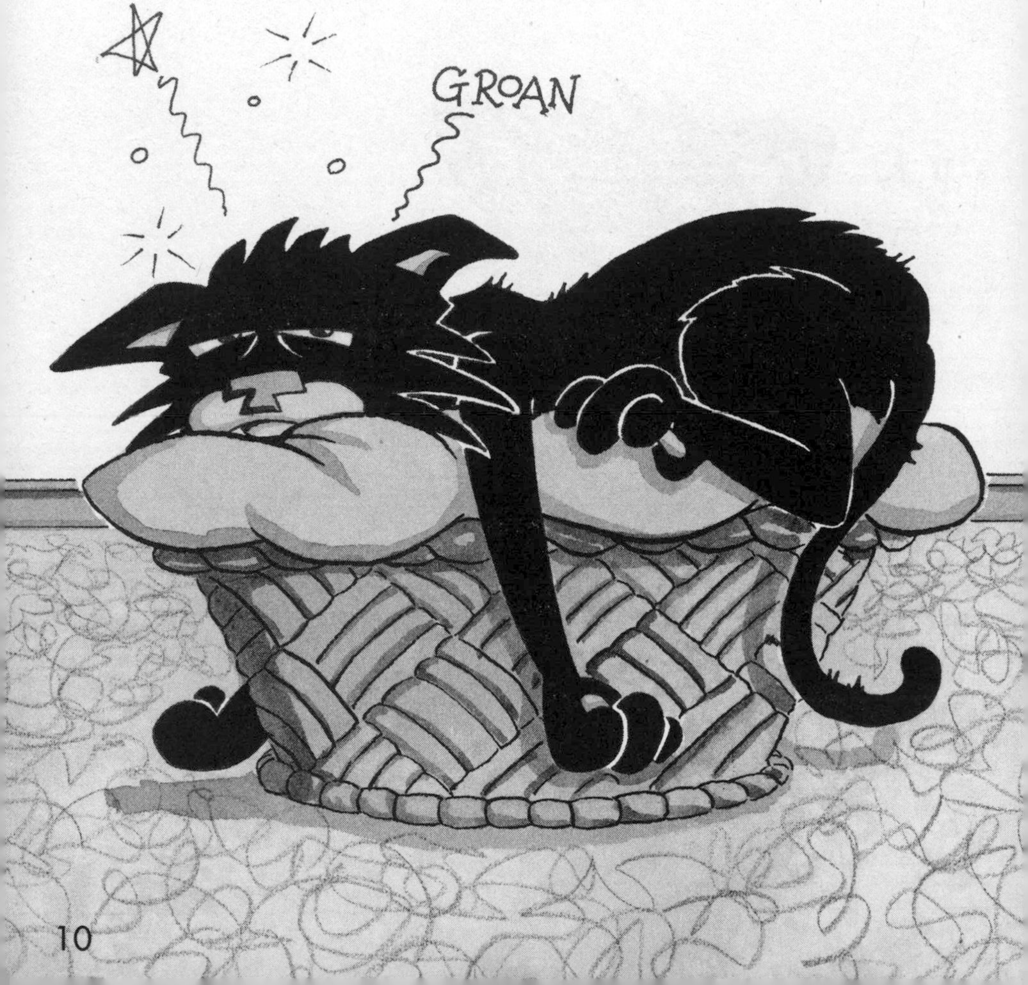
GROAN

And worst of all . . . Kitty is just not eating her food.

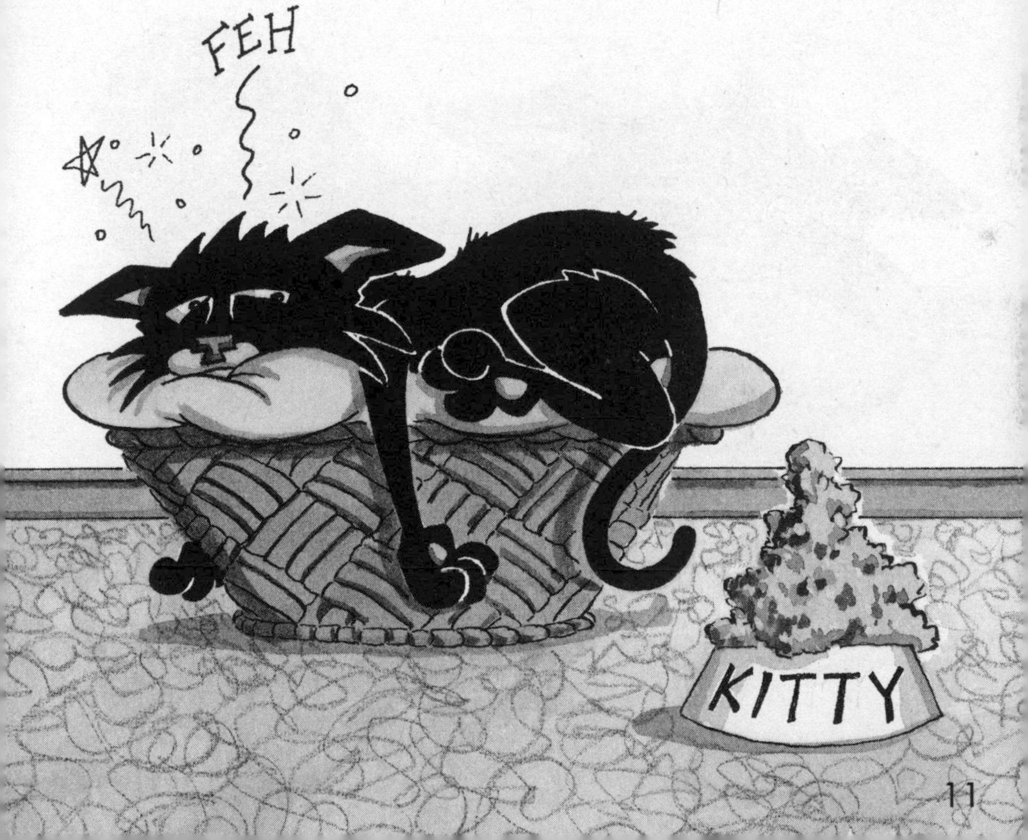
FEH
KITTY

Kitty, I don't understand why you're not eating. I've watched grown men cry trying to beat you at a hot dog eating contest. I once saw you swallow an entire liver and pineapple pizza in one gulp. I've seen you consume an entire meatloaf the size of a car in just five minutes. It was horrifying.

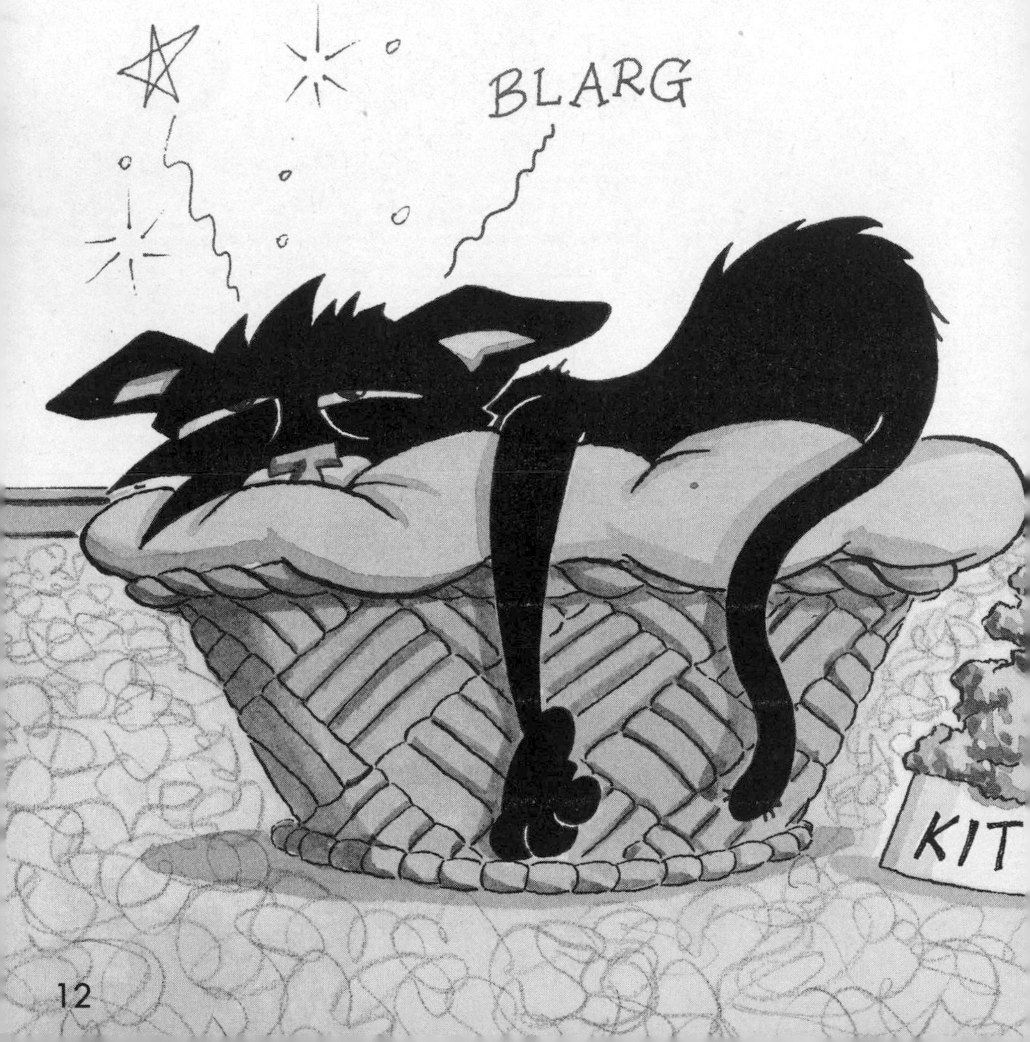
BLARG
KIT

This is the warning poster that hangs over the meat counter of every grocery store in the county.

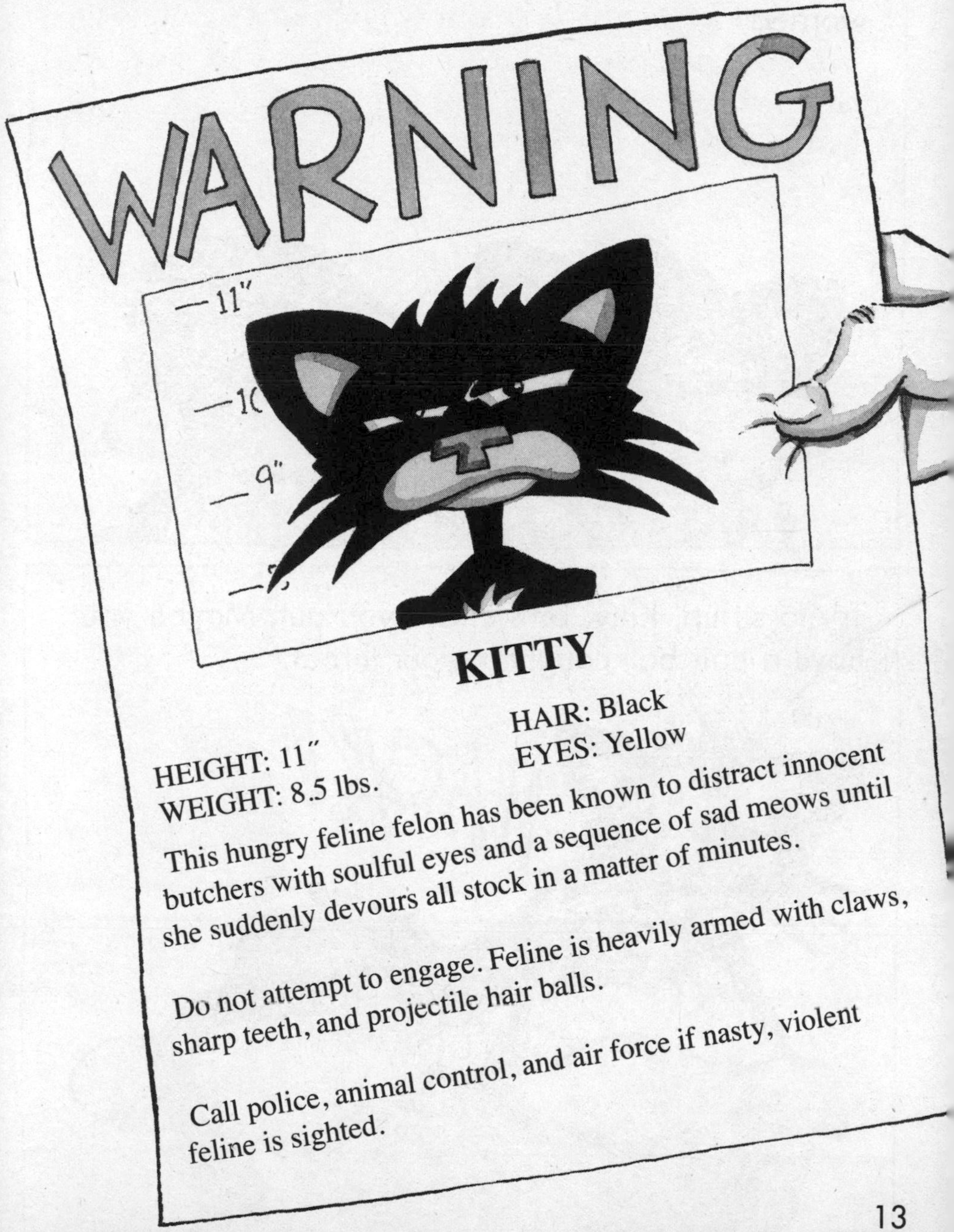
WARNING
11"
10
9"
KITTY
HAIR: Black
EYES: Yellow
HEIGHT: 11"
WEIGHT: 8.5 lbs.
This hungry feline felon has been known to distract innocent butchers with soulful eyes and a sequence of sad meows until she suddenly devours all stock in a matter of minutes.
Do not attempt to engage. Feline is heavily armed with claws, sharp teeth, and projectile hair balls.
Call police, animal control, and air force if nasty, violent feline is sighted.

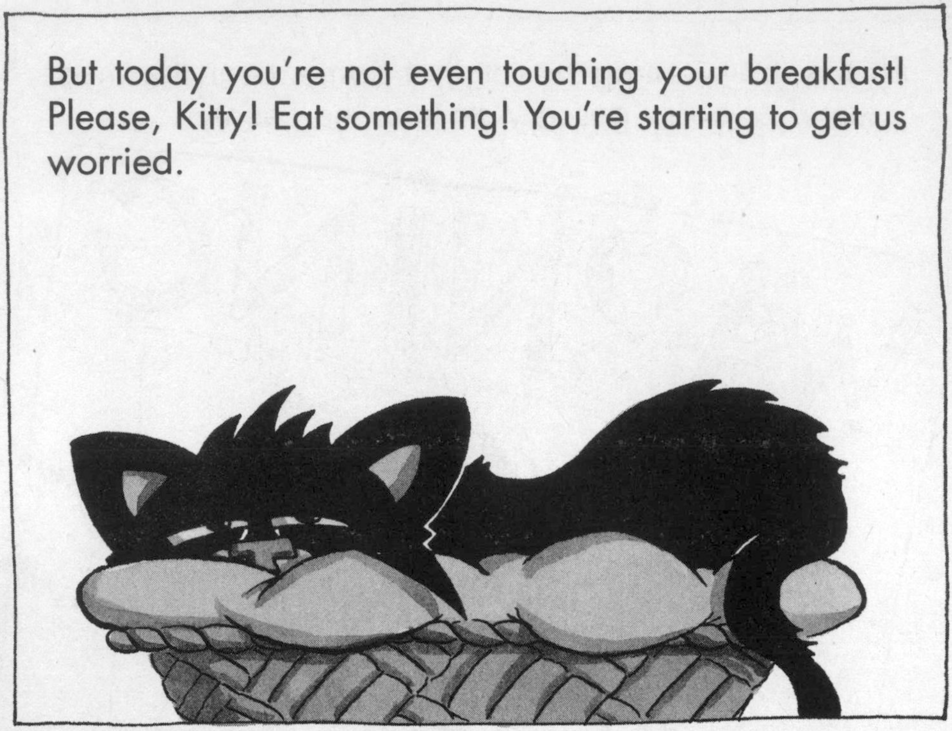
But today you're not even touching your breakfast! Please, Kitty! Eat something! You're starting to get us worried.

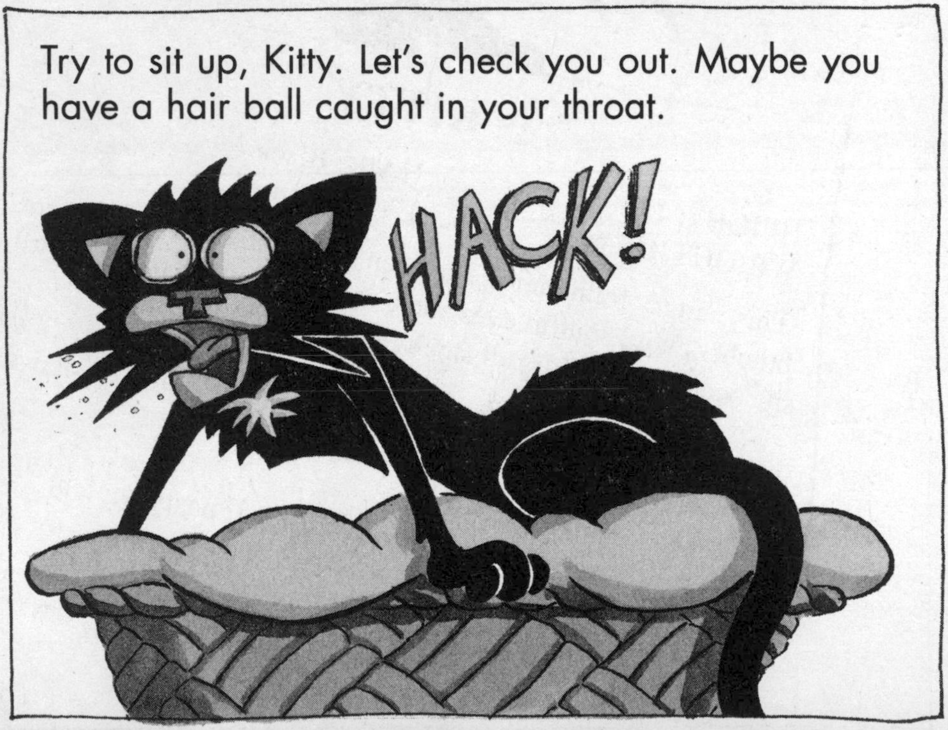
Try to sit up, Kitty. Let's check you out. Maybe you have a hair ball caught in your throat.
HACK!

Nothing? Hmmmm . . . I think I should feel your belly just to see if you have any lumps.

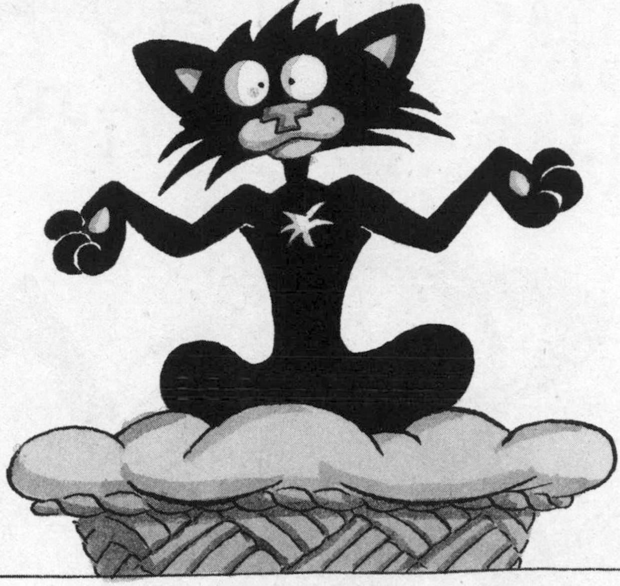

Hold still, Kitty. I promise this won't hurt one bit.

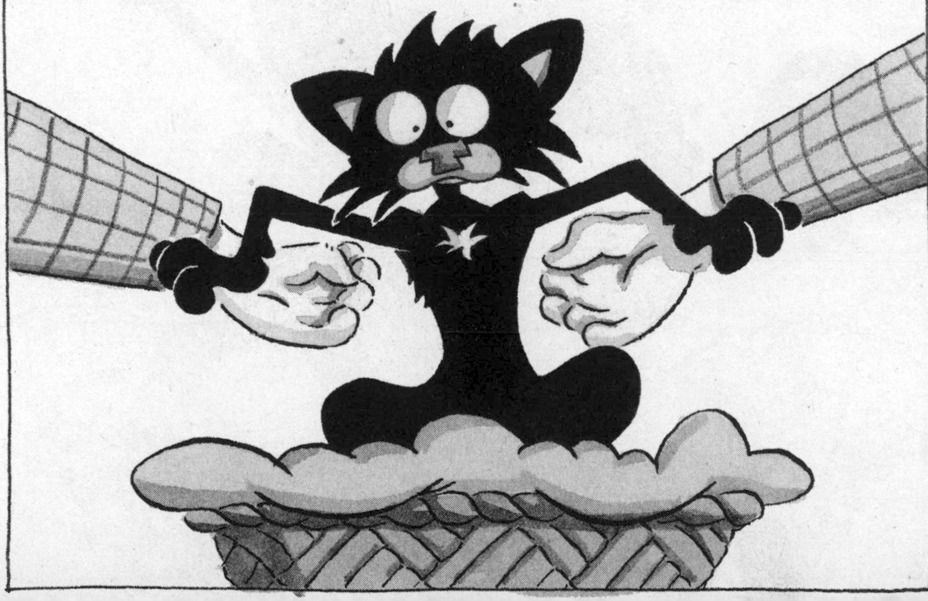

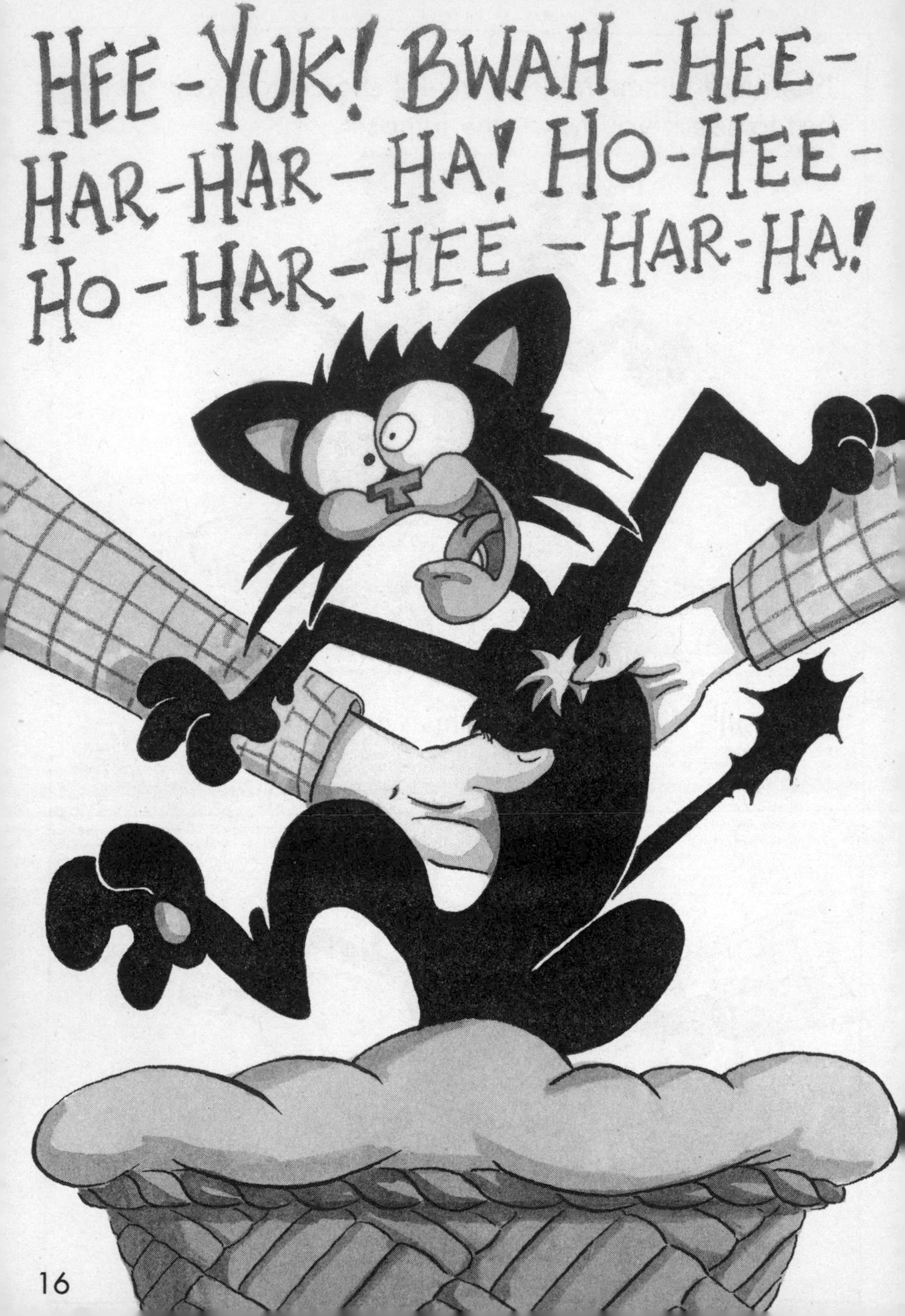
HEE-YUK! BWAH-HEE-HAR-HAR-HA! HO-HEE-HO-HAR-HEE-HAR-HA!

Sorry about that, Kitty. I honestly had no idea you were so ticklish.

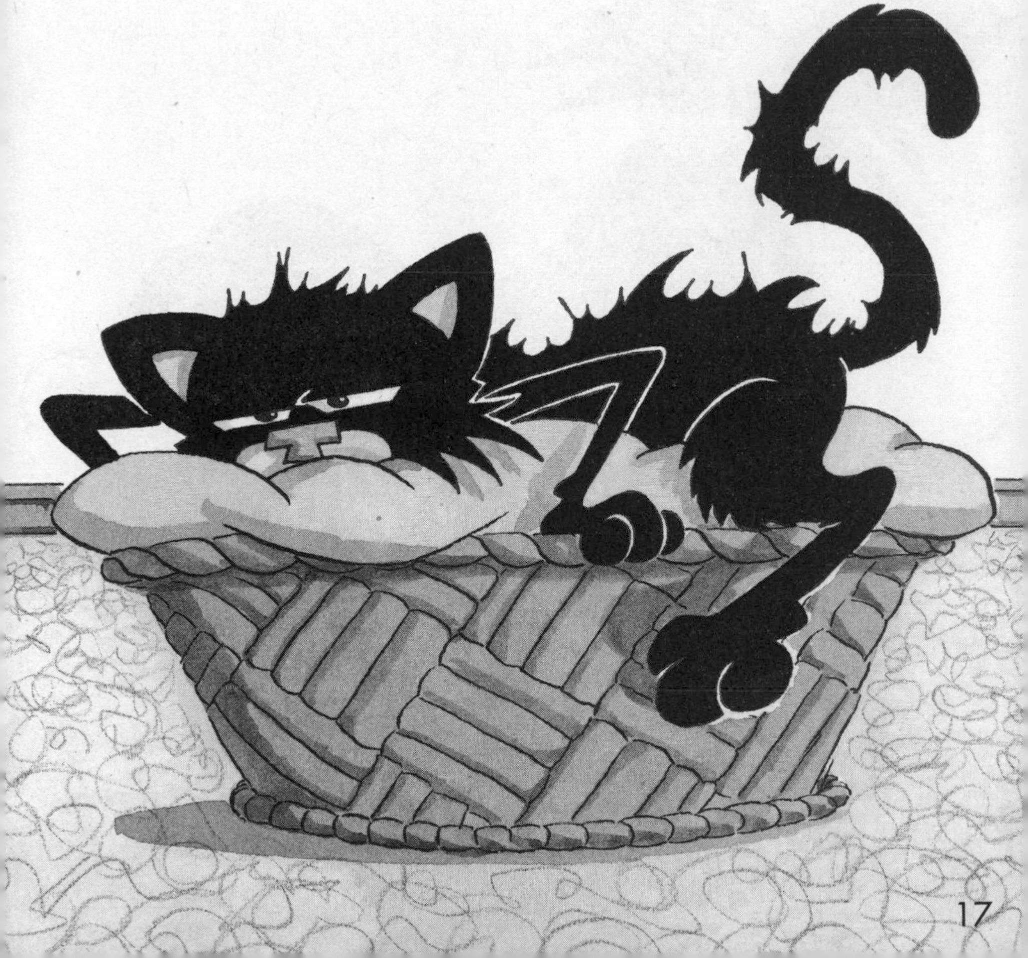

I think that maybe it's time to take your temperature, Kitty.

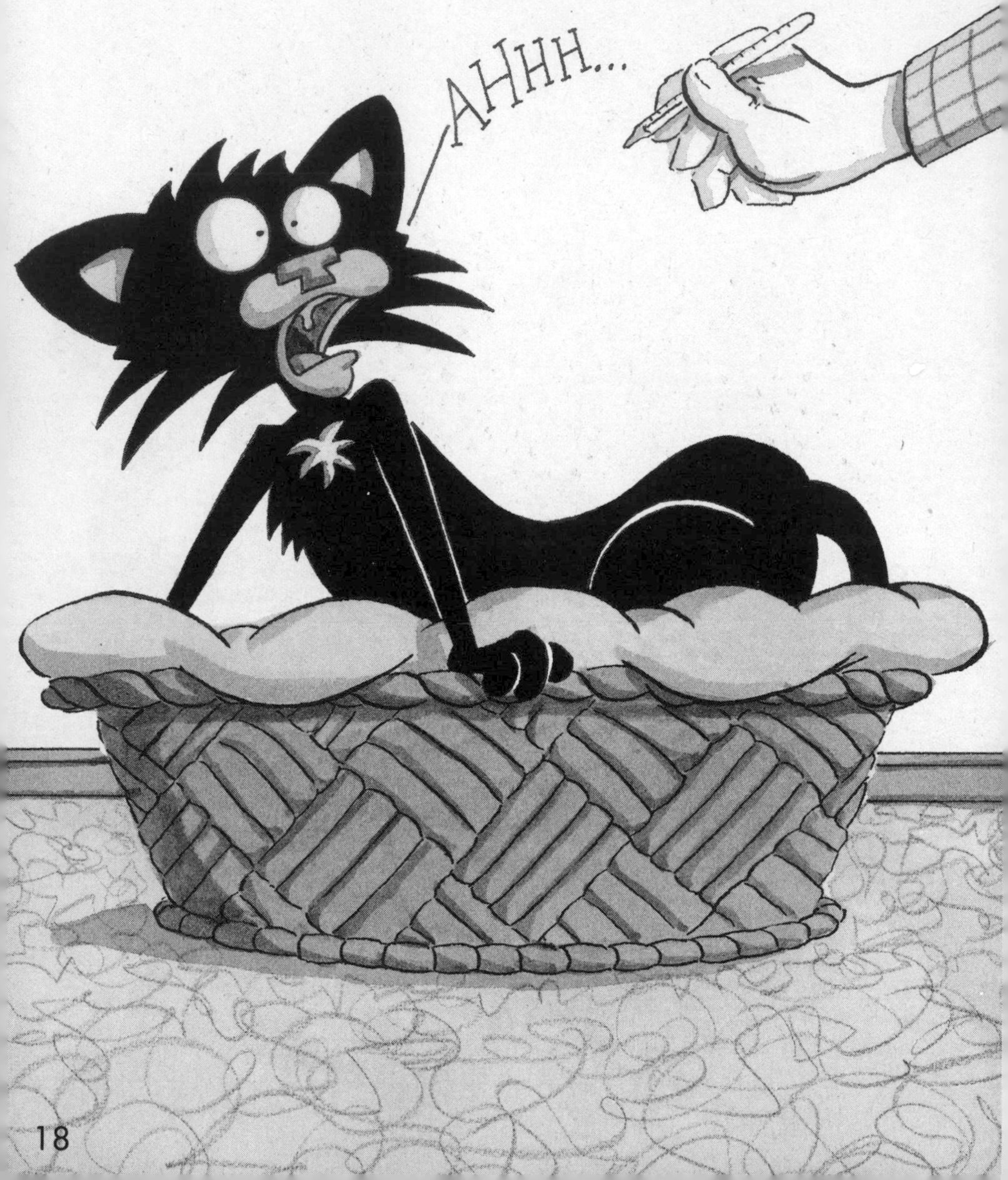
AHHH...

Uhhhh . . . Sorry, Kitty. It's not that kind of thermometer.

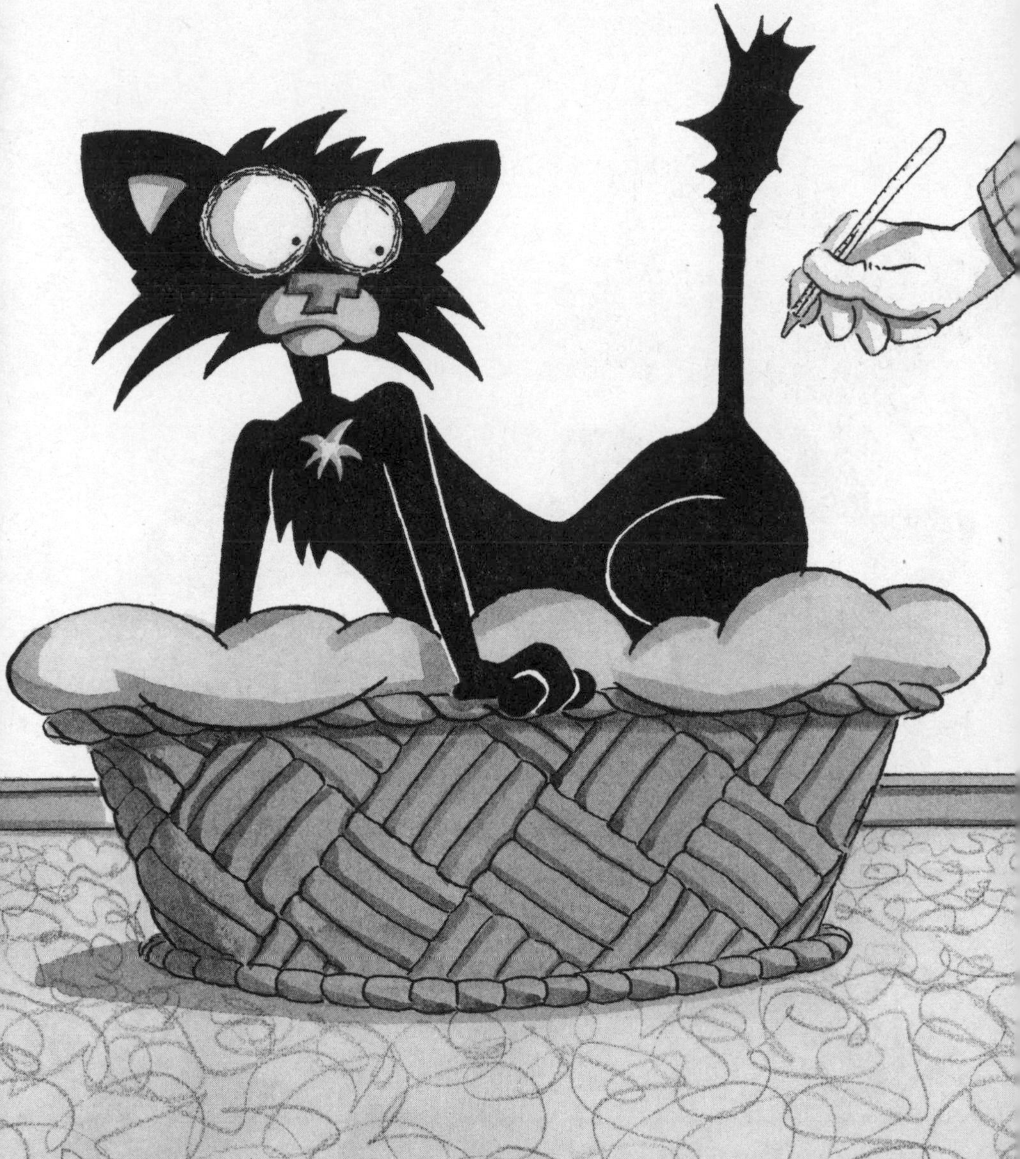

That is not helpful, Kitty.

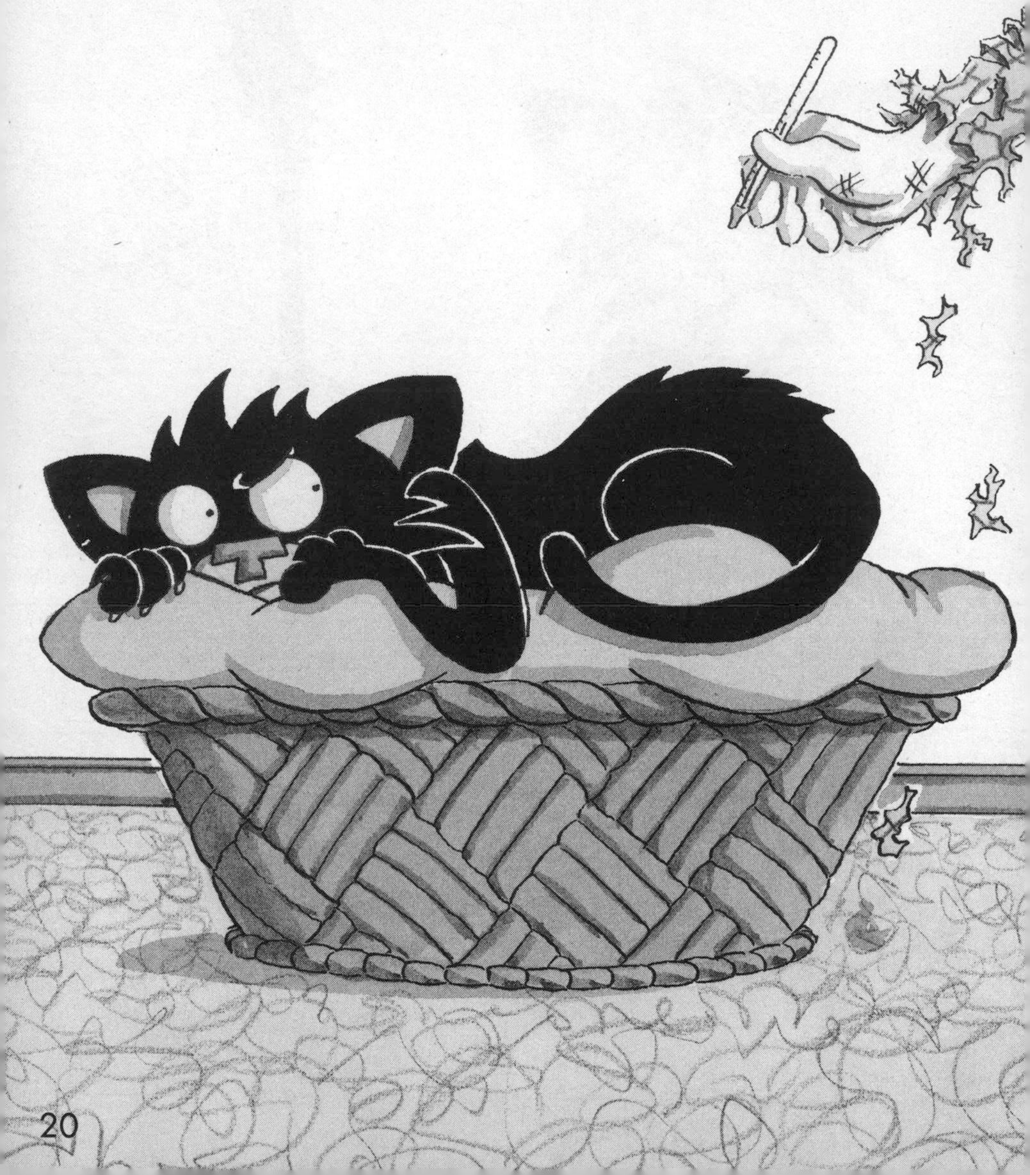

Look, Kitty, you're obviously not feeling well, and we have no idea what's wrong. But we know that something IS wrong. It could be serious. It could be nothing. But if you're not going to let me take your temperature, then someone else will have to.

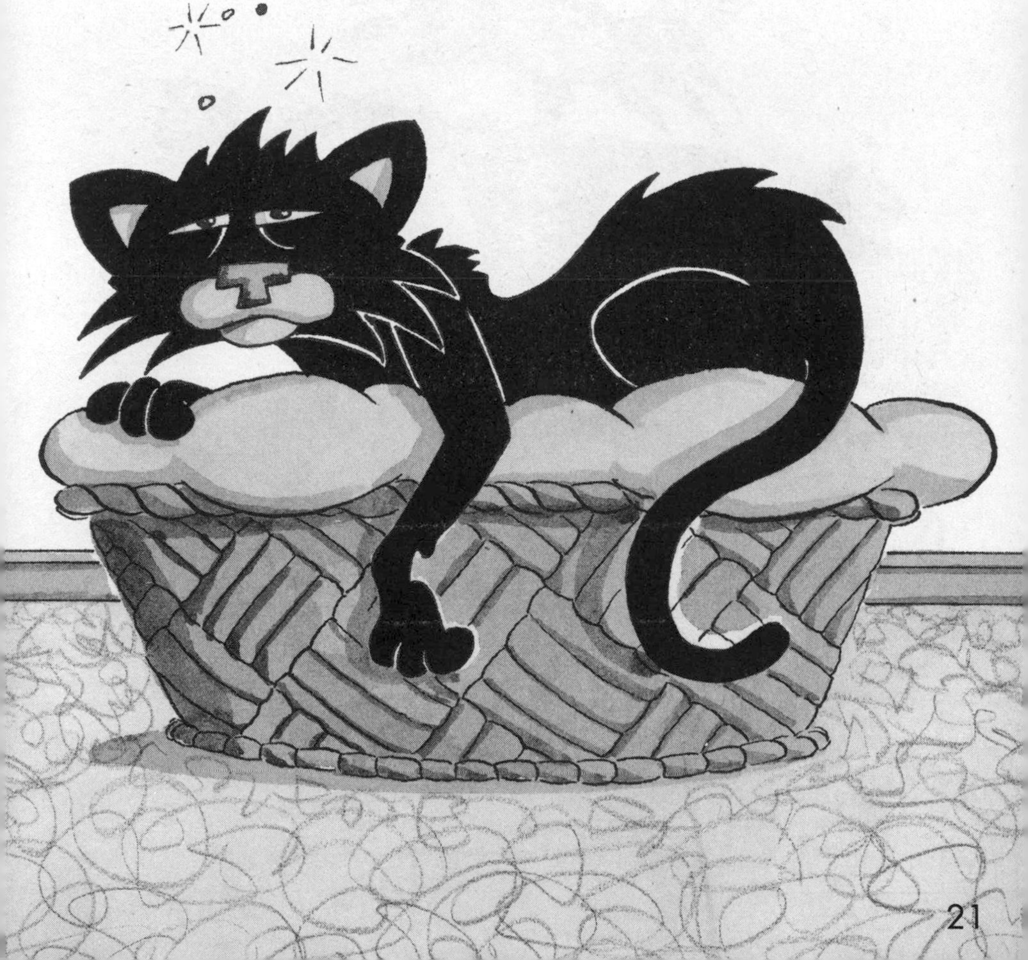

I guess we're just going to have to take you to the . . .

VET.

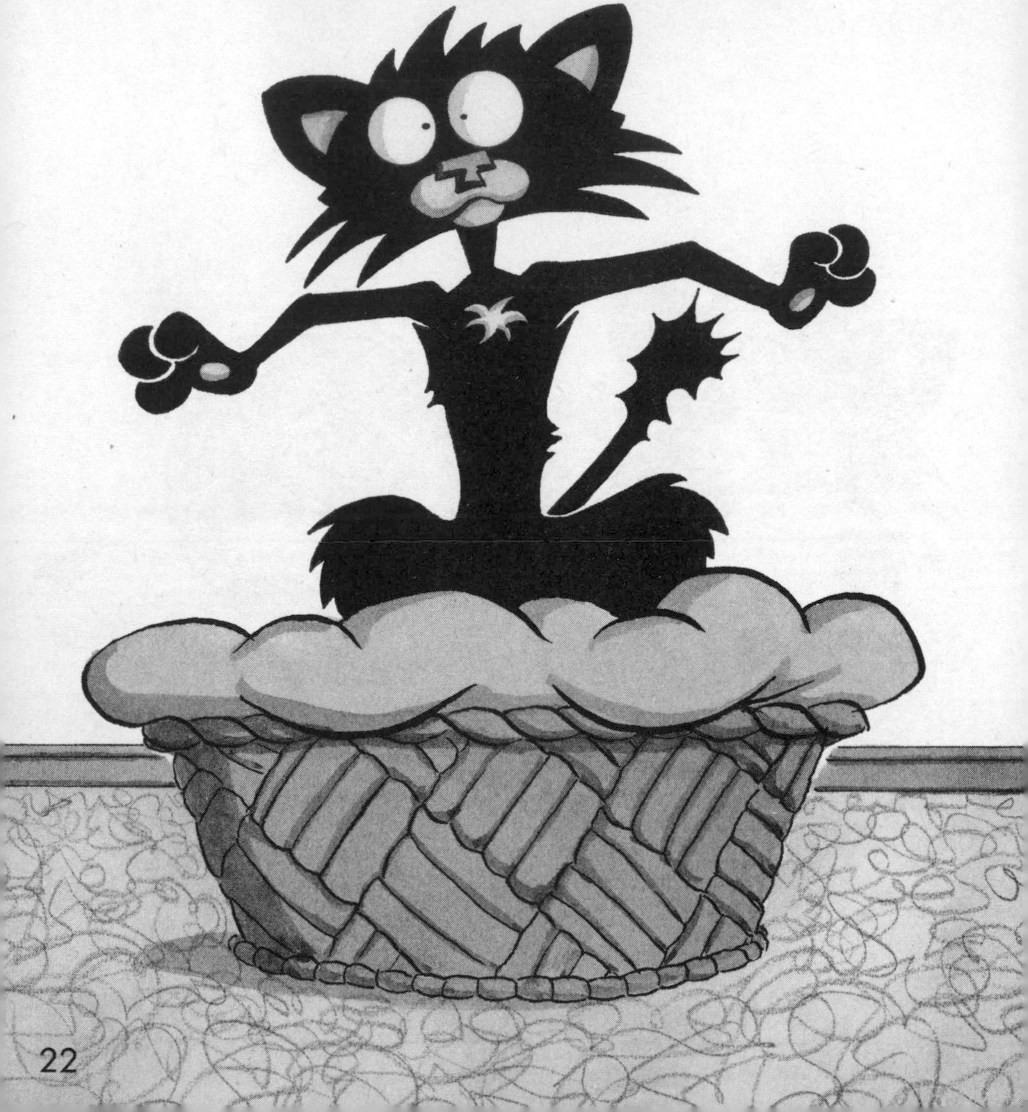

Great.
Well, I guess she has a little energy left in her after all.

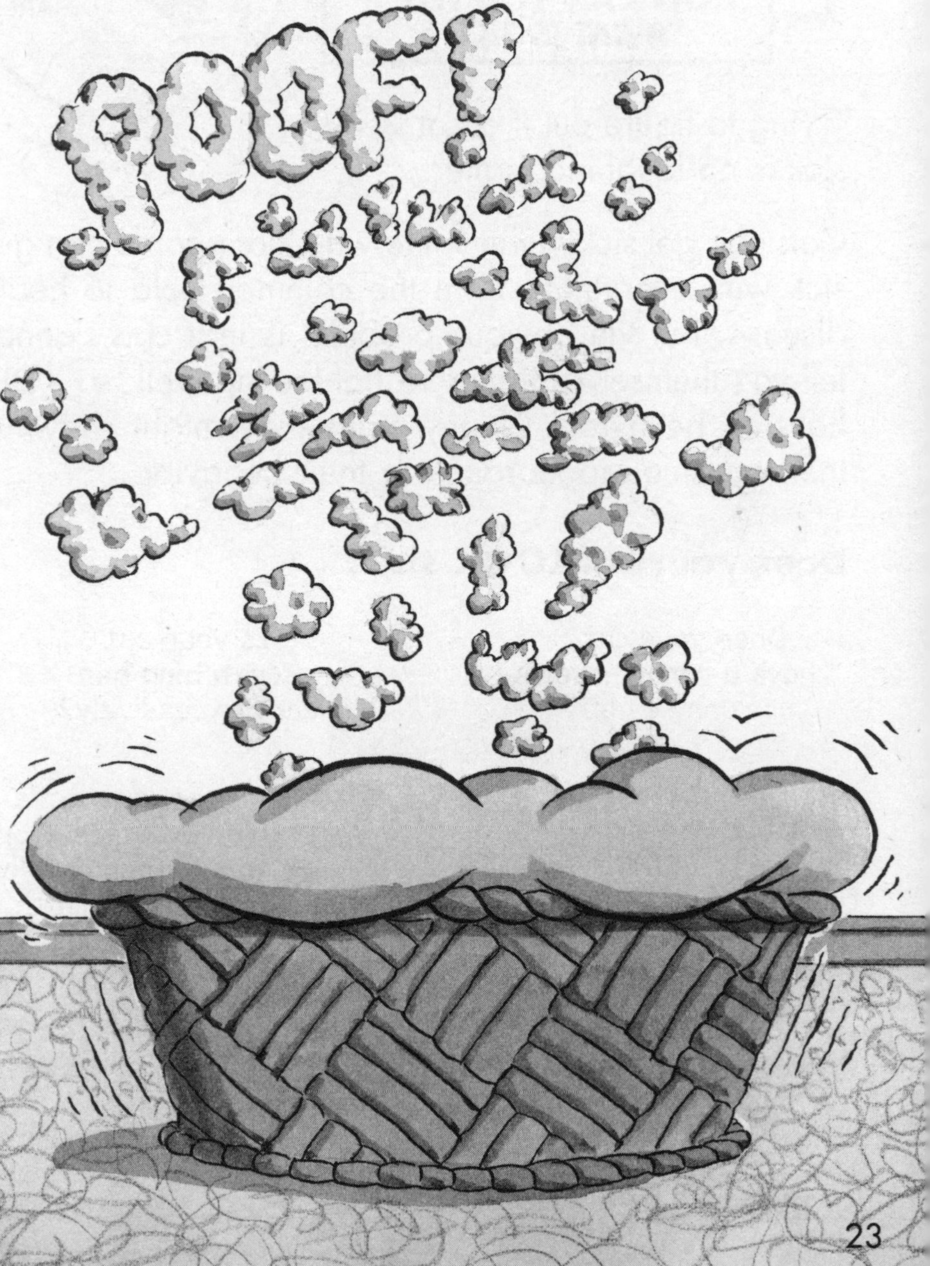
POOF!

UNCLE MURRAY'S FUN FACTS

HOW CAN YOU TELL IF A CAT IS SICK?

They're all pretty sick in the head if you ask me! HAR! HAR!

Trying to figure out if a cat is sick is no laughing matter.

Sorry.

Cats can get sick in the same way that people can get sick with everything from the common cold to heart disease. But the obvious problem is that cats cannot tell you themselves if they're not feeling well, so YOU have to be aware of any signs they might show in their physical appearance or their behavior.

Does your cat LOOK sick?

Does your cat have a runny nose or runny eyes?

Is your cat scratching her ears excessively?

When you pet your cat, do you feel odd bumps under her fur or her skin?

Does your cat's fur look messy or dirty when usually it looks smooth and clean?

Is your cat breathing funny?

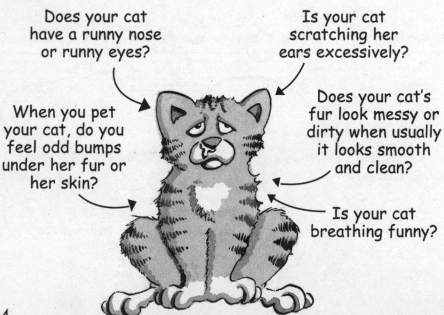

Is your cat ACTING sick?

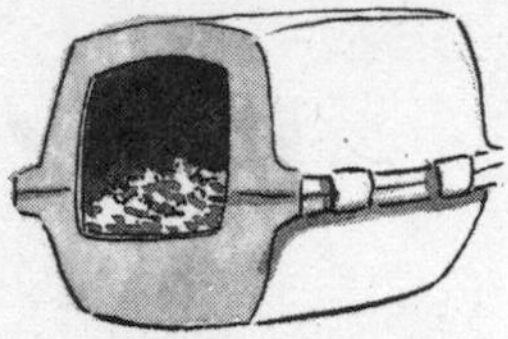

- Is your cat using the litter box a lot more or a lot less than usual?
- Is your cat acting dizzy or is she tilting her head to one side a lot?

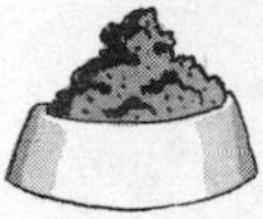

- Is your cat not eating or even losing weight?

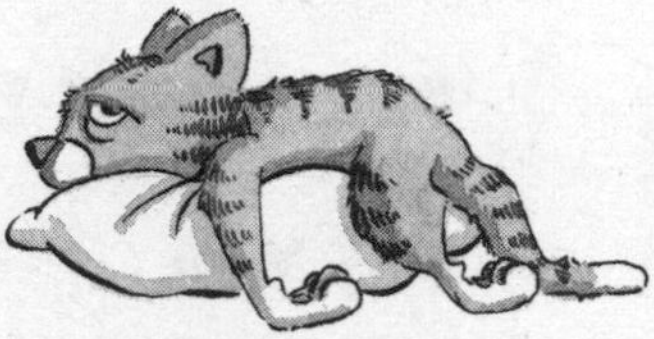

- Look for any sudden change in your cat's personality. If your cat is very active one day but acts unusually tired the next day, there might be a problem.

Sometimes cats will get better all on their own—just like people. But sometimes the problem can be quite serious.

If you even THINK your cat might be sick, the safest thing to do is bring her to an expert who can figure out what is wrong and what to do. And that expert is a veterinarian.

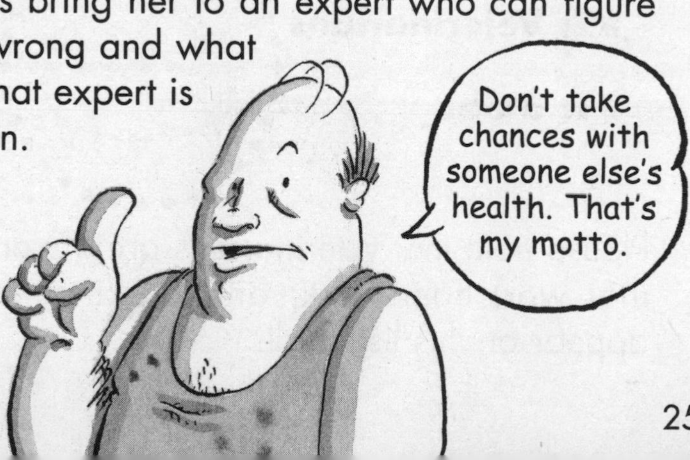
Don't take chances with someone else's health. That's my motto.

•CHAPTER TWO•

HOW TO TAKE KITTY TO THE VET

The following is a list of the Top 10 things cats hate the most.

#10: Spiders

#9: Empty Bowls

#8: Closed Doors

#7: You

#6: Doorbells

#5: Nail Clippers

#4: Other Cats

#3: Dogs

#2: Veterinarians

#1: Baths

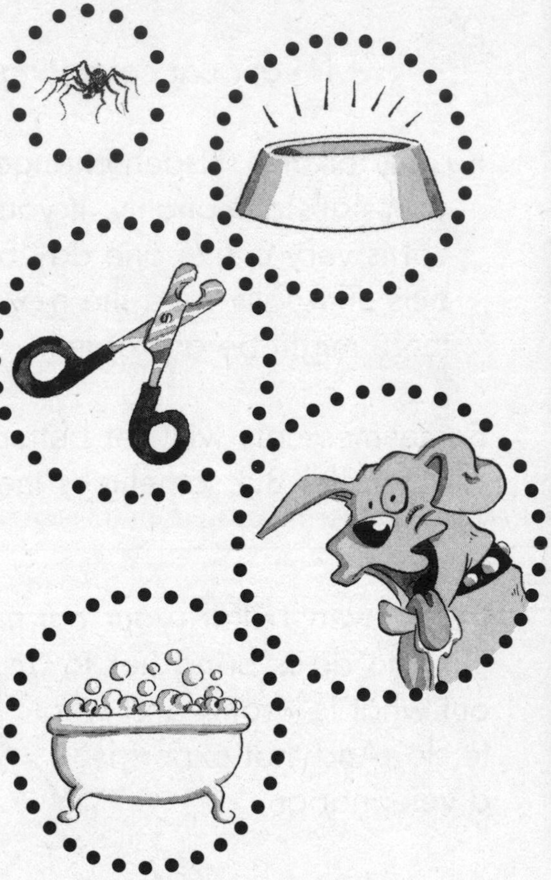

Please note that veterinarians are #2 on this list and that war, homework, and parking tickets do not appear on this list at all.

This means that when it's time for your cat to go to the vet, your cat will really, really, really (*insert the word "really" 1,394,291 more times here*) not want to go to the vet.

This is what happened the last three times we brought Kitty to the vet.

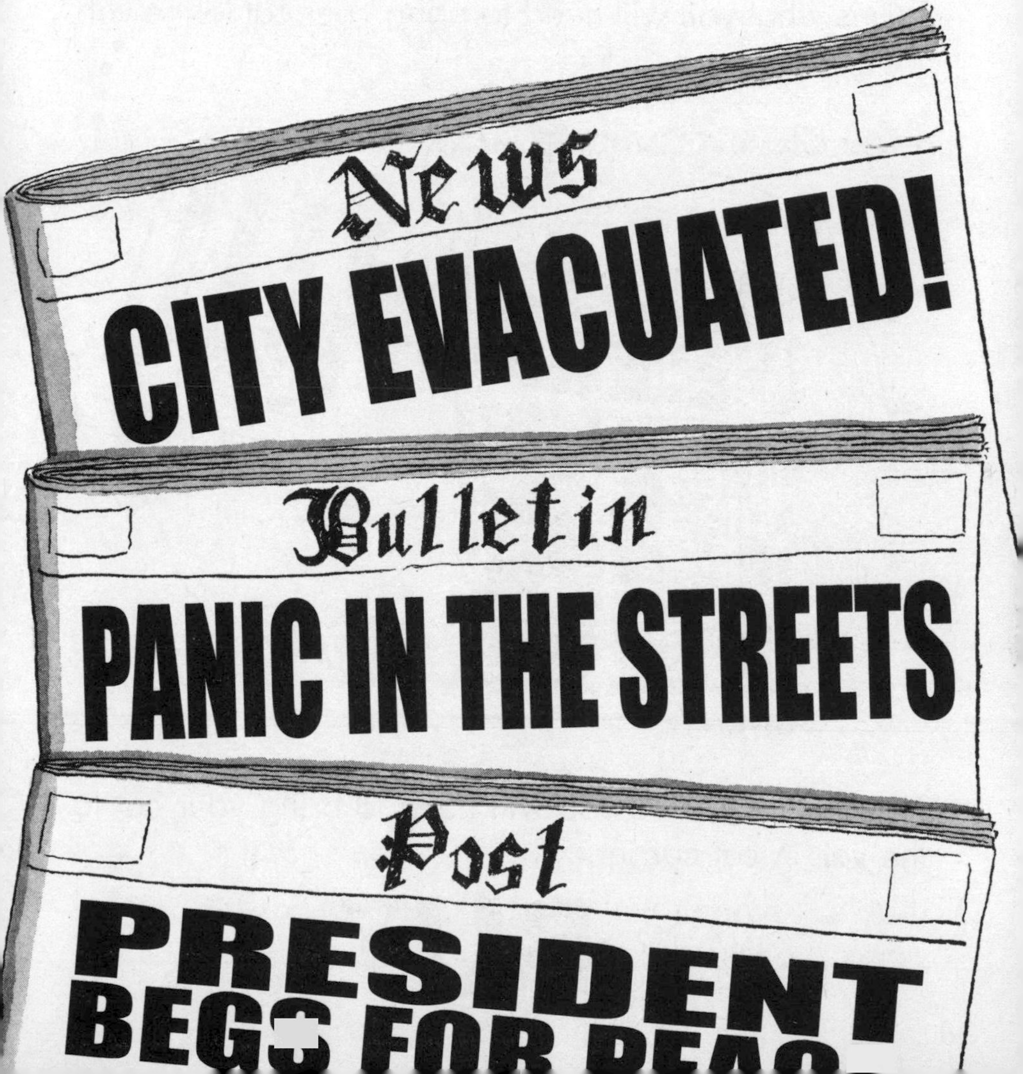
News
CITY EVACUATED!
Bulletin
PANIC IN THE STREETS
Post
PRESIDENT

Please follow these five very important steps when taking a cat to the vet so you can both come out of this alive. Well . . . mostly so YOU can come out of this alive.

•STEP ONE•
GATHER YOUR EQUIPMENT

This is what you will need to bring your cat to the vet.

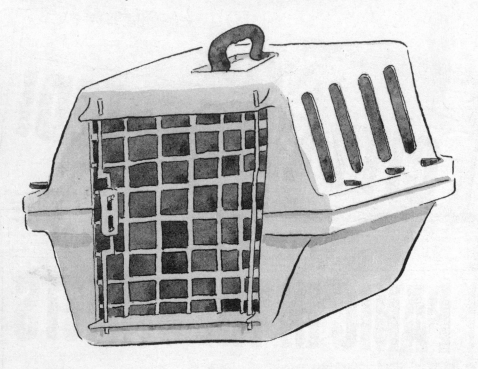

That's it. That is all you will need to bring your cat to the vet. A cat carrier.

BUT . . .

The following is what you will need to get your cat **INTO** the cat carrier . . .

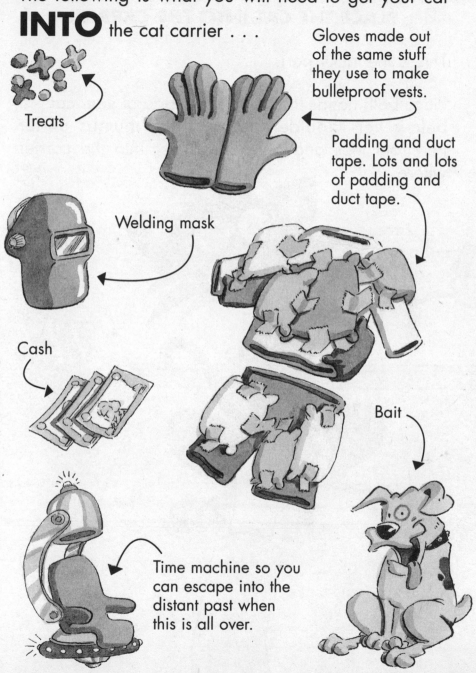

Treats

Gloves made out of the same stuff they use to make bulletproof vests.

Padding and duct tape. Lots and lots of padding and duct tape.

Welding mask

Cash

Bait

Time machine so you can escape into the distant past when this is all over.

•STEP TWO•
PLACE THE CAT INTO THE CARRIER

This is the tricky part.

Place both hands firmly on either side of your cat just below her shoulders. Hook your thumbs under her front legs and gently lead her into the carrier where . . .

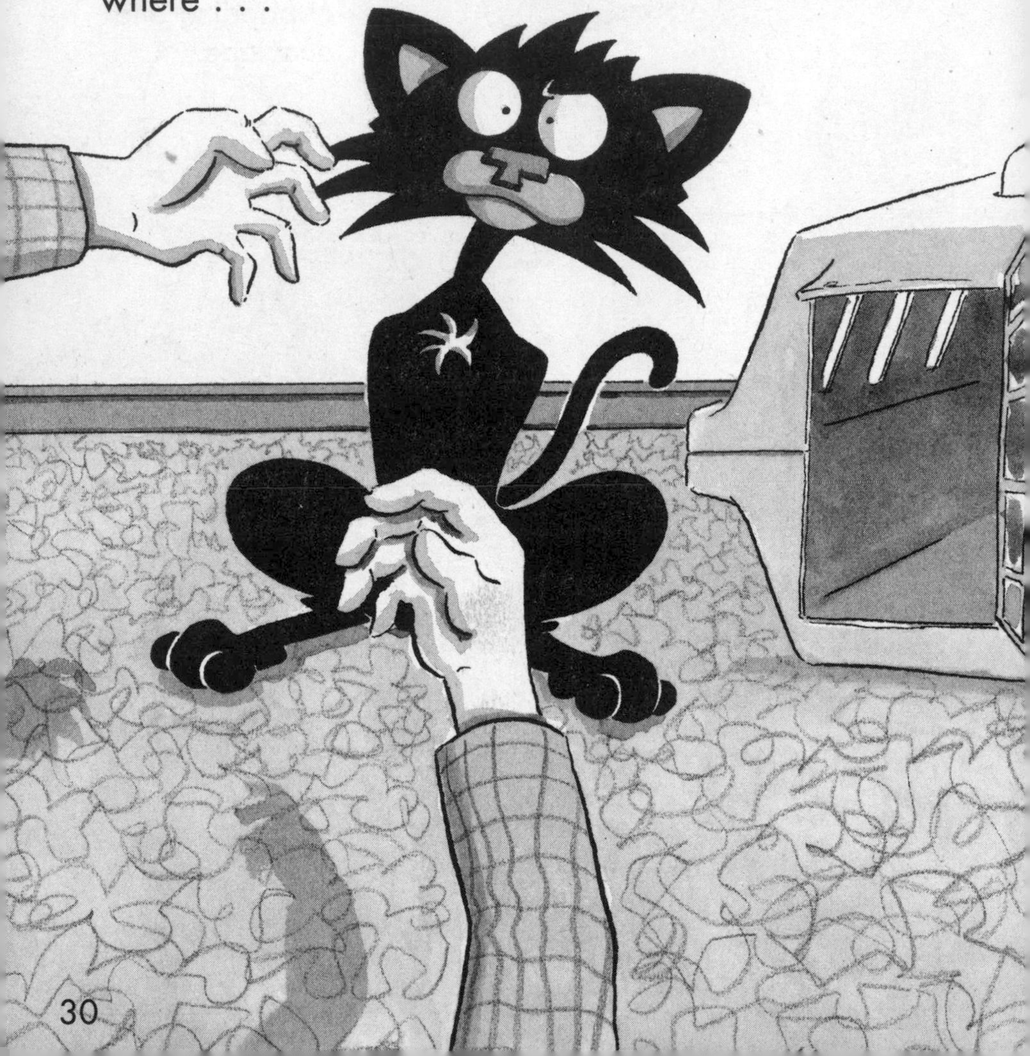

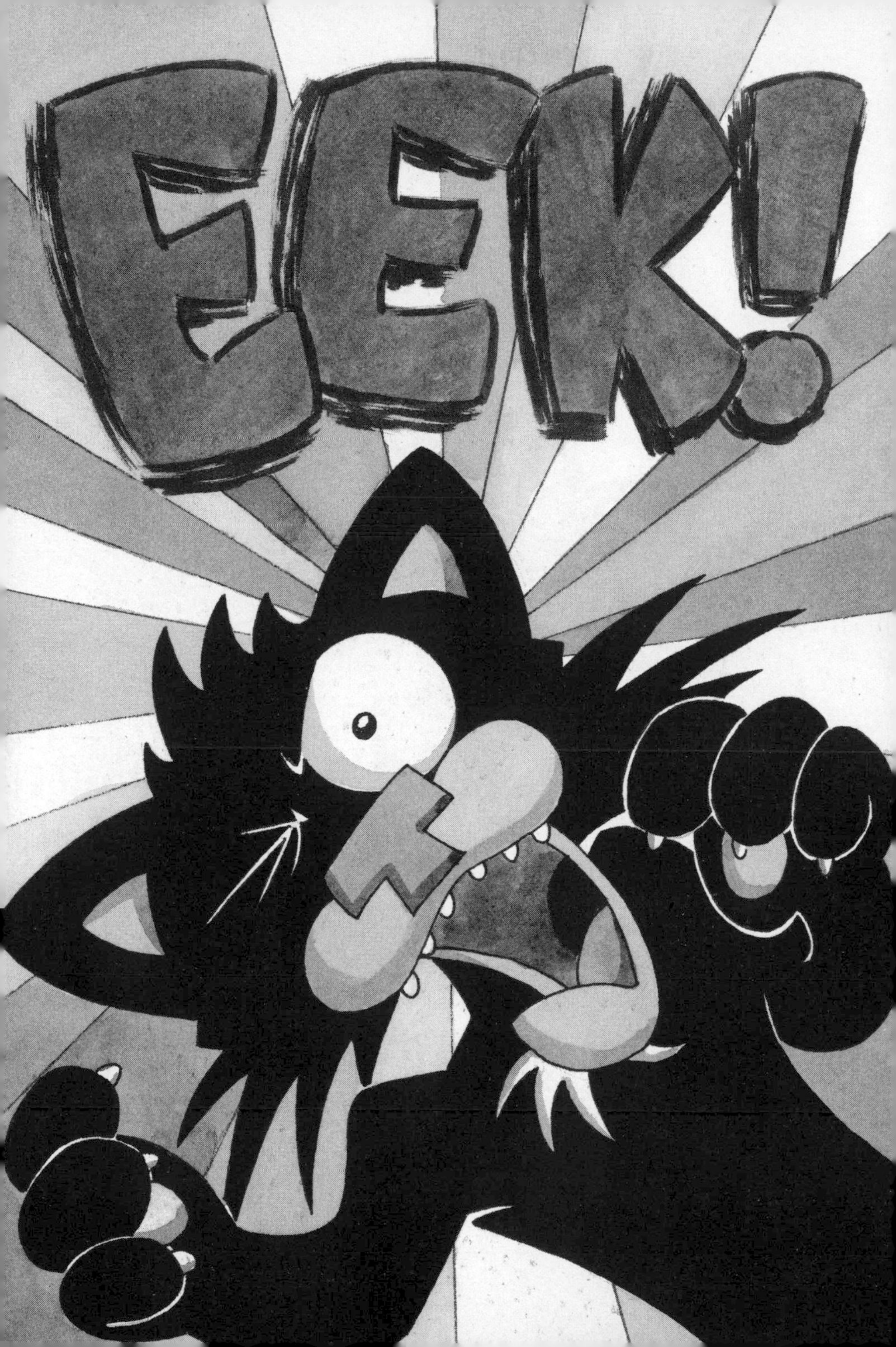
EEK!

If you have not lost too much blood, you may try talking to your cat with a soft, gentle, supportive tone of voice.

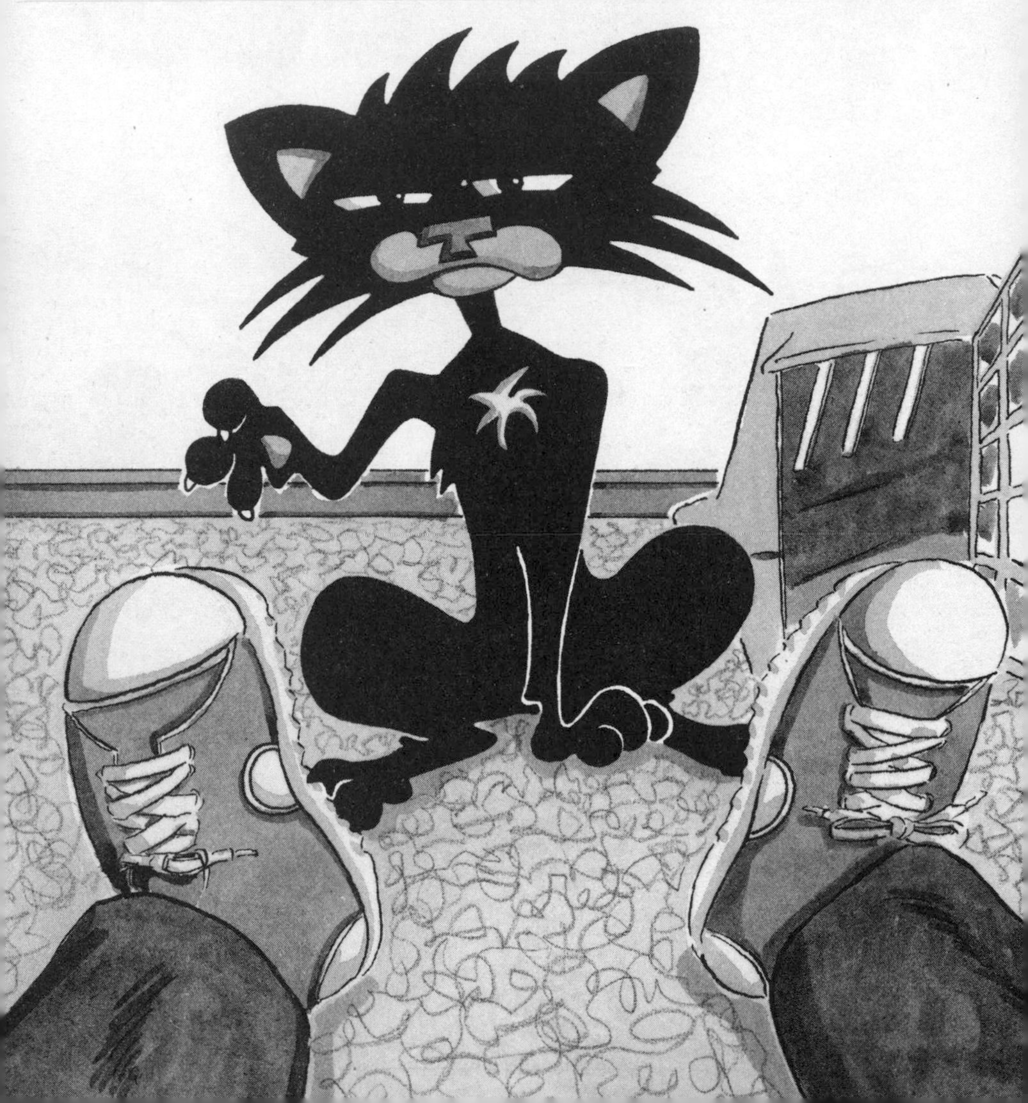

"Hi, Kitty. Aren't you a pretty, little kitty? Yes, you are! Yes, you are! Won't you be a good little, pretty kitty and go into the carrier? You are not well, my precious little jewel, and we need to take you to the nice doctor so you can feel better. Let me lead you into the carrier, my sweet, little, precious, little, pretty kitty cat so we can . . .

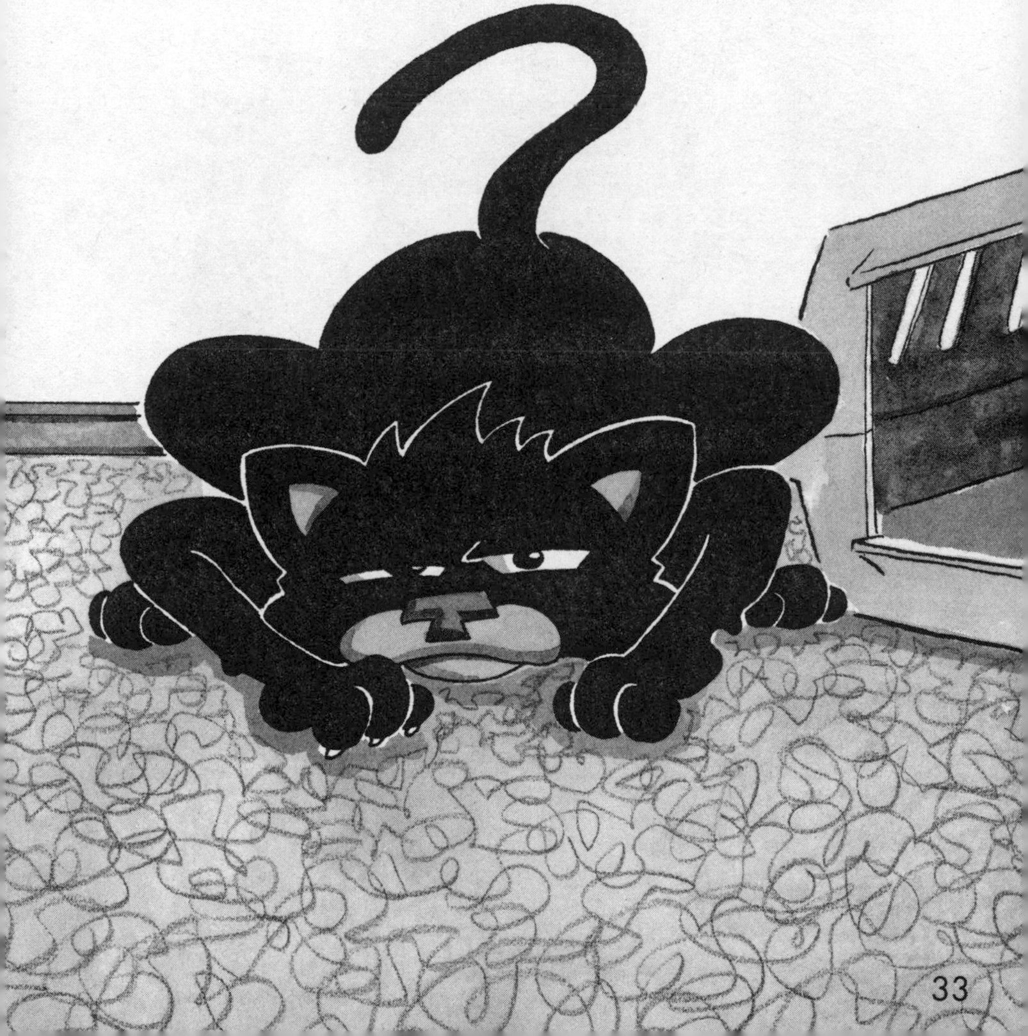

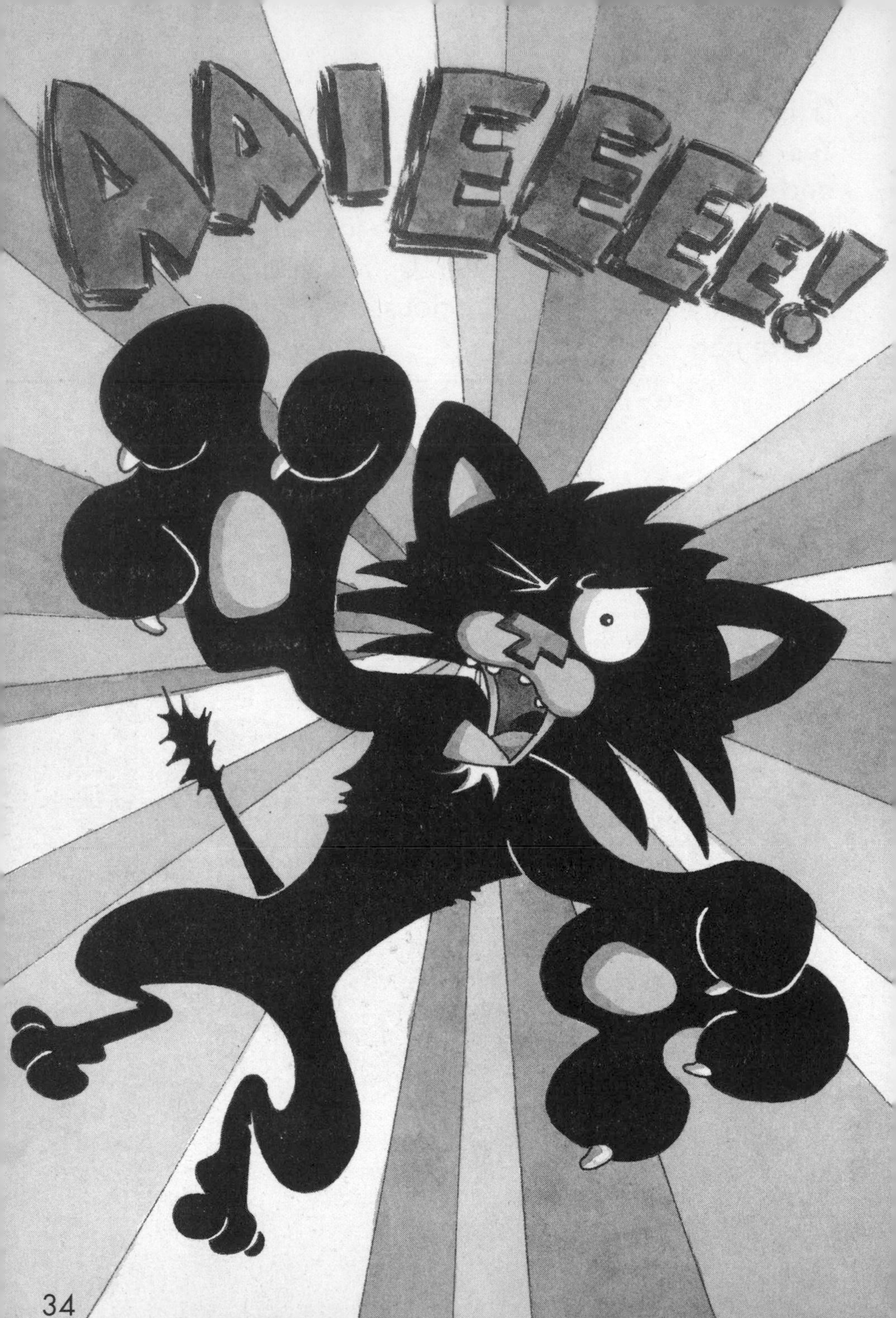
AAIEEEEE!

If the subtle method should fail (and it will), try using a strong, harsh tone of voice to let your cat know that YOU are the one in charge and that YOU should be taken seriously.

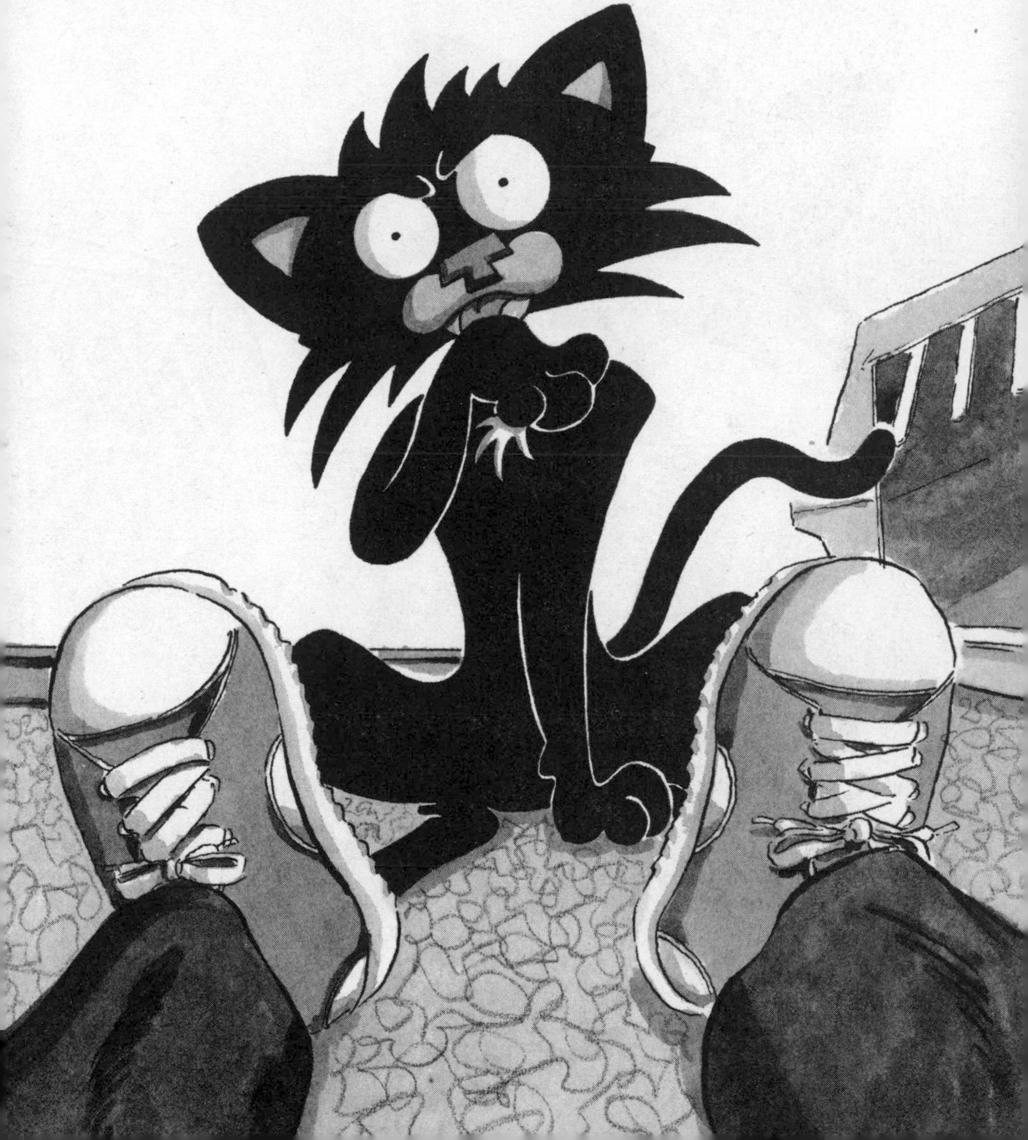

HEY, YOU!! YEAH, YOU!!!

DO YOU KNOW WHO I AM? I'M THE BOSS AROUND HERE! THAT'S WHO! AND THAT MEANS I'M IN CHARGE! I MAKE THE RULES!

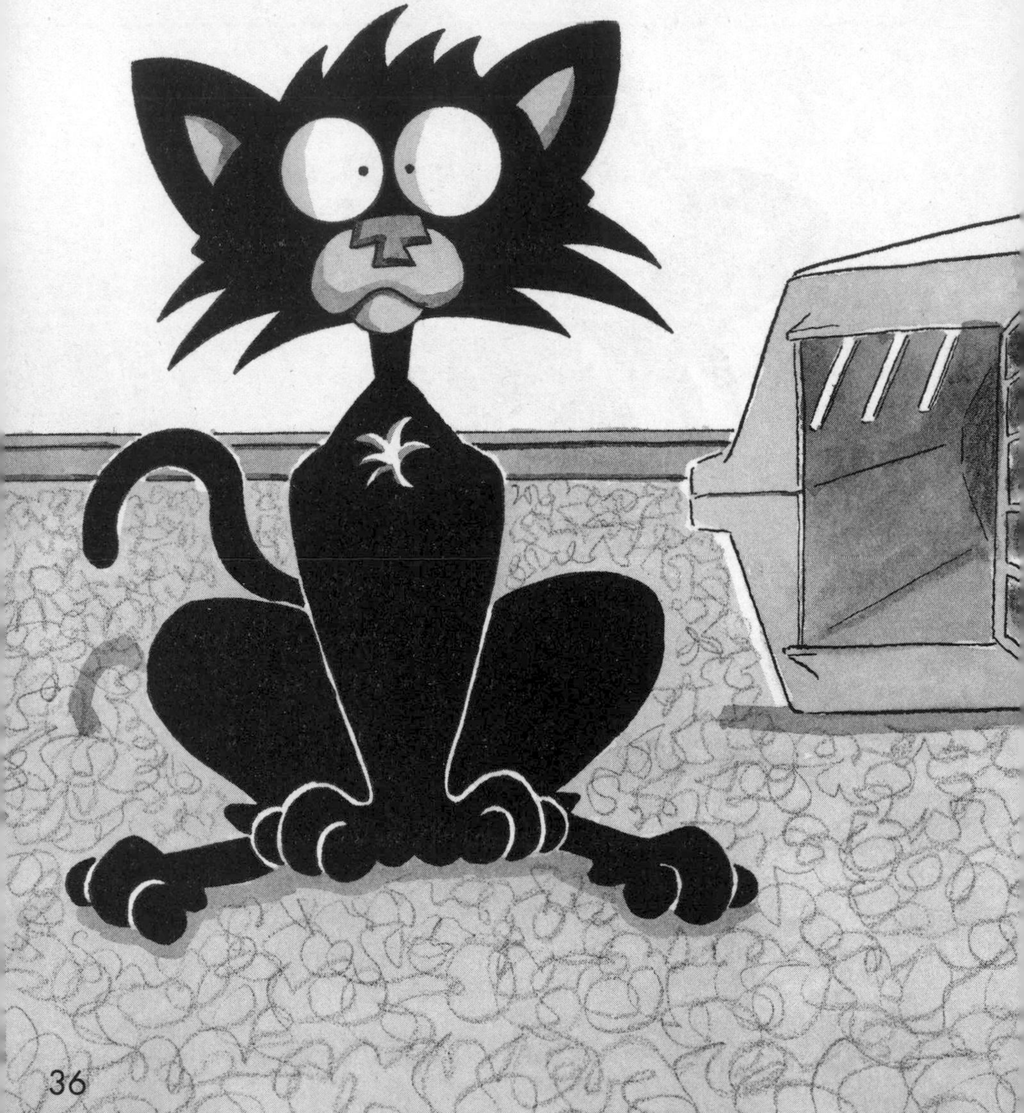

SO IF I SAY "JUMP," YOU ASK ME "HOW HIGH?" AND IF I SAY "CRAWL ON YOUR BELLY," YOU ASK ME "FOR HOW LONG?" AND IF I SAY "GET IN THAT CARRIER," YOU . . .

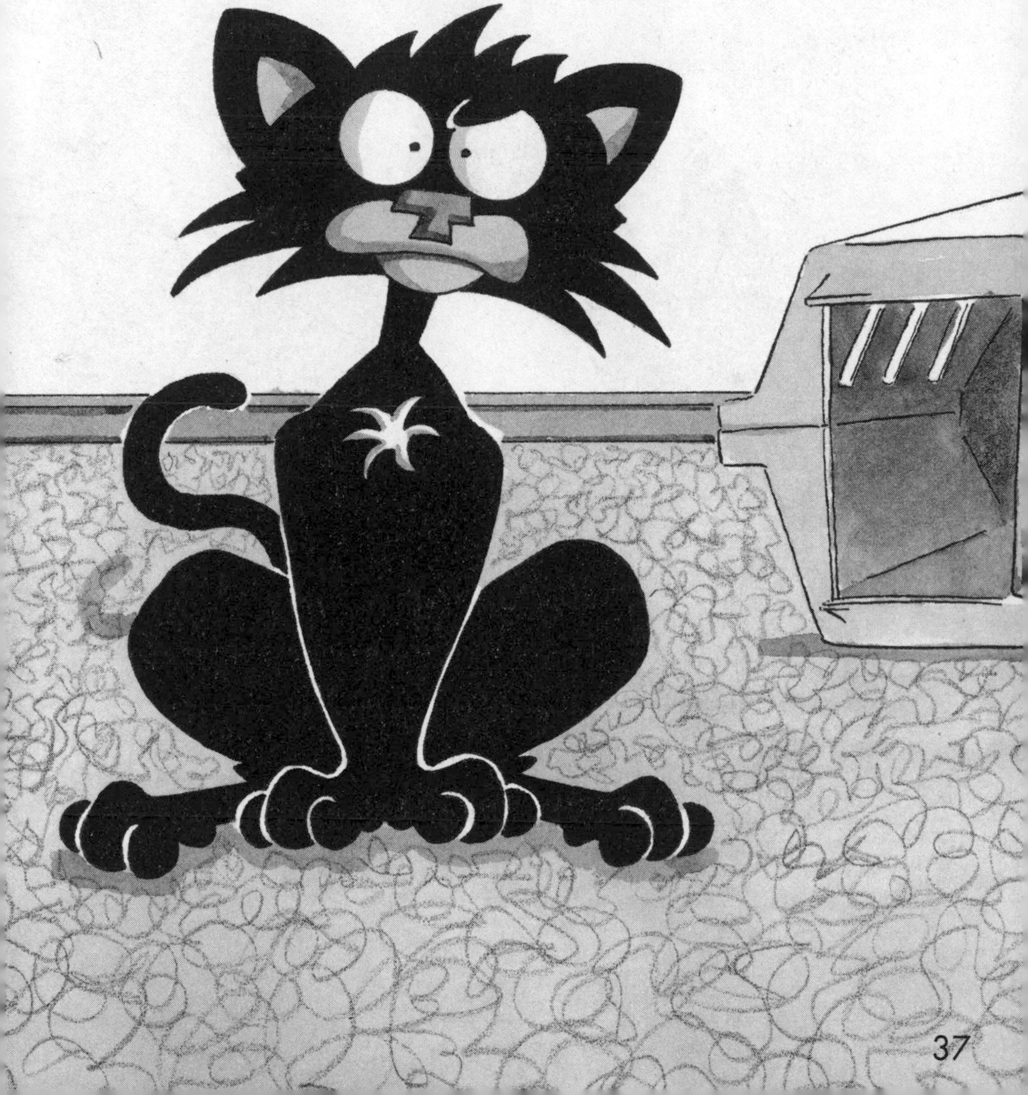

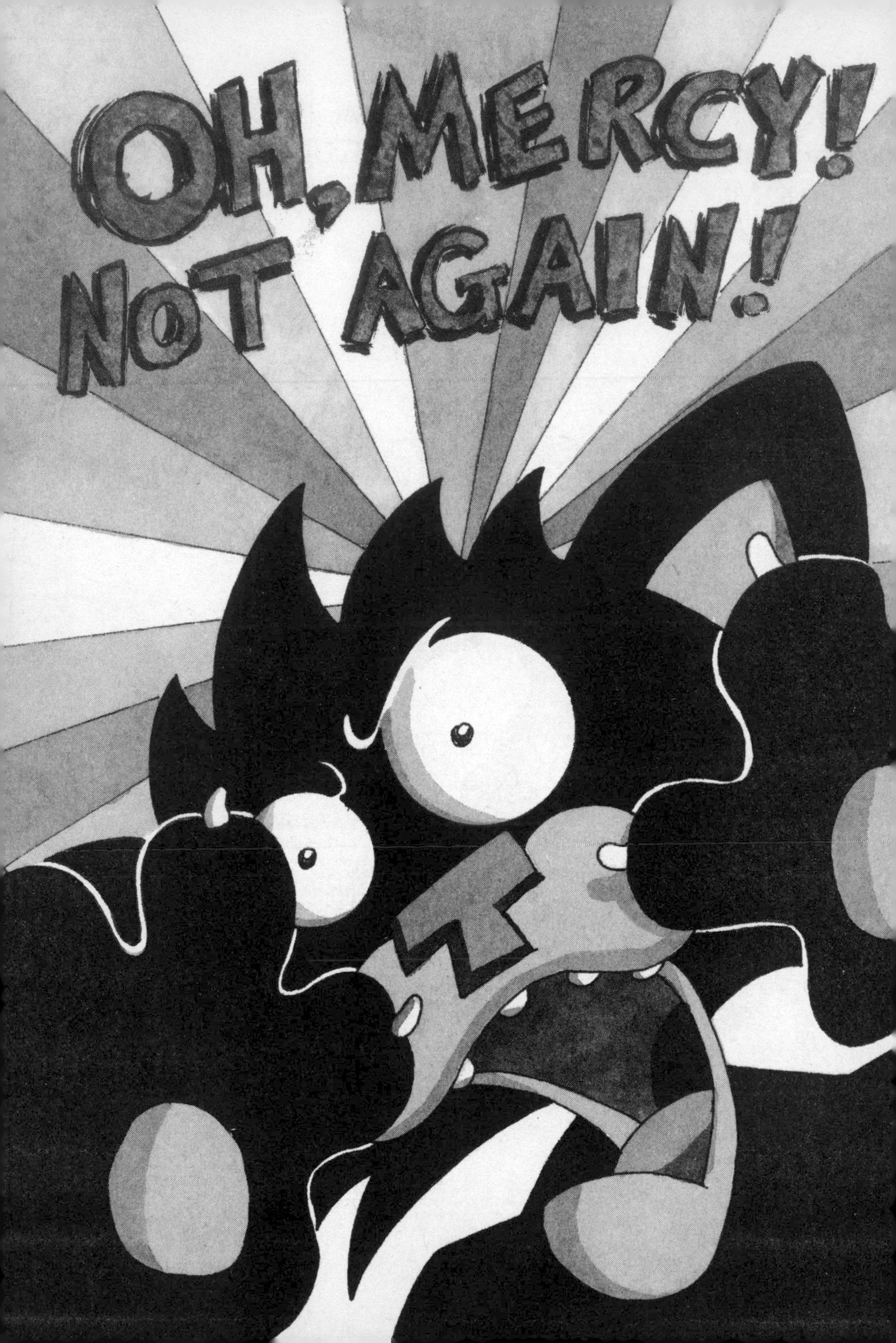
OH, MERCY! NOT AGAIN!

If it appears that communication has completely broken down, you may want to try a different approach.

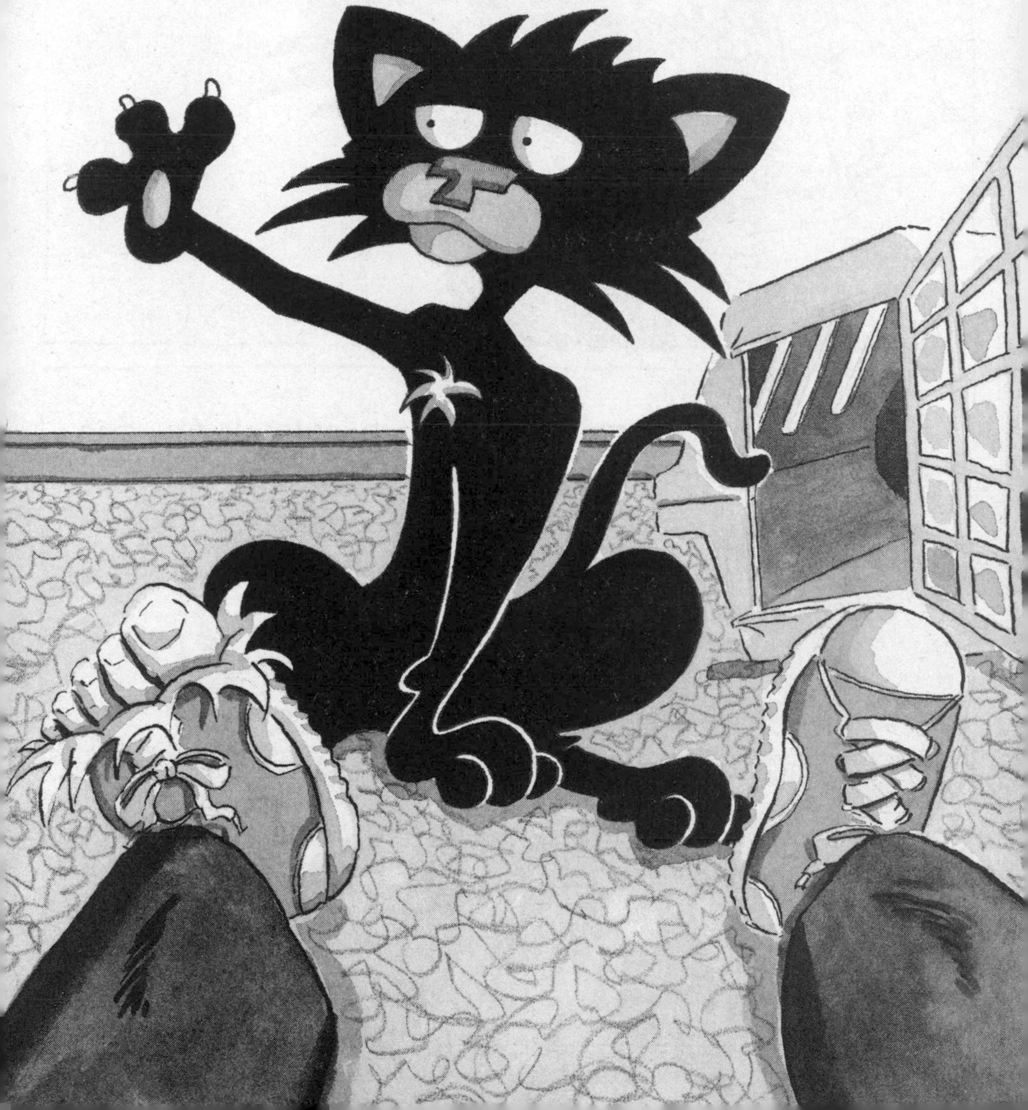

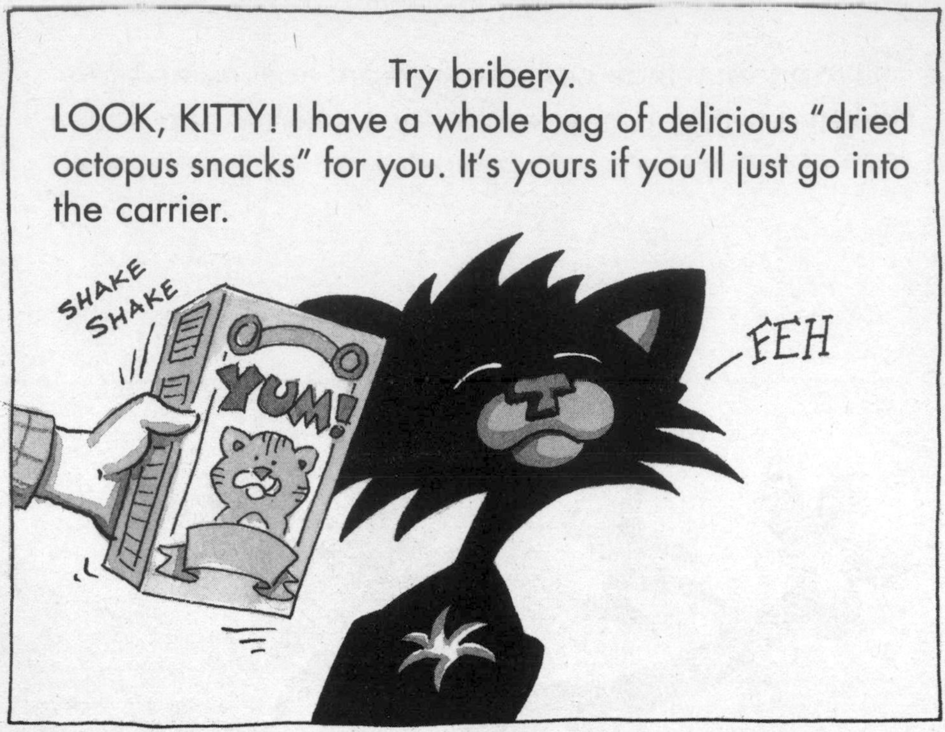
Try bribery.
LOOK, KITTY! I have a whole bag of delicious "dried octopus snacks" for you. It's yours if you'll just go into the carrier.
SHAKE
SHAKE
YUM!
FEH

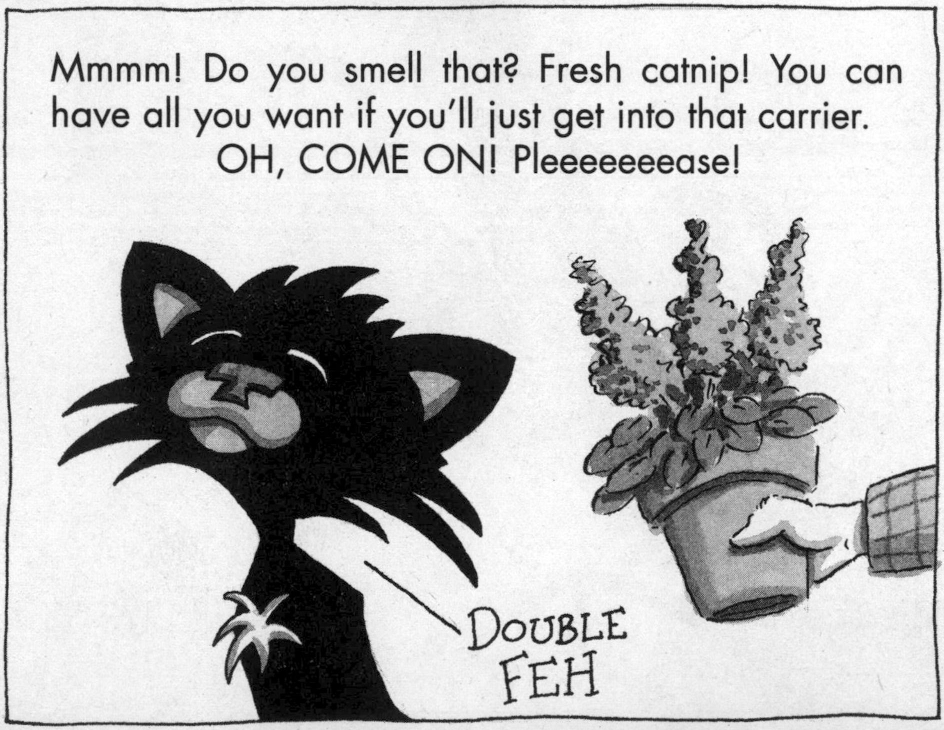
Mmmm! Do you smell that? Fresh catnip! You can have all you want if you'll just get into that carrier.
OH, COME ON! Pleeeeeeease!
DOUBLE FEH

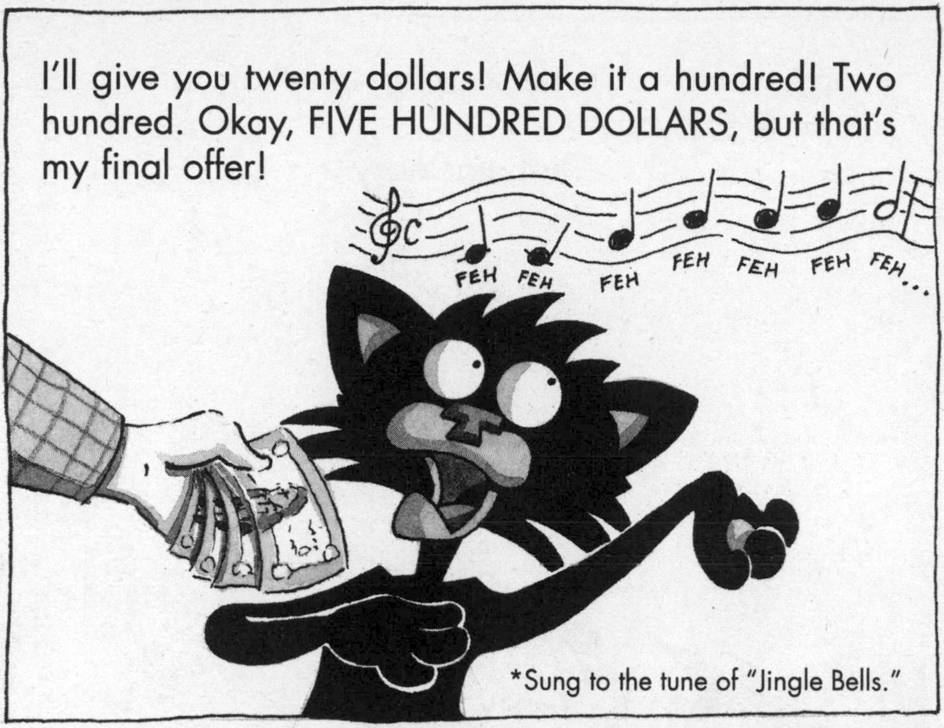
I'll give you twenty dollars! Make it a hundred! Two hundred. Okay, FIVE HUNDRED DOLLARS, but that's my final offer!
FEH FEH FEH FEH FEH FEH FEH...
*Sung to the tune of "Jingle Bells."

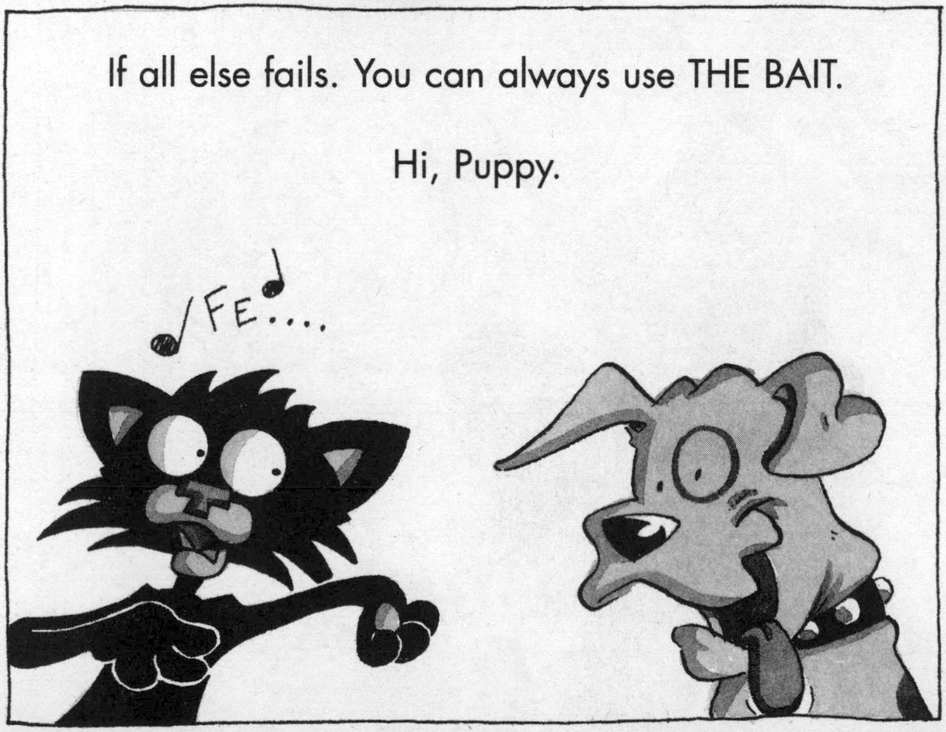
If all else fails. You can always use THE BAIT.
Hi, Puppy.
FE....

Puppy, would you mind stepping into that carrier over there? Thank you.

That was easy.

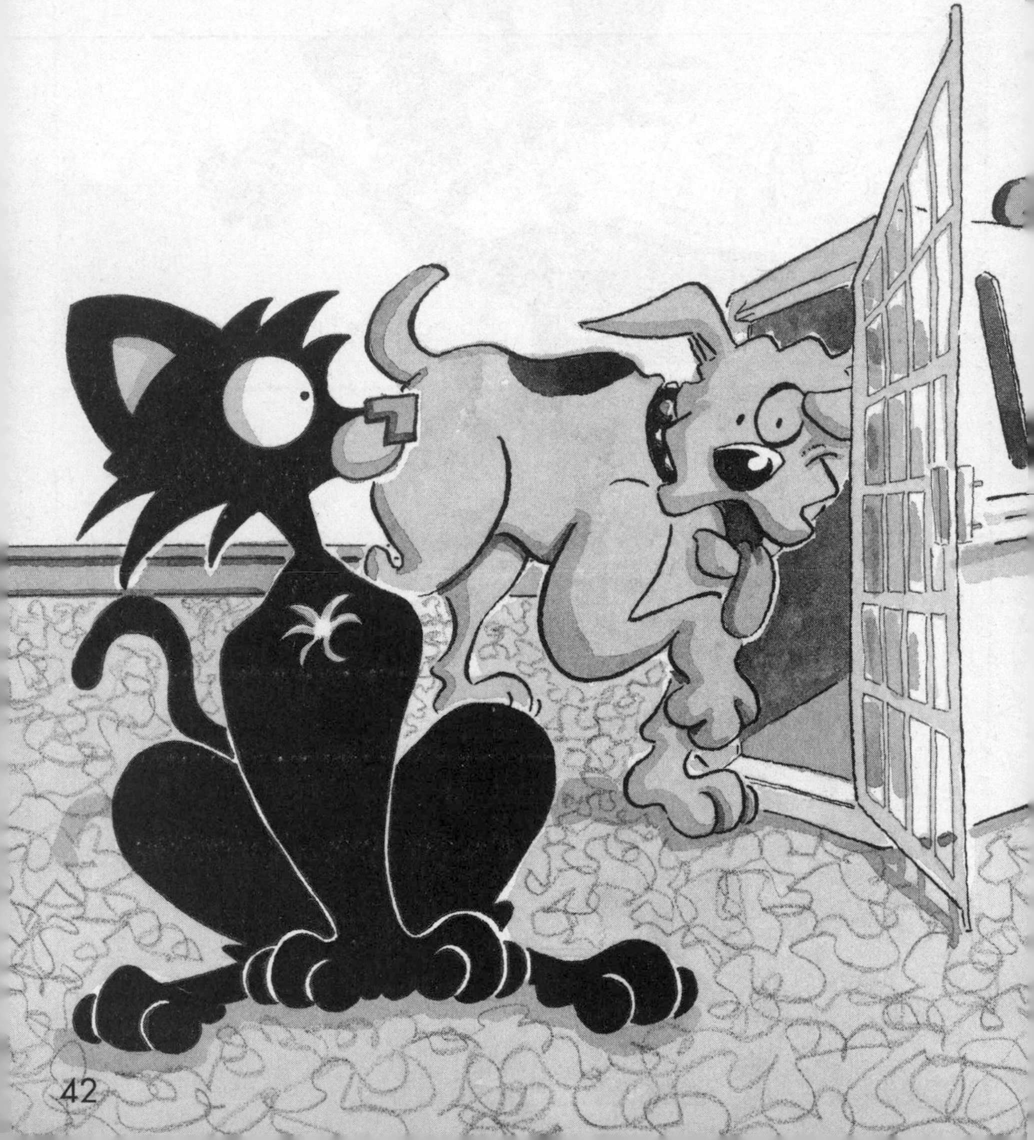

Hi, Kitty. Did I tell you that I happened to see Puppy eating all of your toys this morning? It's true. I watched him do it. He put all of your toys, one by one, into his mouth. And then he ate them. All of them. He especially ate all of your favorite toys.

He says they were delicious.

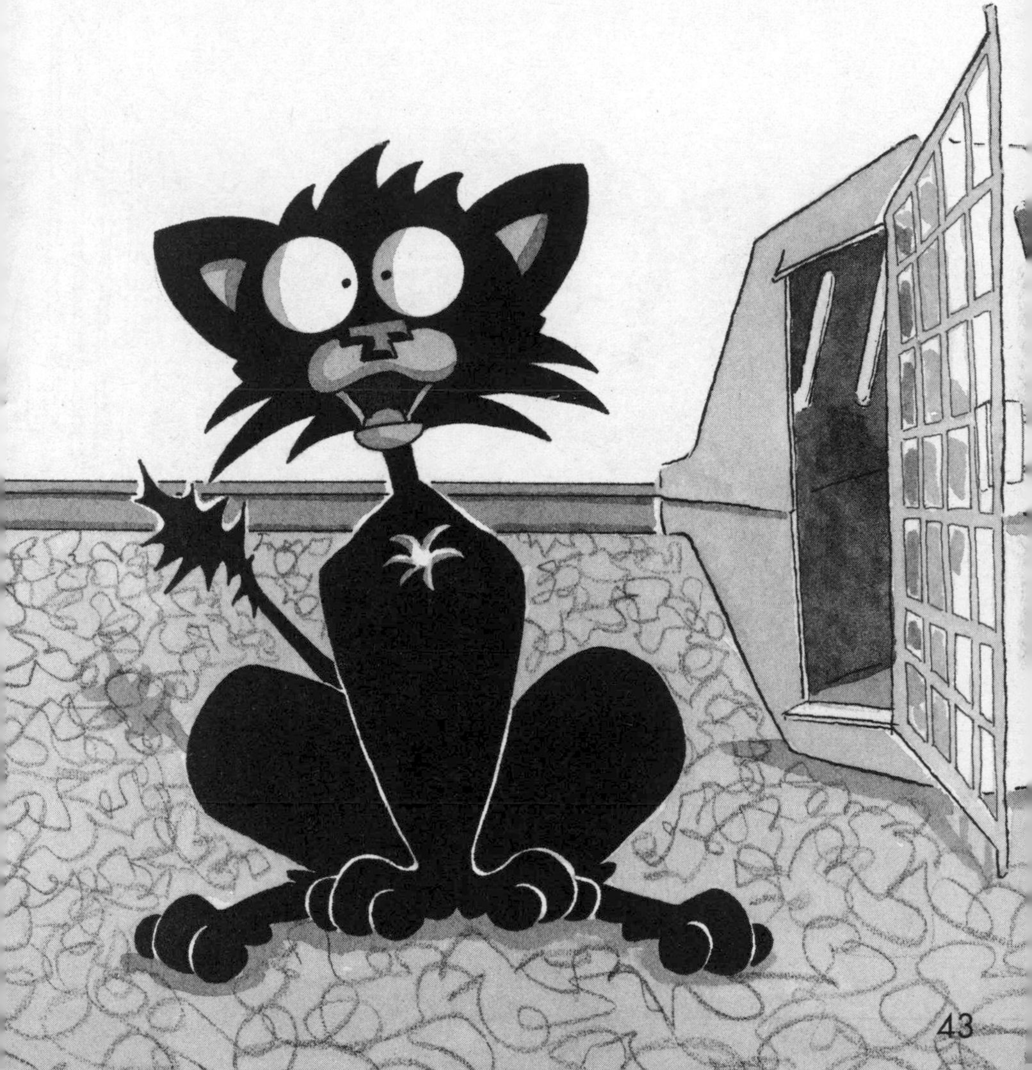

So, in conclusion, Kitty, all of your toys are now inside of Puppy. And Puppy? He is inside of this carrier.

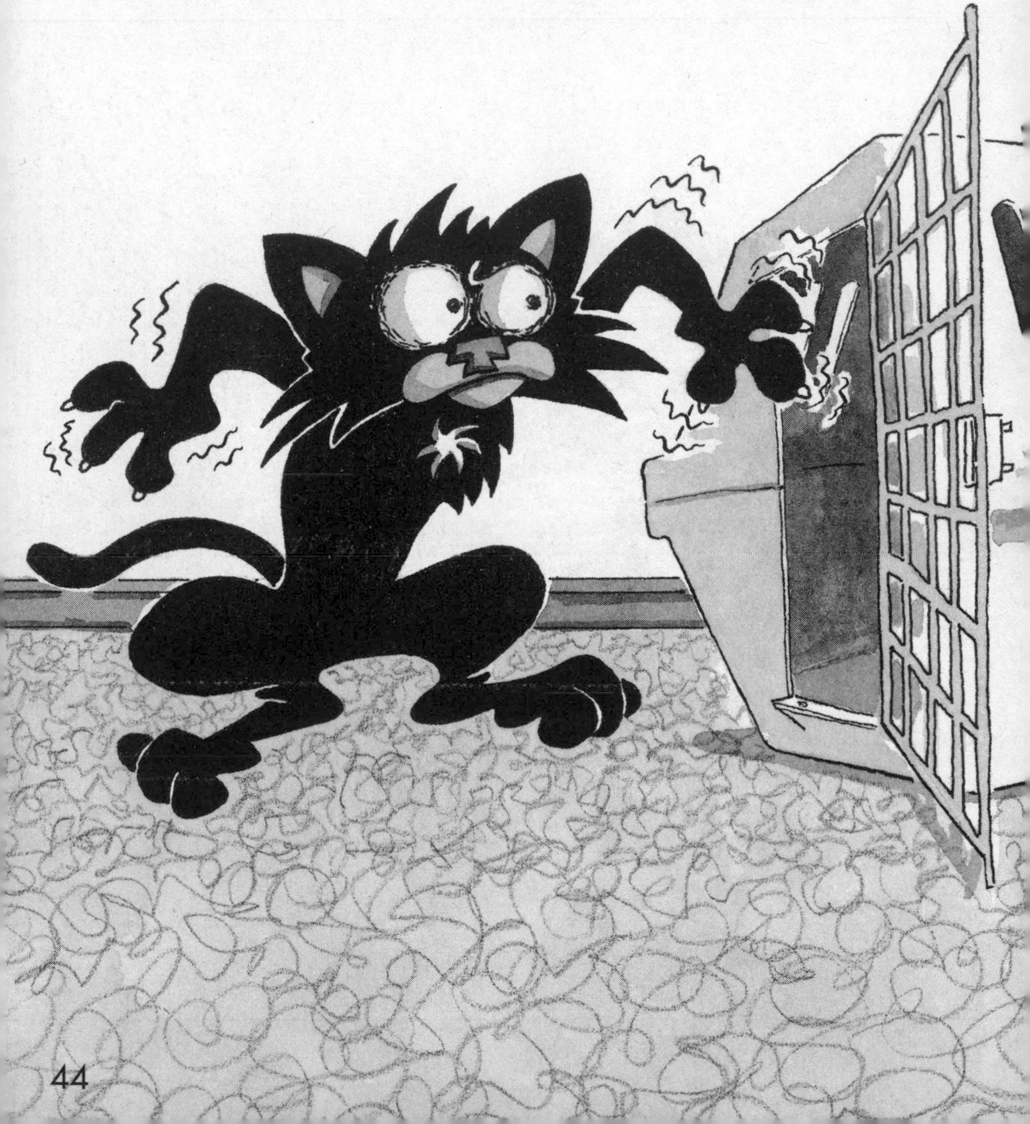

IT WORKED!

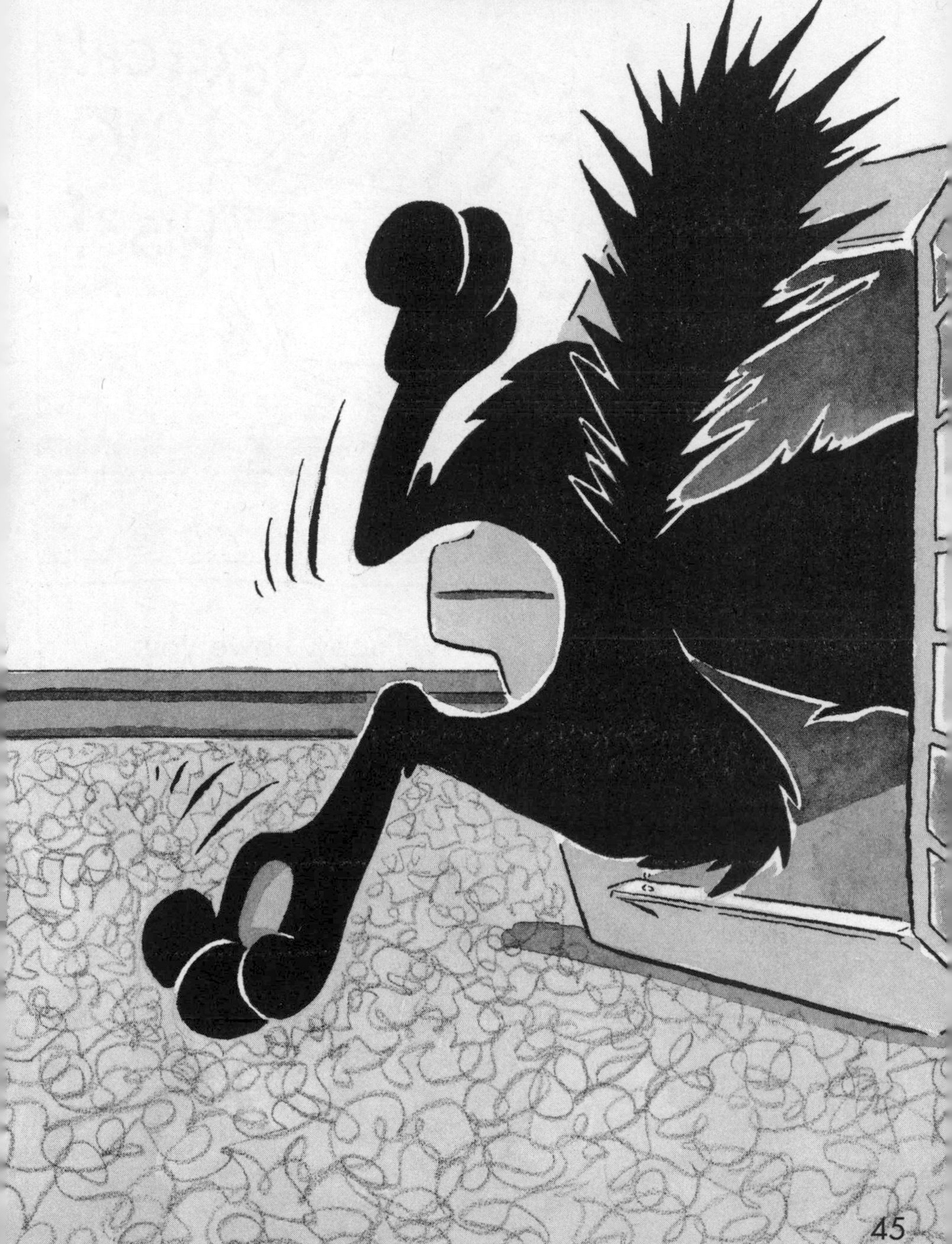

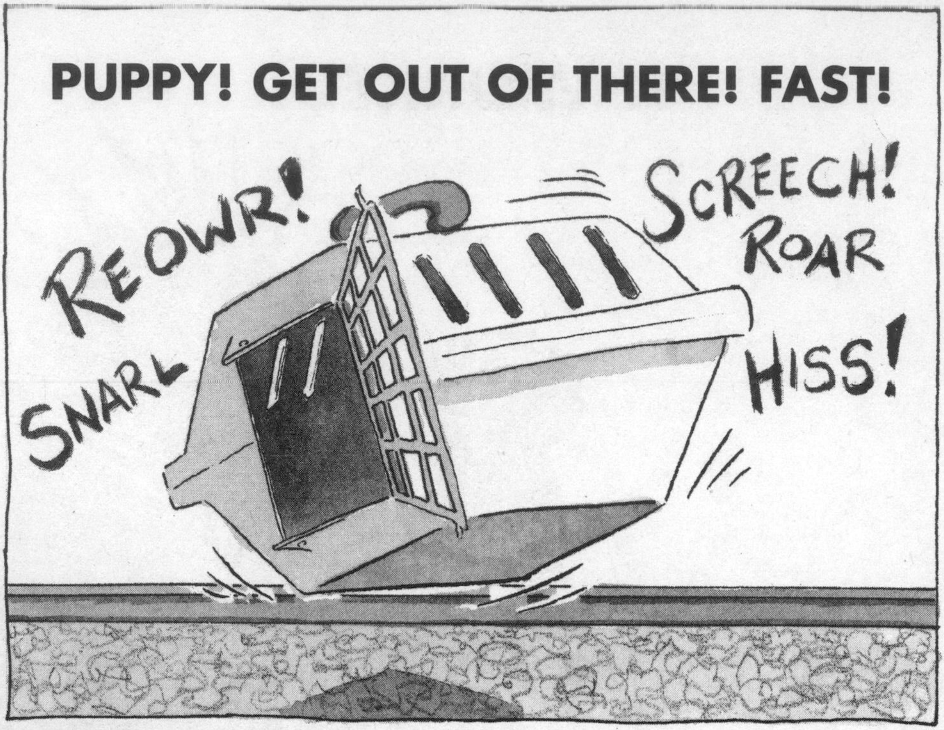
PUPPY! GET OUT OF THERE! FAST!
REOWR!
SCREECH!
ROAR
SNARL
HISS!

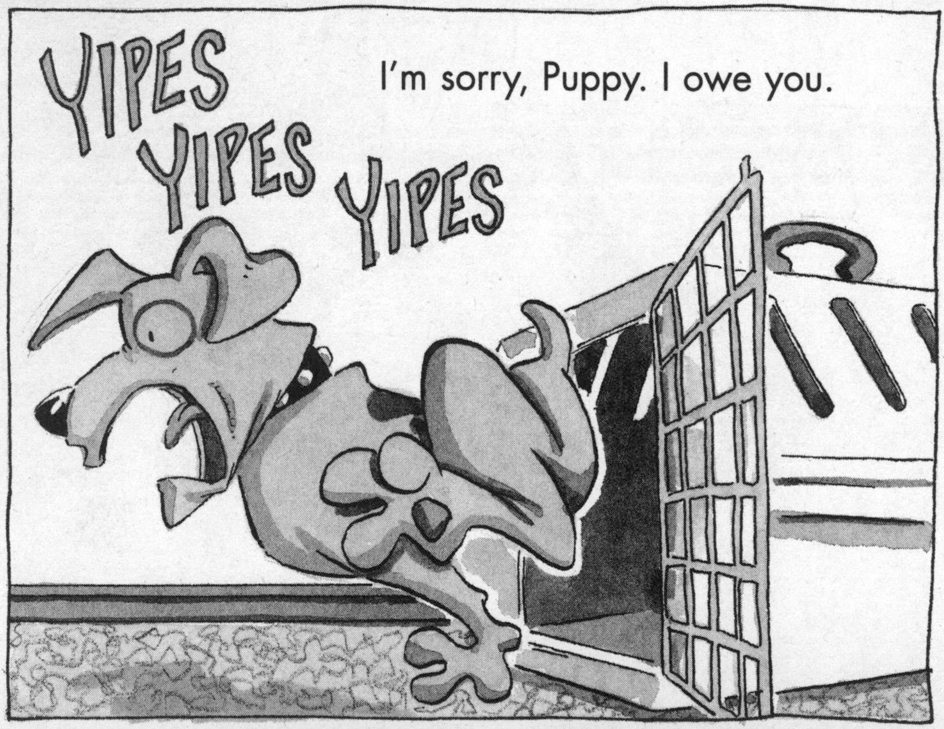
YIPES
YIPES
YIPES
I'm sorry, Puppy. I owe you.

QUICK!
SHUT THE DOOR!

Whew!

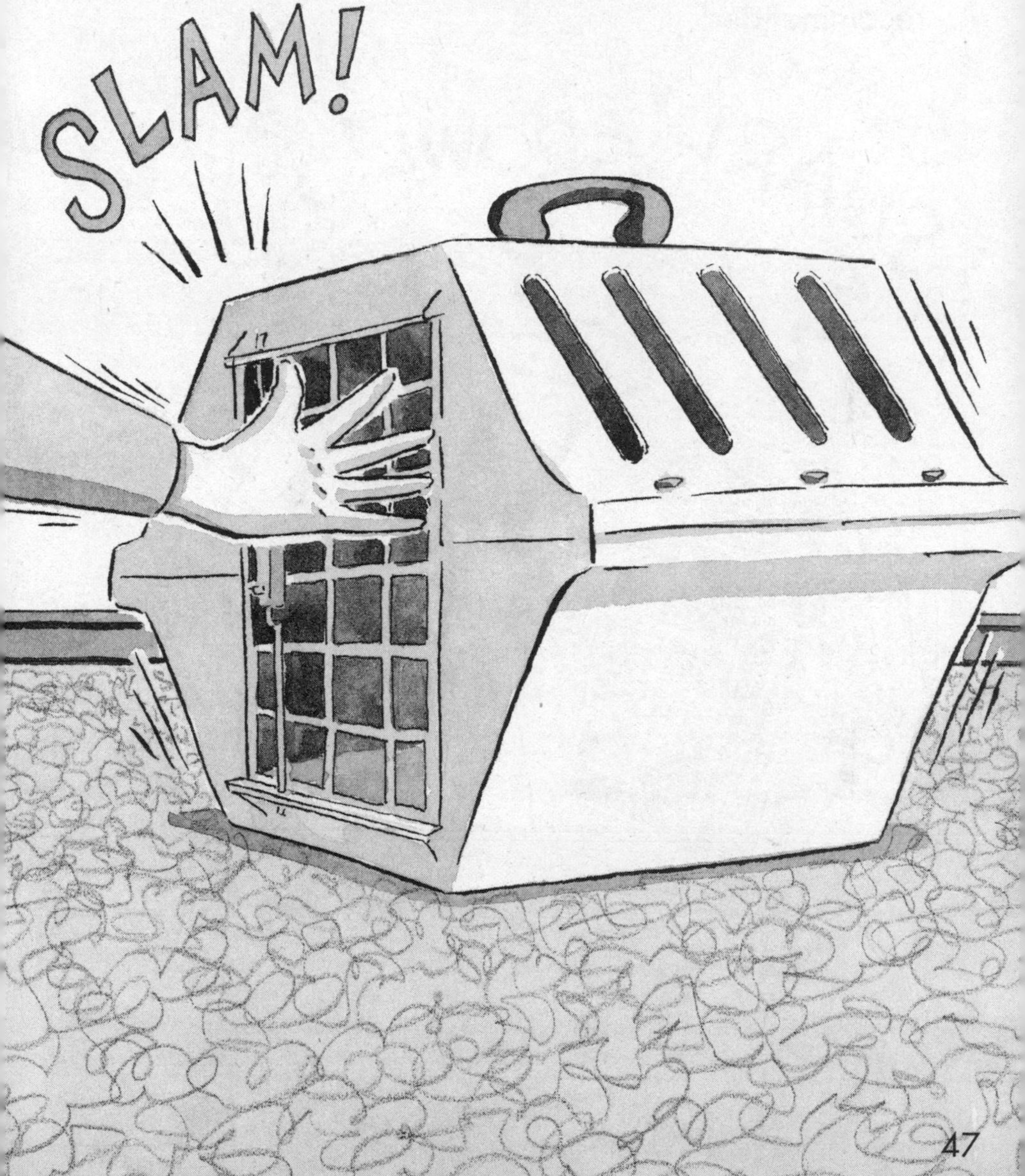
SLAM!

•STEP THREE•
TRANSPORTATION

Use fireplace tongs, a hockey stick, a crowbar, or any kind of long, sturdy pole to transport carrier with cat inside to vet. A police escort is optional, but highly recommended.

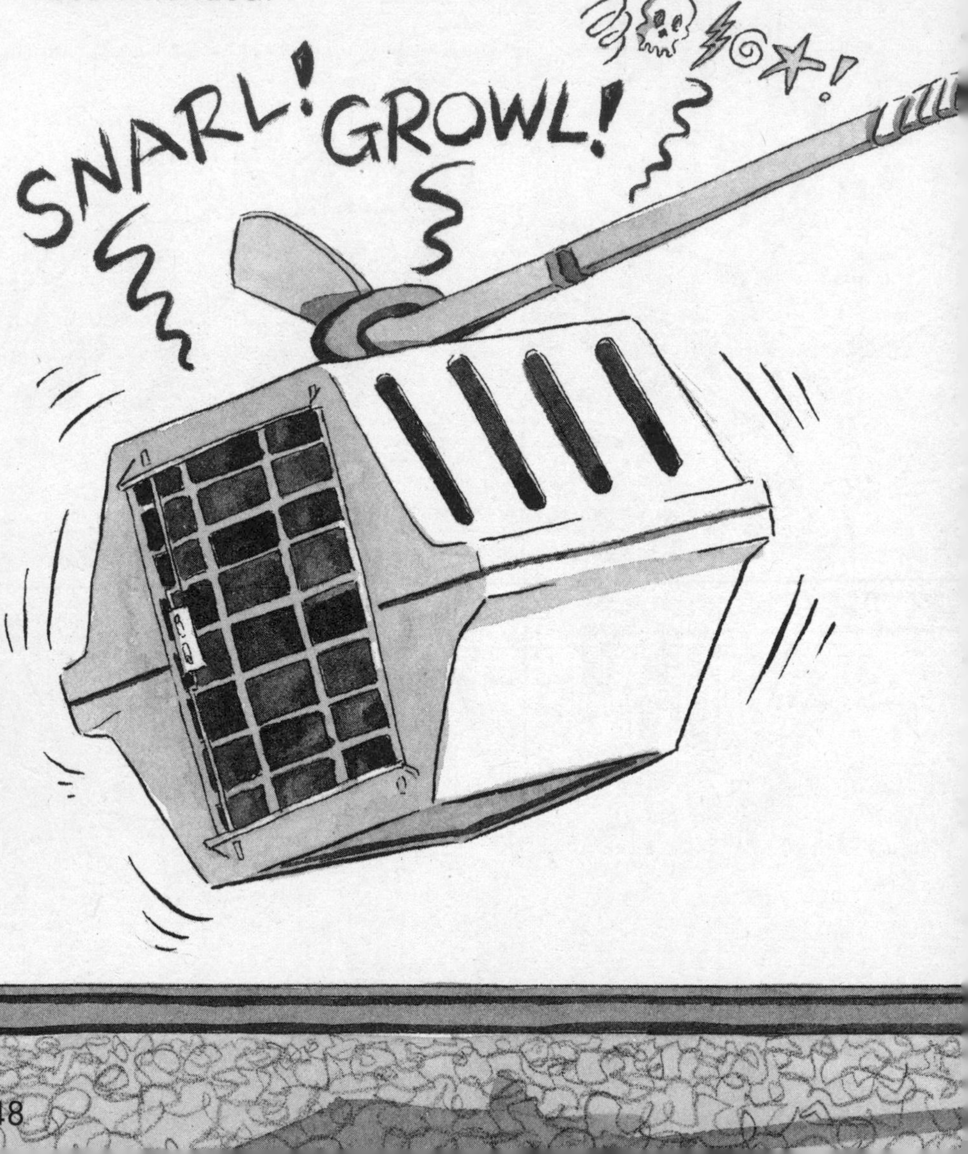
SNARL!
GROWL!

•STEP FOUR•
LOGIC

Ask yourself why you own a cat in the first place.

The following is a list of animals that will not try to murder you when you bring them to the vet.

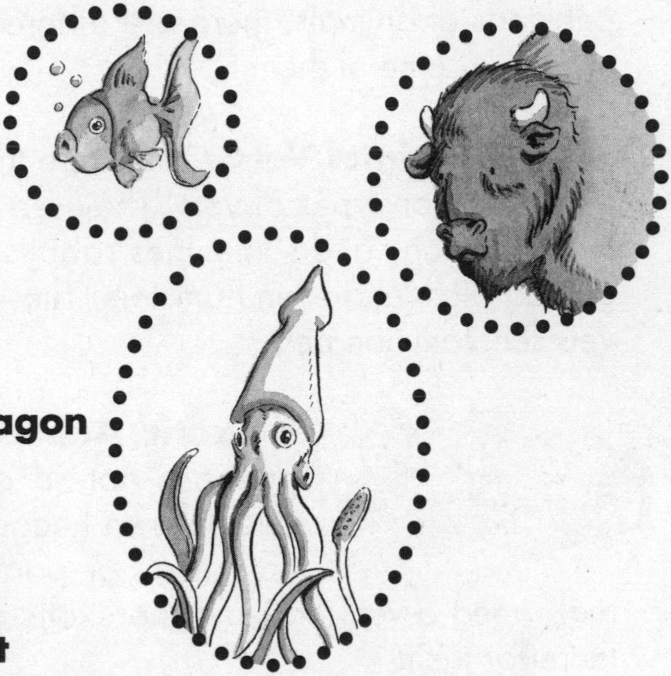

Dog

Buffalo

Goldfish

Hamster

Tarantula

Komodo Dragon

Giant Squid

Guinea Pig

Vampire Bat

Pretty much every other animal in the world other than cats.

•STEP FIVE•
REPEAT

Repeat Step Four as often as necessary until you come to your senses and buy a gerbil.

UNCLE MURRAY'S FUN FACTS

WHAT IS A VETERINARIAN?

Someone who doesn't eat meat?

Essentially, a veterinarian—or "vet," for short—is a doctor for animals. But just as there are lots of different kinds of animals, there are different kinds of vets. Here are some of them.

• **Small Animal Vets**—These are the most common types of vets. They see cats and dogs and sometimes rabbits, guinea pigs, and even hamsters. These vets see common pets.

• **Exotic Animal Vets**—Some pets are not so common. Some people own hedgehogs or ferrets or snakes or parrots. These animals need a vet, too. And the exotic animal vets are there for them.

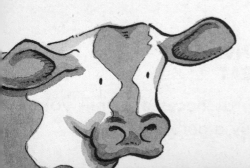

• What about farm animals? These animals are seen by the **Large Animal Vets**. These are the vets who do the most house calls because you can't bring a herd of cows or horses into a doctor's office. You could try. But it wouldn't be a good idea.

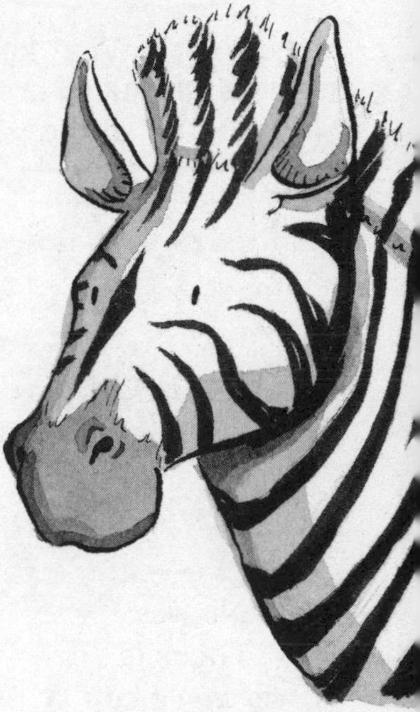

• Zoo animals? They're seen by **Wild Animal Vets**, of course. These vets have to be knowledgeable of a whole wide variety of unusual animals, from apes and bats to yaks and zebras.

• And lastly, there are the **Specialists**, vets who specialize their study and care in a single species of animal, like a cat, or even in a single body part, like a cat's heart. These doctors often do important research that helps all of the other vets take care of their patients.

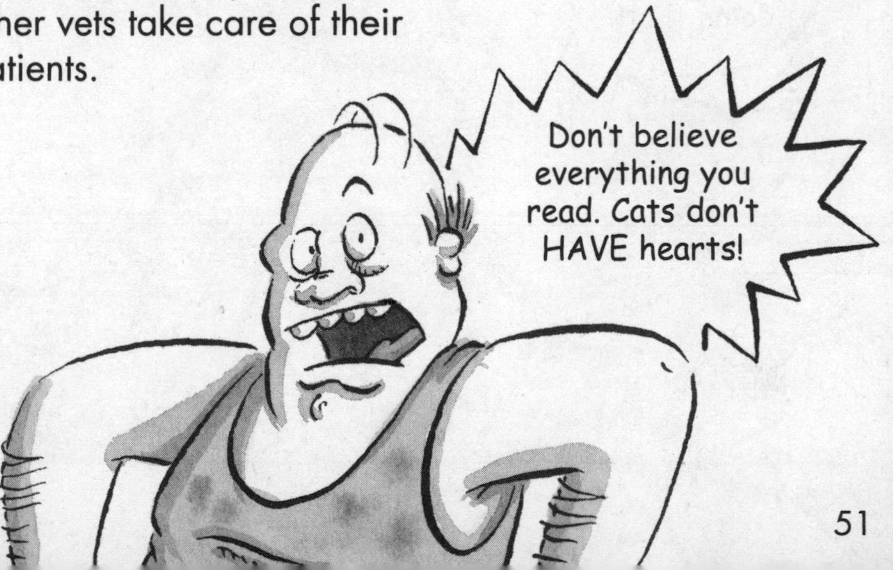
Don't believe everything you read. Cats don't HAVE hearts!

•CHAPTER THREE•

AT THE VET

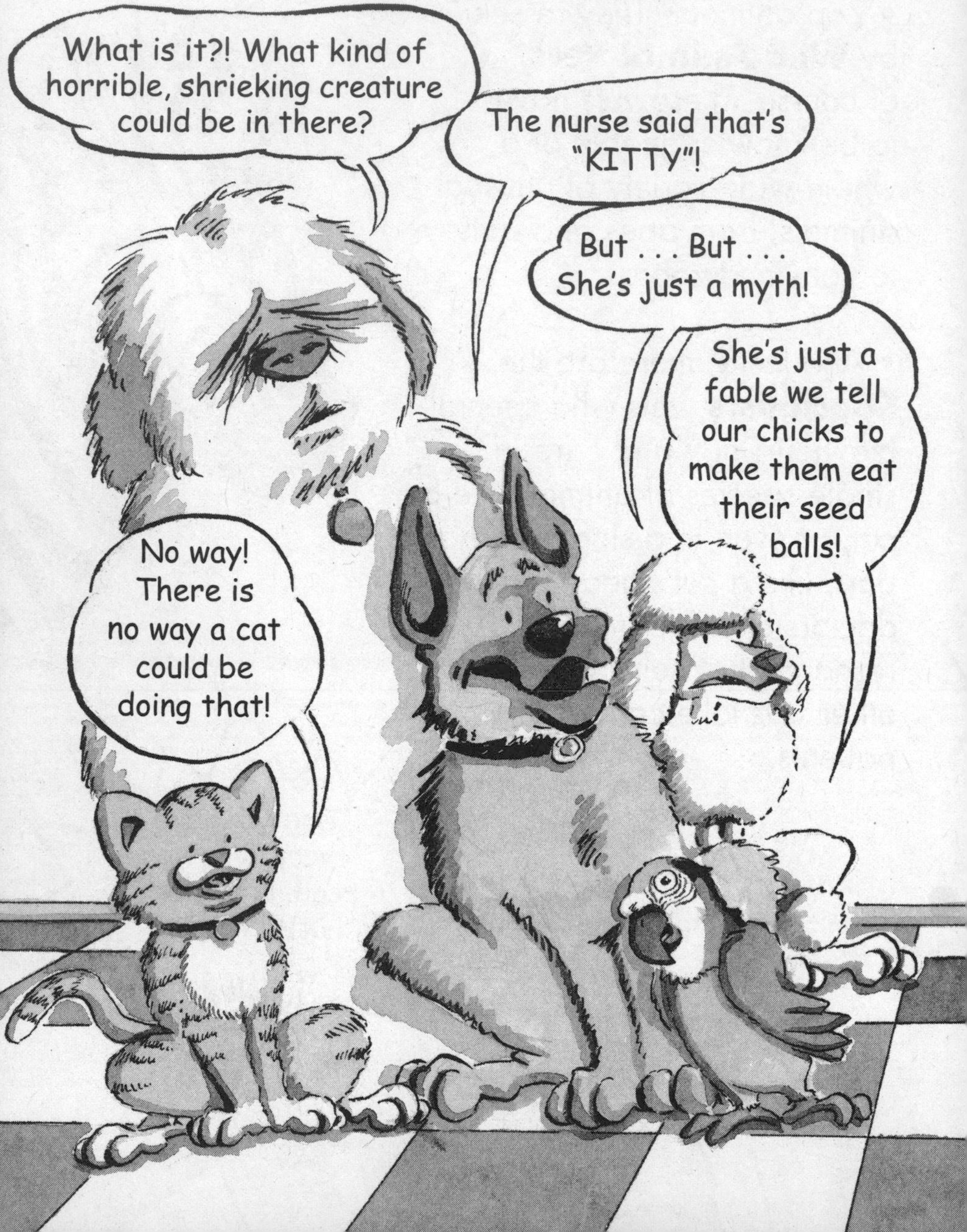

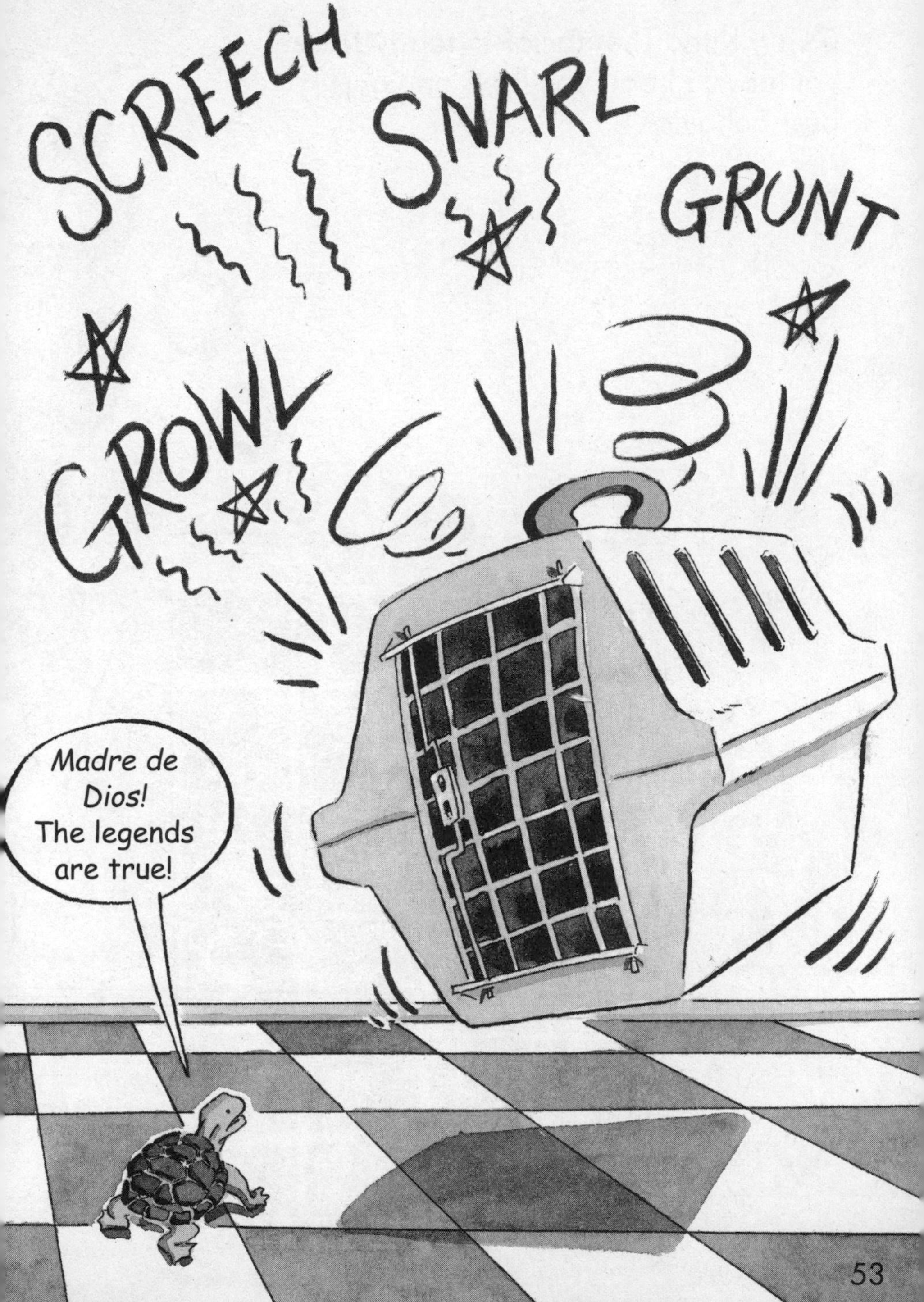
SCREECH
SNARL
GRUNT
GROWL
Madre de Dios! The legends are true!

Okay, Kitty. The doctor is ready to see you now. I hope you'll be on your best behavior.

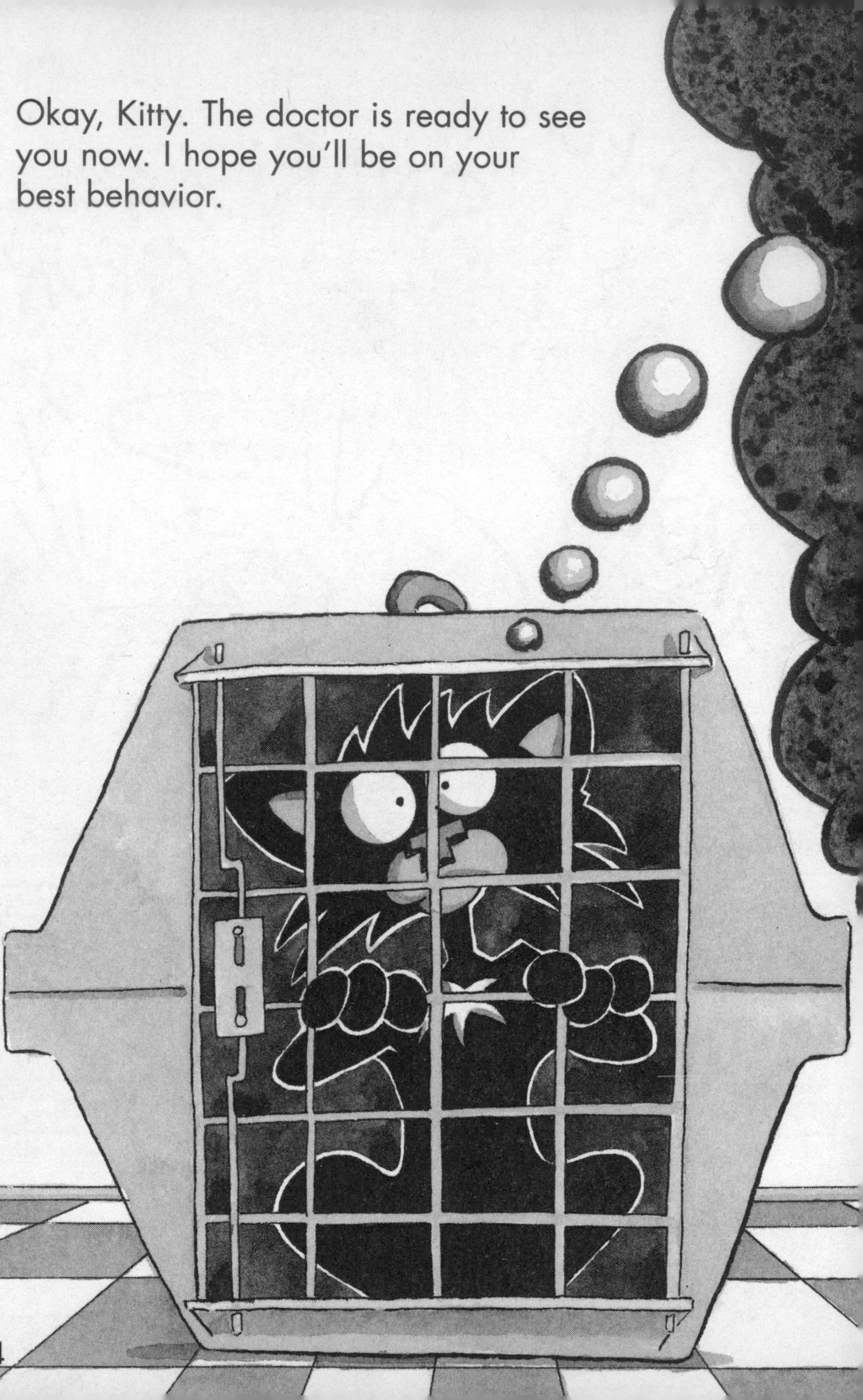

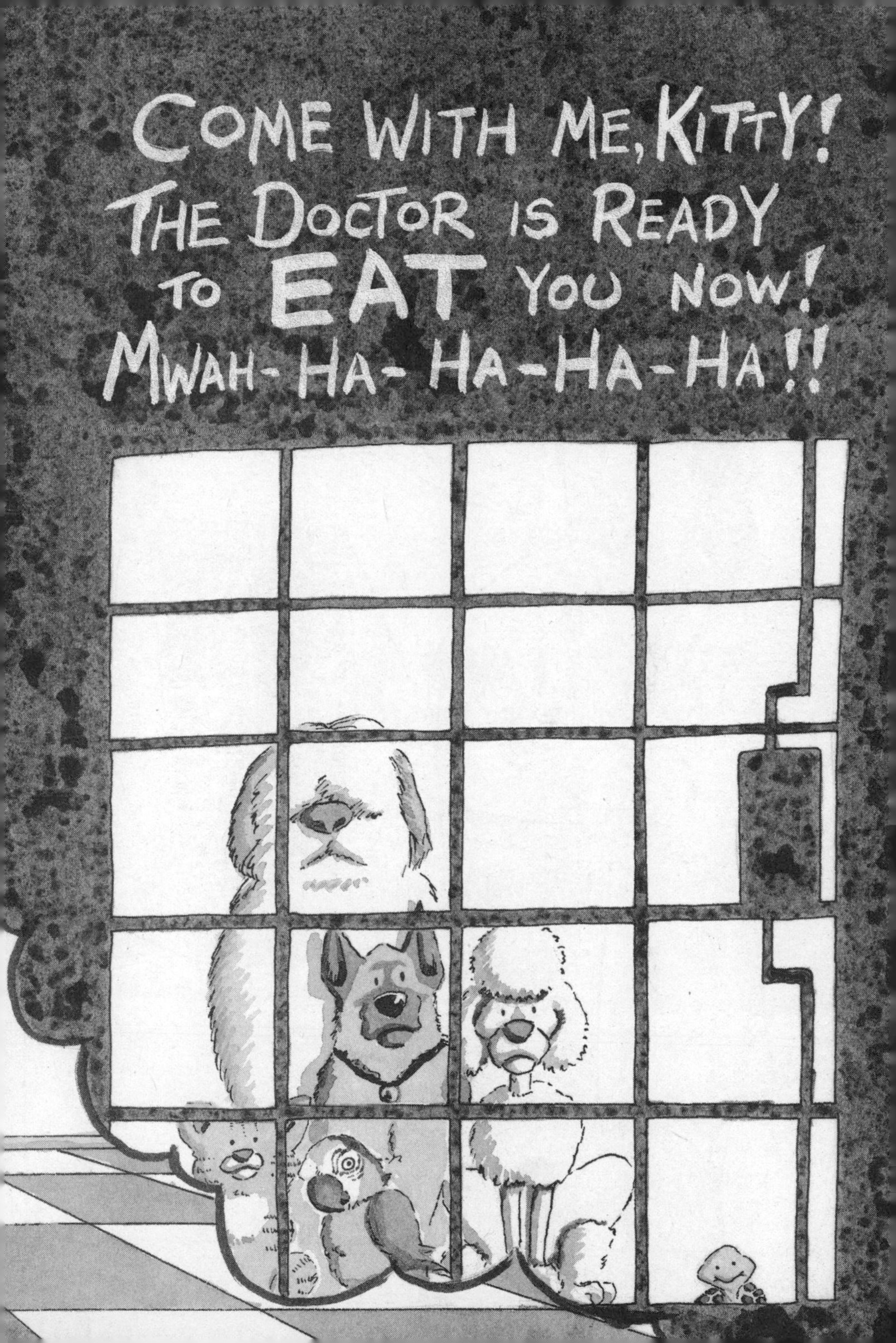
COME WITH ME, KITTY! THE DOCTOR IS READY TO EAT YOU NOW! MWAH-HA-HA-HA-HA!!

The reason we're here, Doc, is because Kitty stopped eating all of a sudden and we just don't know why. We're all terribly worried.

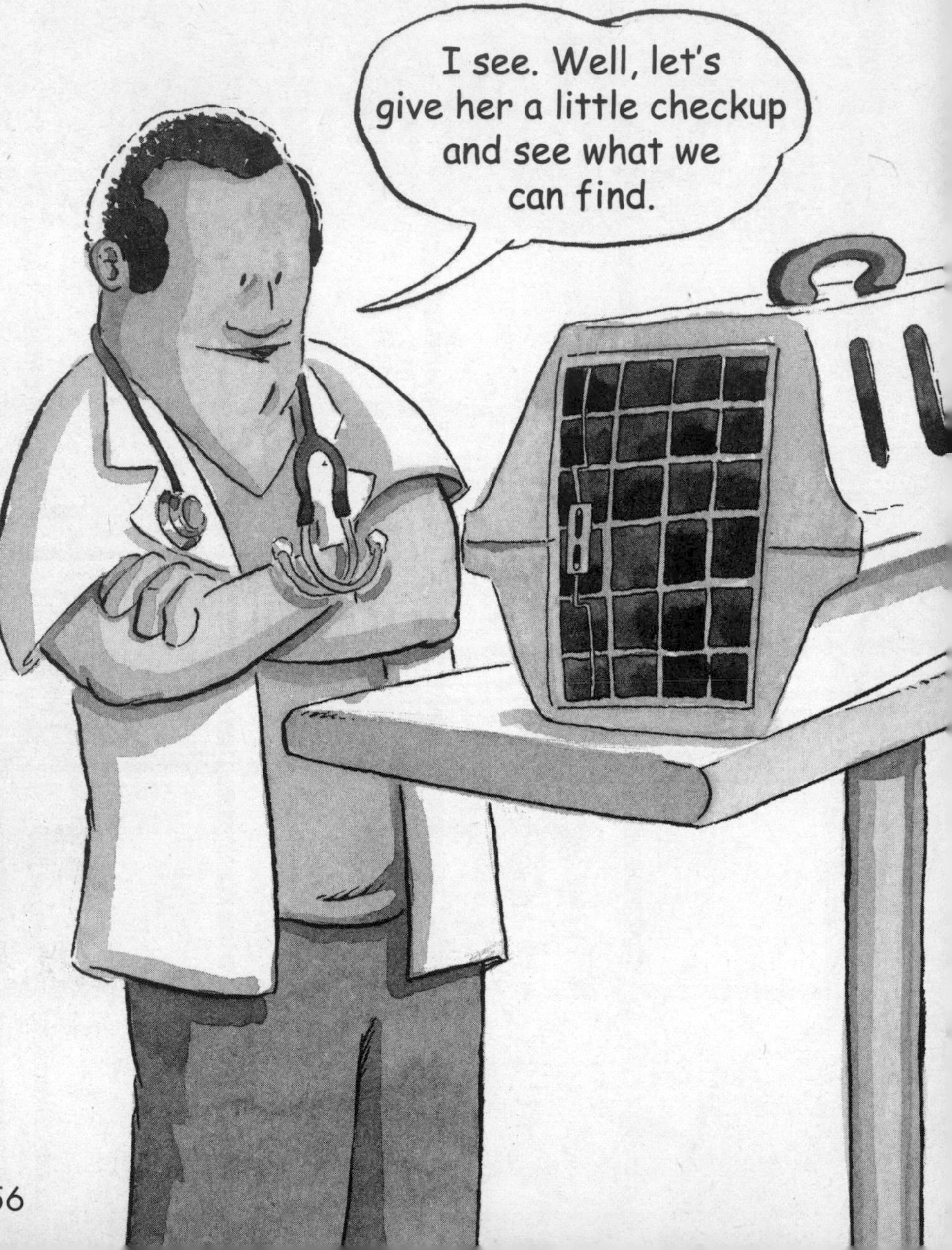
I see. Well, let's give her a little checkup and see what we can find.

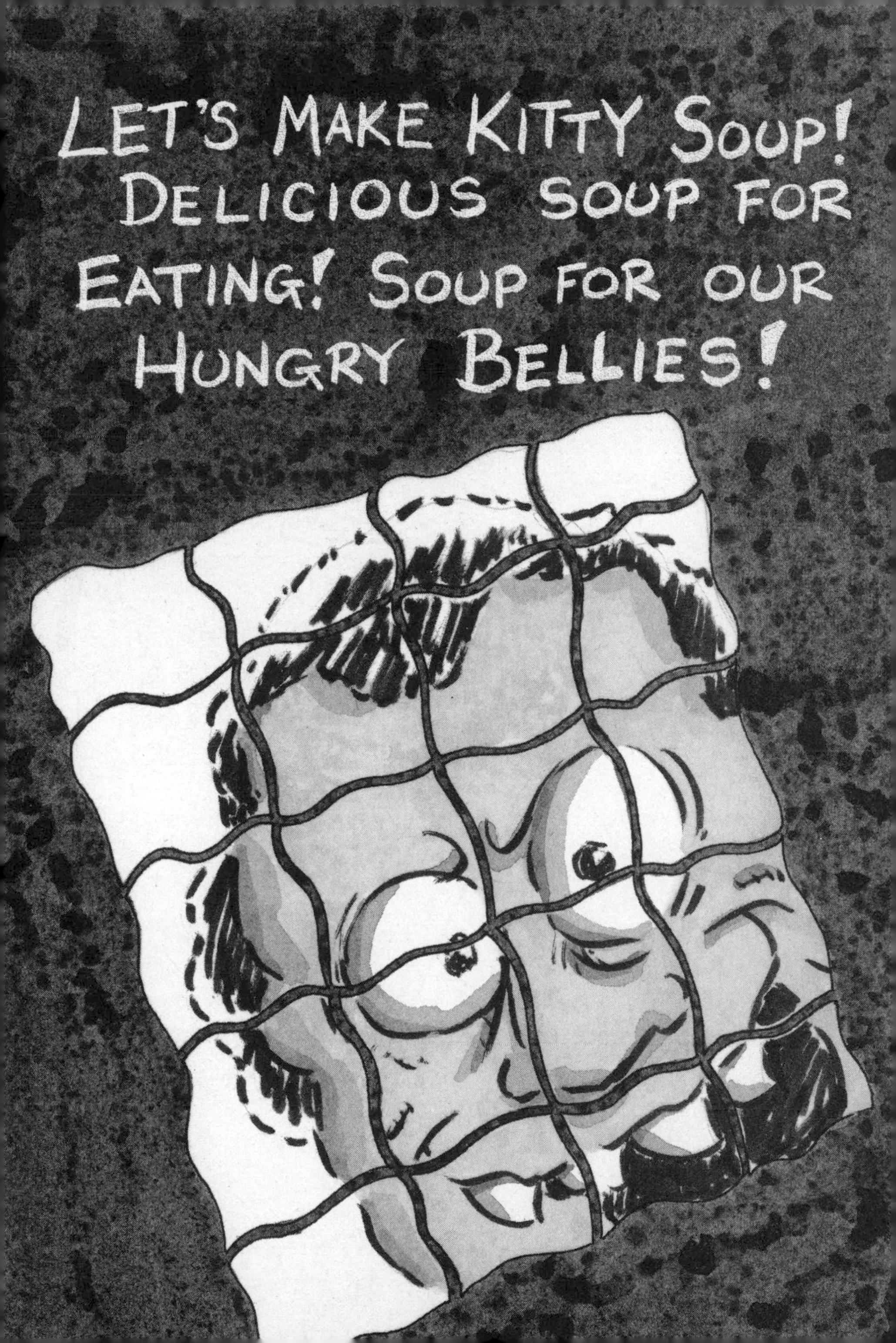
LET'S MAKE KITTY SOUP!
DELICIOUS SOUP FOR
EATING! SOUP FOR OUR
HUNGRY BELLIES!

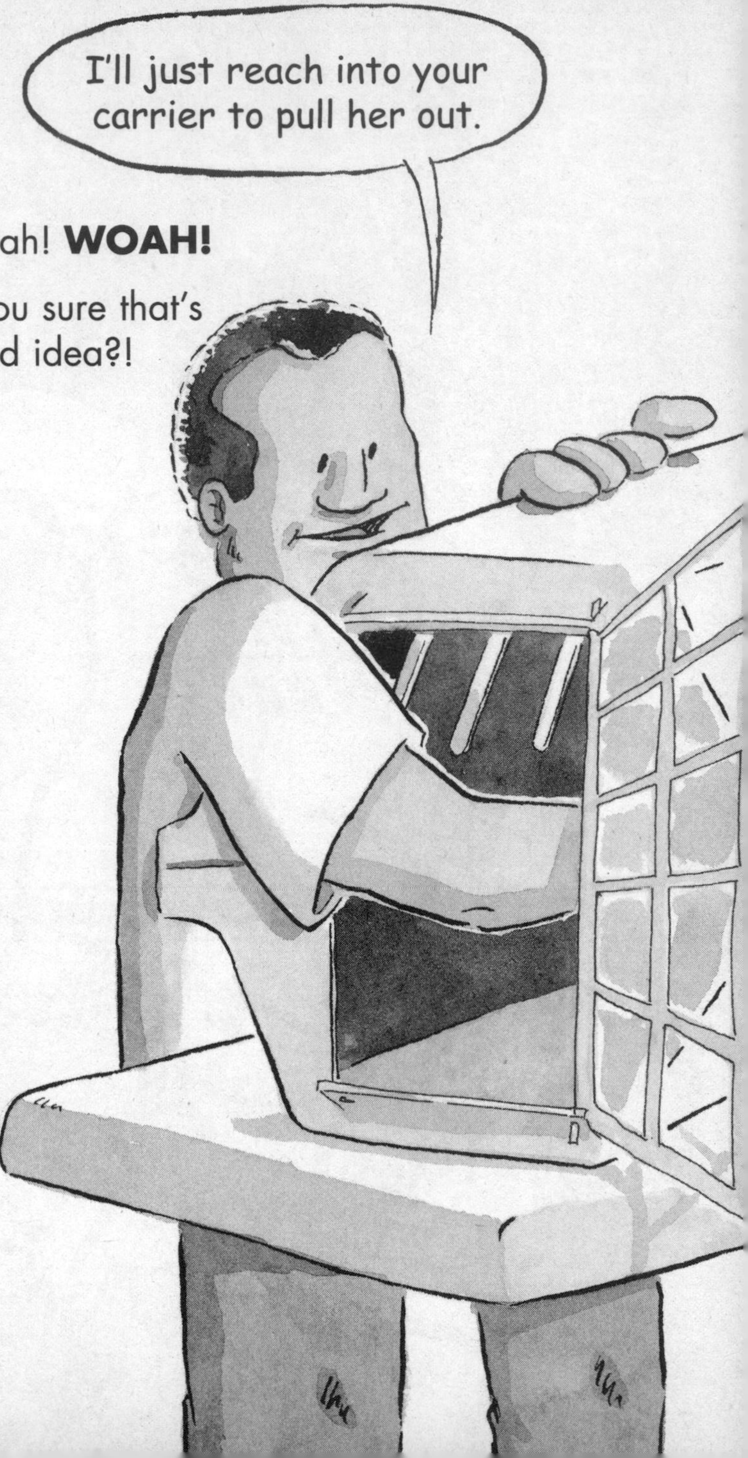
I'll just reach into your carrier to pull her out.

Woah! Woah! **WOAH!**

Doc, are you sure that's such a good idea?!

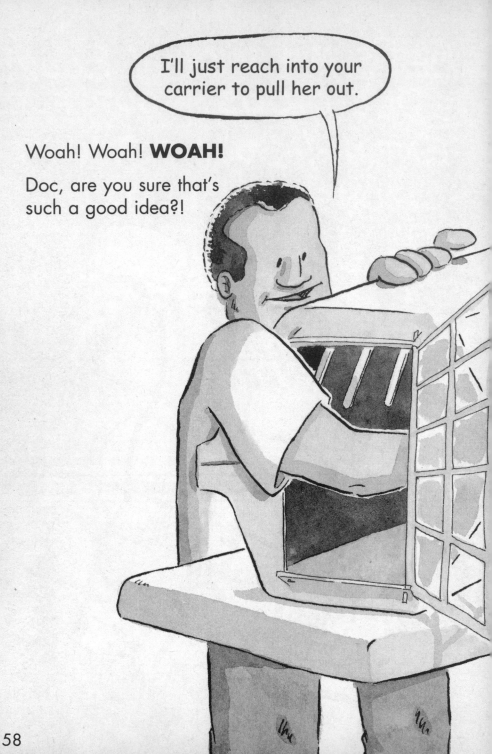

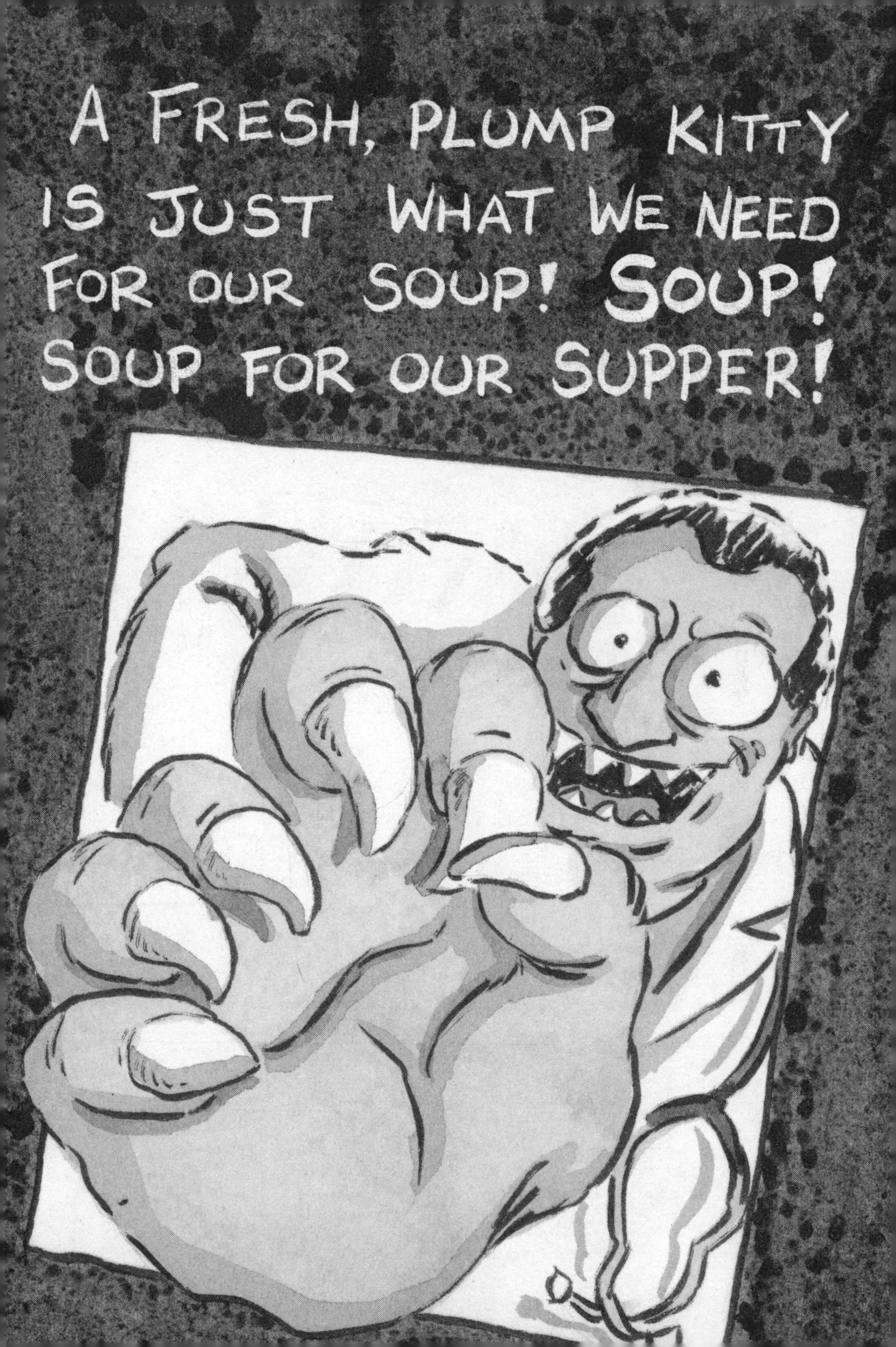
A FRESH, PLUMP KITTY IS JUST WHAT WE NEED FOR OUR SOUP! SOUP! SOUP FOR OUR SUPPER!

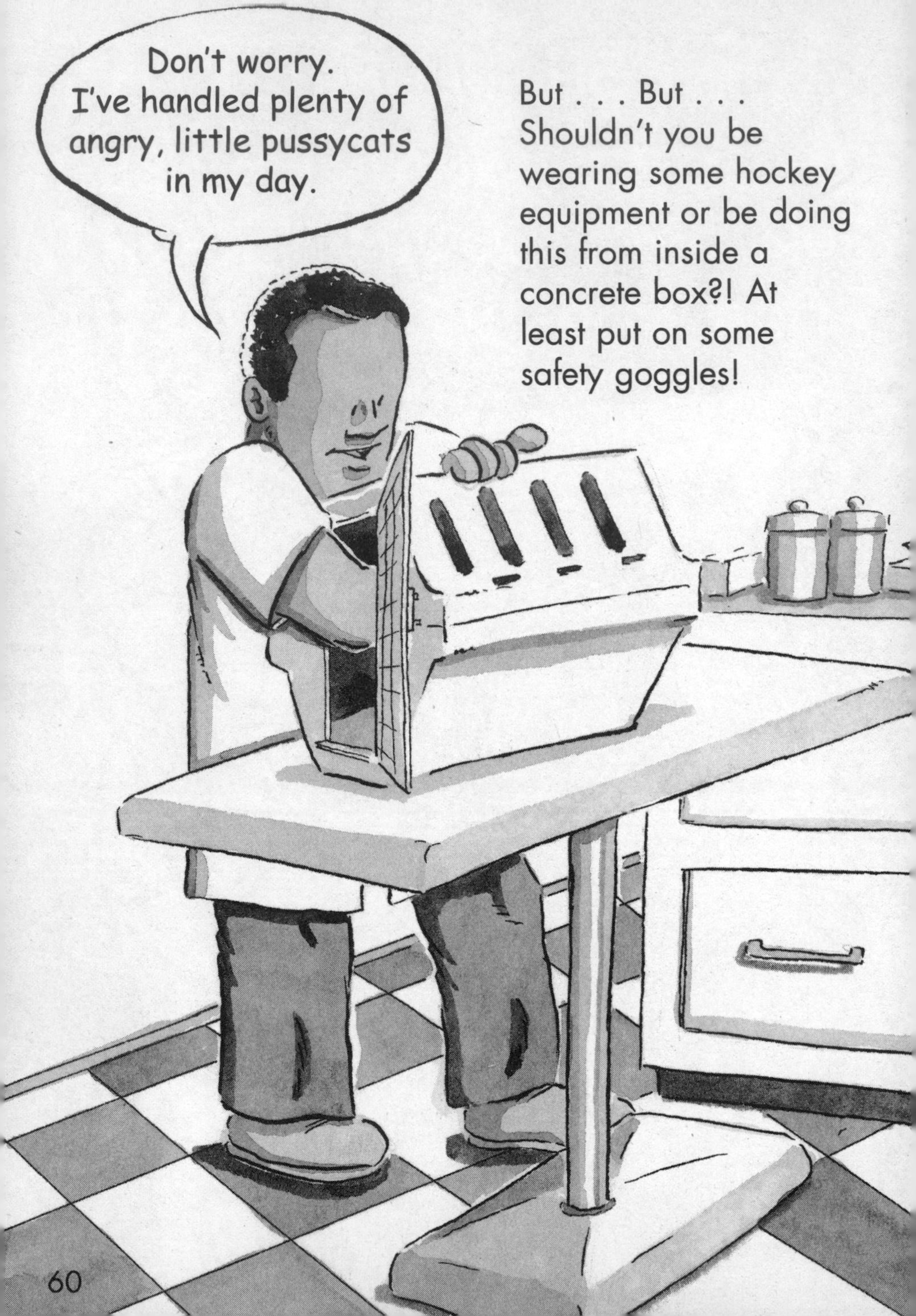
Don't worry. I've handled plenty of angry, little pussycats in my day.

But . . . But . . . Shouldn't you be wearing some hockey equipment or be doing this from inside a concrete box?! At least put on some safety goggles!

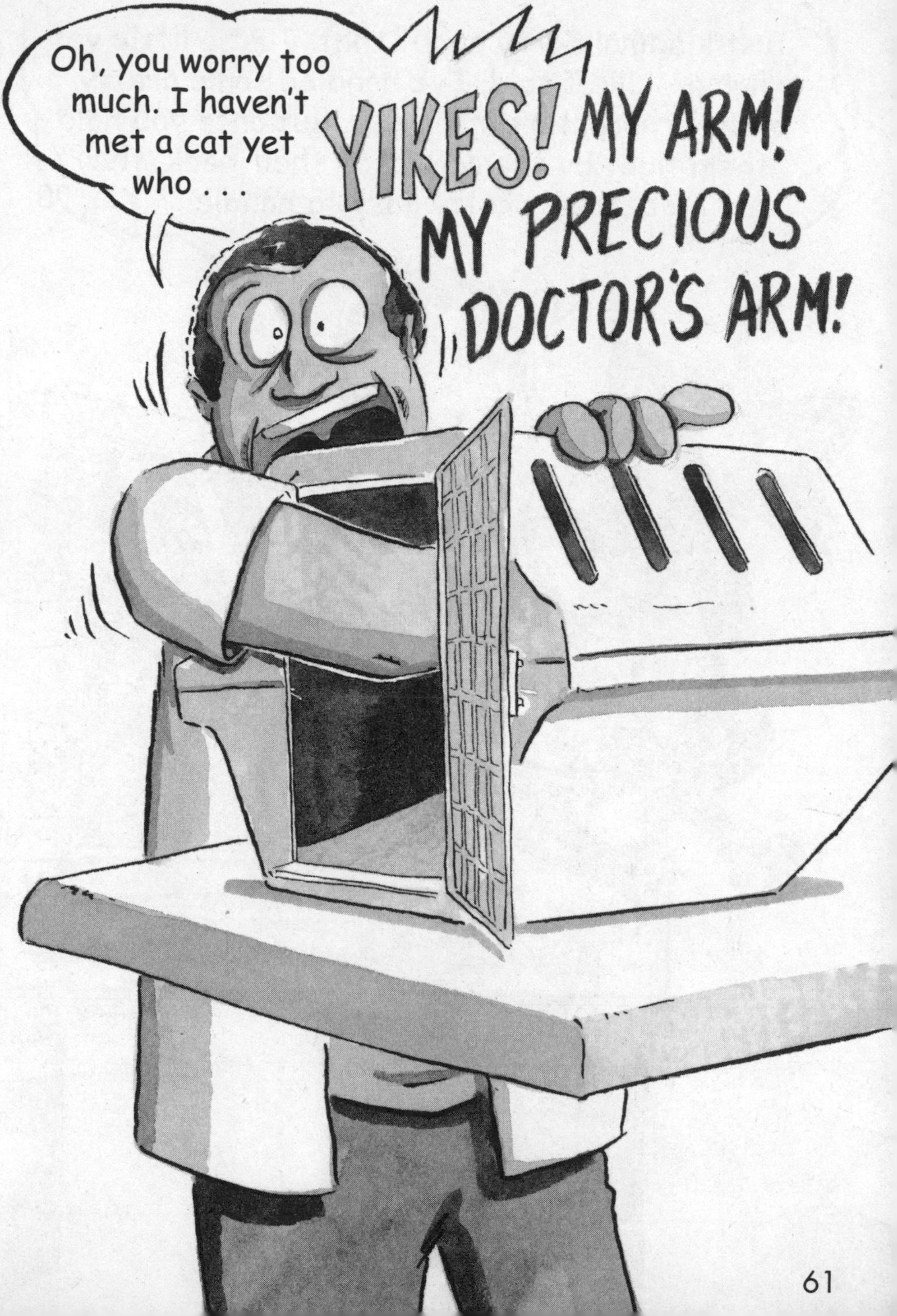
Oh, you worry too much. I haven't met a cat yet who . . .
YIKES! MY ARM! MY PRECIOUS DOCTOR'S ARM!

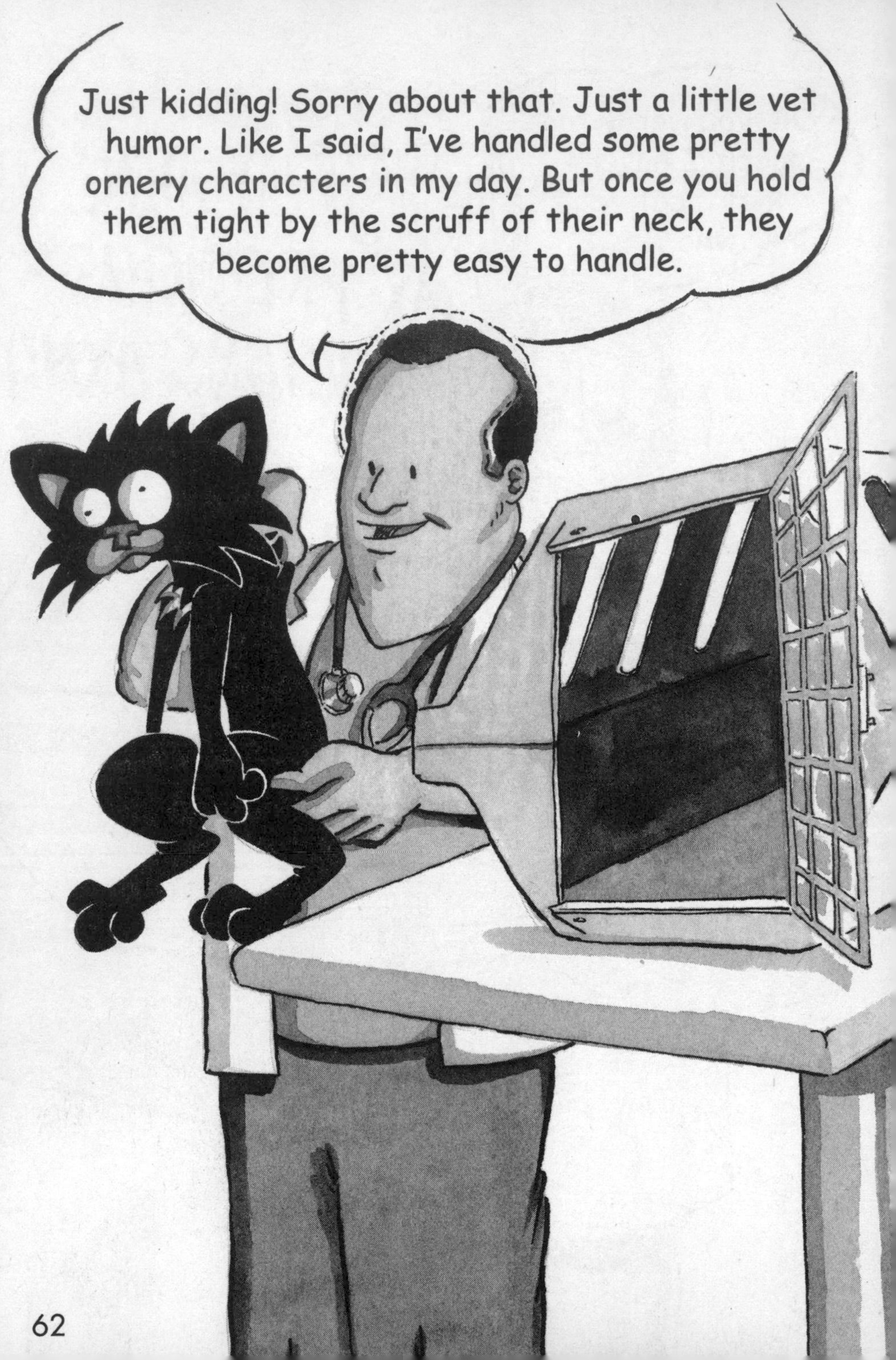
Just kidding! Sorry about that. Just a little vet humor. Like I said, I've handled some pretty ornery characters in my day. But once you hold them tight by the scruff of their neck, they become pretty easy to handle.

This is by far the most amazing thing I've ever seen.

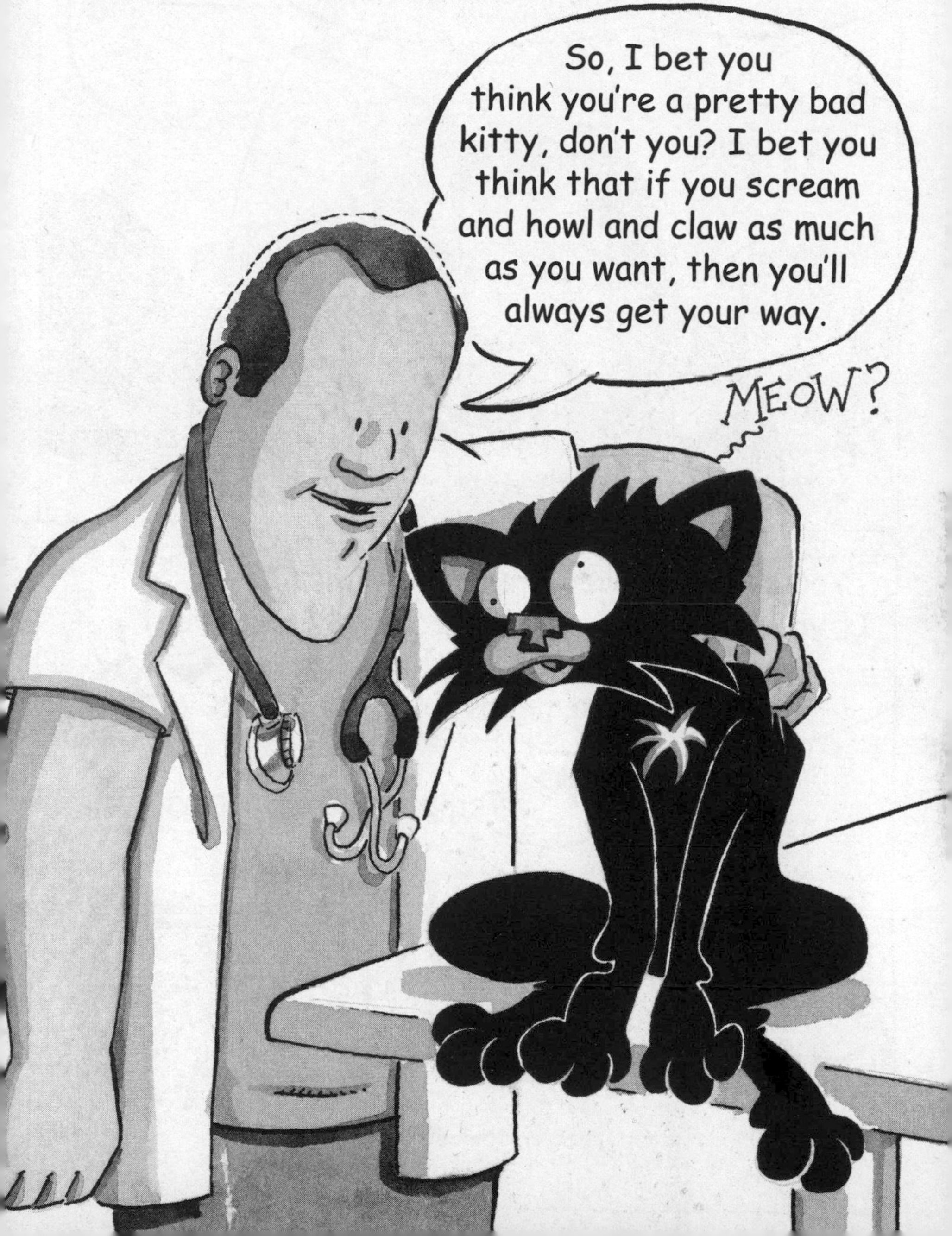
So, I bet you think you're a pretty bad kitty, don't you? I bet you think that if you scream and howl and claw as much as you want, then you'll always get your way.
MEOW?

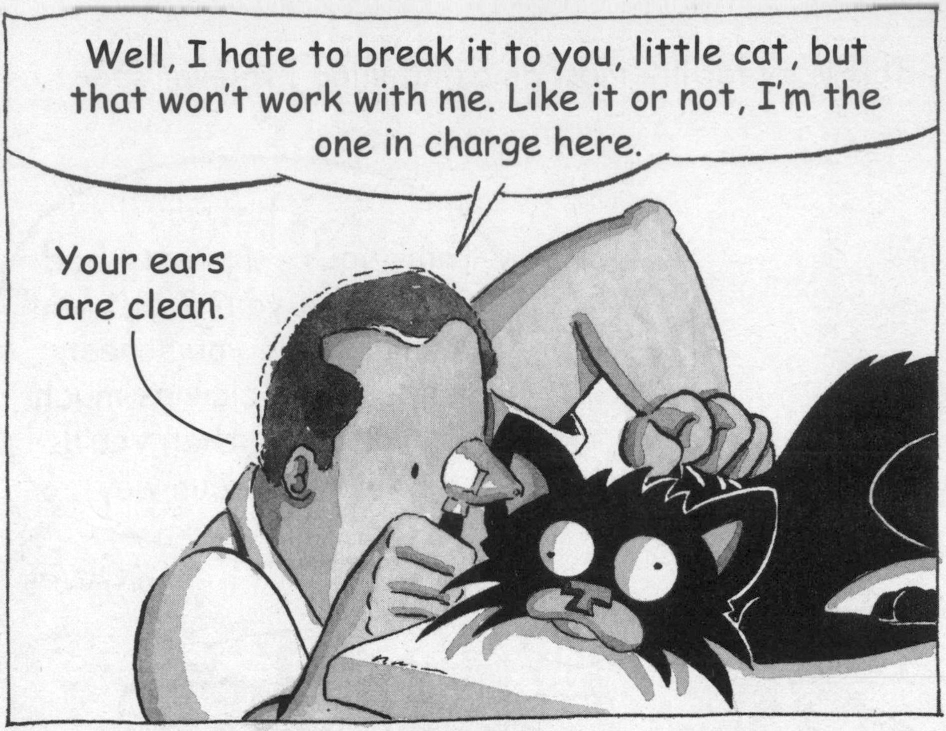
Well, I hate to break it to you, little cat, but that won't work with me. Like it or not, I'm the one in charge here.
Your ears are clean.

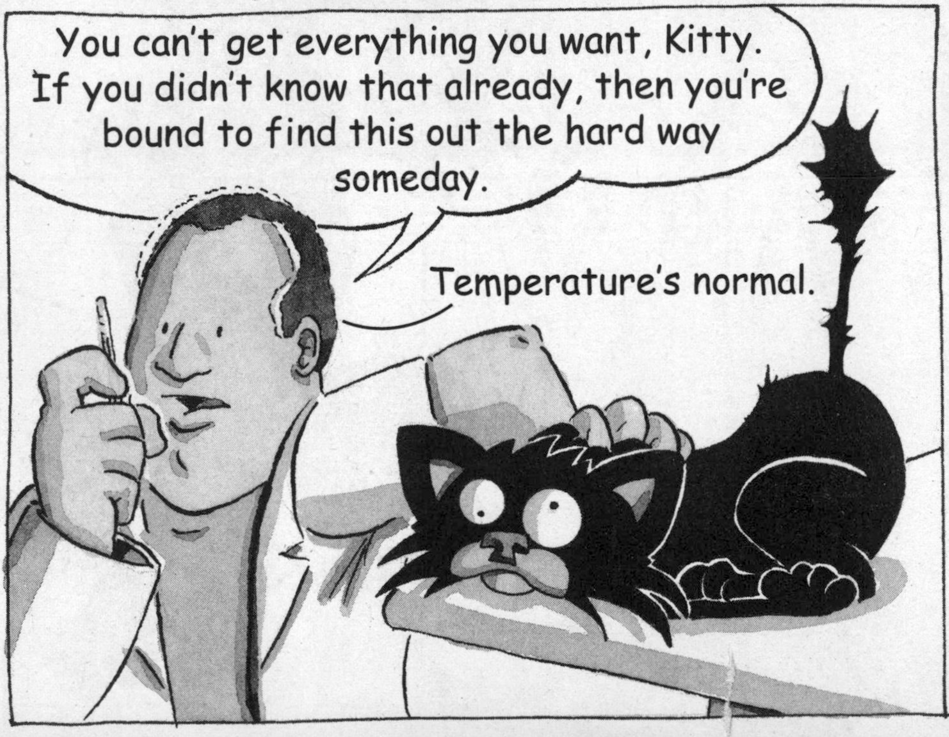
You can't get everything you want, Kitty. If you didn't know that already, then you're bound to find this out the hard way someday.
Temperature's normal.

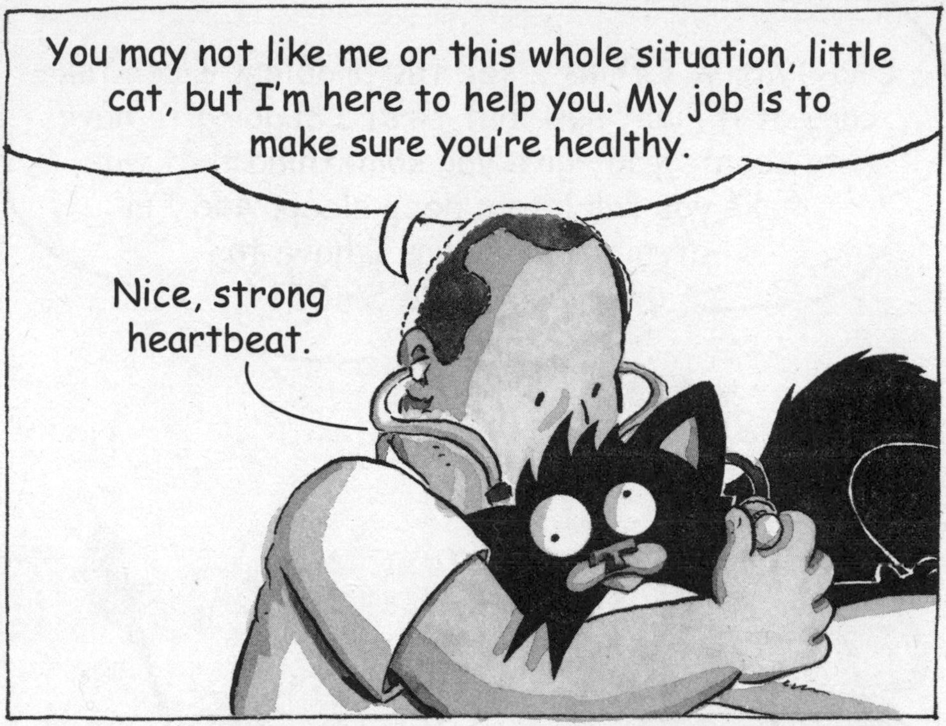
You may not like me or this whole situation, little cat, but I'm here to help you. My job is to make sure you're healthy.
Nice, strong heartbeat.

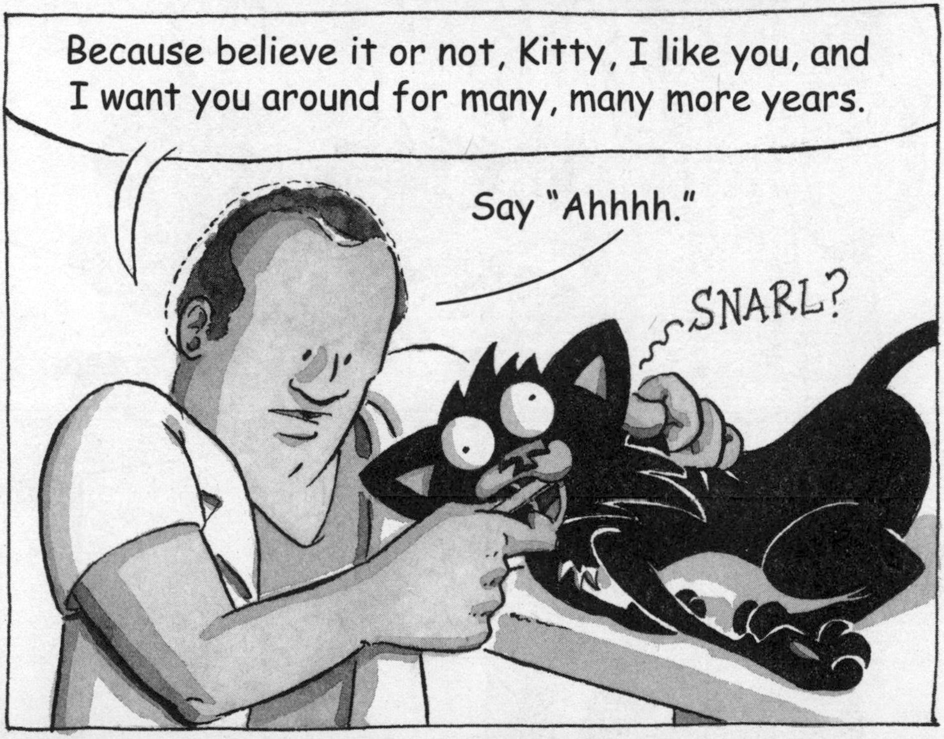
Because believe it or not, Kitty, I like you, and I want you around for many, many more years.
Say "Ahhhh."
SNARL?

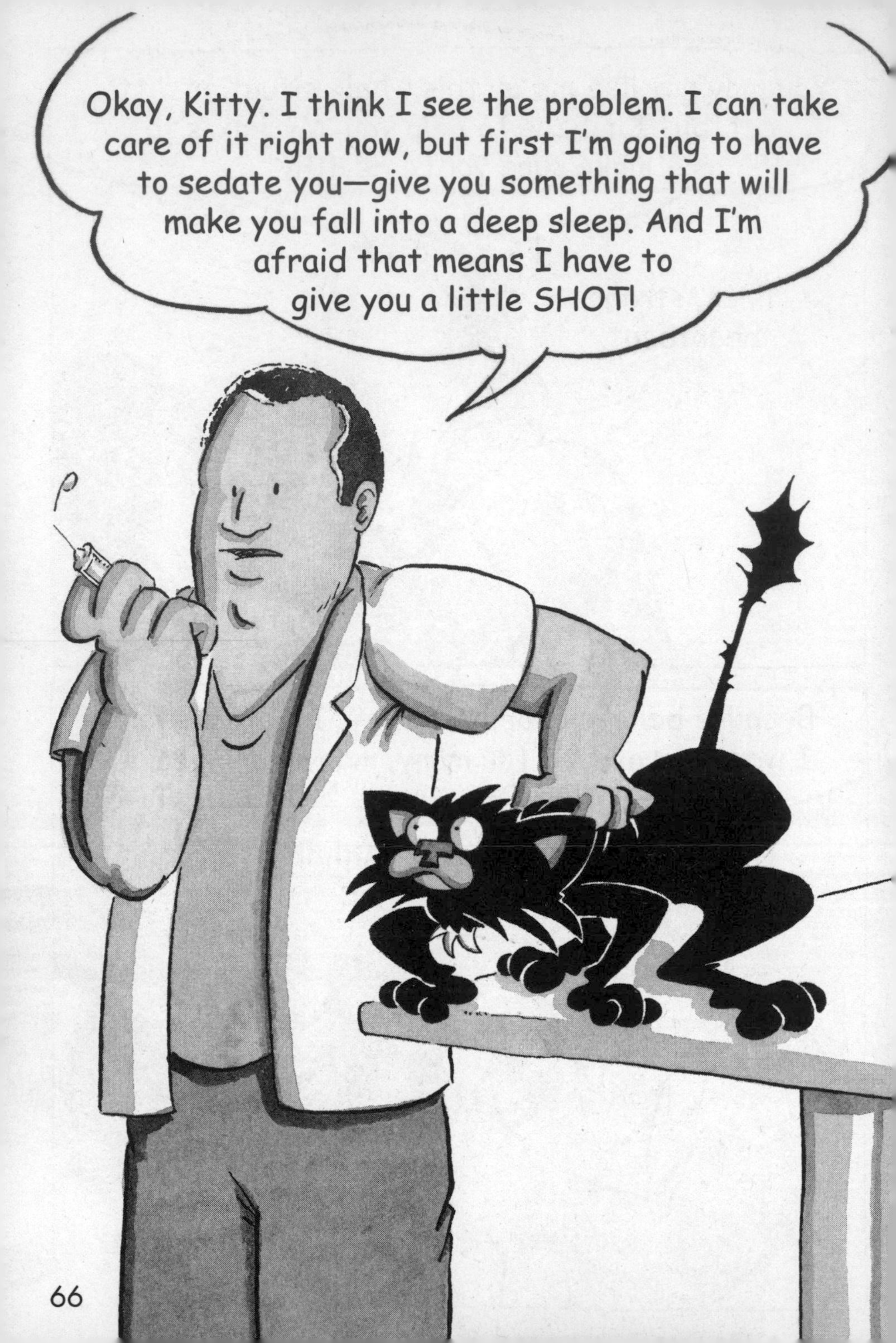
Okay, Kitty. I think I see the problem. I can take care of it right now, but first I'm going to have to sedate you—give you something that will make you fall into a deep sleep. And I'm afraid that means I have to give you a little SHOT!

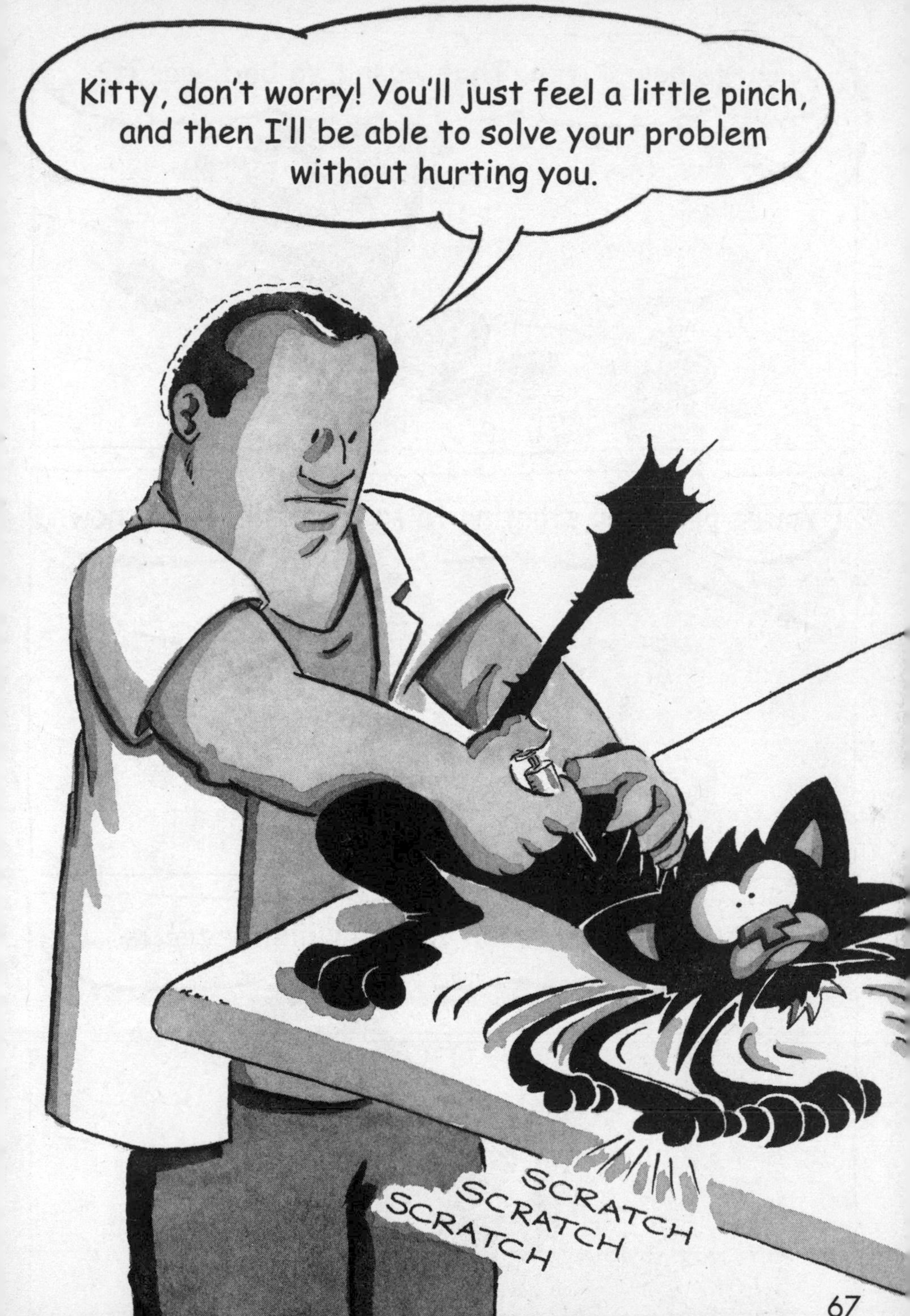
Kitty, don't worry! You'll just feel a little pinch, and then I'll be able to solve your problem without hurting you.
SCRATCH
SCRATCH
SCRATCH

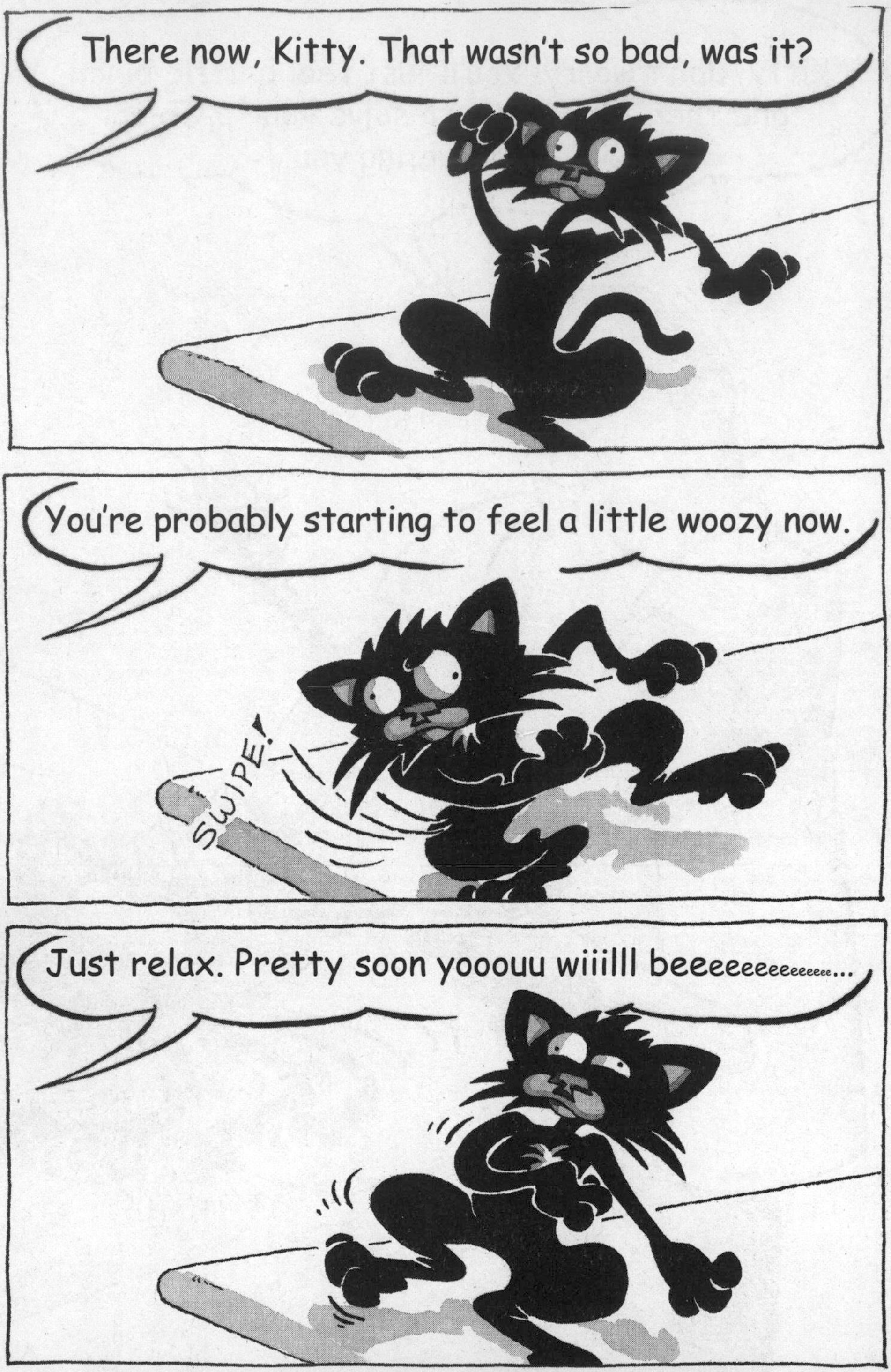
There now, Kitty. That wasn't so bad, was it?
You're probably starting to feel a little woozy now.
SWIPE!
Just relax. Pretty soon yooouu wiiilll beeeeeeeeeeeee...

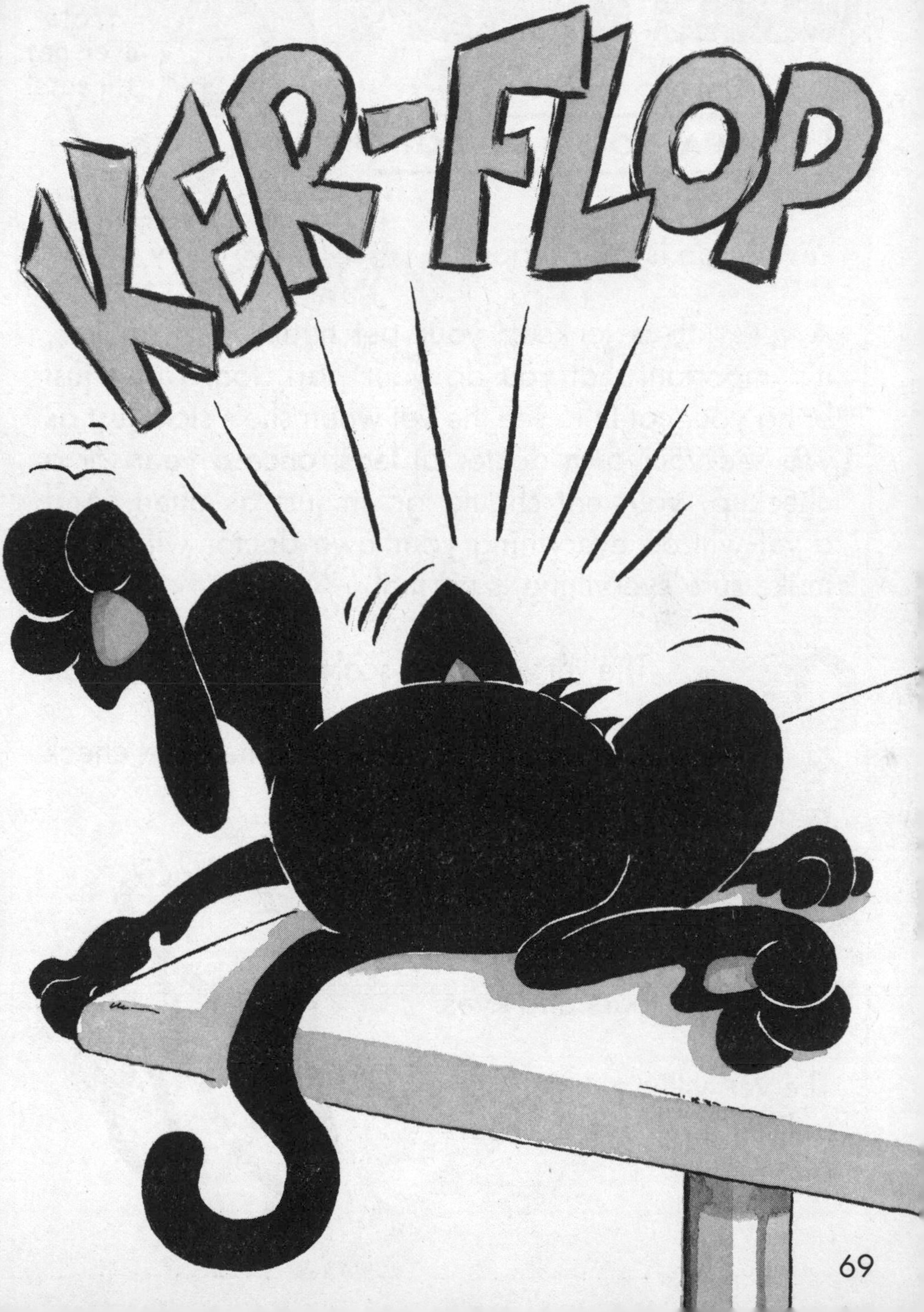
KER-FLOP

UNCLE MURRAY'S FUN FACTS

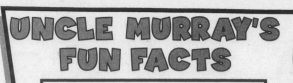

WHAT DOES A VET DO?

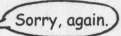

A vet frets over pet threats!

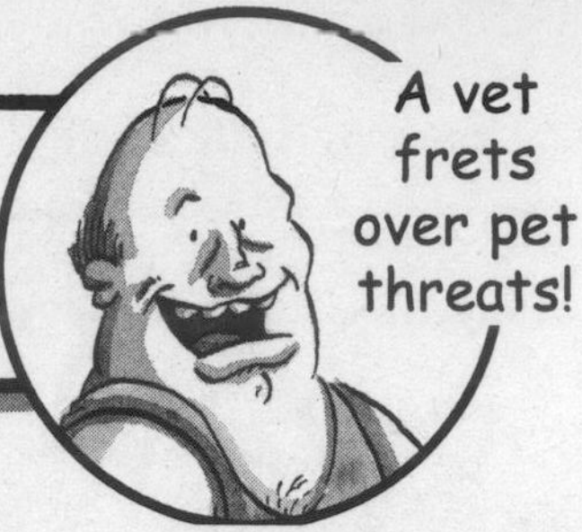

A vet's job is very serious.

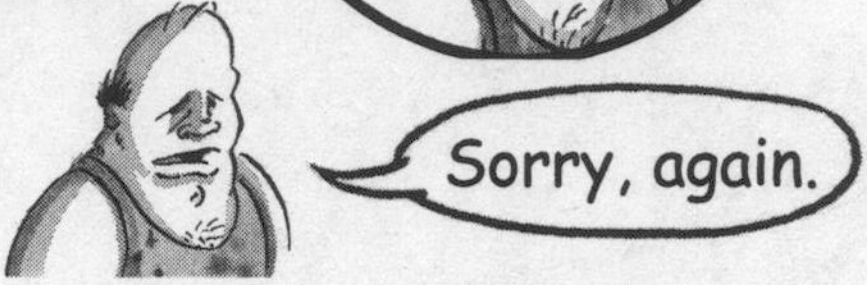

Sorry, again.

A vet's job is to keep your pet healthy. To do this, it's important that you do your part, too. Don't just bring your cat in to see the vet when she's sick. Just as you see your own doctor at least once a year for a checkup, your cat should go in just as often. And a vet will do everything your own doctor will do to make sure everything is normal.

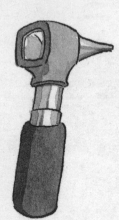

The vet will use a scale to weigh your cat.

The vet will use a thermometer to check your cat's temperature.

The vet will use an otoscope to check inside your cat's ears and eyes.

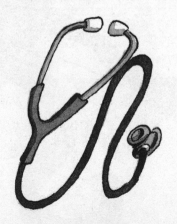

The vet will use a stethoscope to listen to your cat's heart and lungs.

The vet will look inside your cat's mouth to see her teeth and peer down her throat. (Only your cat probably won't say "Ahhh!")

The vet will gently press down on and feel the area around your cat's belly to check for anything unusual.

And, yes, a vet will give your cat shots just like your doctor gives to you. Cats need vaccinations to prevent them from contracting certain serious diseases.

Your cat may not like these visits to the vet, but they're important. Every visit to the vet ensures that your cat will live a longer and healthier life.

Do cats get a sticker or a toy at the end of their appointments? Once I got a yo-yo!

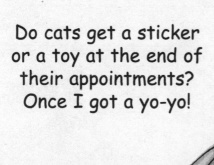

•CHAPTER FOUR•

PUSSYCAT PARADISE

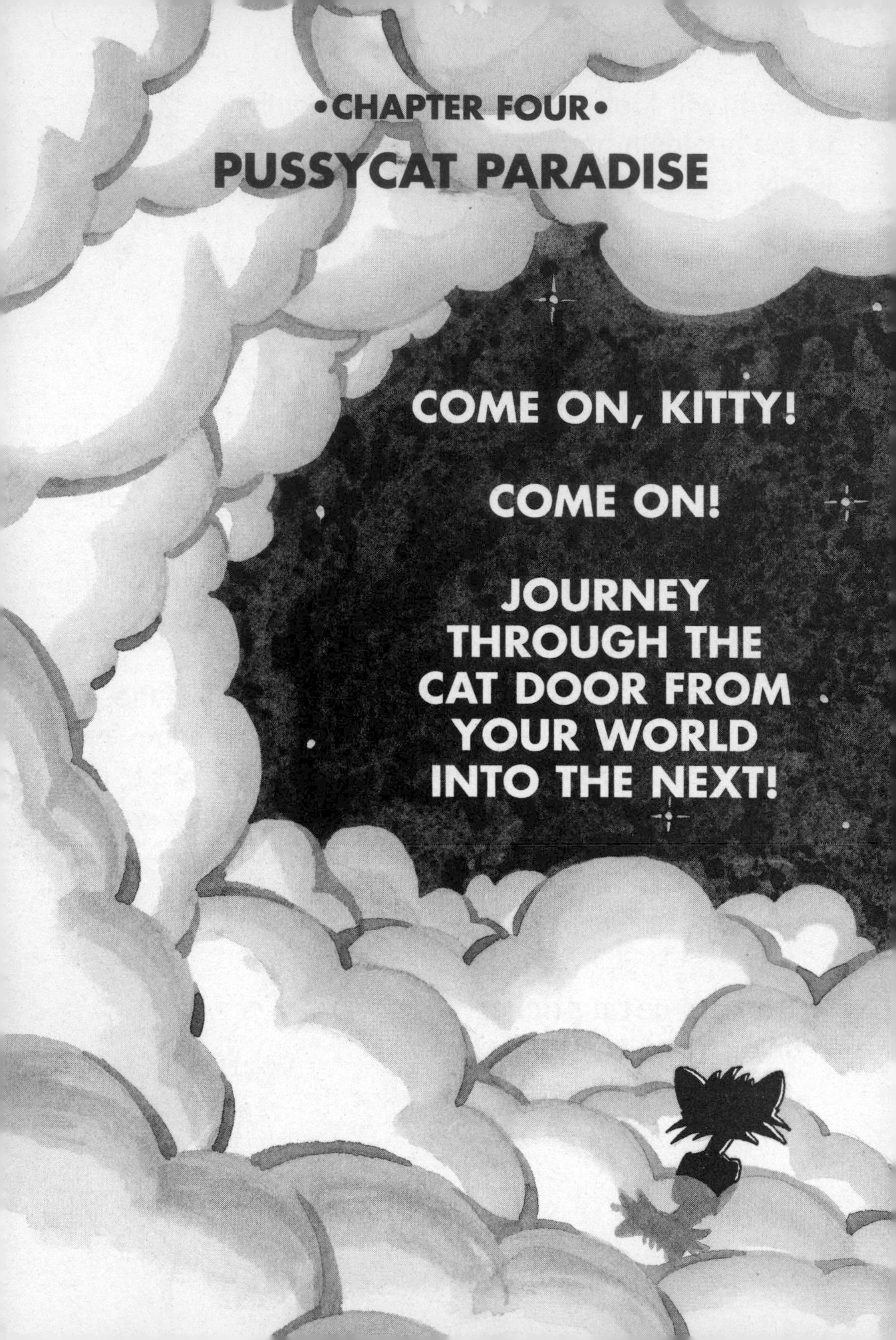
COME ON, KITTY!
COME ON!
JOURNEY THROUGH THE CAT DOOR FROM YOUR WORLD INTO THE NEXT!

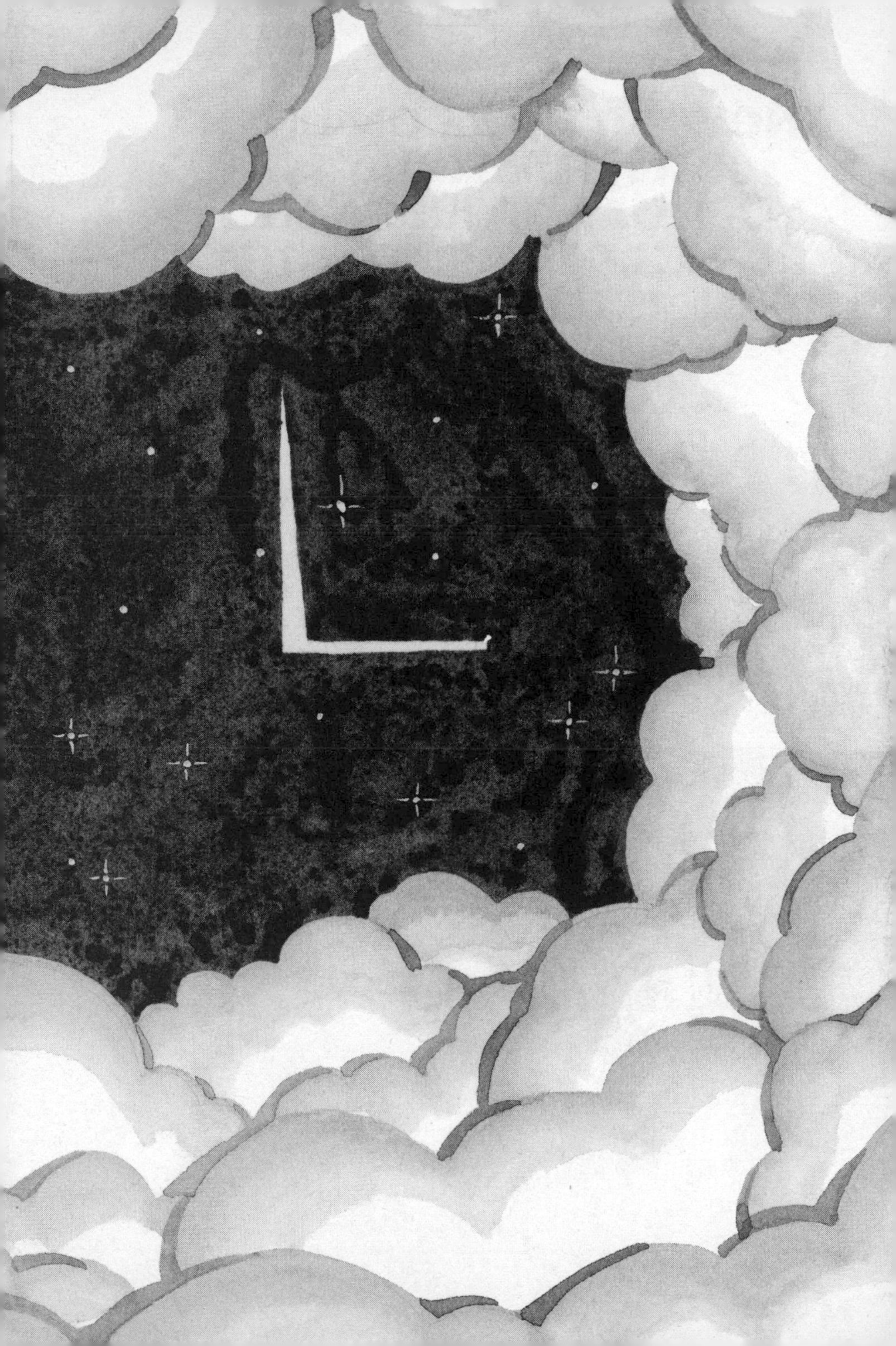

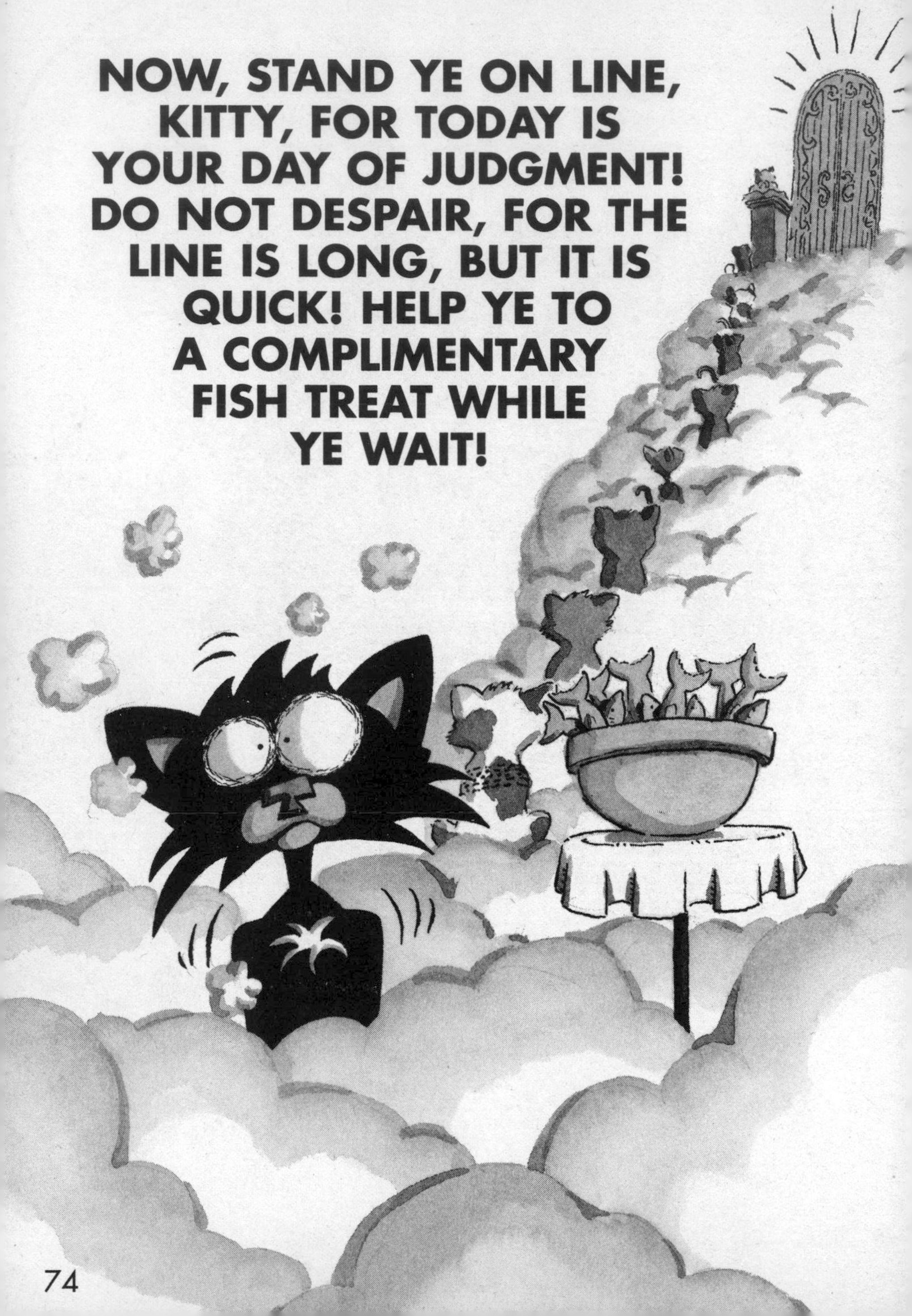
NOW, STAND YE ON LINE, KITTY, FOR TODAY IS YOUR DAY OF JUDGMENT! DO NOT DESPAIR, FOR THE LINE IS LONG, BUT IT IS QUICK! HELP YE TO A COMPLIMENTARY FISH TREAT WHILE YE WAIT!

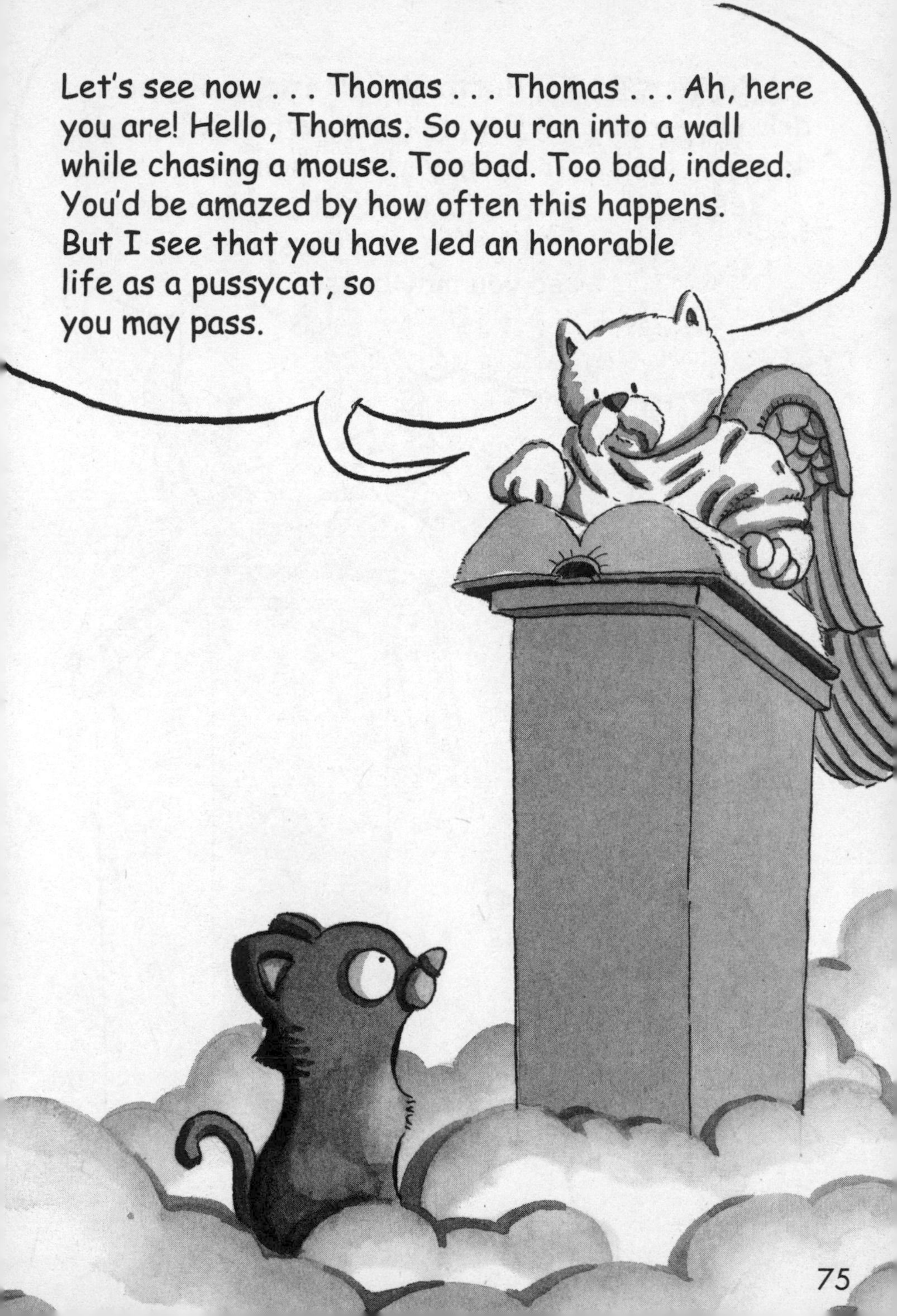
Let's see now . . . Thomas . . . Thomas . . . Ah, here you are! Hello, Thomas. So you ran into a wall while chasing a mouse. Too bad. Too bad, indeed. You'd be amazed by how often this happens. But I see that you have led an honorable life as a pussycat, so you may pass.

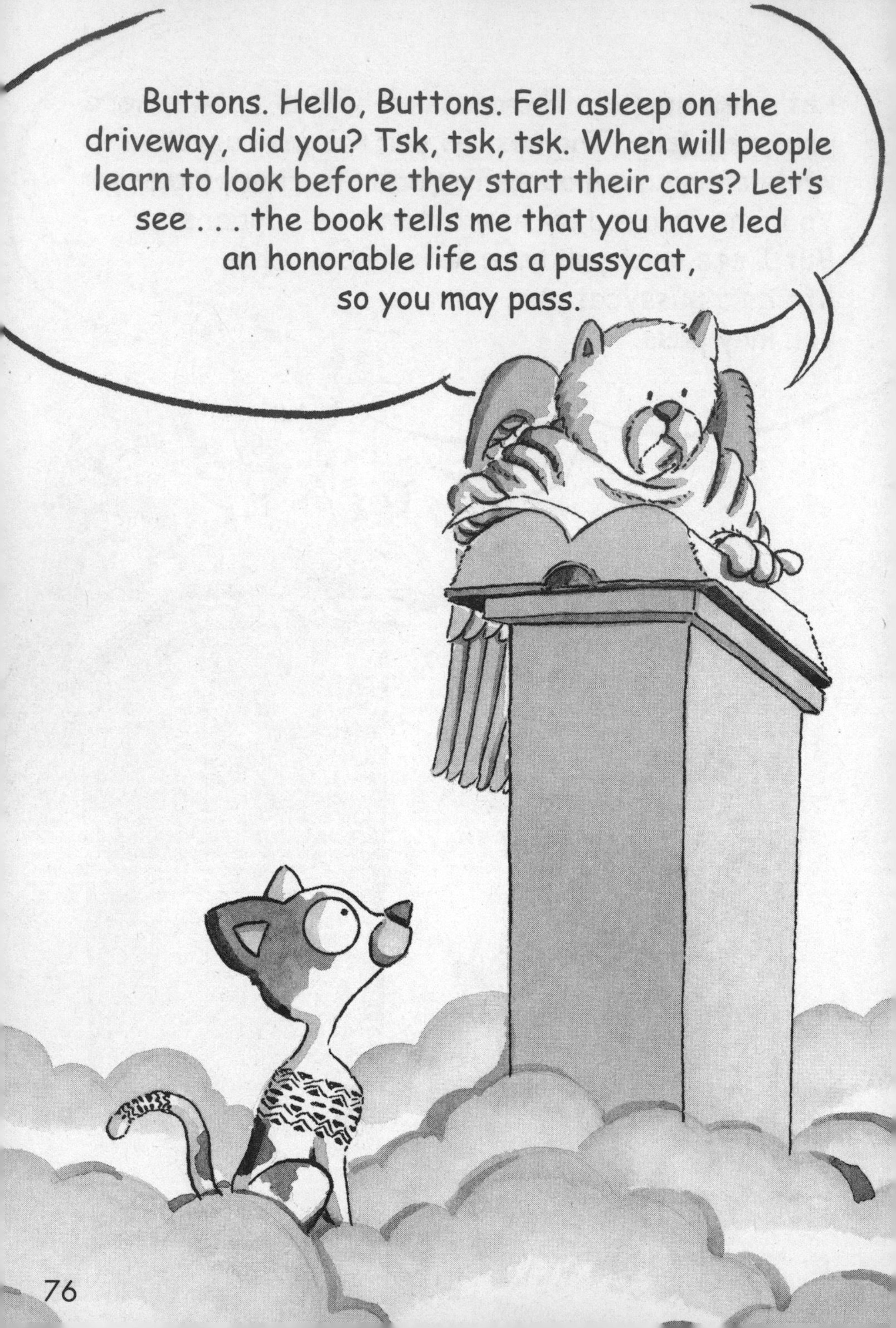
Buttons. Hello, Buttons. Fell asleep on the driveway, did you? Tsk, tsk, tsk. When will people learn to look before they start their cars? Let's see . . . the book tells me that you have led an honorable life as a pussycat, so you may pass.

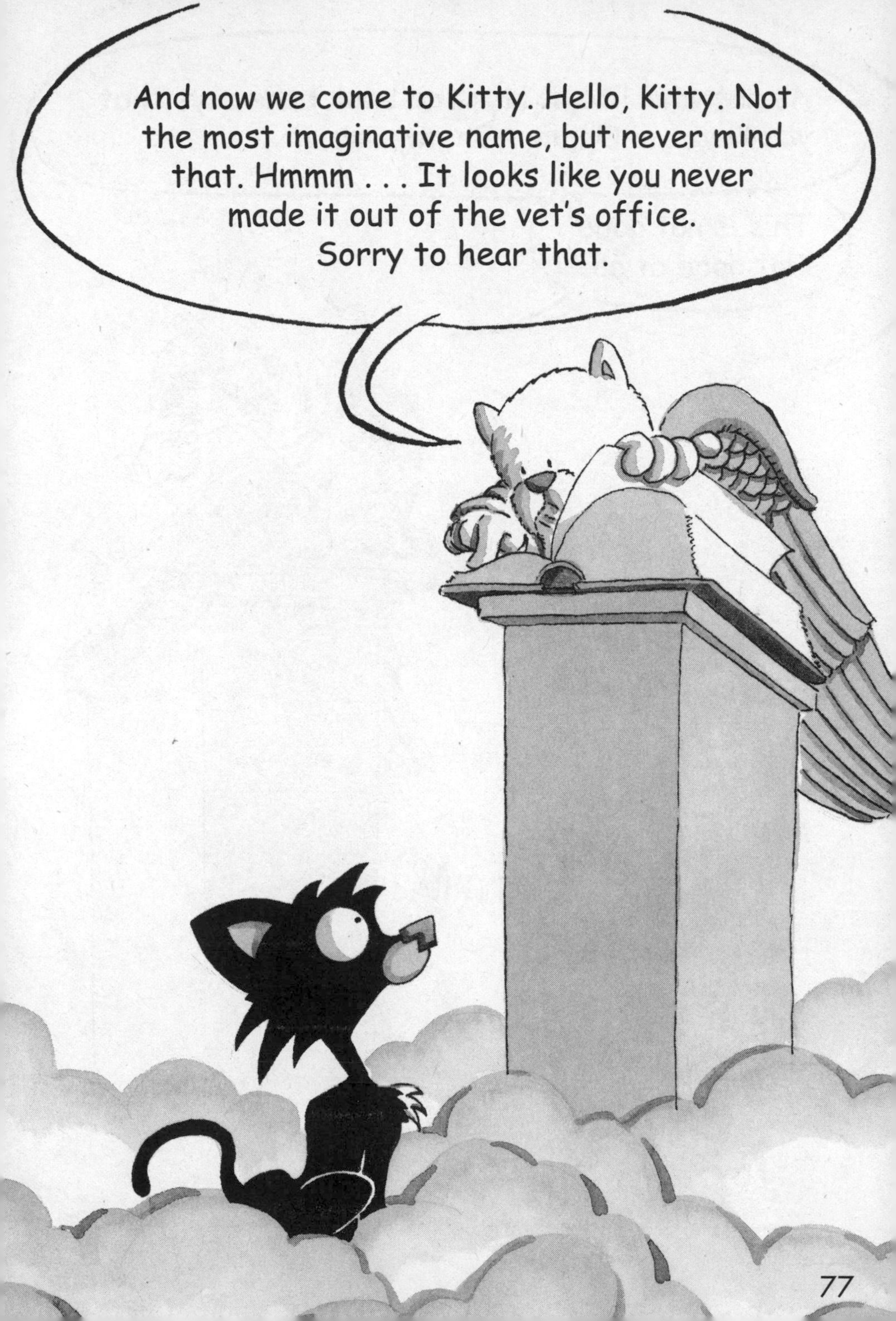
And now we come to Kitty. Hello, Kitty. Not the most imaginative name, but never mind that. Hmmm . . . It looks like you never made it out of the vet's office. Sorry to hear that.

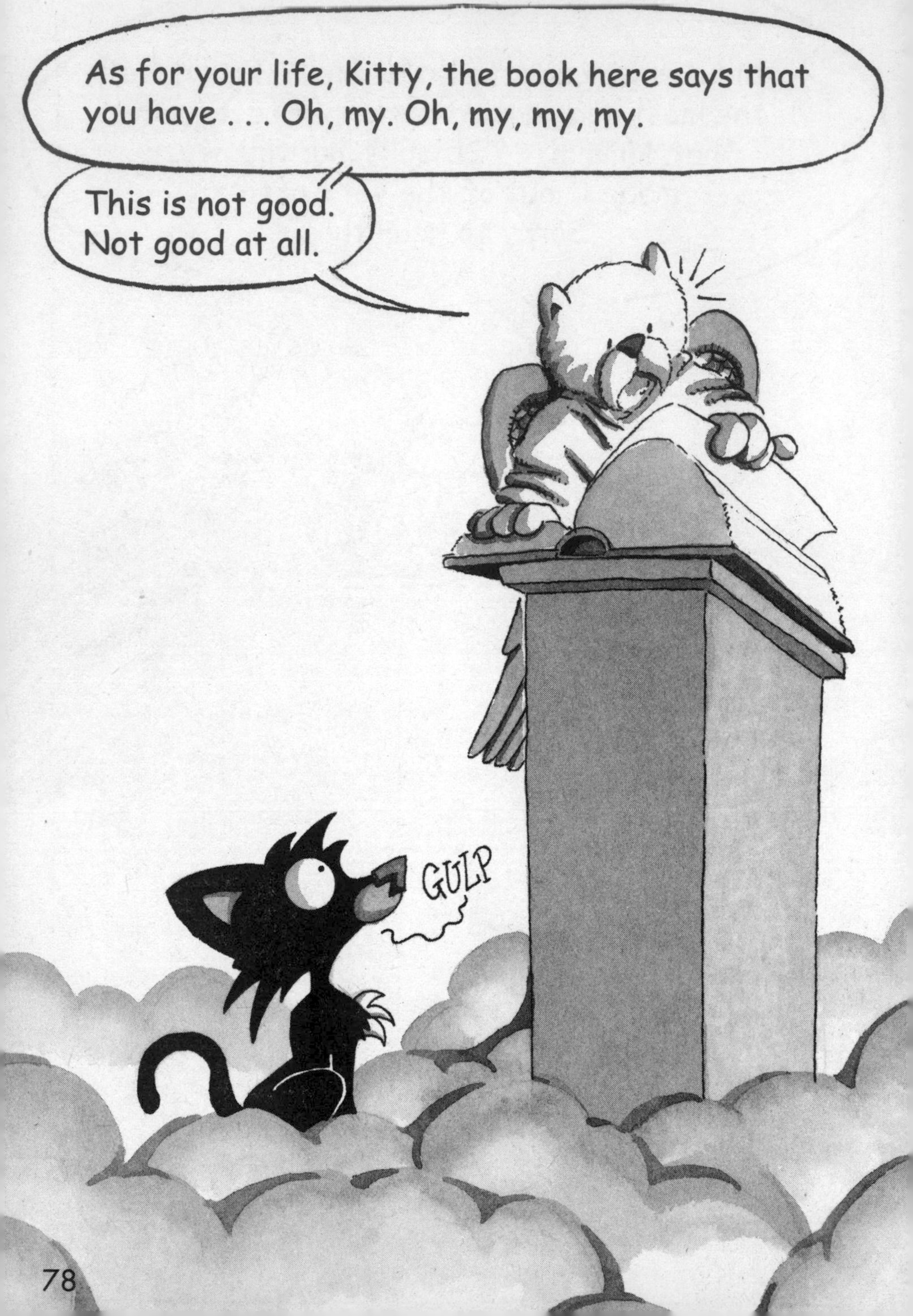
As for your life, Kitty, the book here says that you have . . . Oh, my. Oh, my, my, my.
This is not good. Not good at all.
GULP

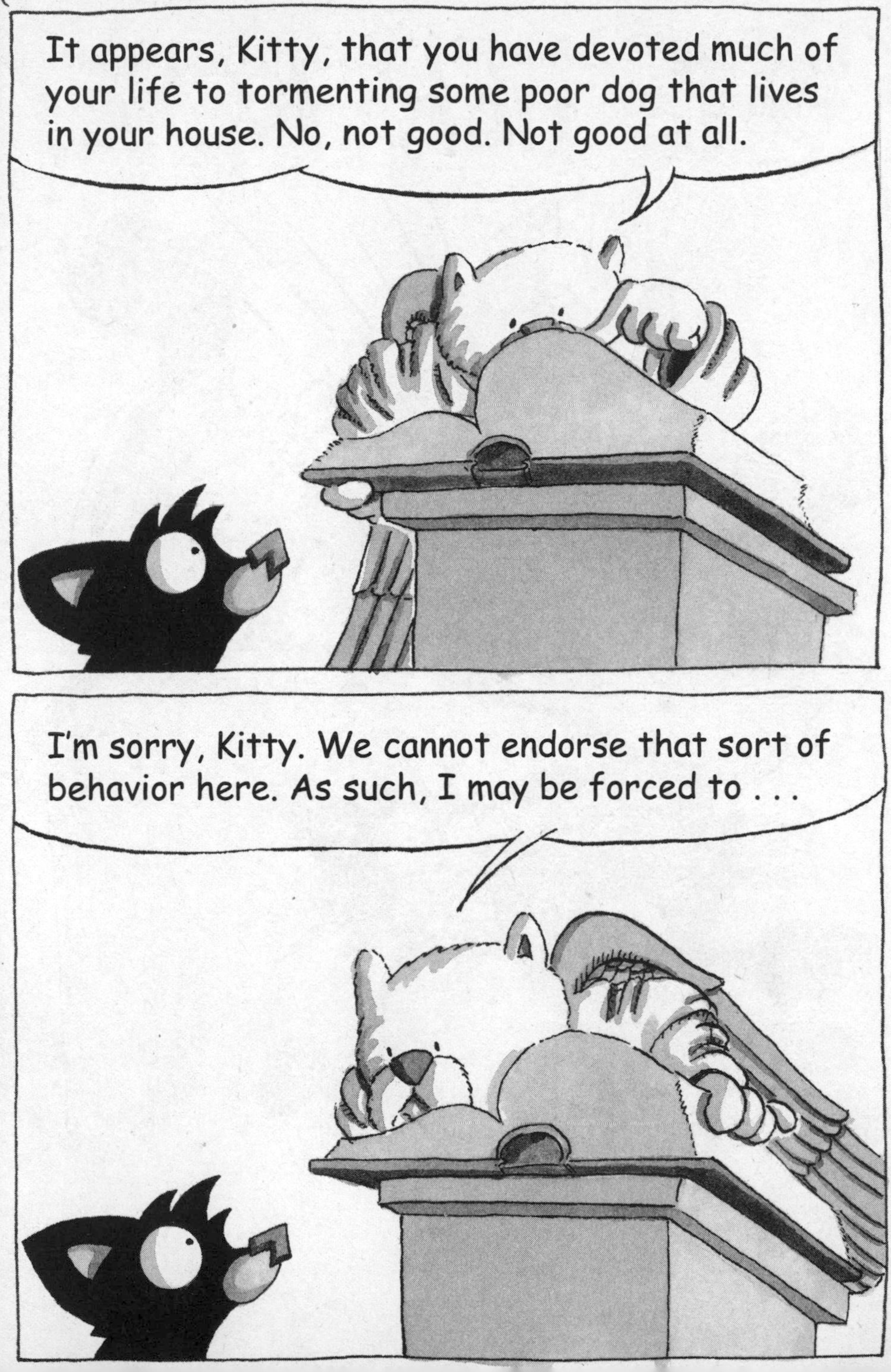
It appears, Kitty, that you have devoted much of your life to tormenting some poor dog that lives in your house. No, not good. Not good at all.
I'm sorry, Kitty. We cannot endorse that sort of behavior here. As such, I may be forced to . . .

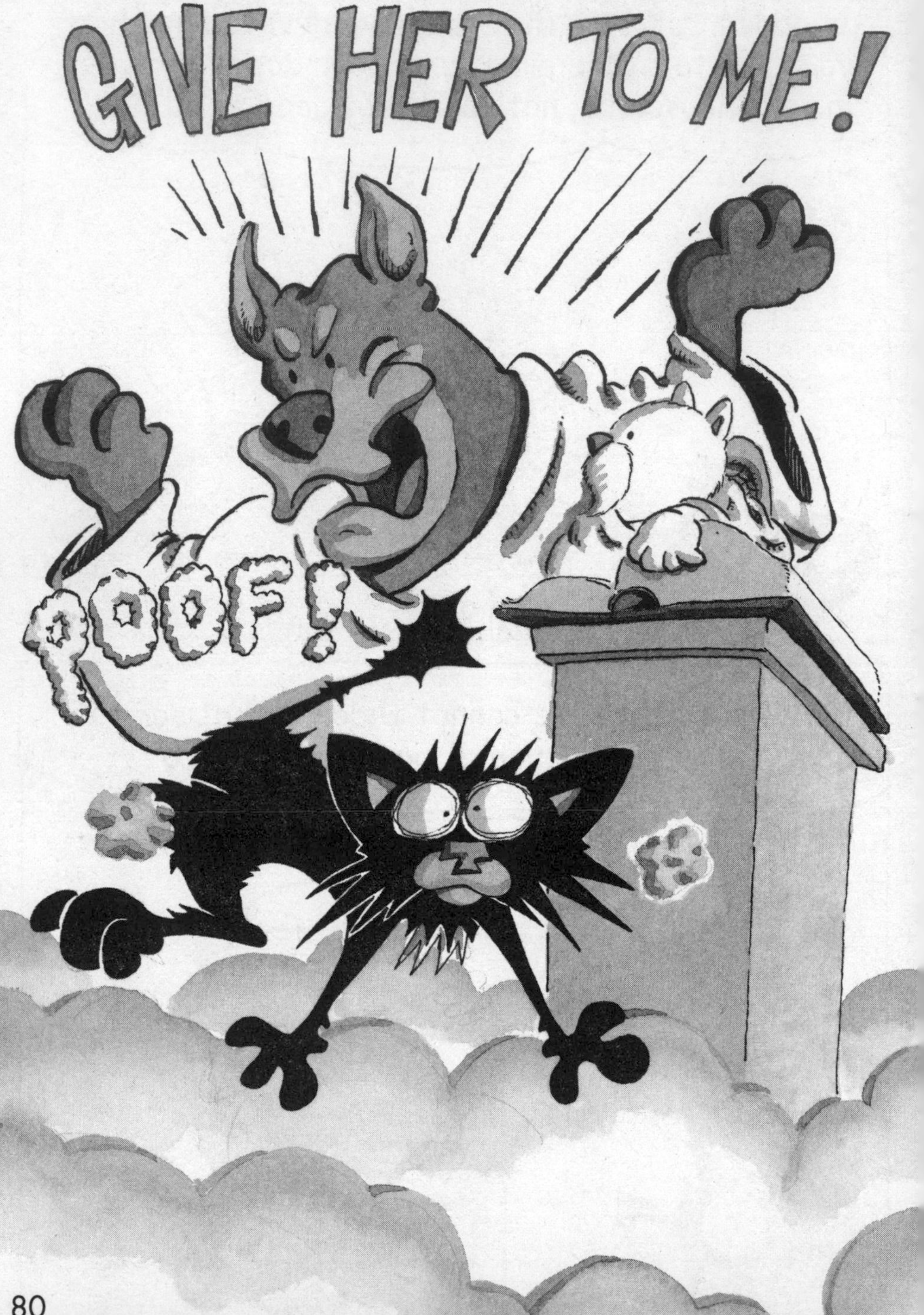
GIVE HER TO ME!
POOF!

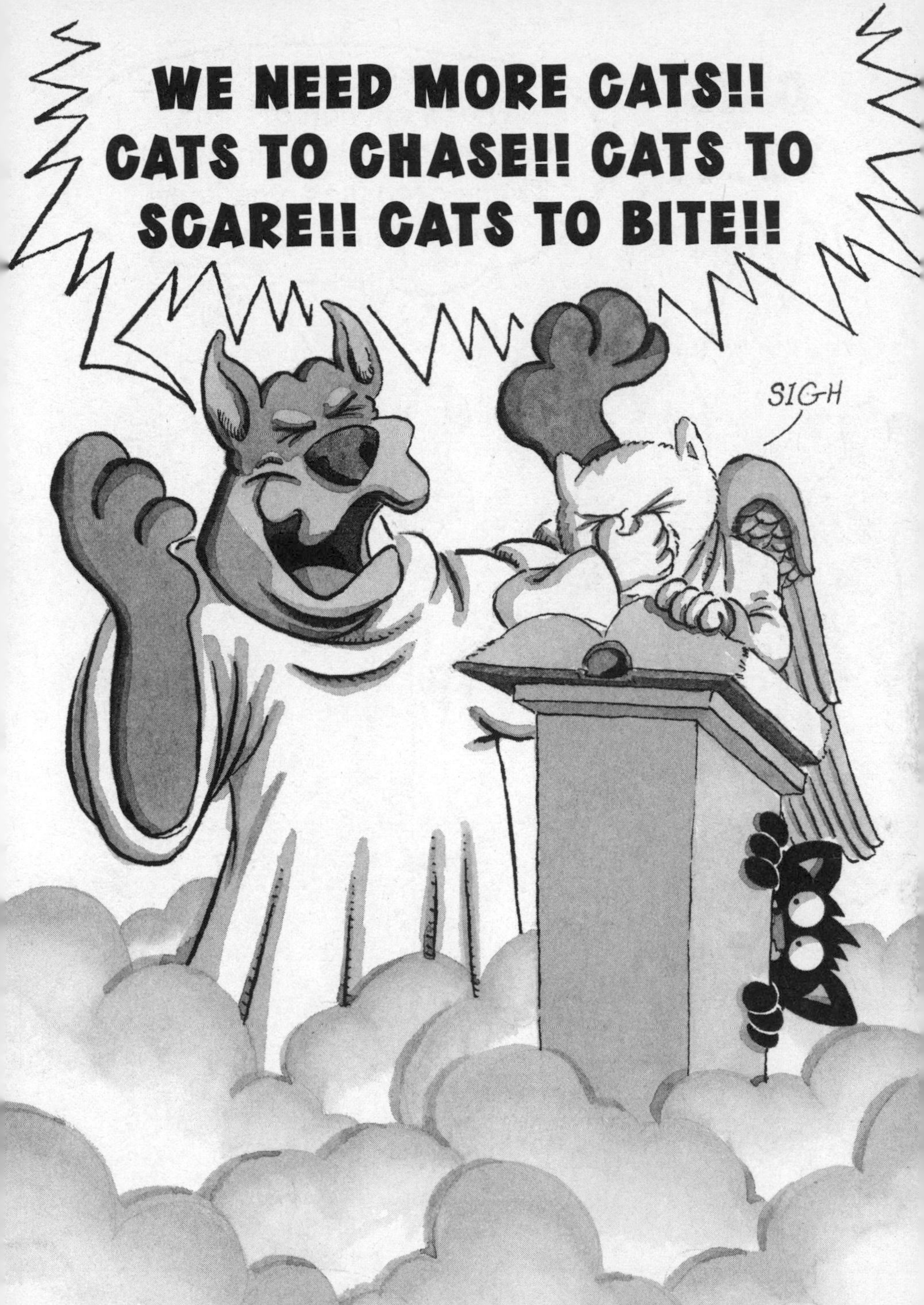
WE NEED MORE CATS!! CATS TO CHASE!! CATS TO SCARE!! CATS TO BITE!!
SIGH

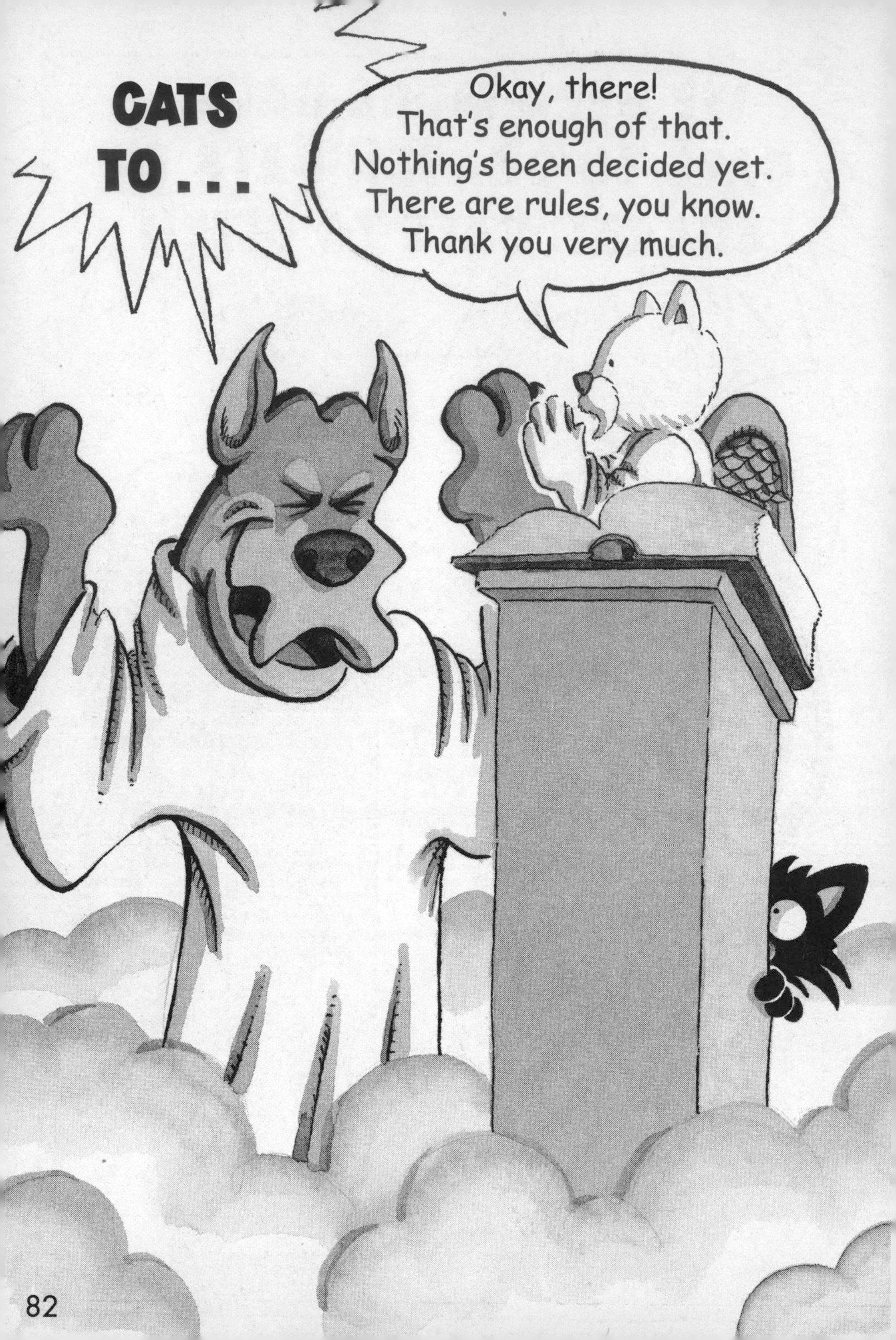
CATS TO . . .
Okay, there!
That's enough of that.
Nothing's been decided yet.
There are rules, you know.
Thank you very much.

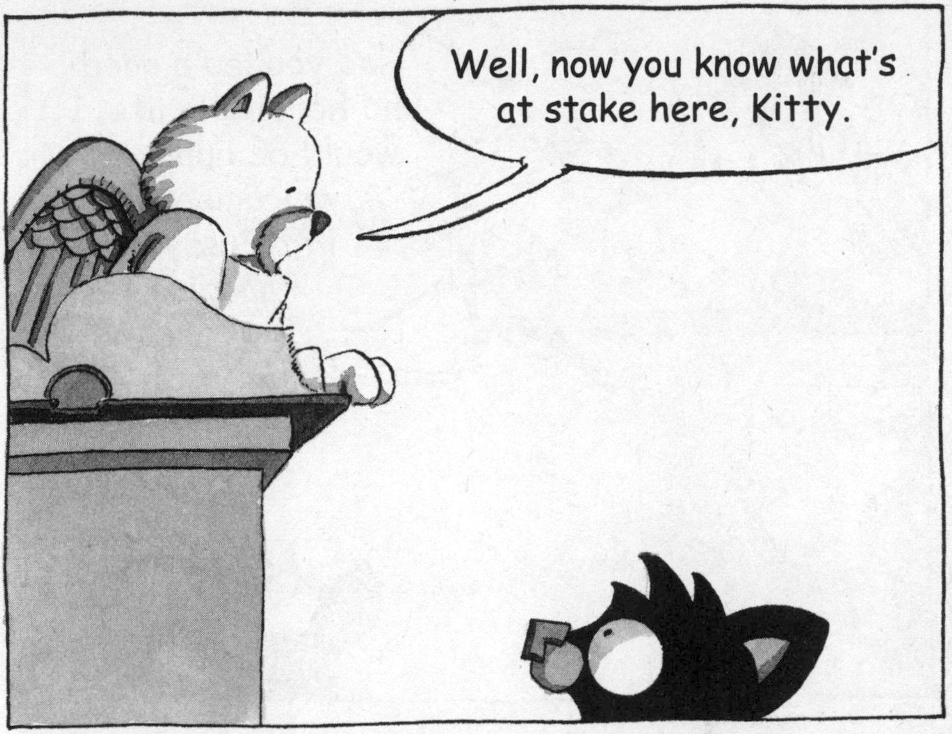
Well, now you know what's at stake here, Kitty.

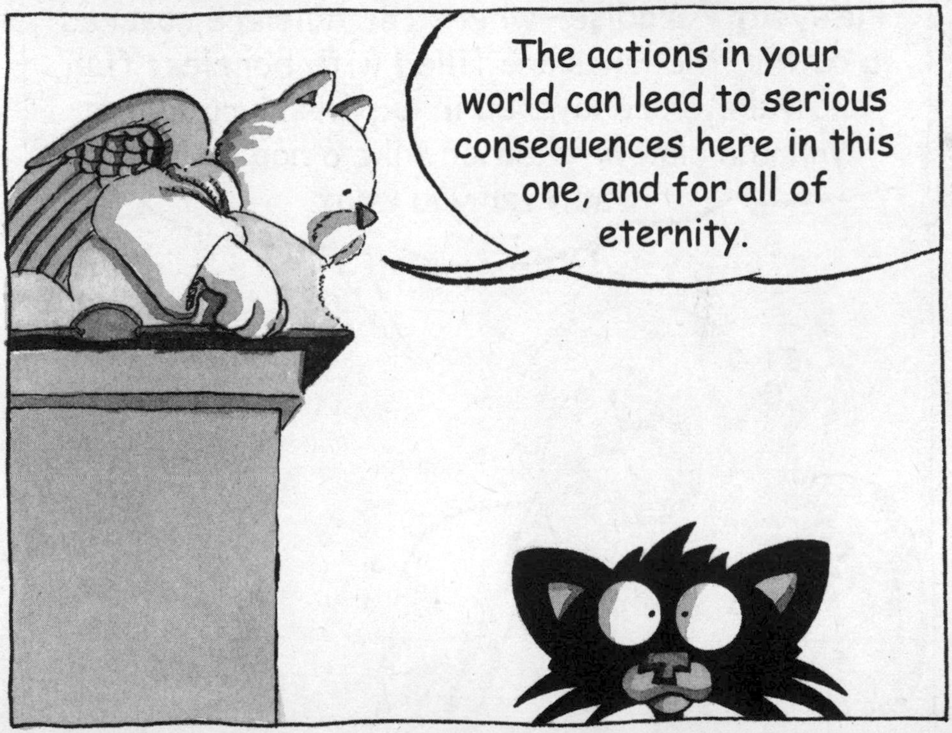
The actions in your world can lead to serious consequences here in this one, and for all of eternity.

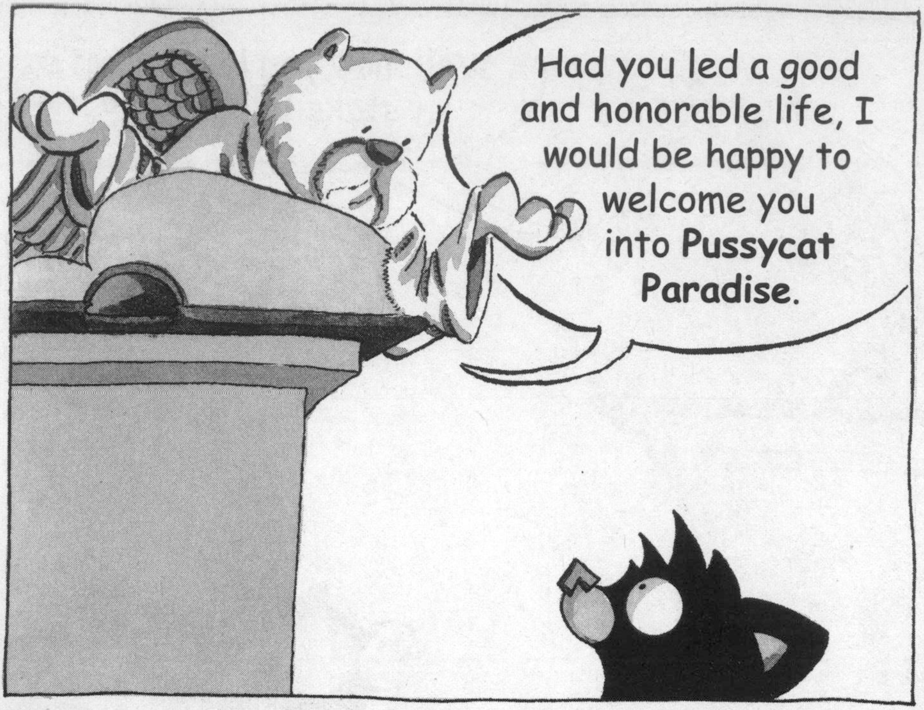
Had you led a good and honorable life, I would be happy to welcome you into **Pussycat Paradise**.

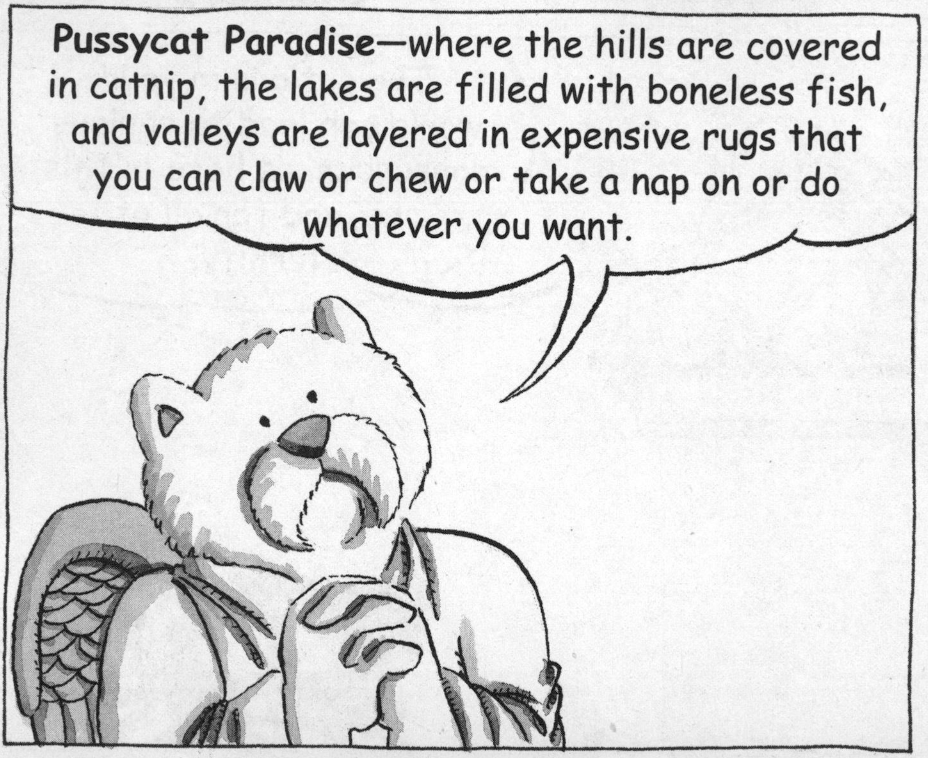
Pussycat Paradise—where the hills are covered in catnip, the lakes are filled with boneless fish, and valleys are layered in expensive rugs that you can claw or chew or take a nap on or do whatever you want.

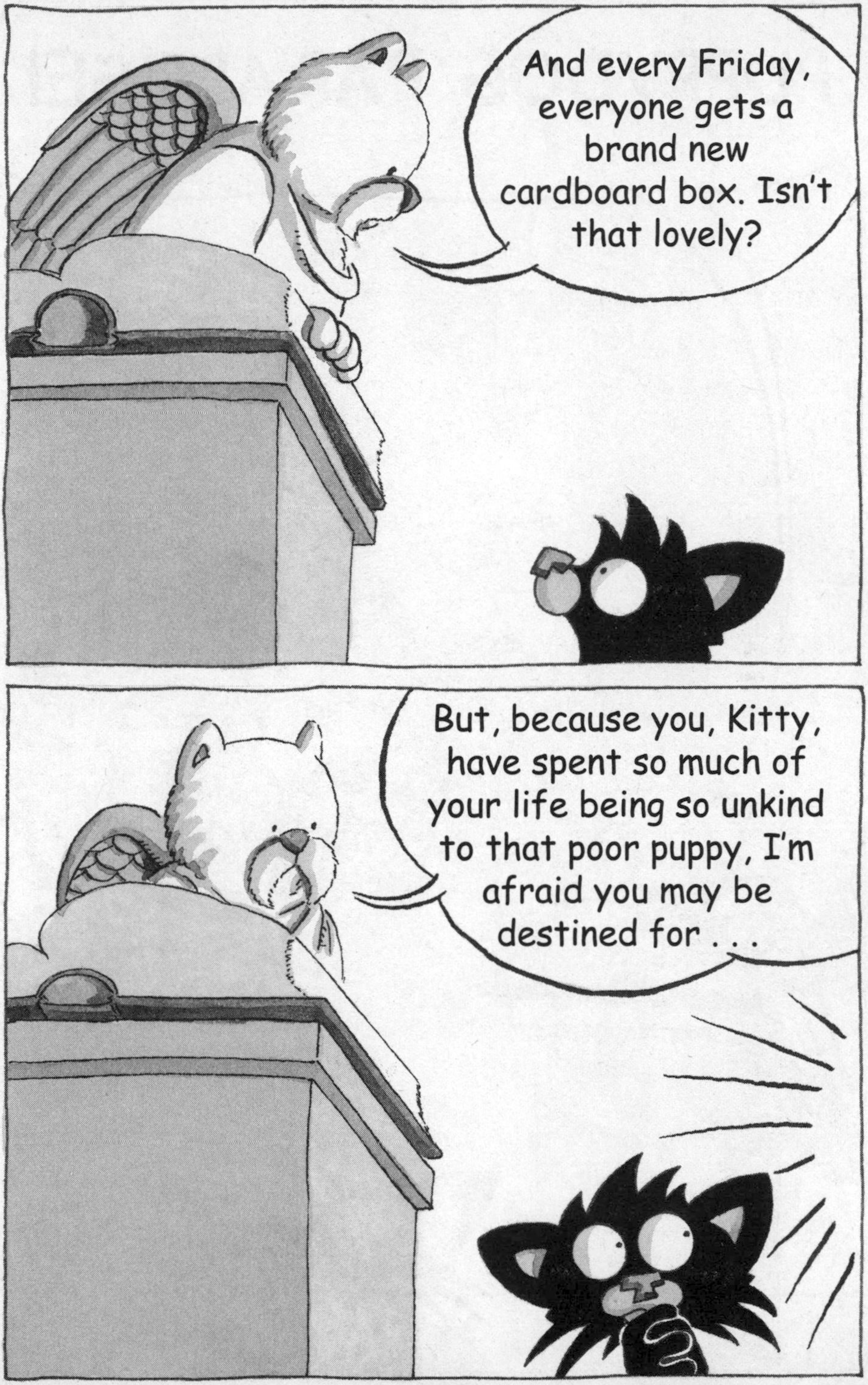
And every Friday, everyone gets a brand new cardboard box. Isn't that lovely?
But, because you, Kitty, have spent so much of your life being so unkind to that poor puppy, I'm afraid you may be destined for . . .

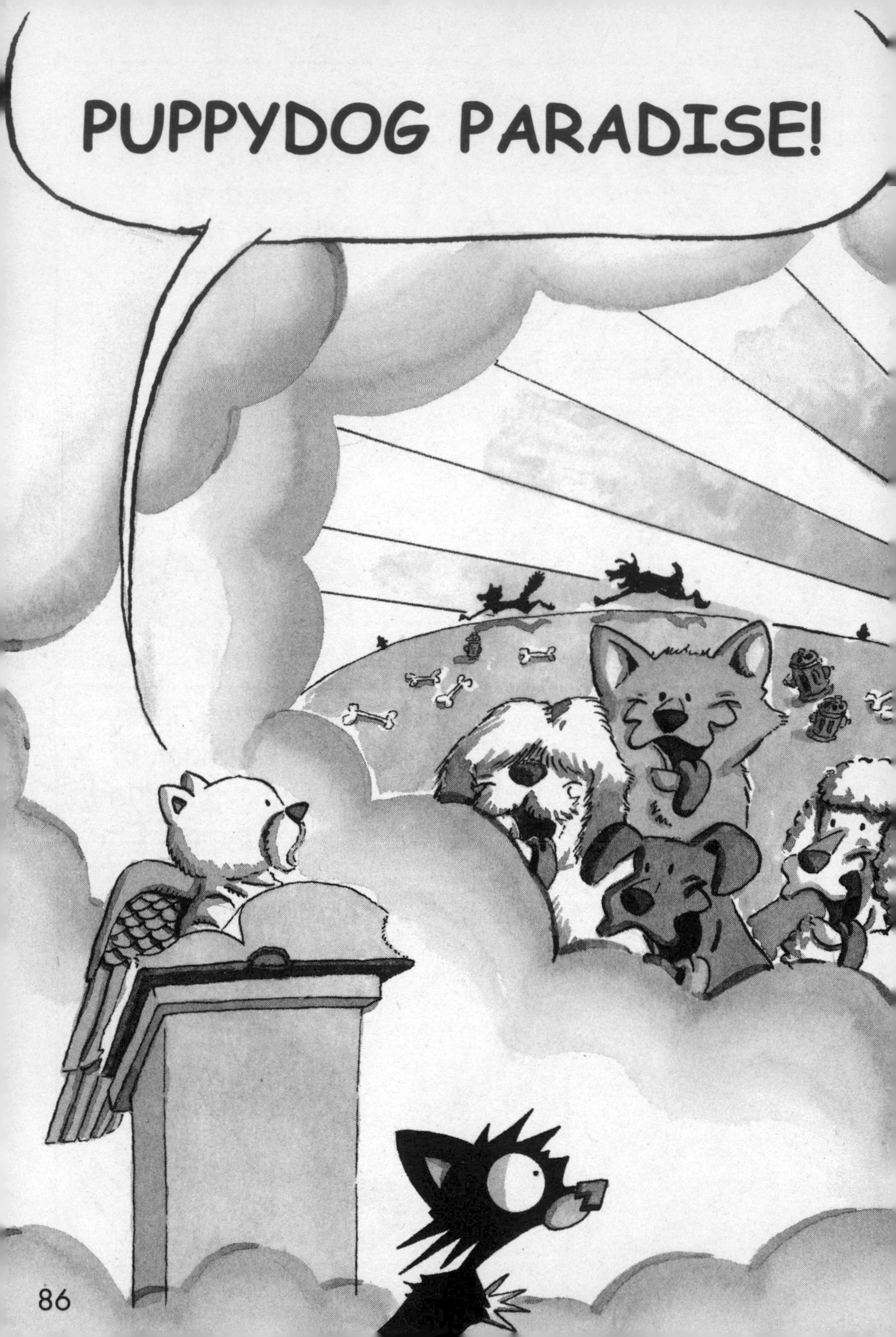
PUPPYDOG PARADISE!

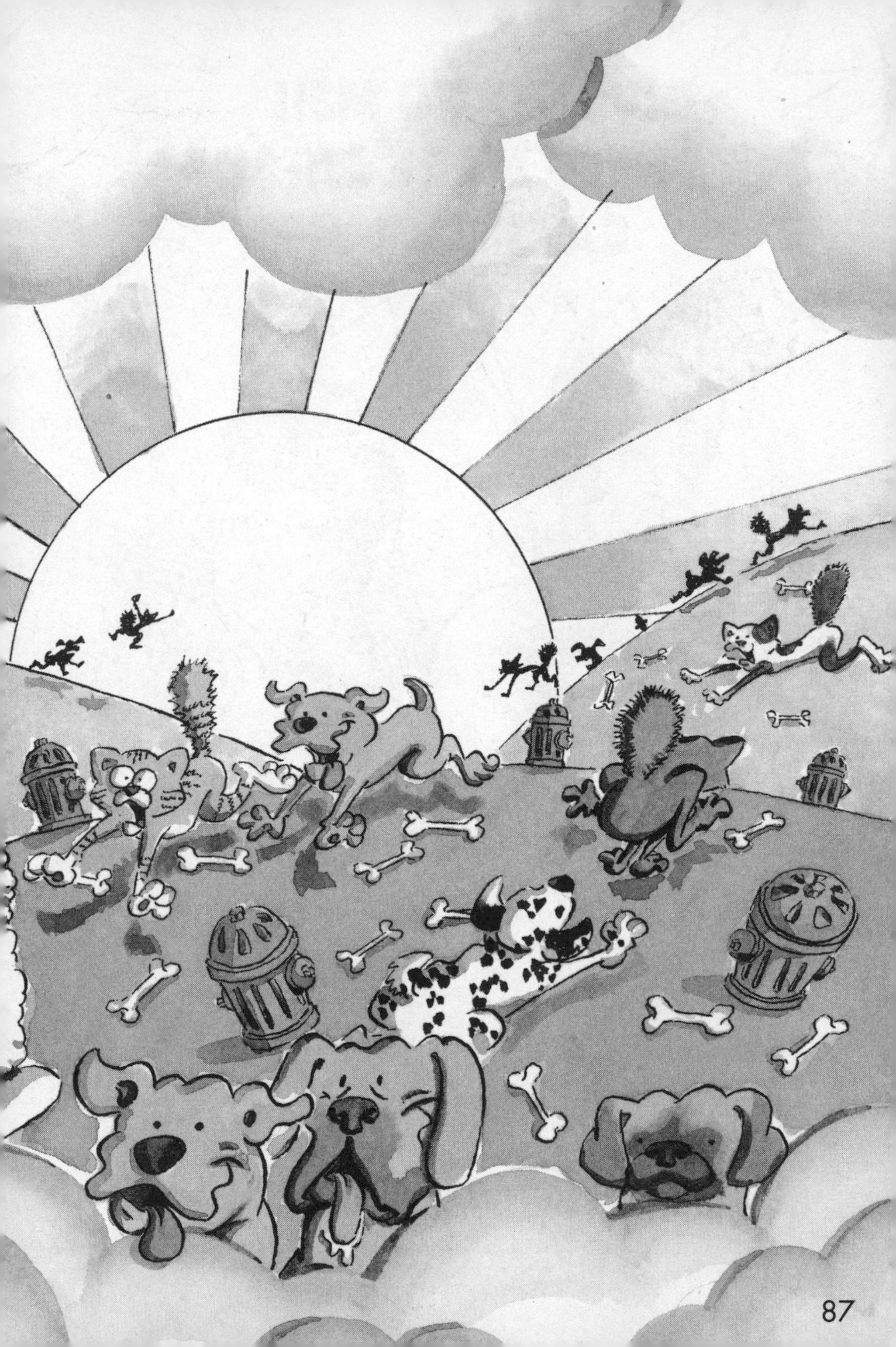

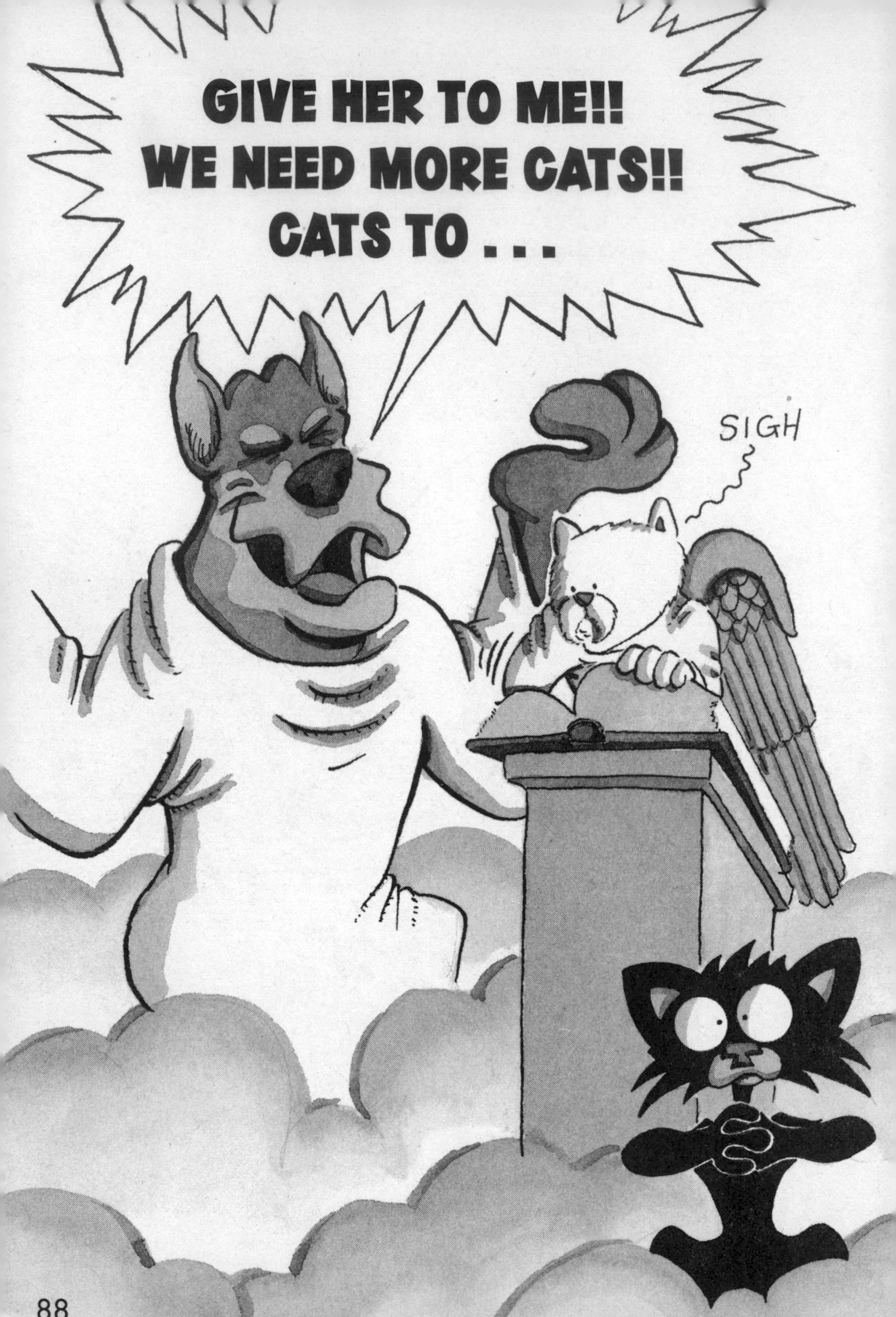
GIVE HER TO ME!! WE NEED MORE CATS!! CATS TO . . .
SIGH

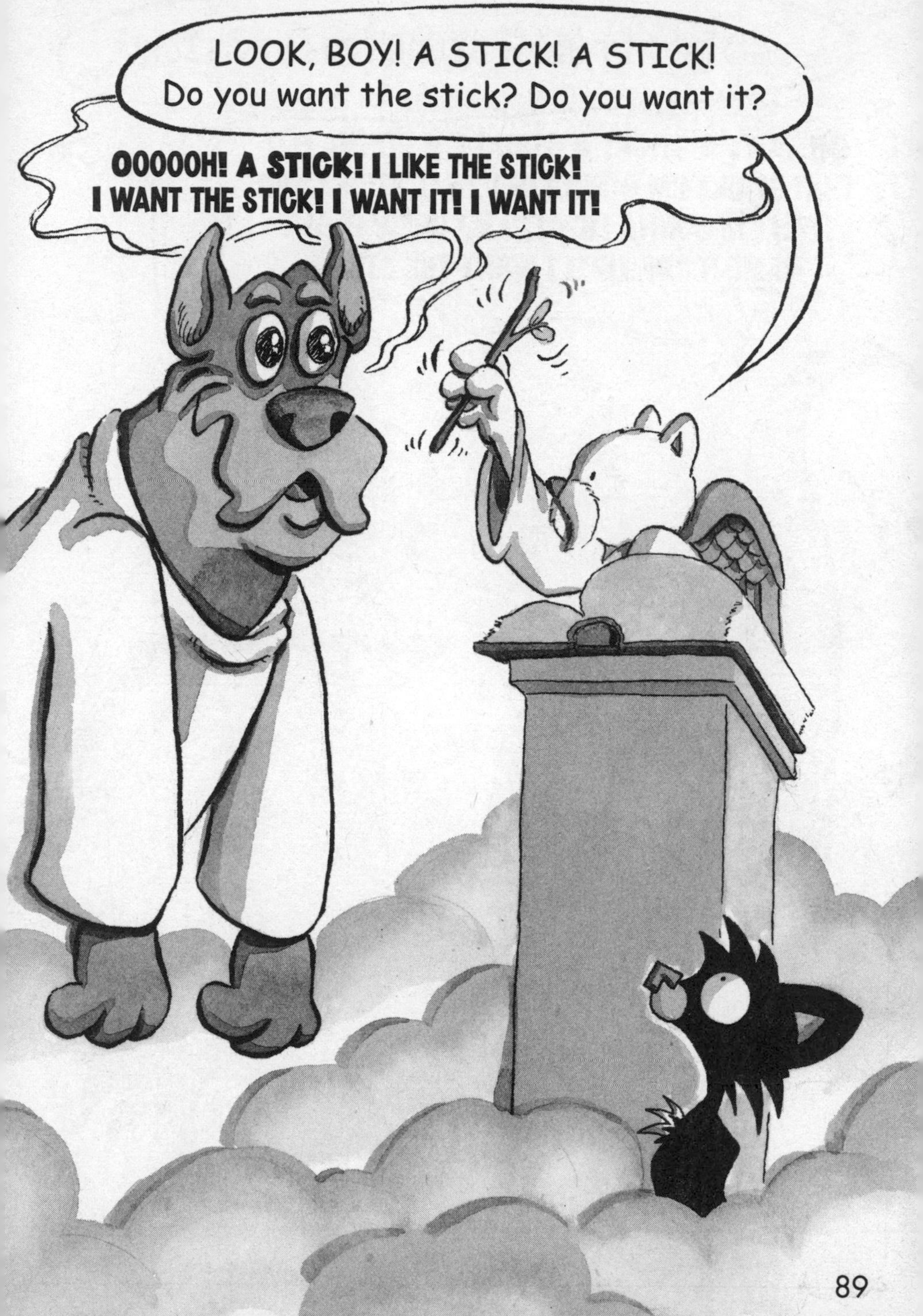
LOOK, BOY! A STICK! A STICK!
Do you want the stick? Do you want it?
OOOOOH! A STICK! I LIKE THE STICK!
I WANT THE STICK! I WANT IT! I WANT IT!

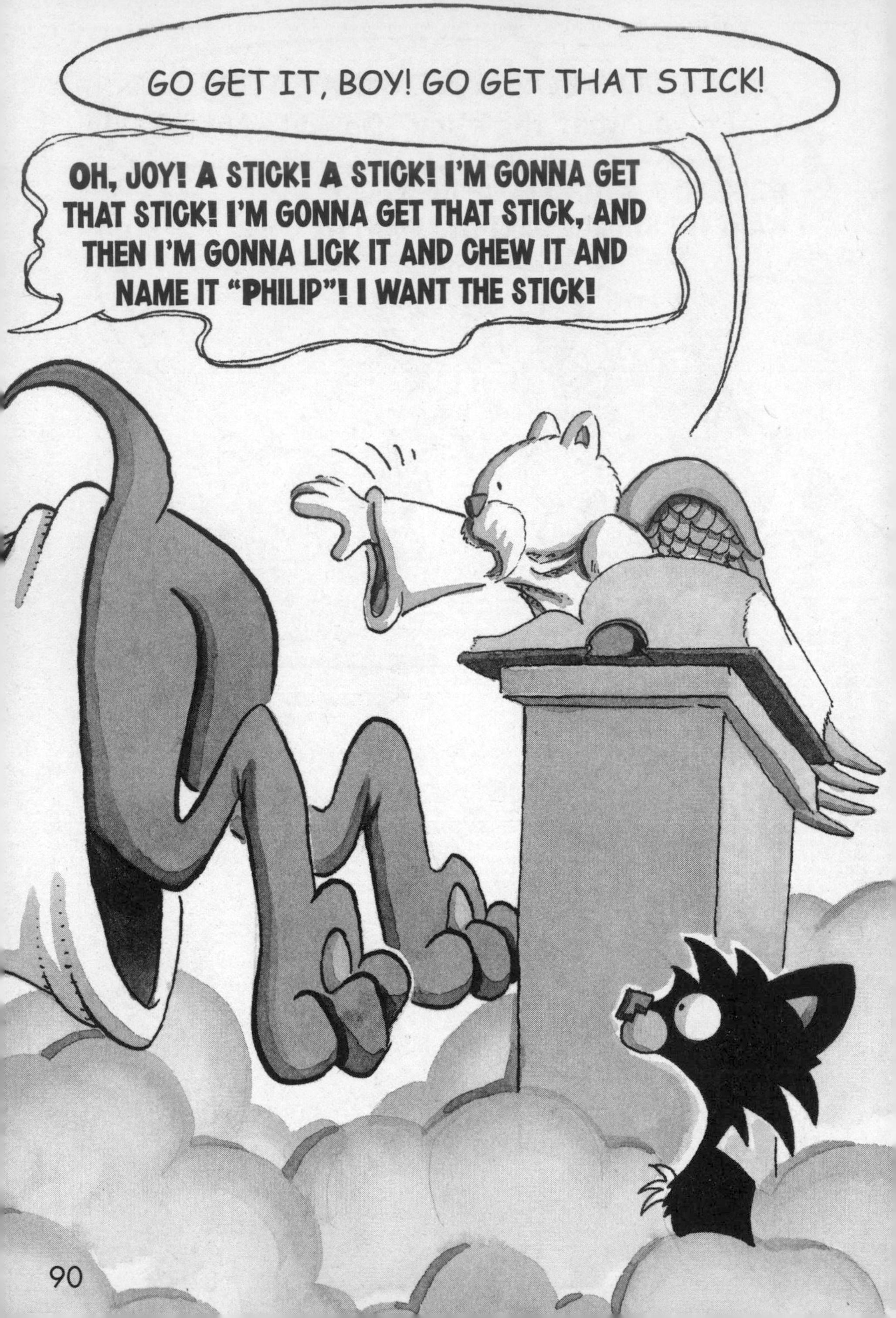
GO GET IT, BOY! GO GET THAT STICK!
OH, JOY! A STICK! A STICK! I'M GONNA GET THAT STICK! I'M GONNA GET THAT STICK, AND THEN I'M GONNA LICK IT AND CHEW IT AND NAME IT "PHILIP"! I WANT THE STICK!

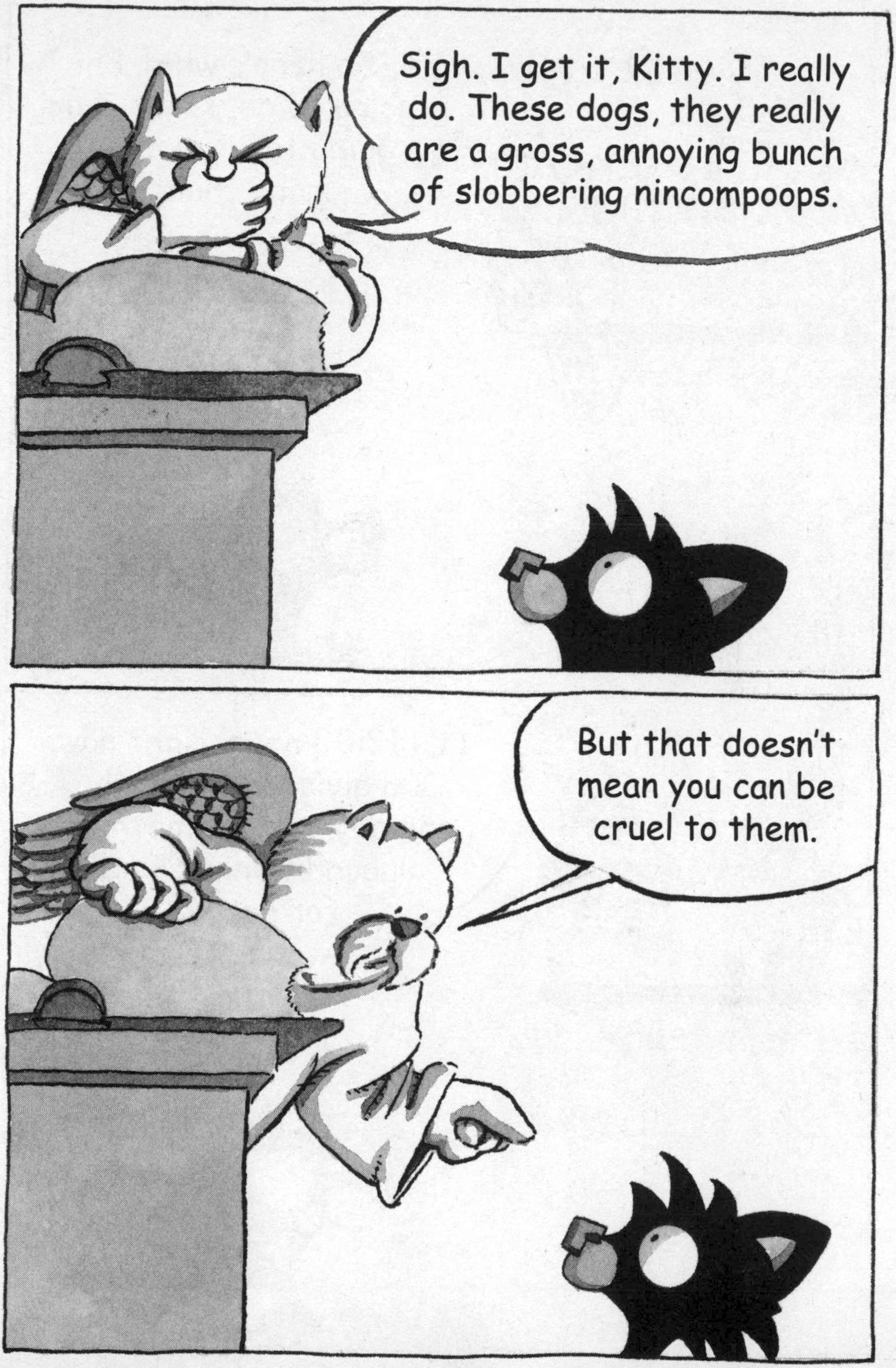
Sigh. I get it, Kitty. I really do. These dogs, they really are a gross, annoying bunch of slobbering nincompoops.
But that doesn't mean you can be cruel to them.

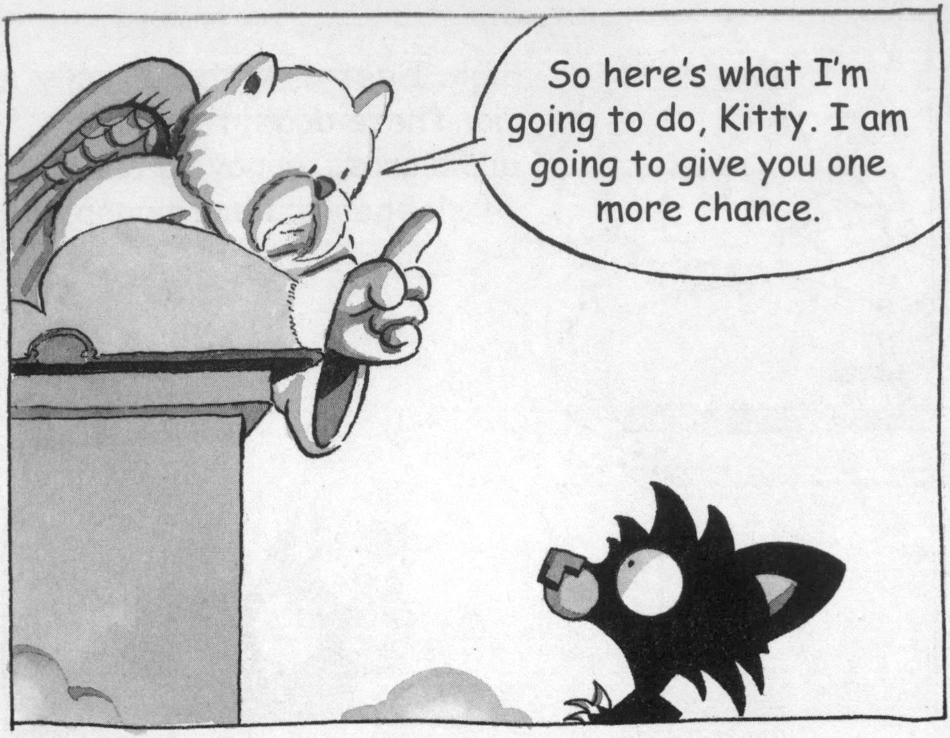
So here's what I'm going to do, Kitty. I am going to give you one more chance.

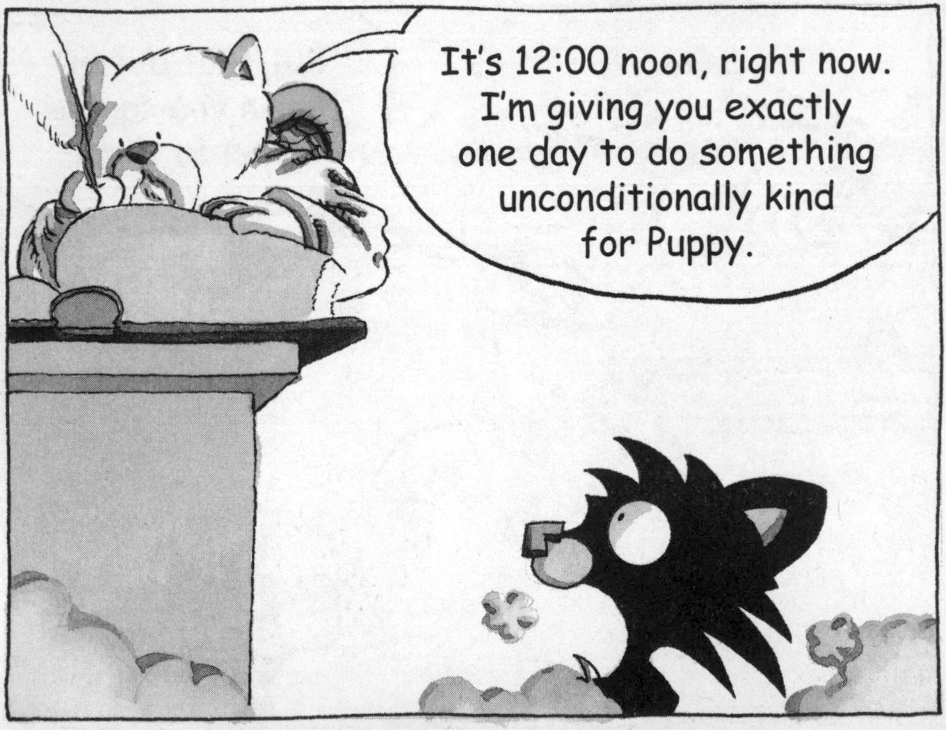
It's 12:00 noon, right now. I'm giving you exactly one day to do something unconditionally kind for Puppy.

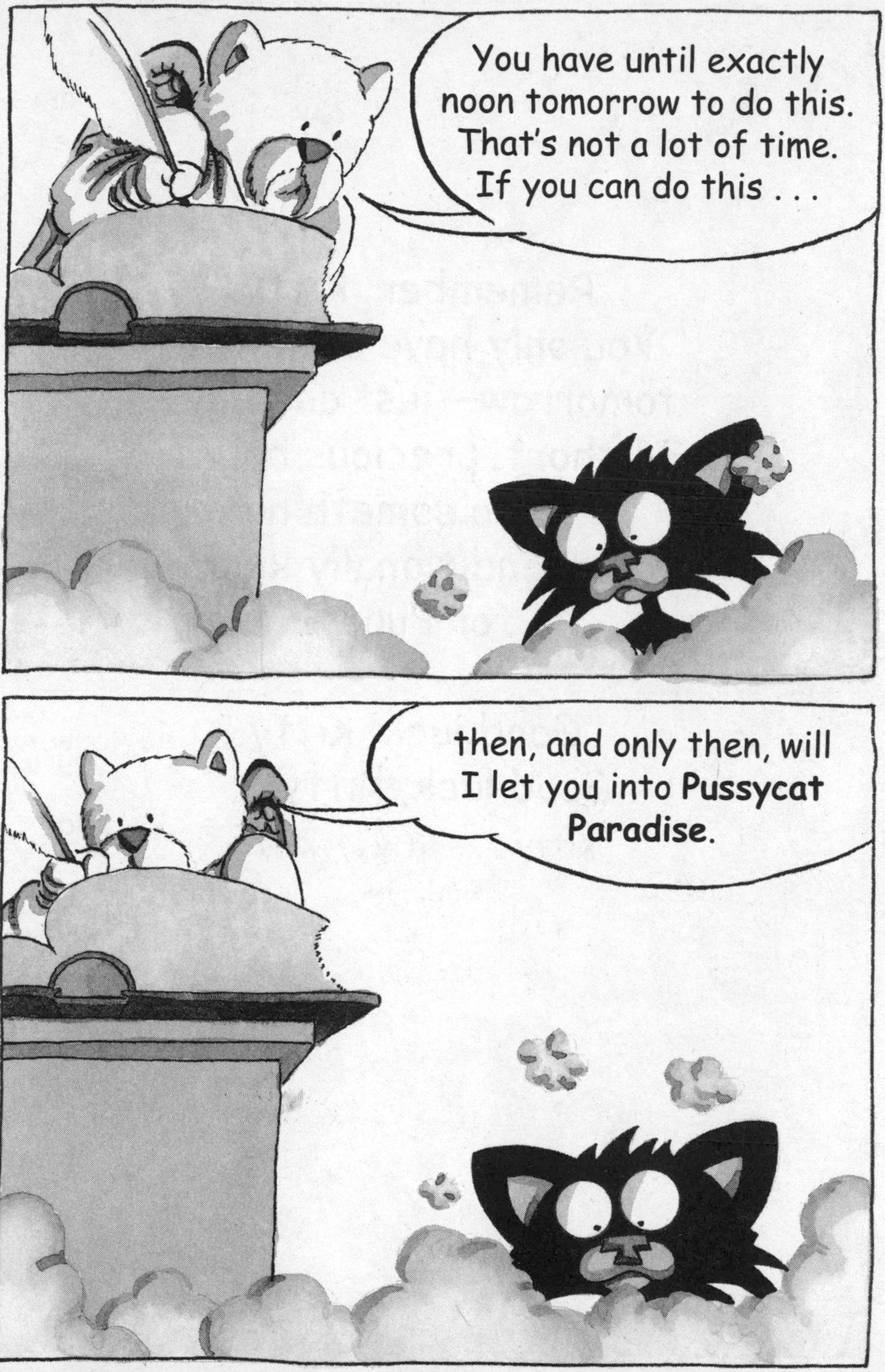
You have until exactly noon tomorrow to do this. That's not a lot of time. If you can do this . . .
then, and only then, will I let you into **Pussycat Paradise**.

Remember, Kitty.
You only have until noon
tomorrow—just one day—
24 short, precious hours—
to do something
unconditionally kind
for Puppy.

Good luck, Kitty.
Good luck, Kitty . . .
Kitty . . . Kitty . . . Kitty . . .
Kitty . . . Kitty . . .

•CHAPTER FIVE•

HOME AGAIN

Kitty . . . Kitty . . . Wake up, Kitty. It's all over. You're home now and back from the vet.

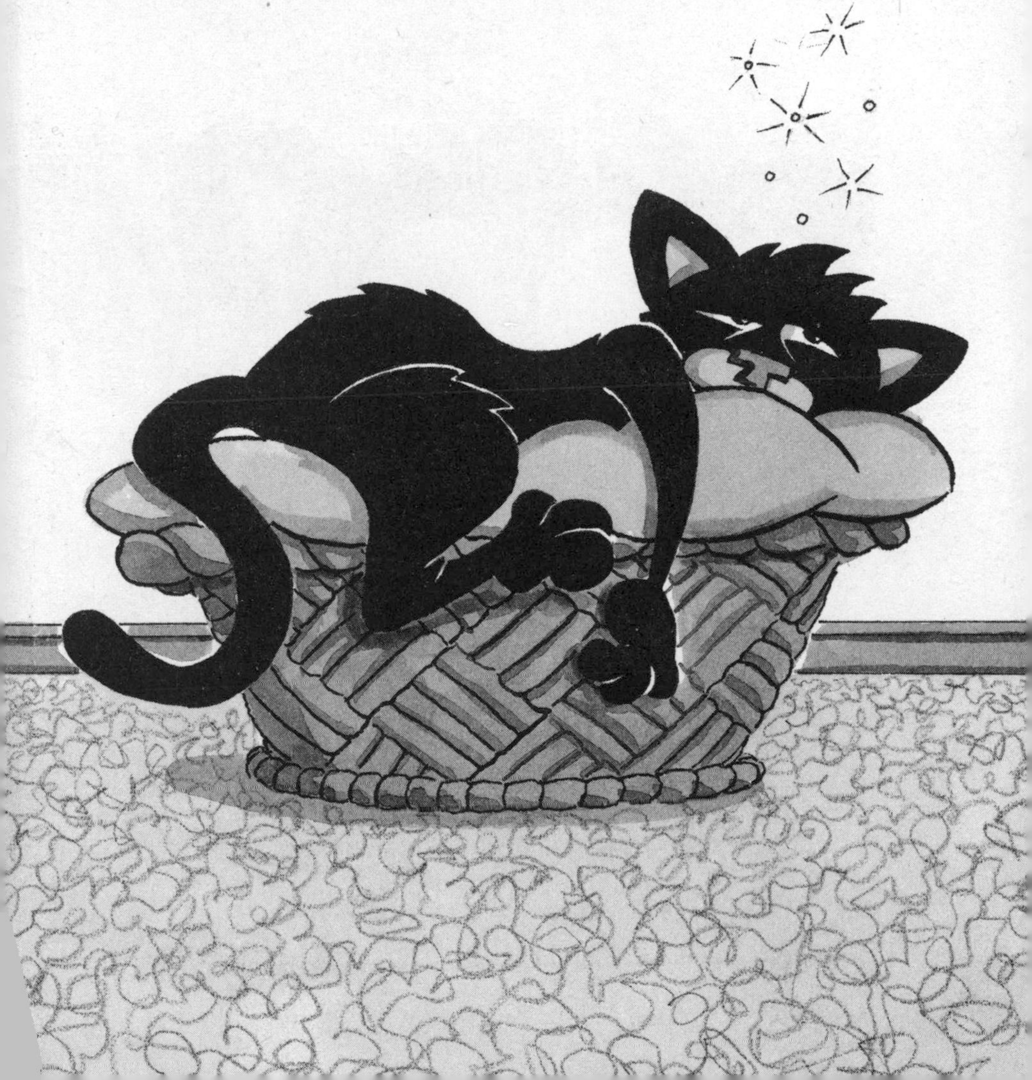

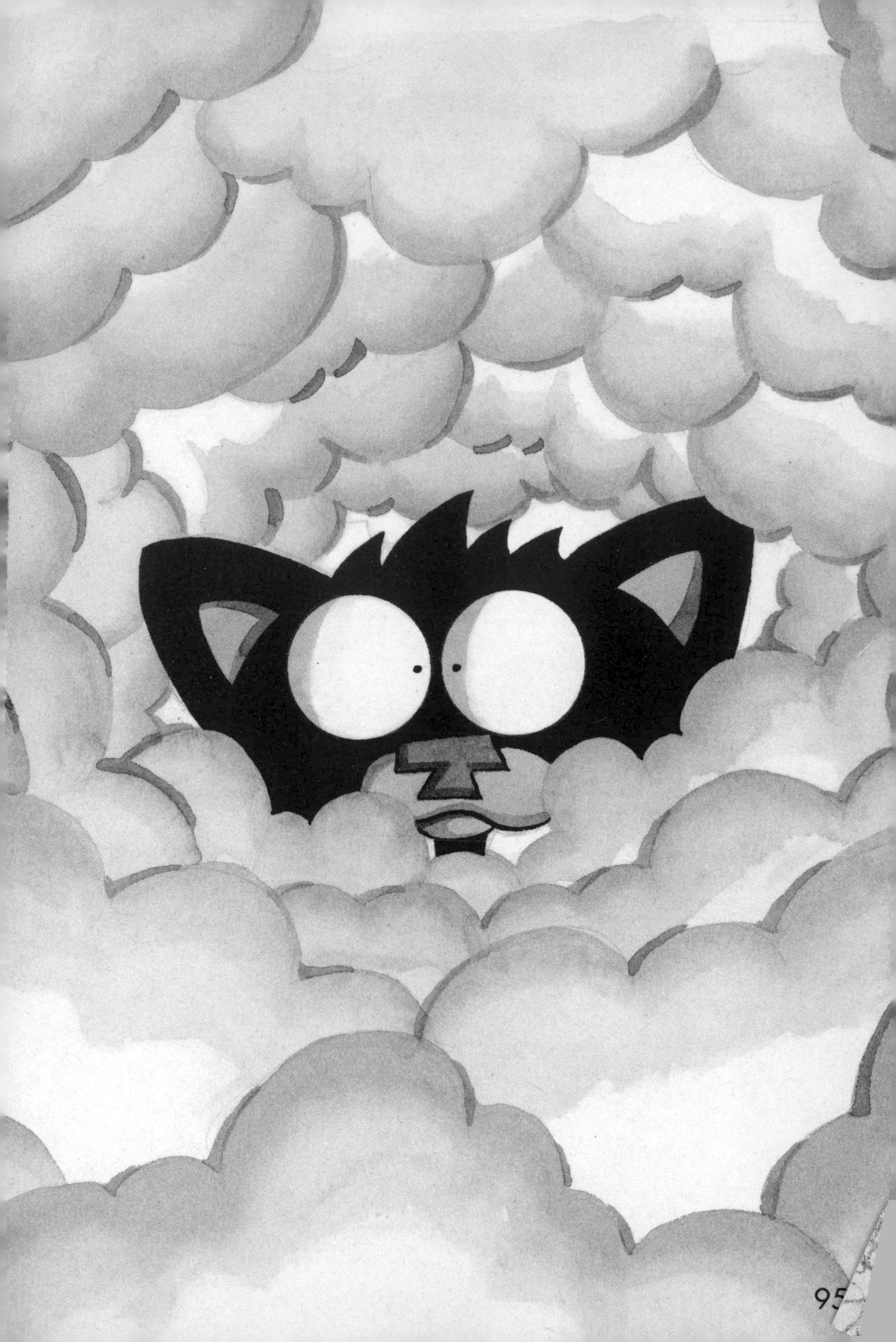

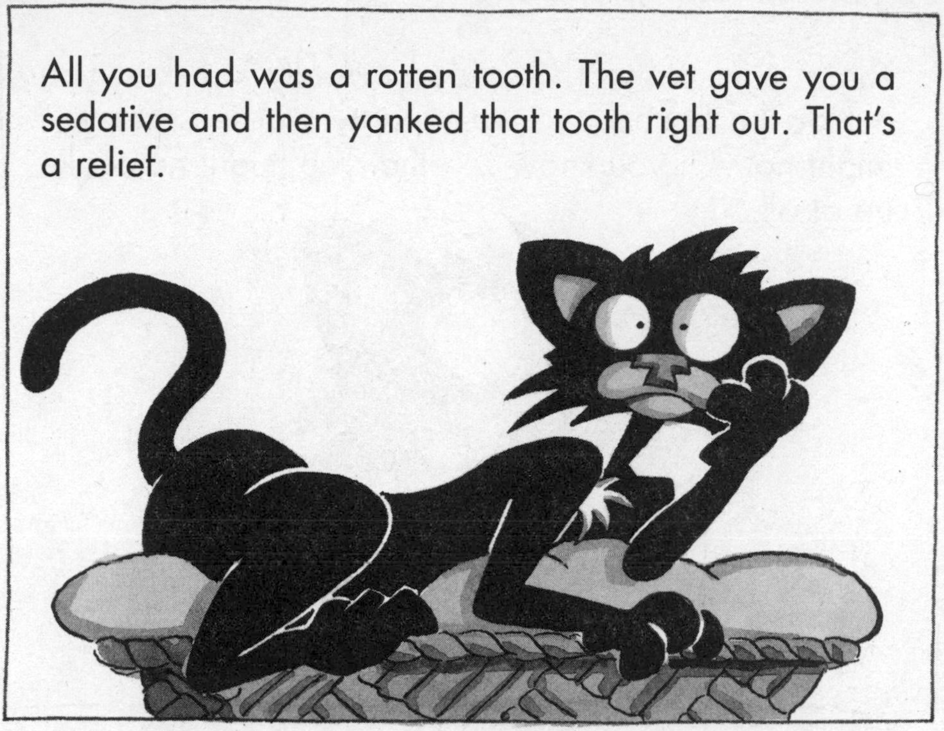
All you had was a rotten tooth. The vet gave you a sedative and then yanked that tooth right out. That's a relief.

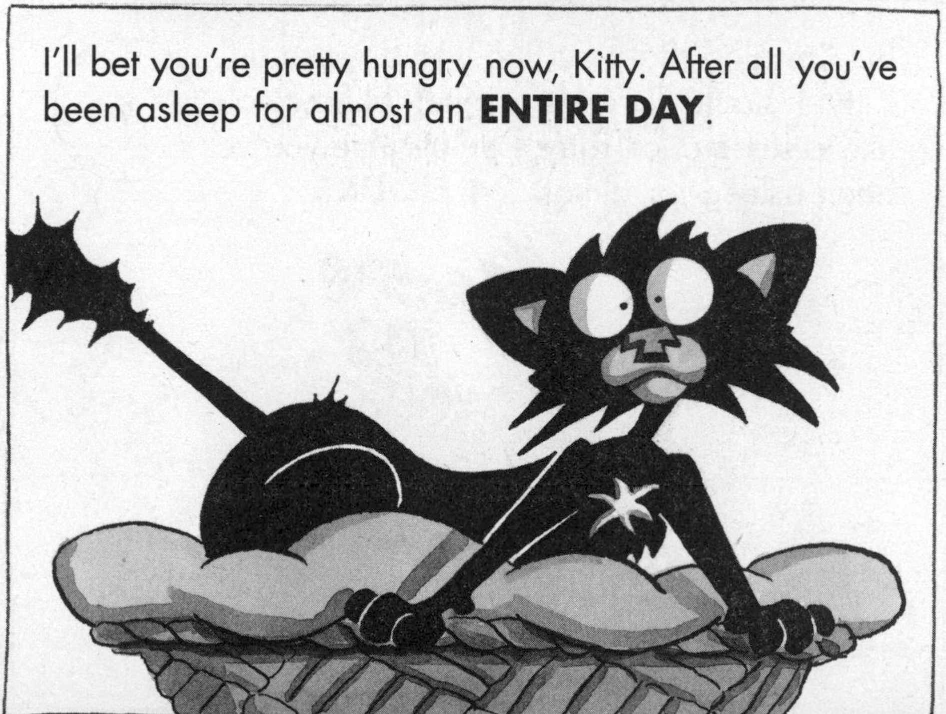
I'll bet you're pretty hungry now, Kitty. After all you've been asleep for almost an **ENTIRE DAY**.

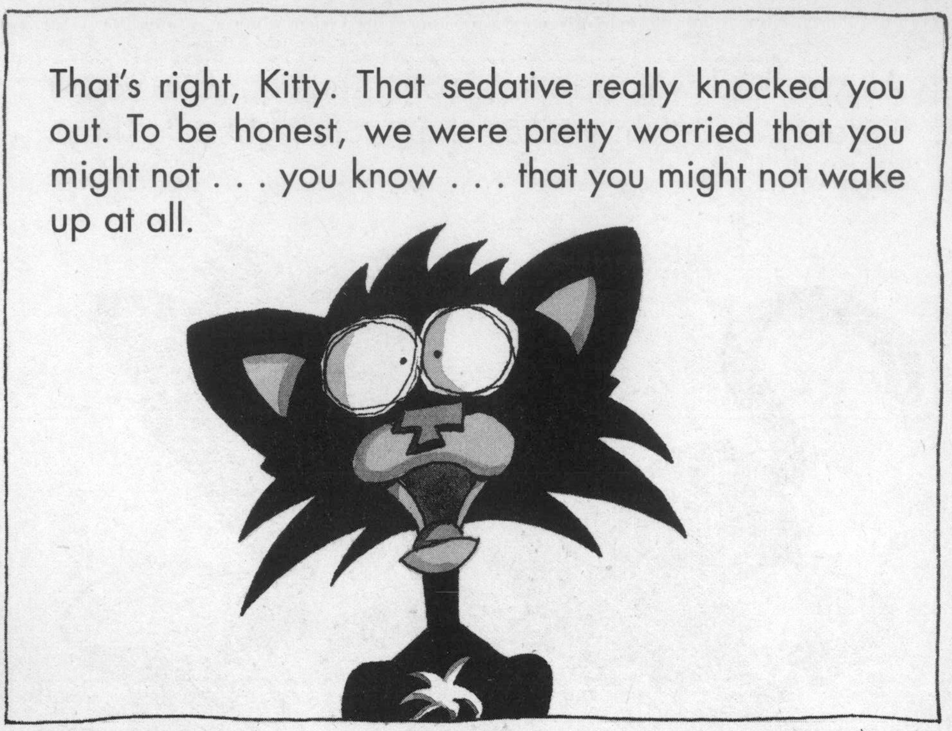
That's right, Kitty. That sedative really knocked you out. To be honest, we were pretty worried that you might not . . . you know . . . that you might not wake up at all.

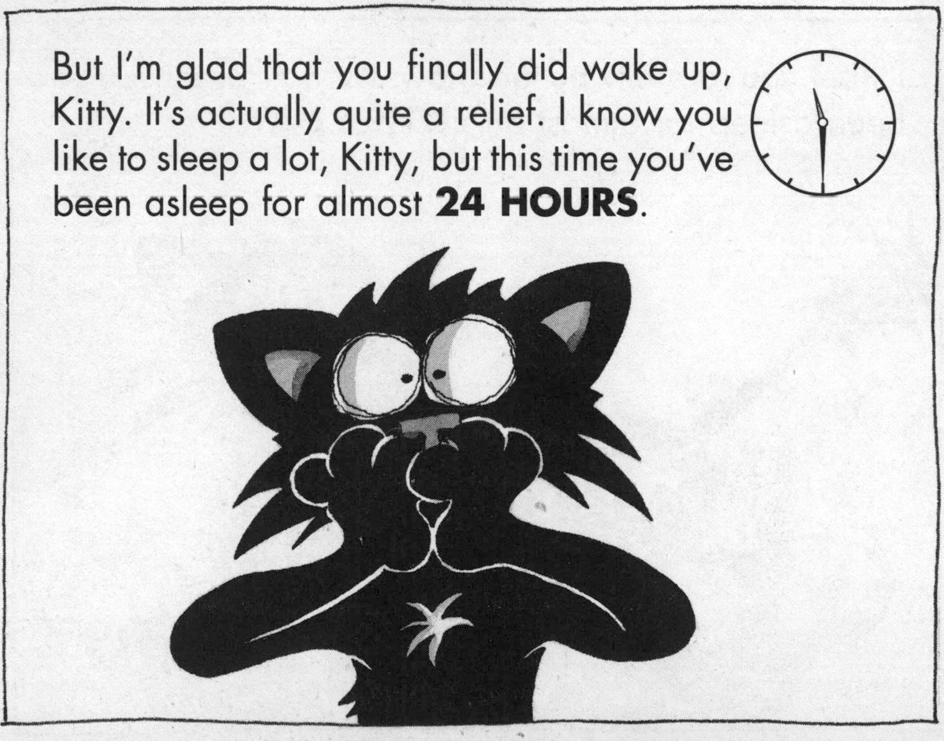
But I'm glad that you finally did wake up, Kitty. It's actually quite a relief. I know you like to sleep a lot, Kitty, but this time you've been asleep for almost **24 HOURS**.

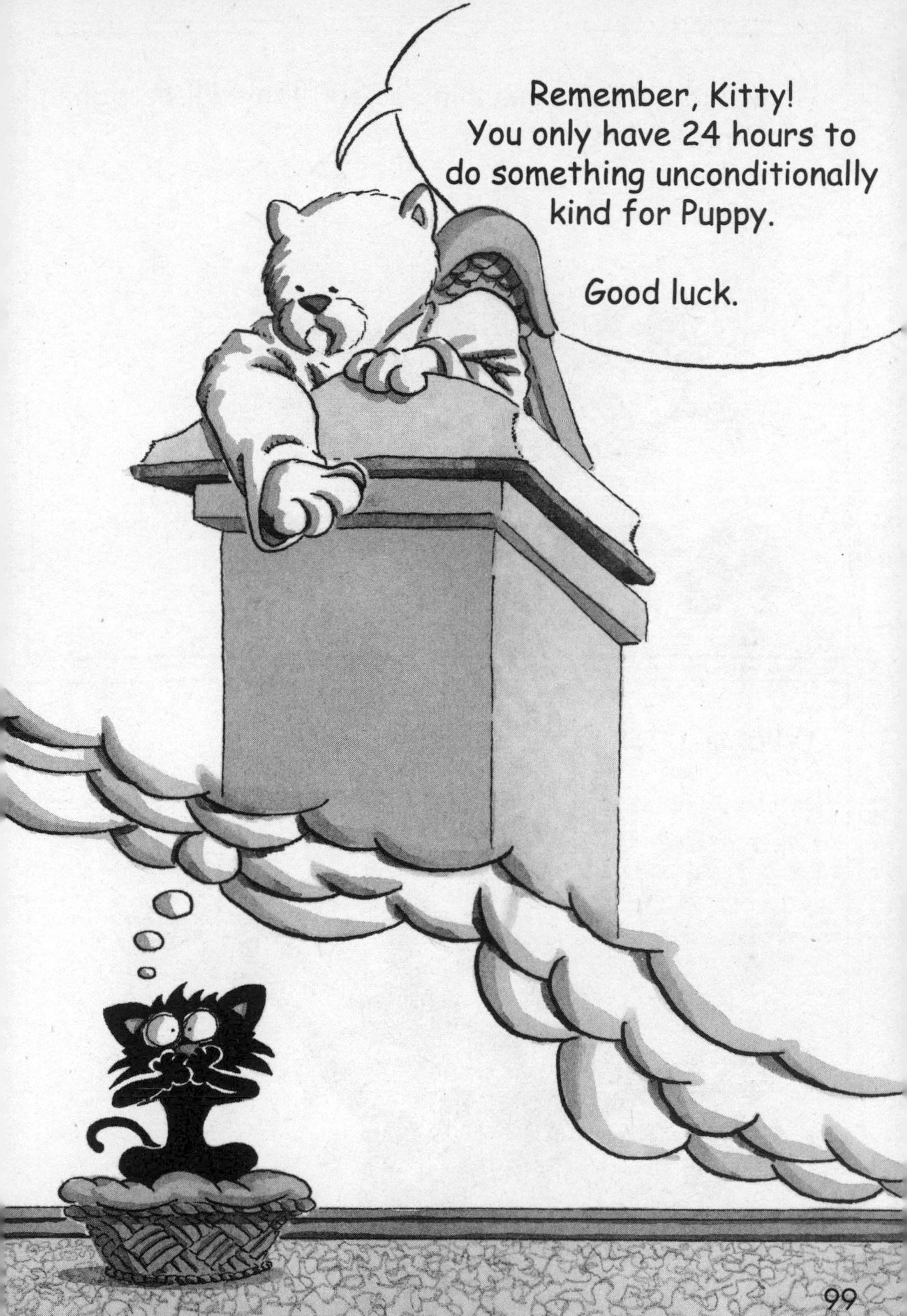
Remember, Kitty!
You only have 24 hours to
do something unconditionally
kind for Puppy.
Good luck.

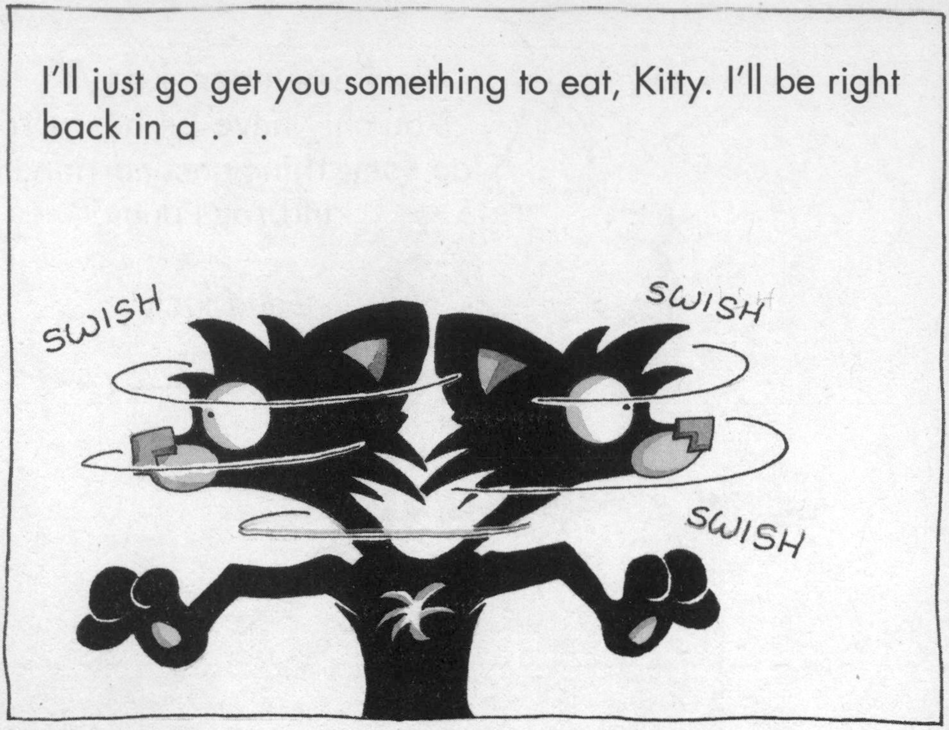
I'll just go get you something to eat, Kitty. I'll be right back in a . . .
SWISH
SWISH
SWISH

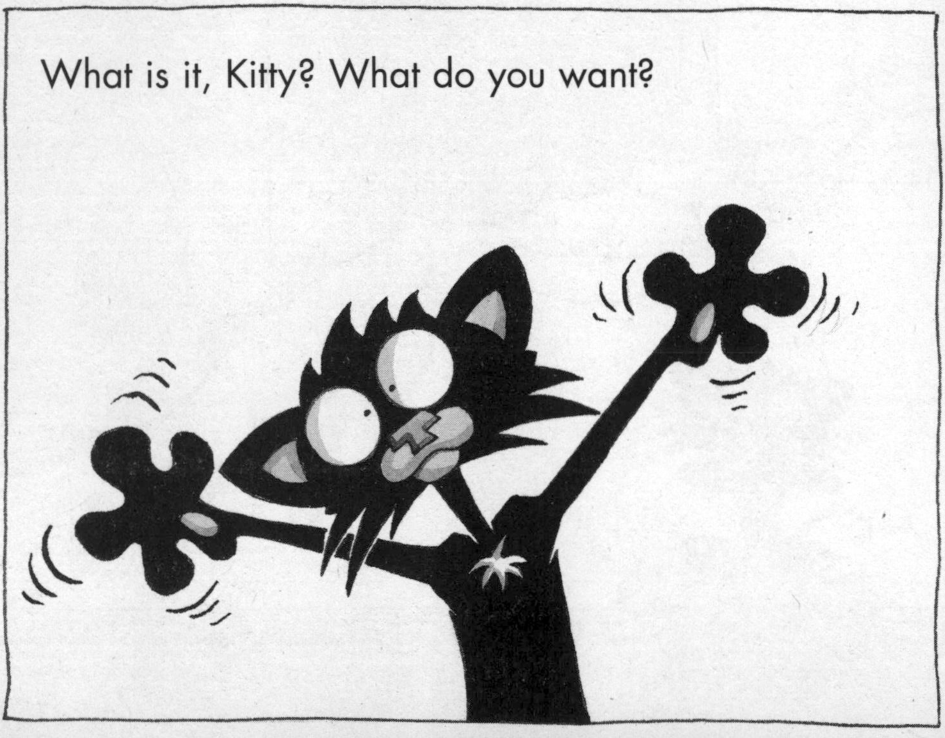
What is it, Kitty? What do you want?

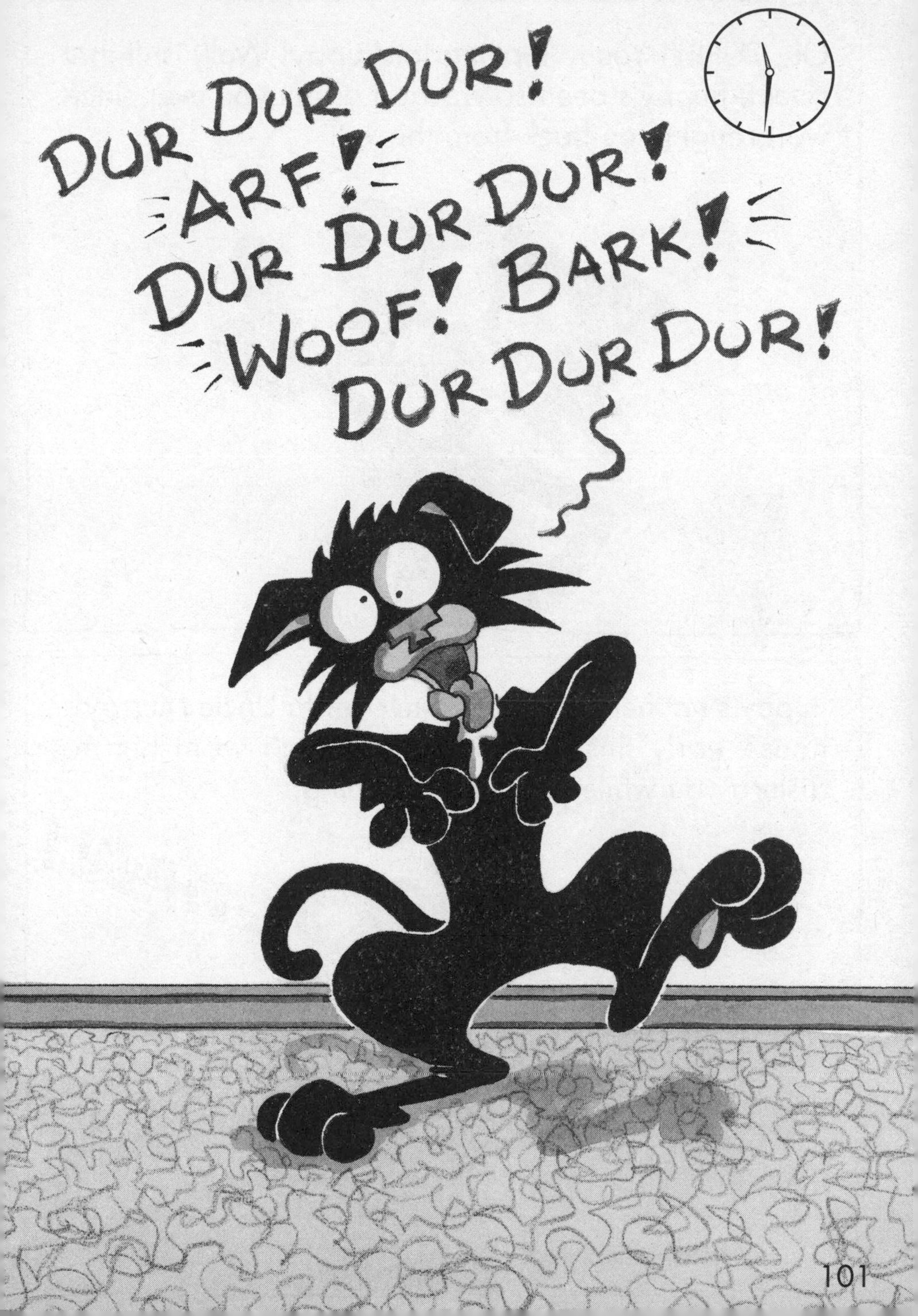
DUR DUR DUR!
ARF!
DUR DUR DUR!
WOOF! BARK!
DUR DUR DUR!

Oh, PUPPY! You're looking for Puppy! Well, isn't that sweet. Puppy's been so worried about you ever since we brought you back from the vet.

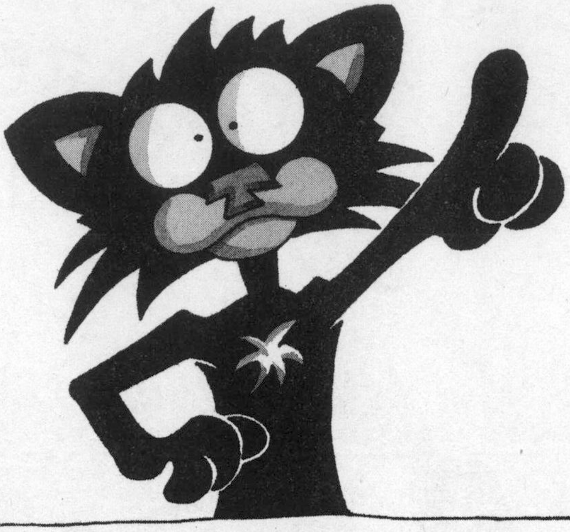

Puppy's not here. We sent him over to Uncle Murray's house early this morning. We didn't want him to disturb you while you were sleeping.

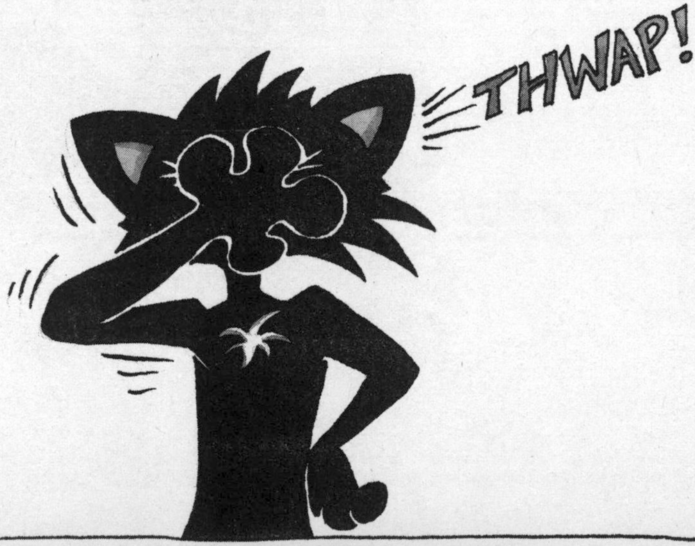
THWAP!

But, don't worry, Kitty. Puppy should be home in a few hours. Gosh, it really is so nice that you actually seem to miss him. I never expected you to . . . HEY! Where are you going?

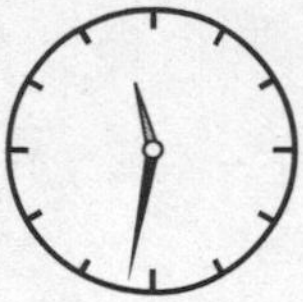

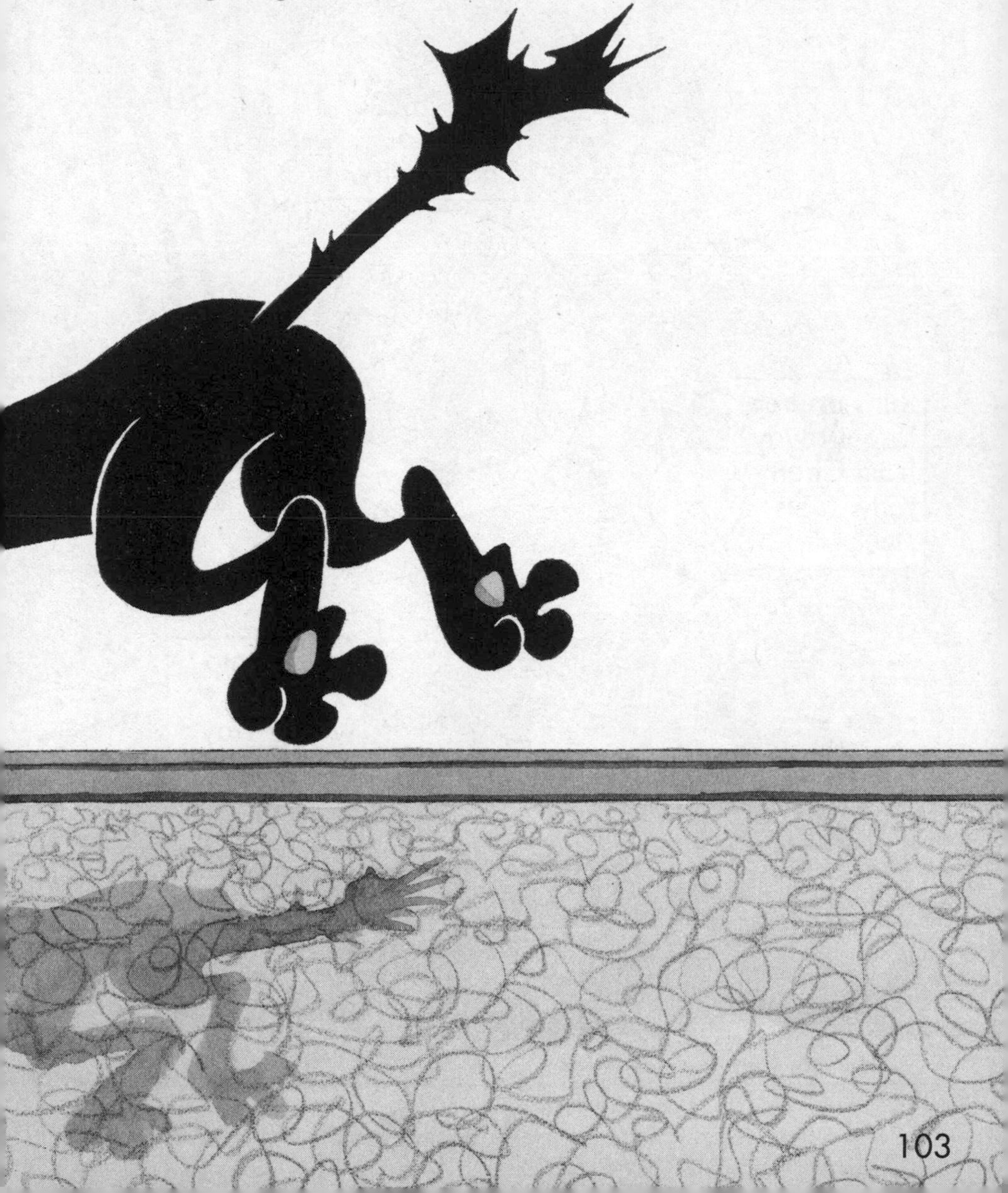

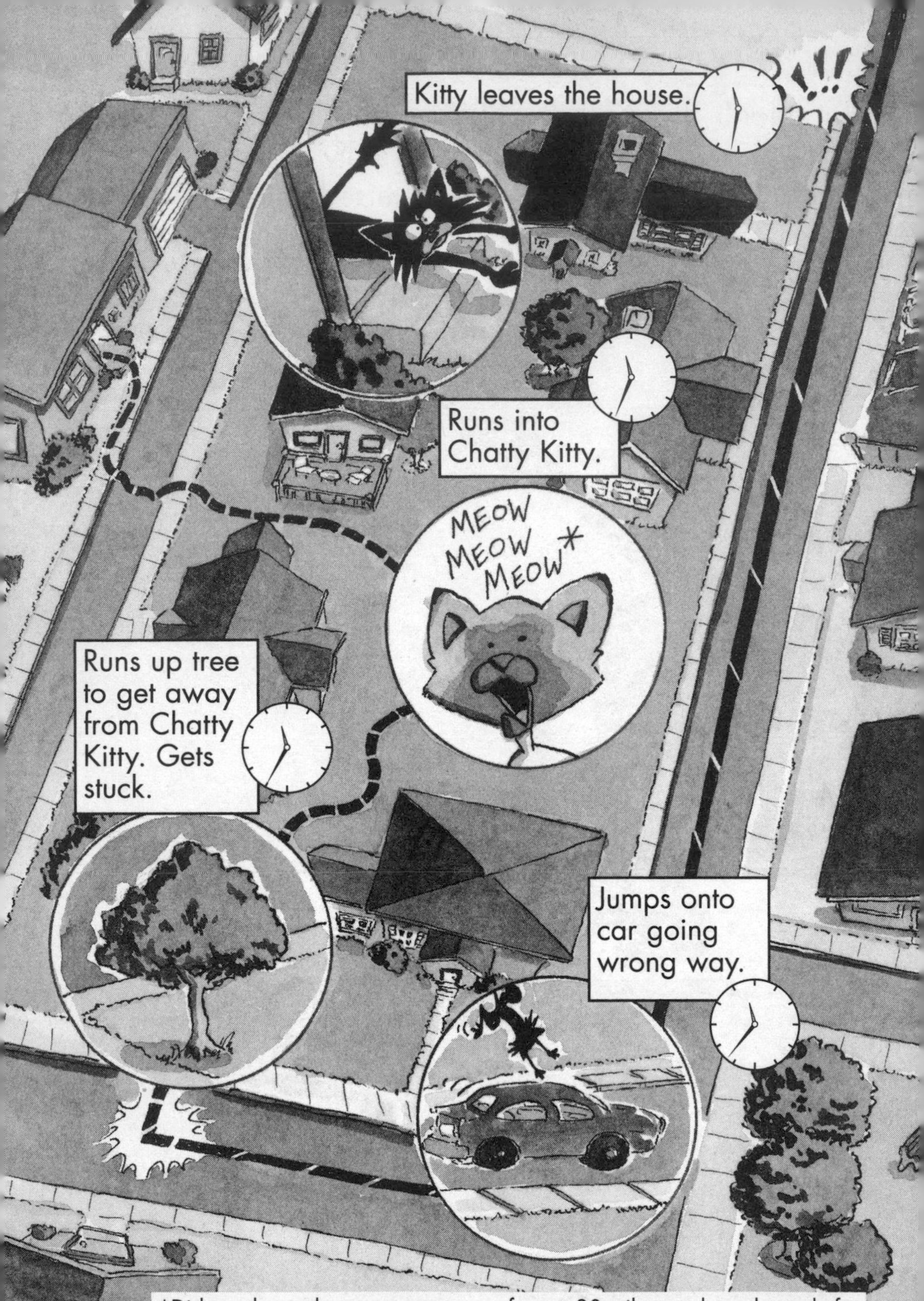
Kitty leaves the house.
!!!
Runs into Chatty Kitty.
MEOW MEOW MEOW*
Runs up tree to get away from Chatty Kitty. Gets stuck.
Jumps onto car going wrong way.

*Did you know that a cat can run as fast as 30 miles per hour, but only for a few seconds? That's just a bit faster than people and elephants, but not quite as fast as reindeer and giraffes.

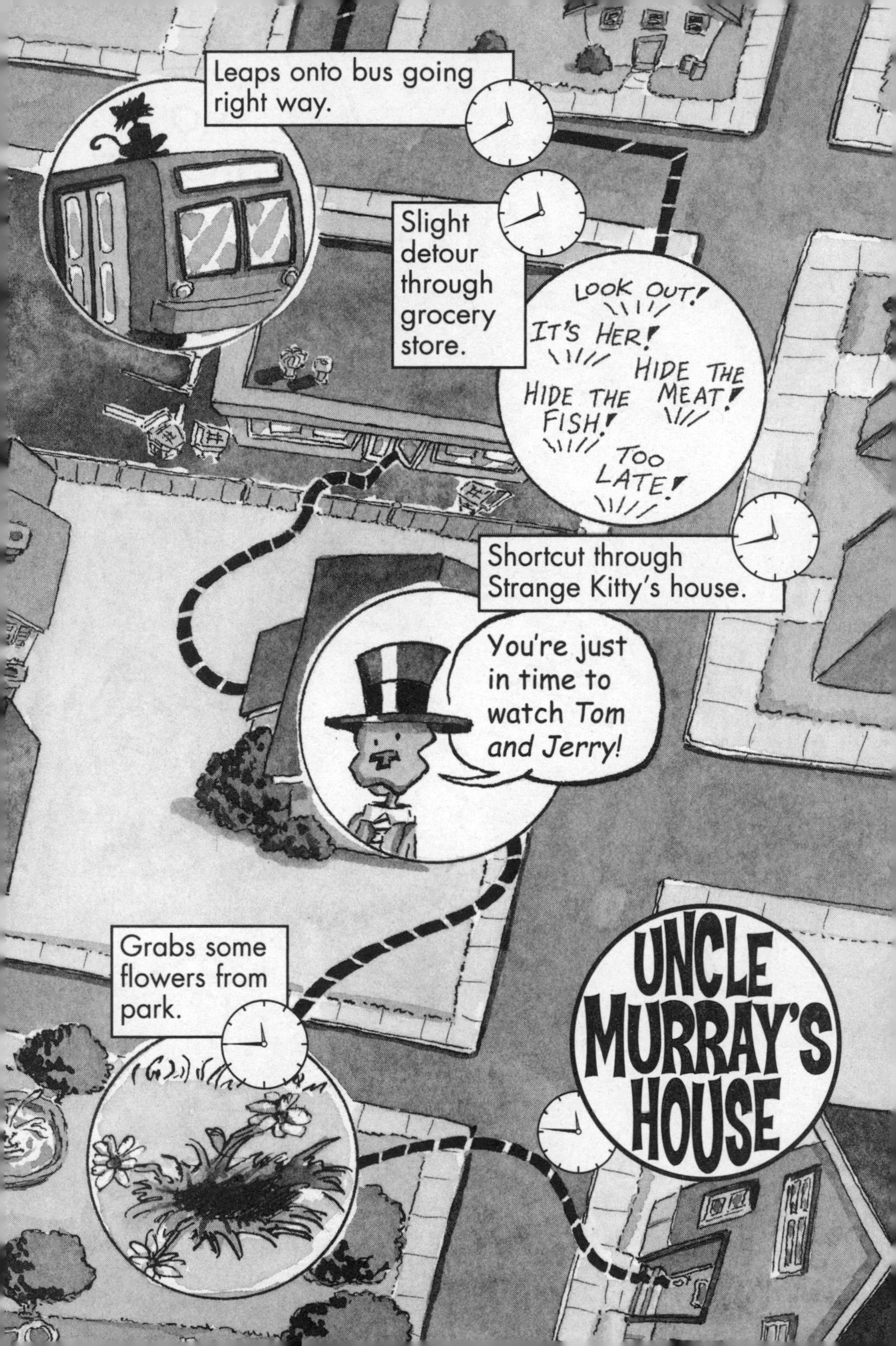
Leaps onto bus going right way.
Slight detour through grocery store.
LOOK OUT!
IT'S HER!
HIDE THE MEAT!
HIDE THE FISH!
TOO LATE!
Shortcut through Strange Kitty's house.
You're just in time to watch *Tom and Jerry*!
Grabs some flowers from park.
UNCLE MURRAY'S HOUSE

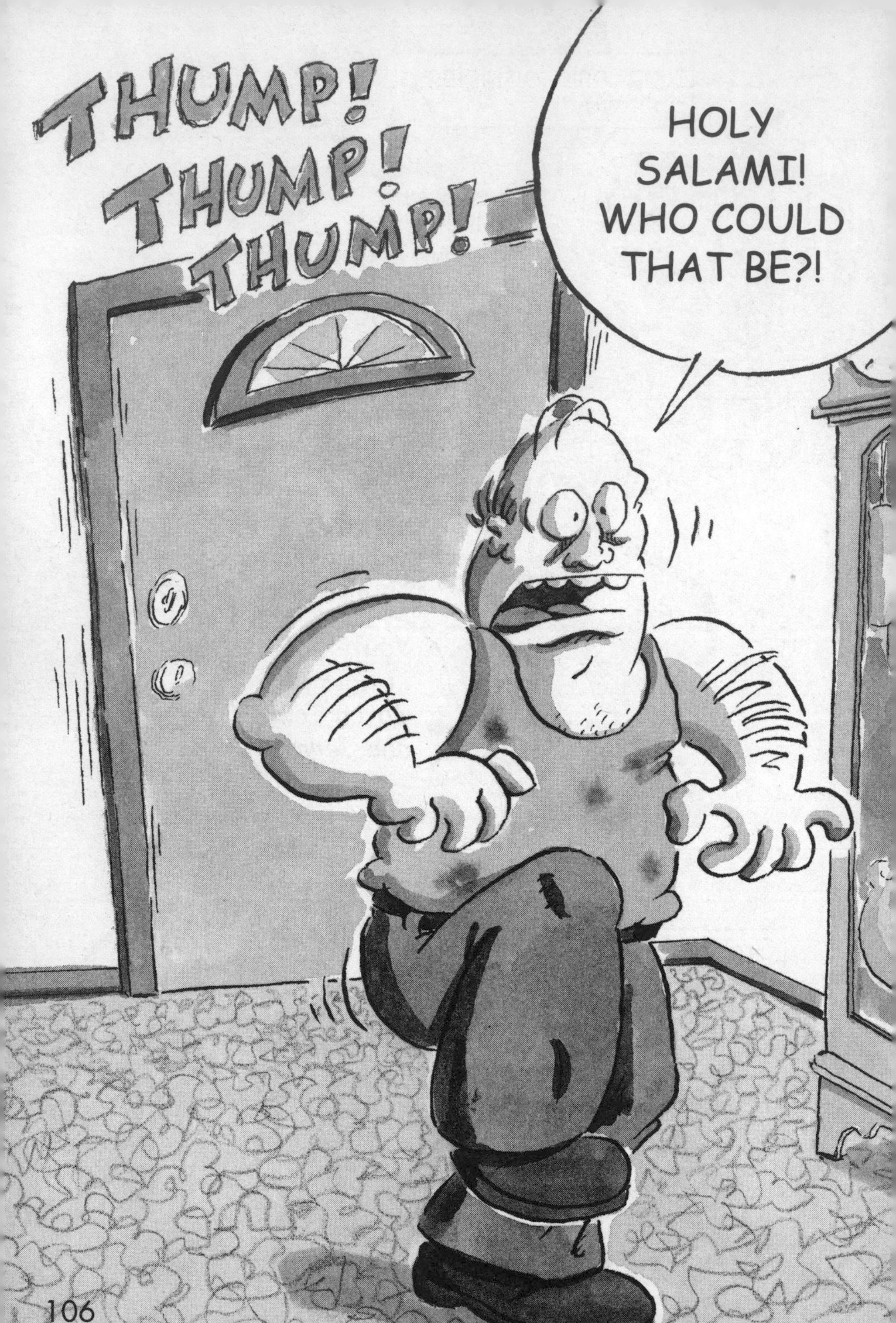
THUMP! THUMP! THUMP!
HOLY SALAMI! WHO COULD THAT BE?!

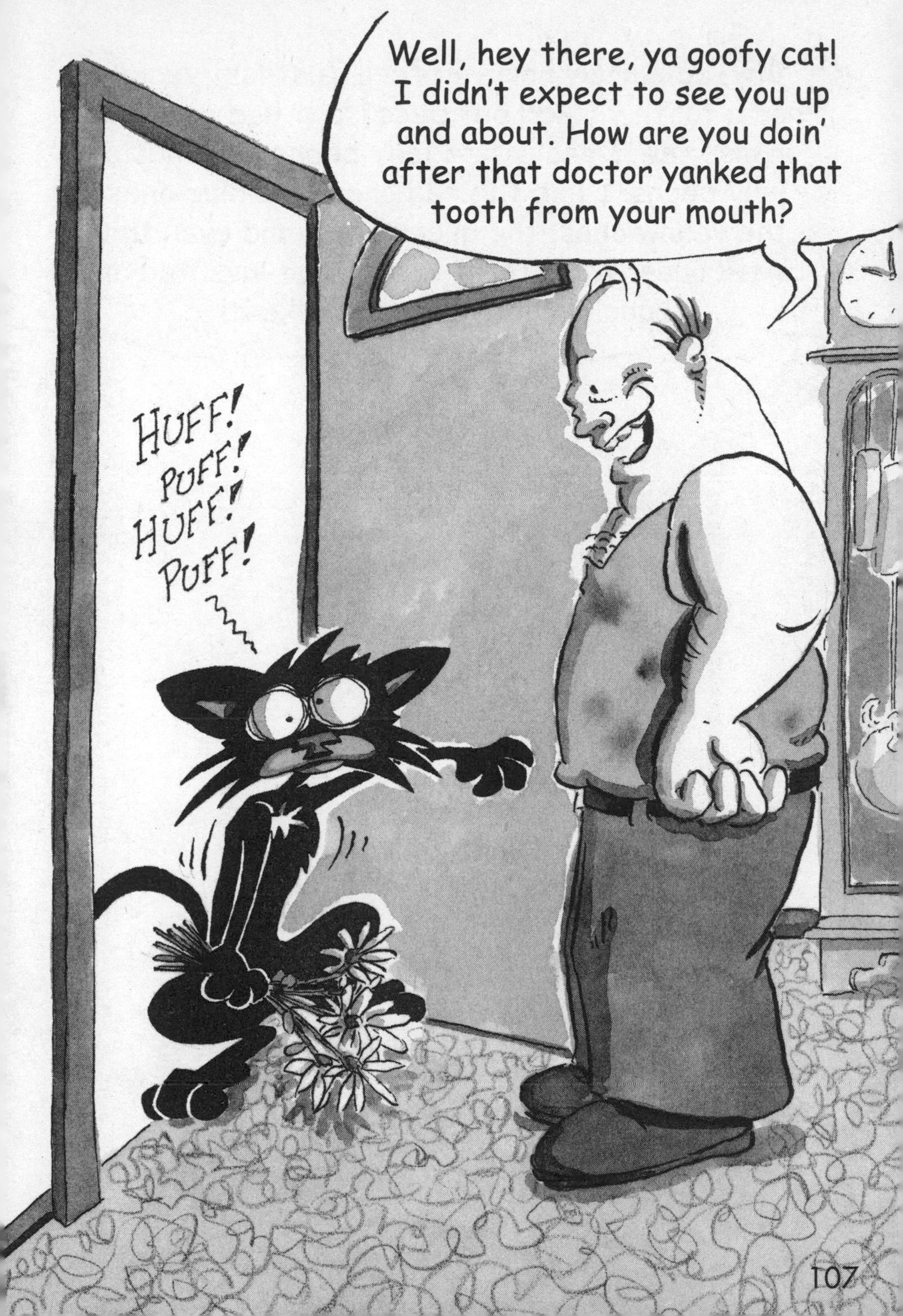
Well, hey there, ya goofy cat! I didn't expect to see you up and about. How are you doin' after that doctor yanked that tooth from your mouth?
HUFF! PUFF! HUFF! PUFF!

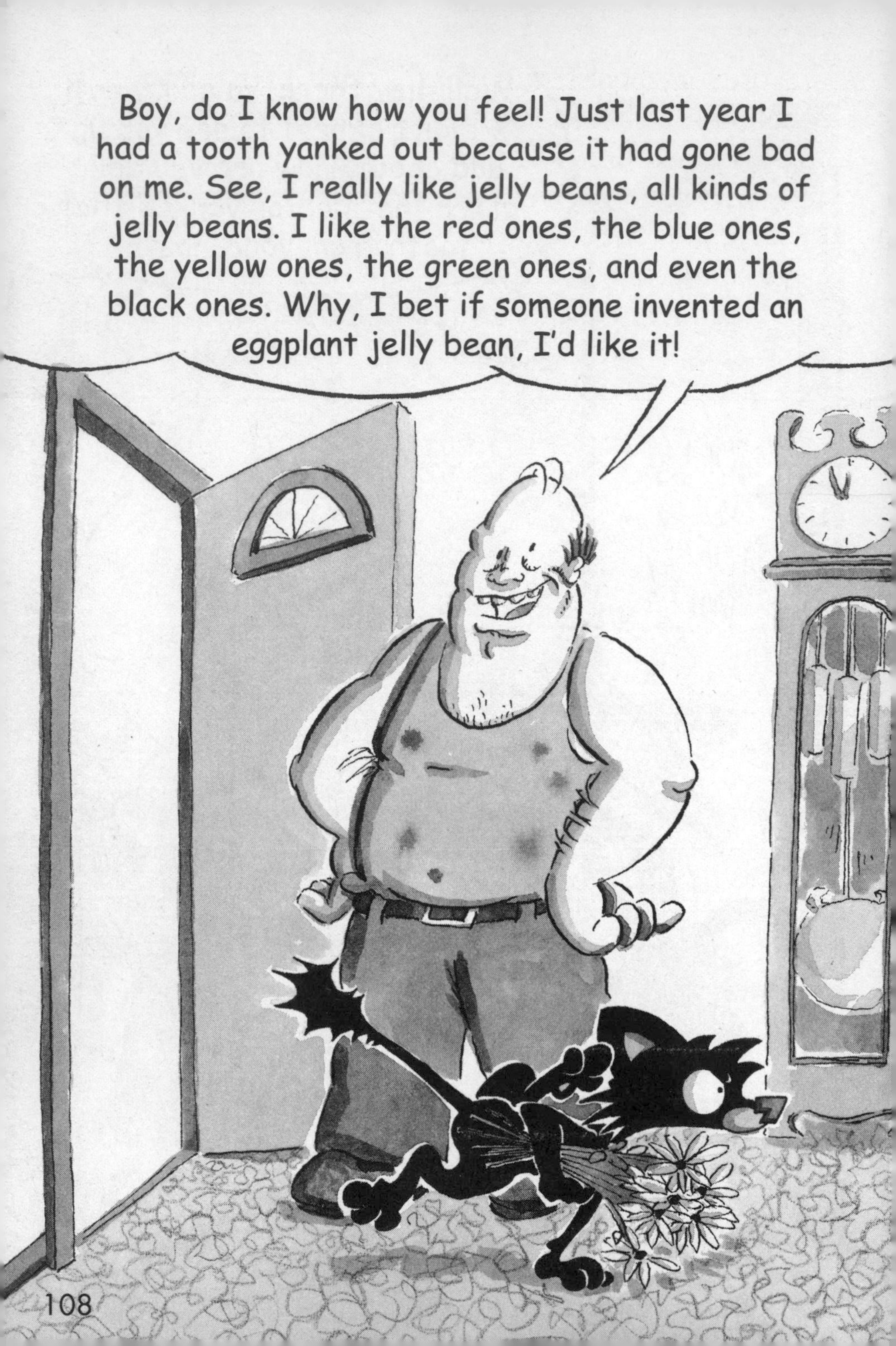
Boy, do I know how you feel! Just last year I had a tooth yanked out because it had gone bad on me. See, I really like jelly beans, all kinds of jelly beans. I like the red ones, the blue ones, the yellow ones, the green ones, and even the black ones. Why, I bet if someone invented an eggplant jelly bean, I'd like it!

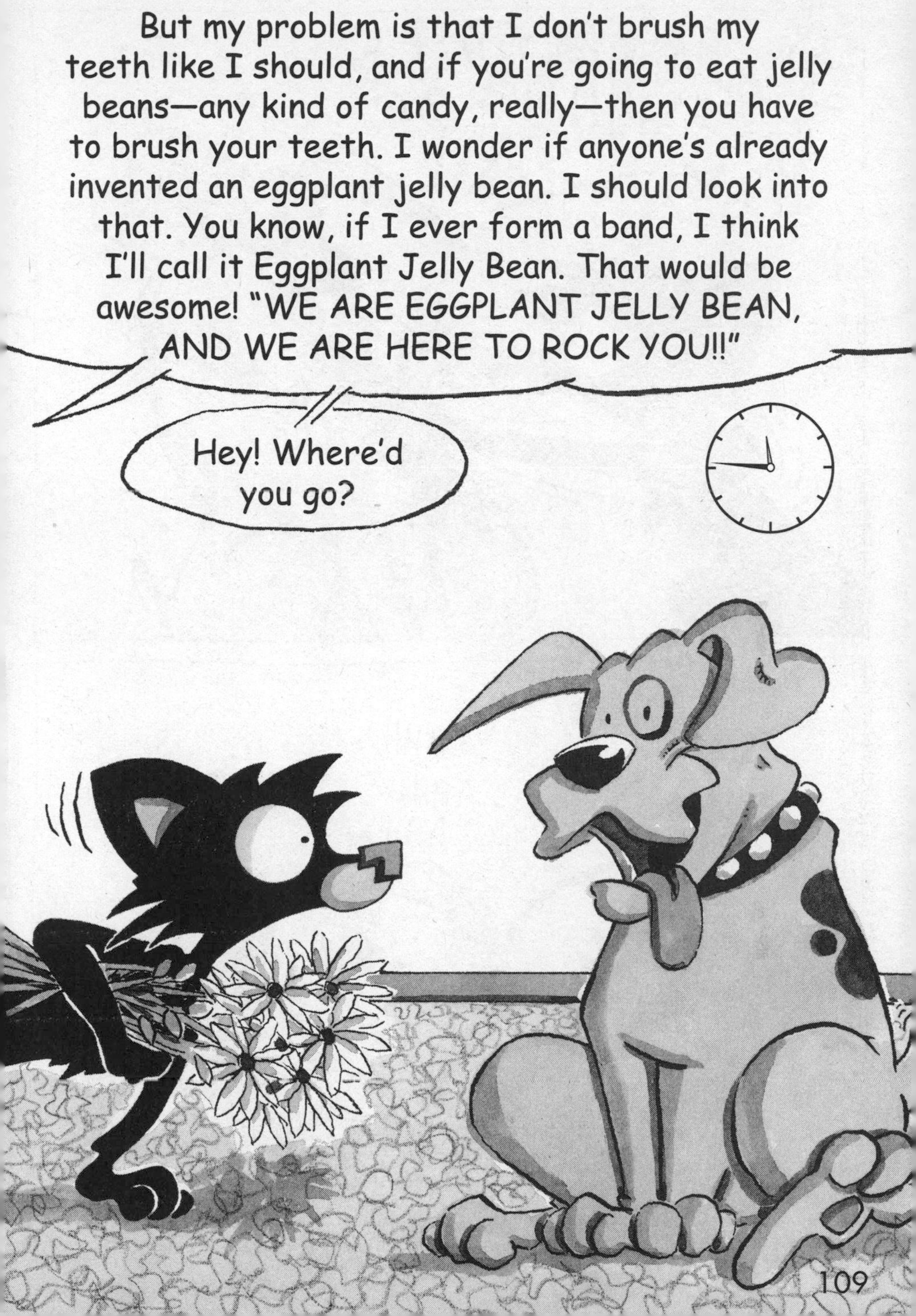
But my problem is that I don't brush my teeth like I should, and if you're going to eat jelly beans—any kind of candy, really—then you have to brush your teeth. I wonder if anyone's already invented an eggplant jelly bean. I should look into that. You know, if I ever form a band, I think I'll call it Eggplant Jelly Bean. That would be awesome! "WE ARE EGGPLANT JELLY BEAN, AND WE ARE HERE TO ROCK YOU!!"
Hey! Where'd you go?

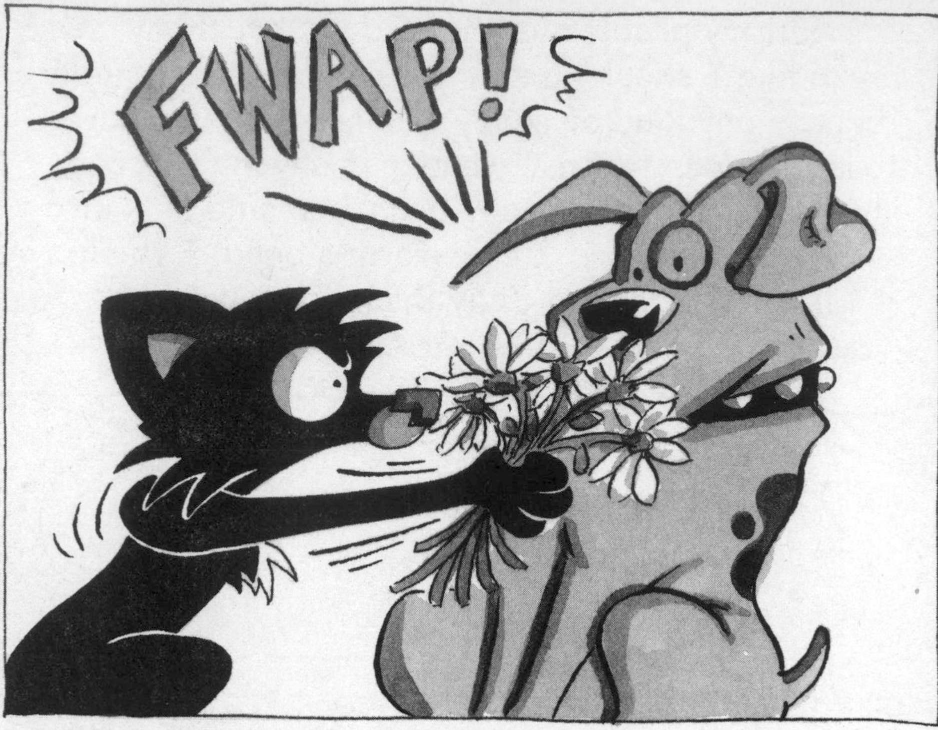
FWAP!

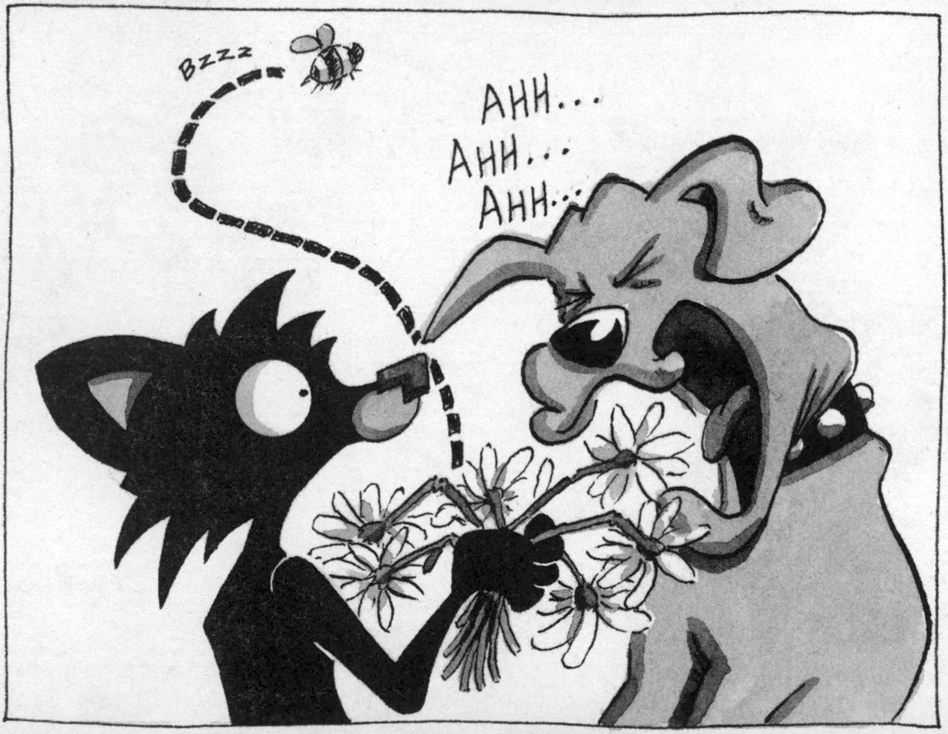
Bzzz
AHH...
AHH...
AHH...

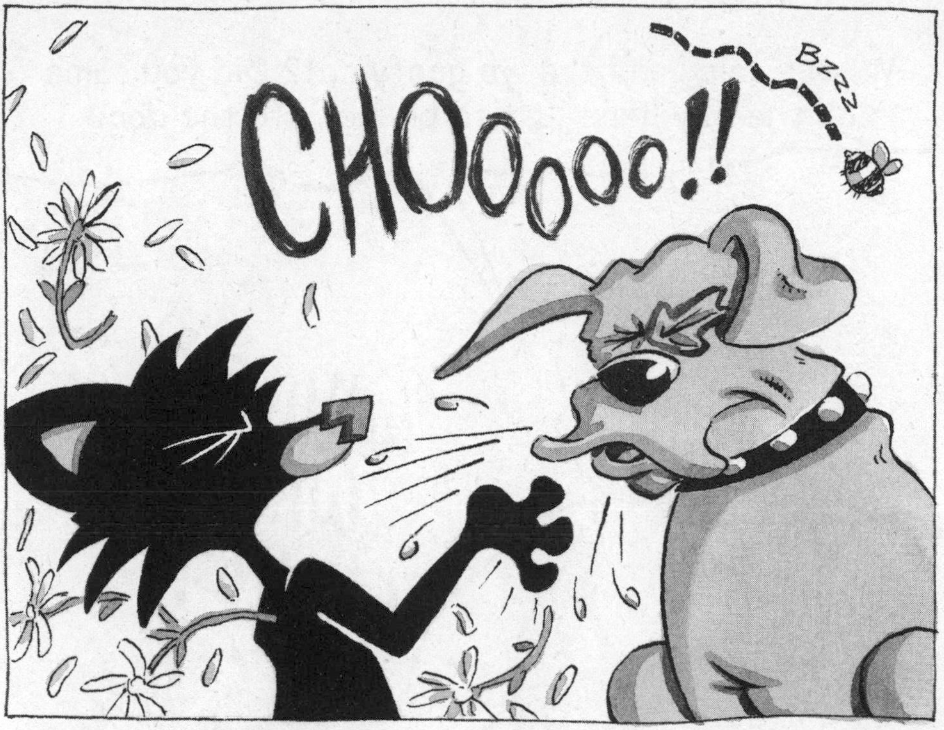
CHOOOOO!!
BZZZ

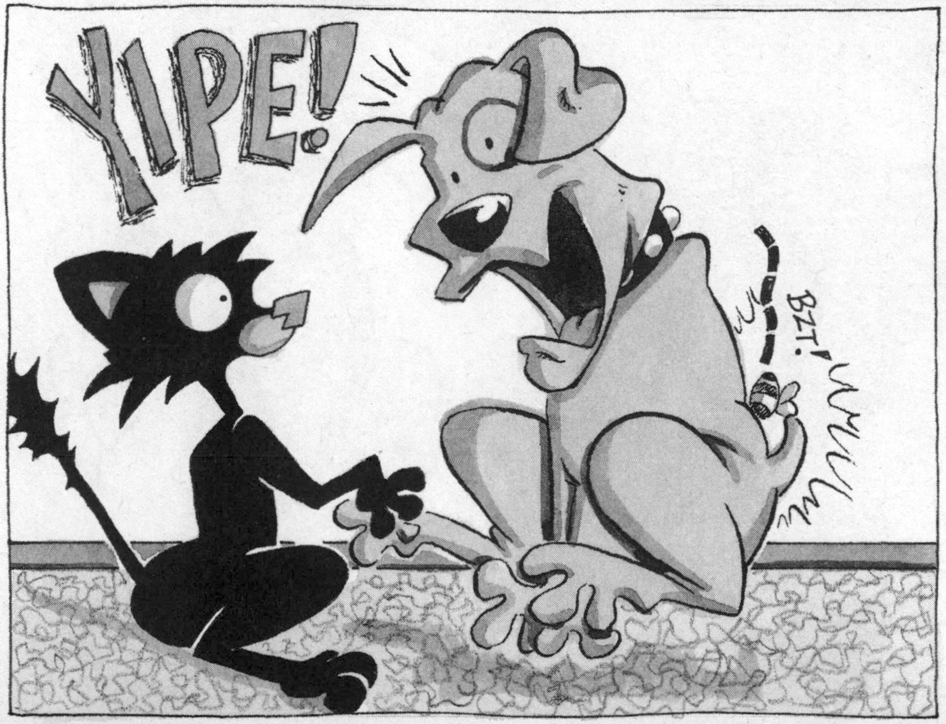
YIPE!
BZT!

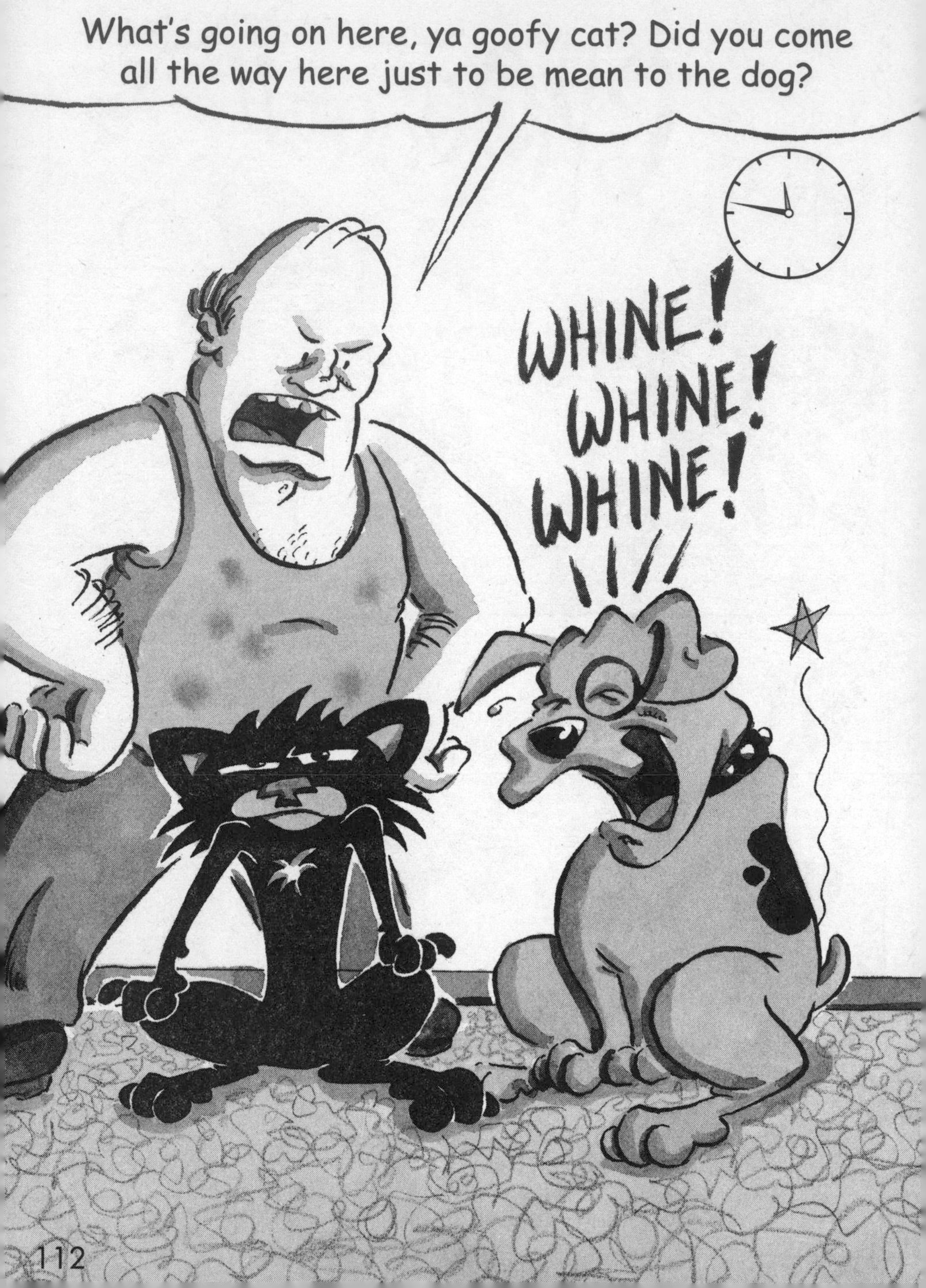
What's going on here, ya goofy cat? Did you come all the way here just to be mean to the dog?
WHINE! WHINE! WHINE!

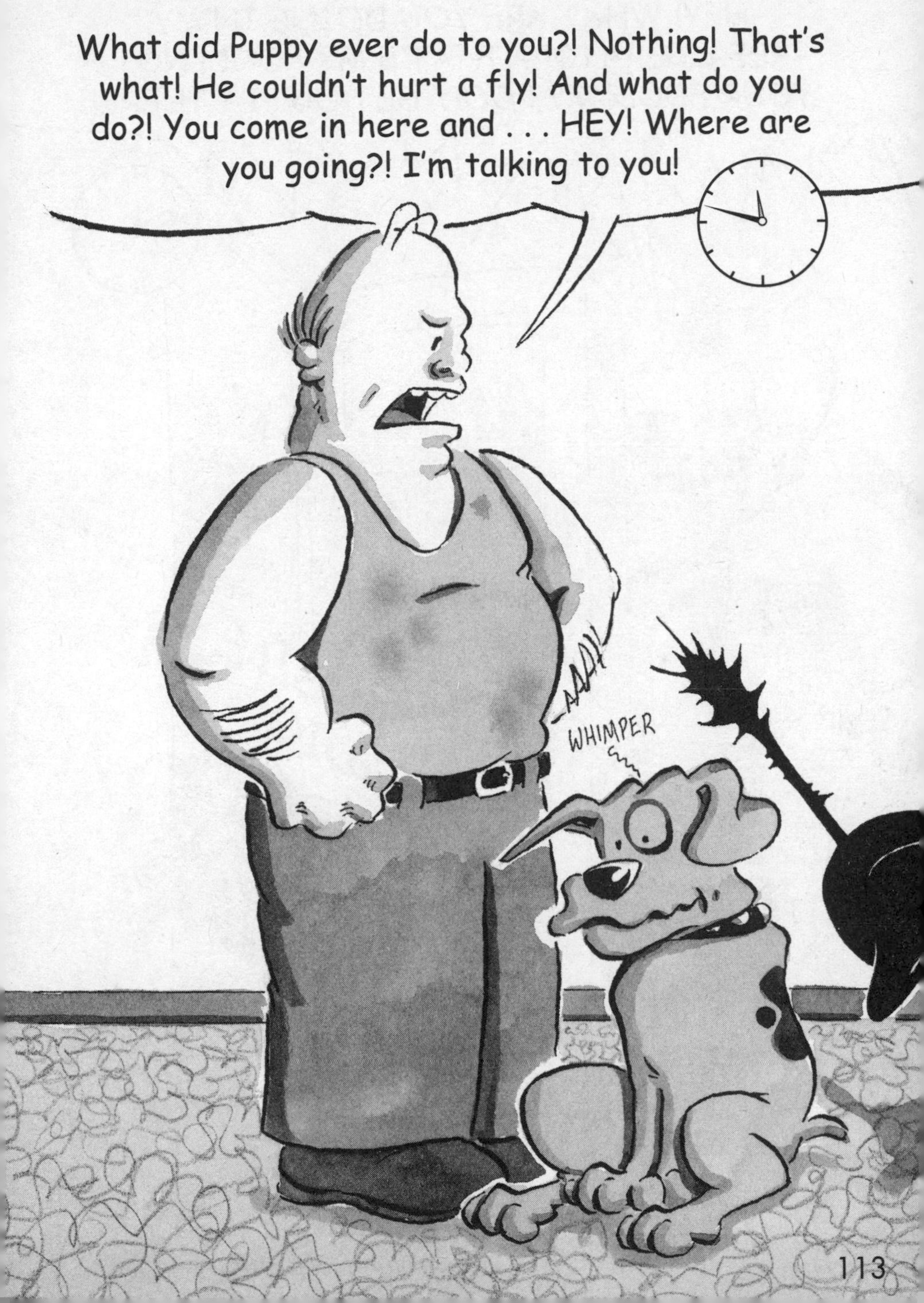
What did Puppy ever do to you?! Nothing! That's what! He couldn't hurt a fly! And what do you do?! You come in here and . . . HEY! Where are you going?! I'm talking to you!
WHIMPER

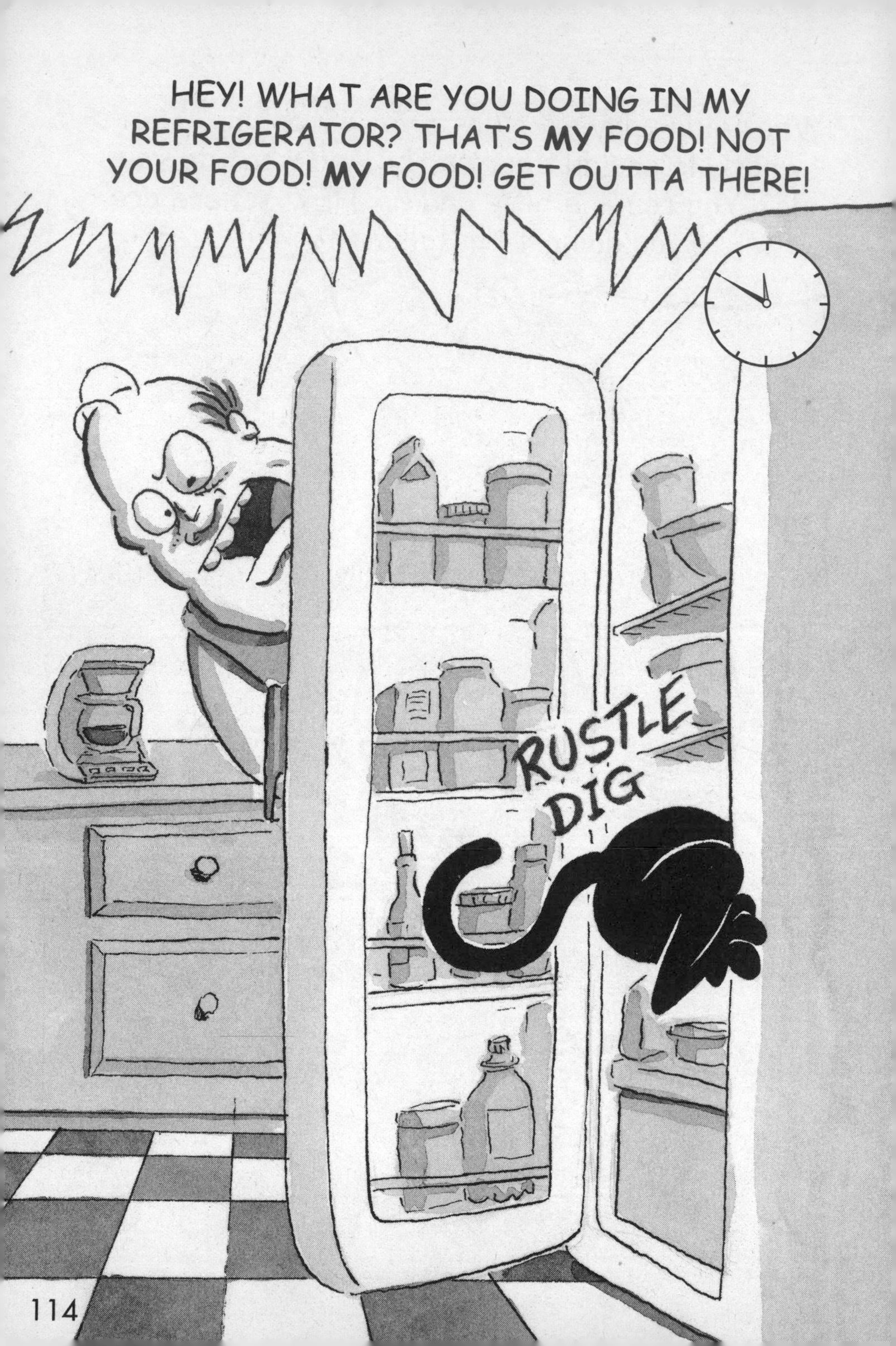
HEY! WHAT ARE YOU DOING IN MY REFRIGERATOR? THAT'S **MY** FOOD! NOT YOUR FOOD! **MY** FOOD! GET OUTTA THERE!
RUSTLE
DIG

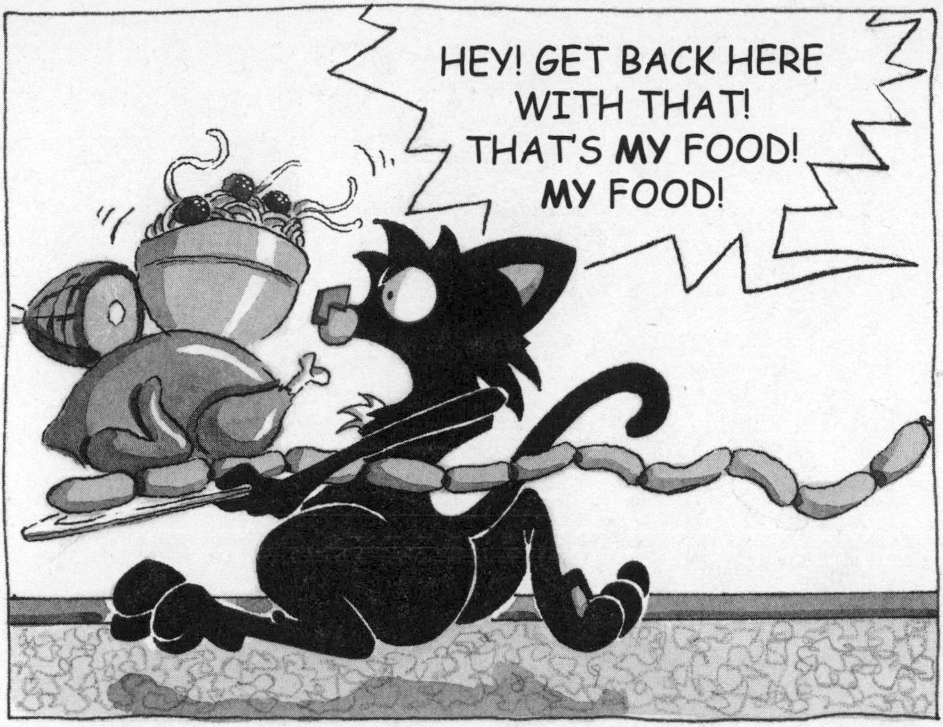
HEY! GET BACK HERE WITH THAT! THAT'S MY FOOD! MY FOOD!

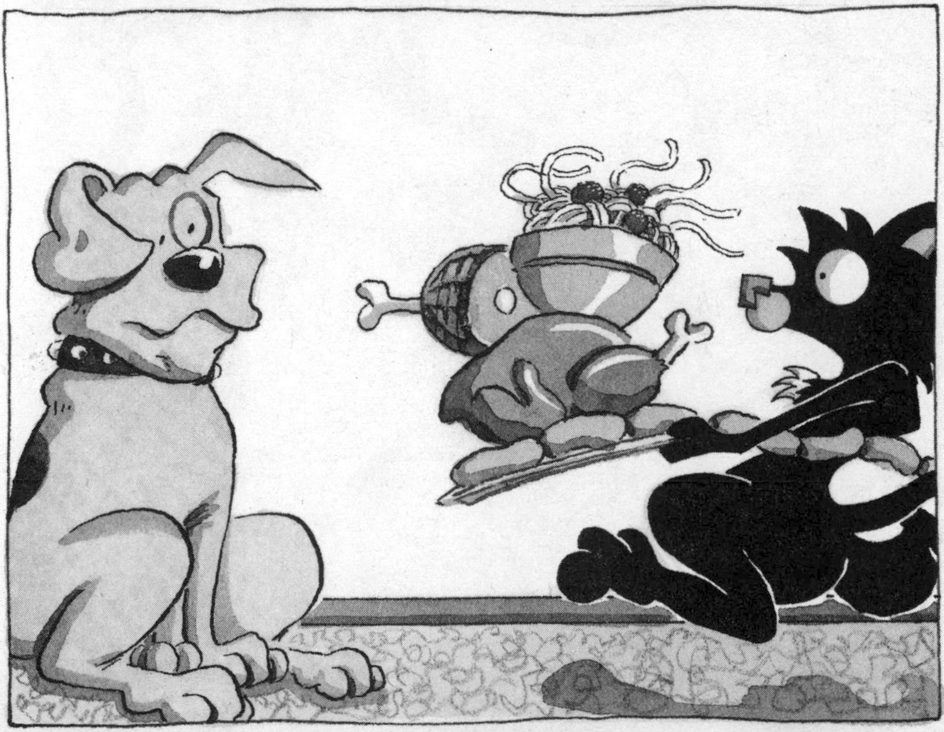

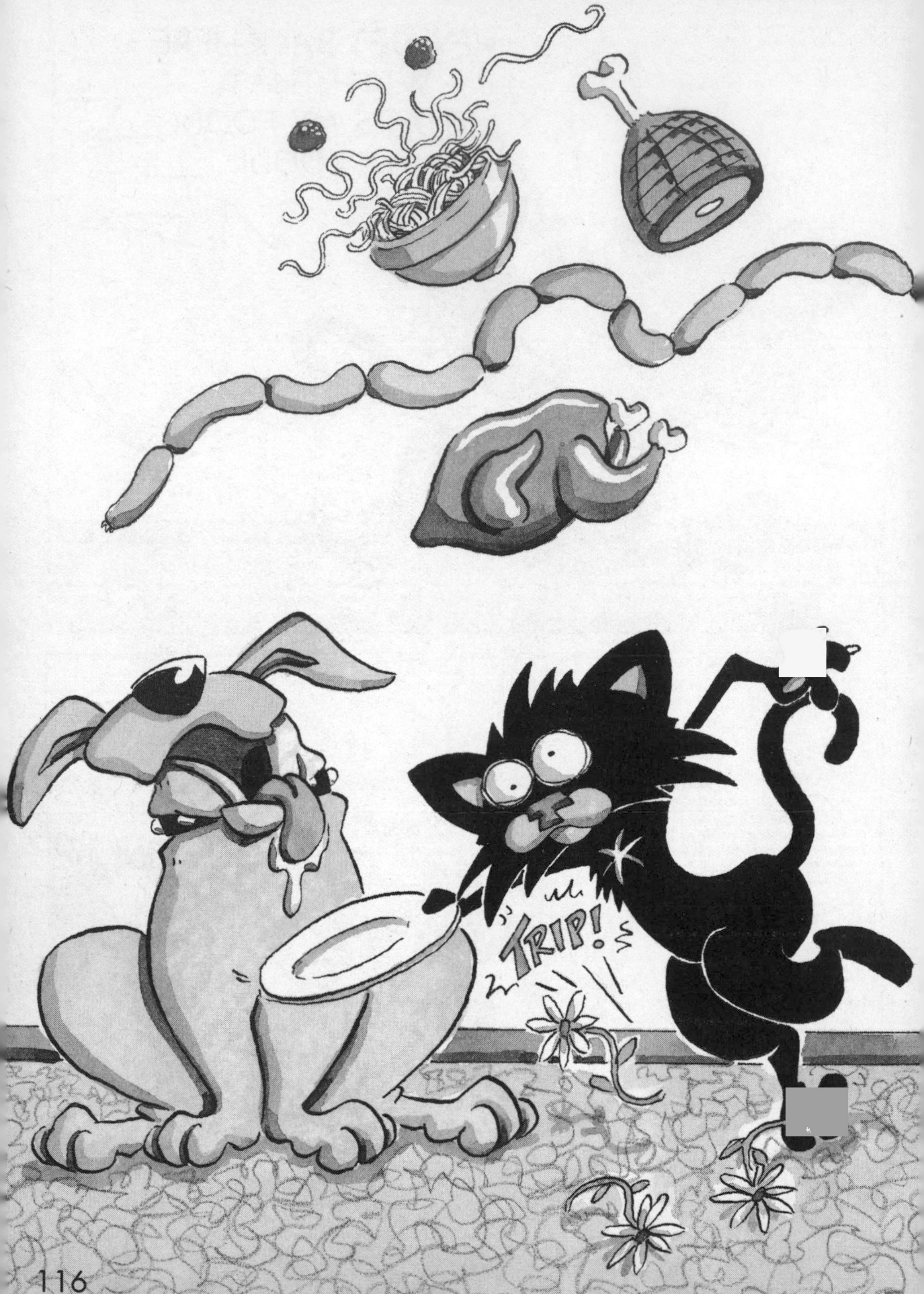
TRIP!

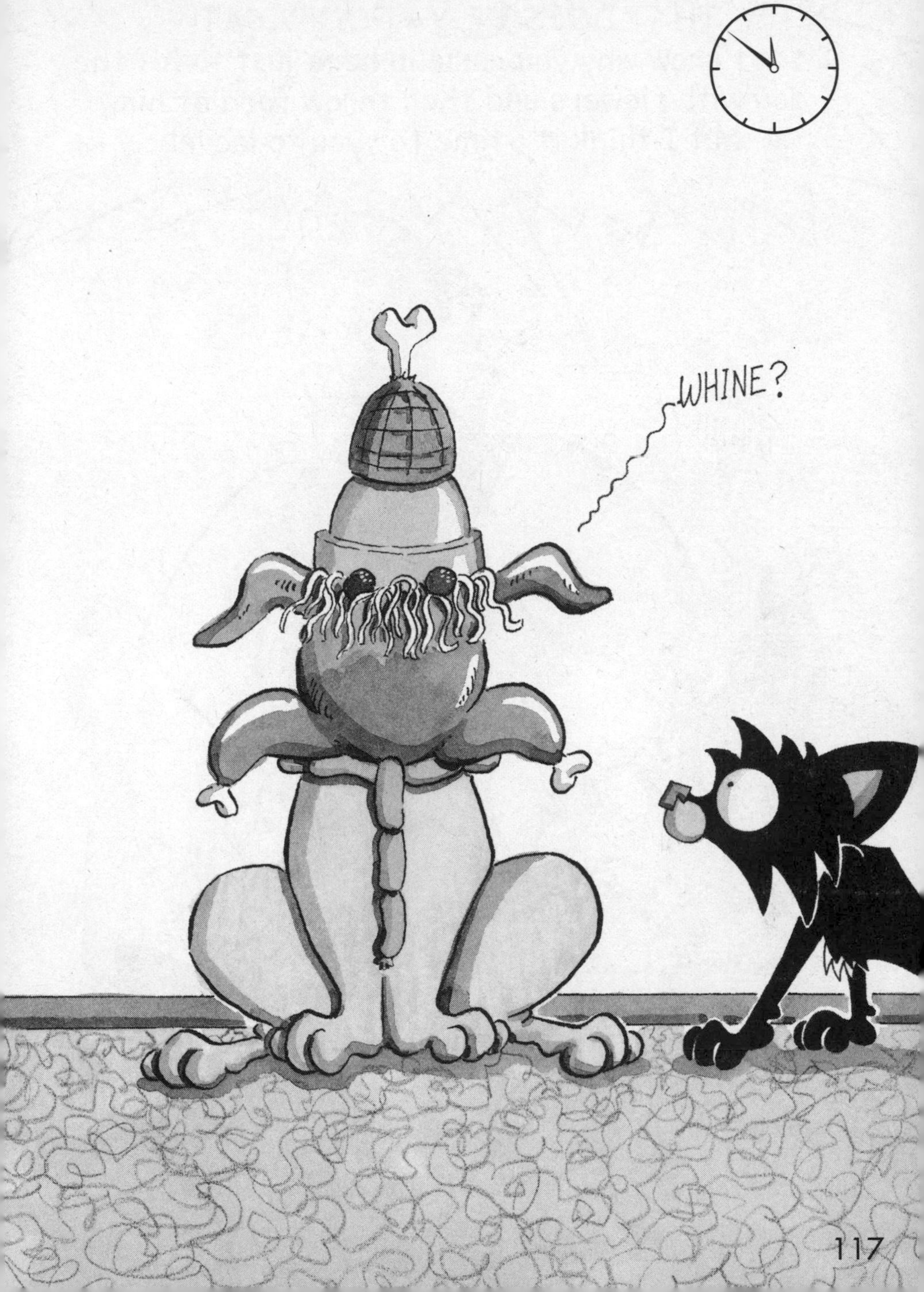
WHINE?

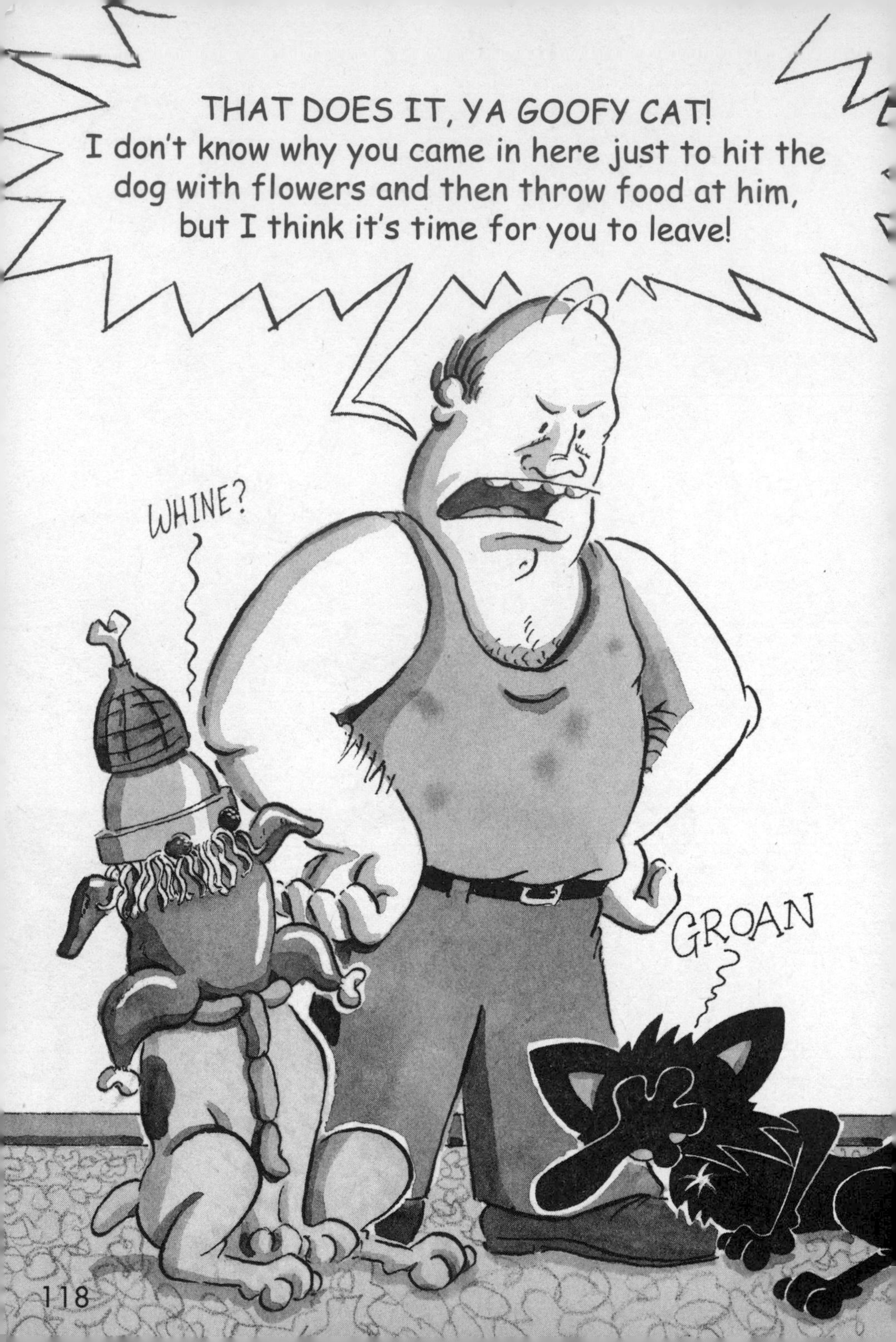
THAT DOES IT, YA GOOFY CAT!
I don't know why you came in here just to hit the dog with flowers and then throw food at him, but I think it's time for you to leave!
WHINE?
GROAN

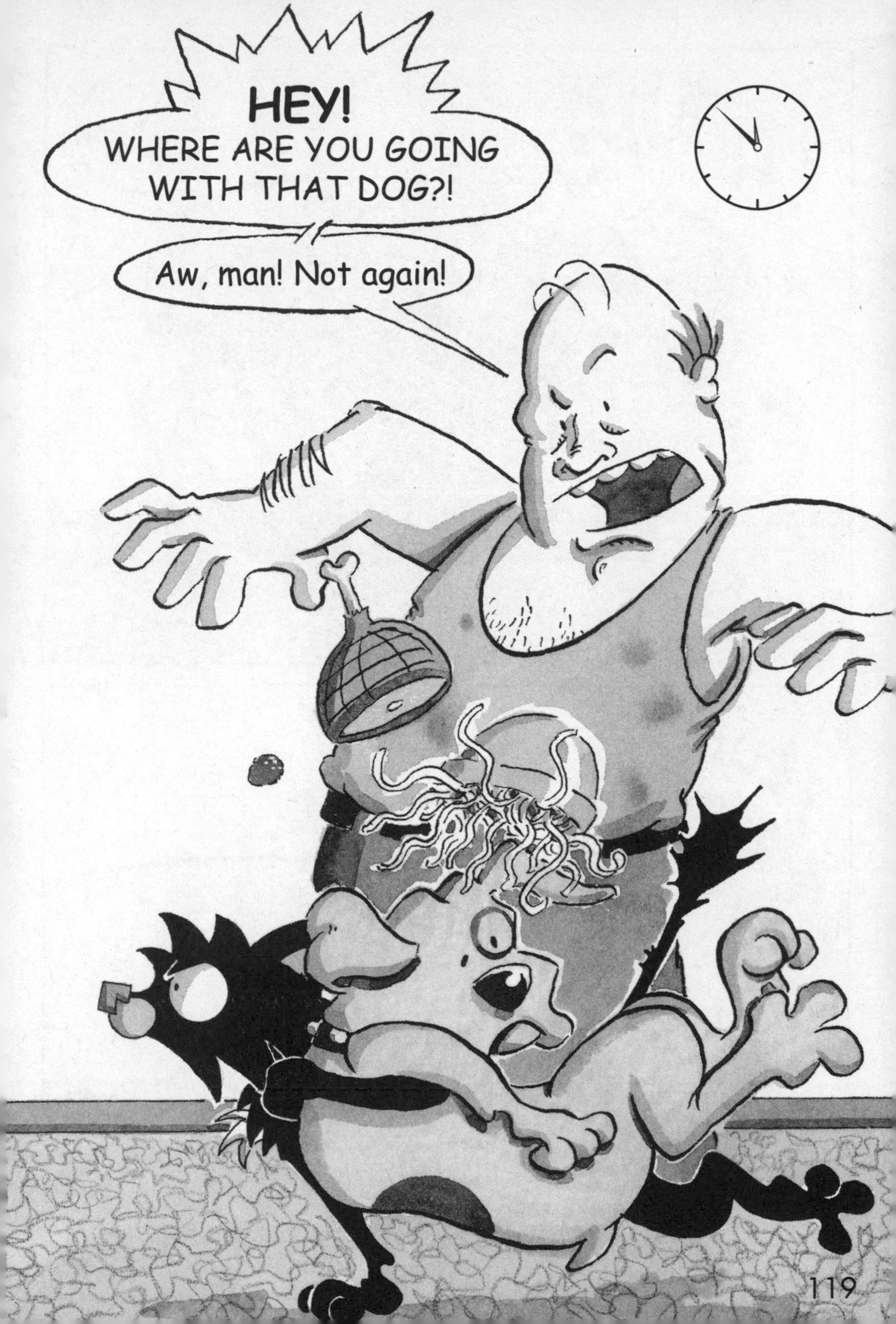
HEY!
WHERE ARE YOU GOING WITH THAT DOG?!
Aw, man! Not again!

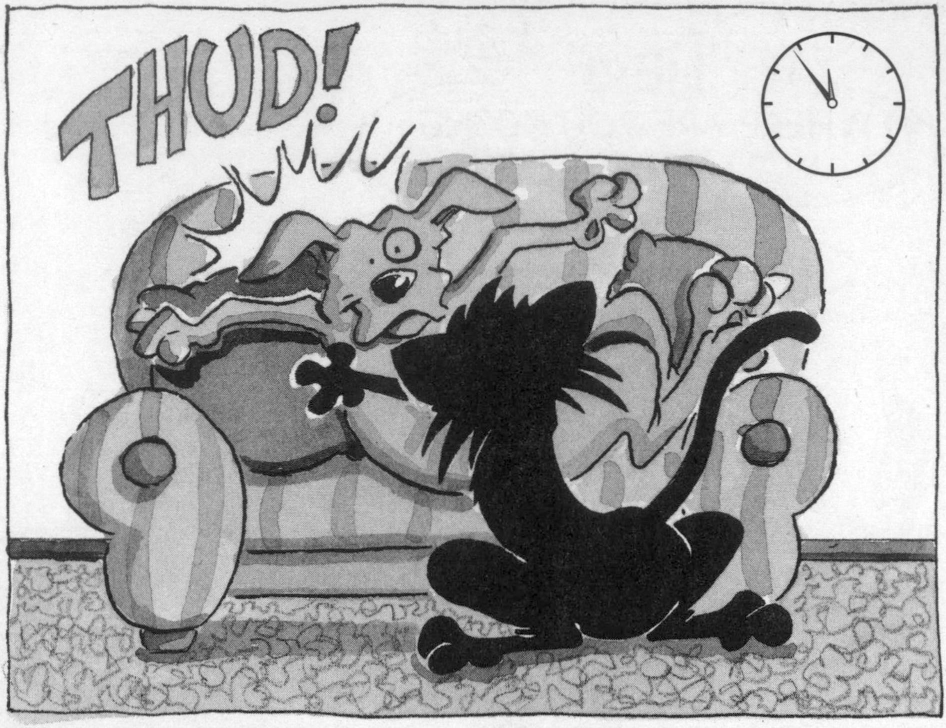
THUD!

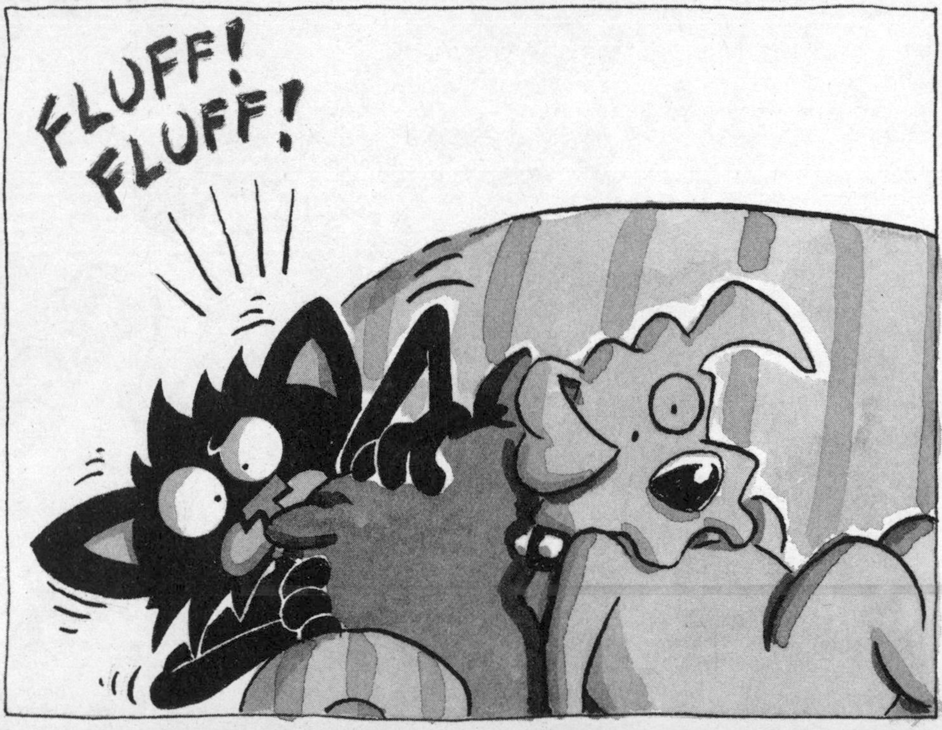
FLUFF!
FLUFF!

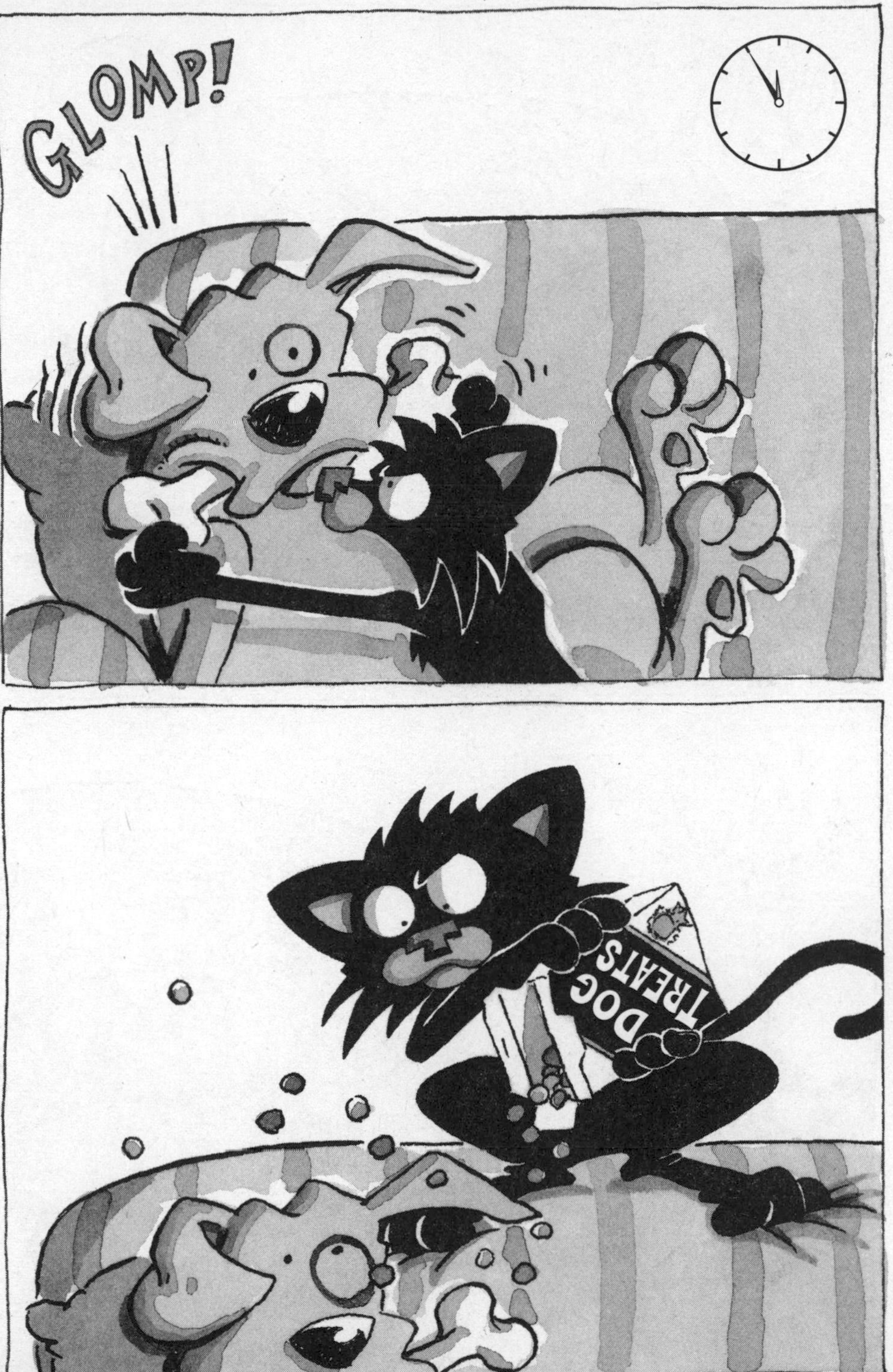
GLOMP!
DOG
TREATS

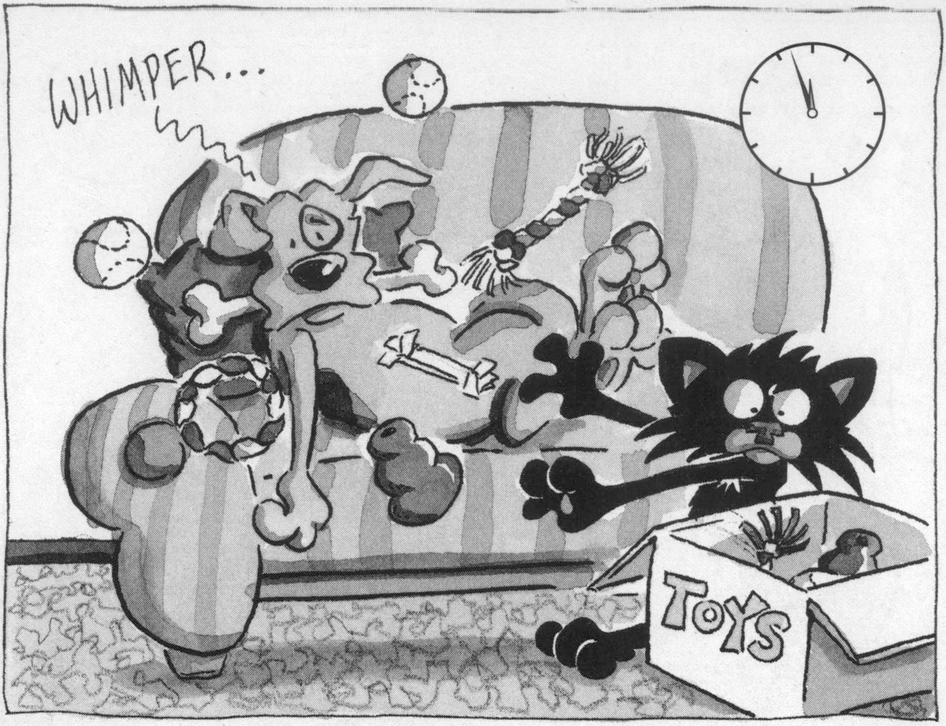
WHIMPER...
TOYS

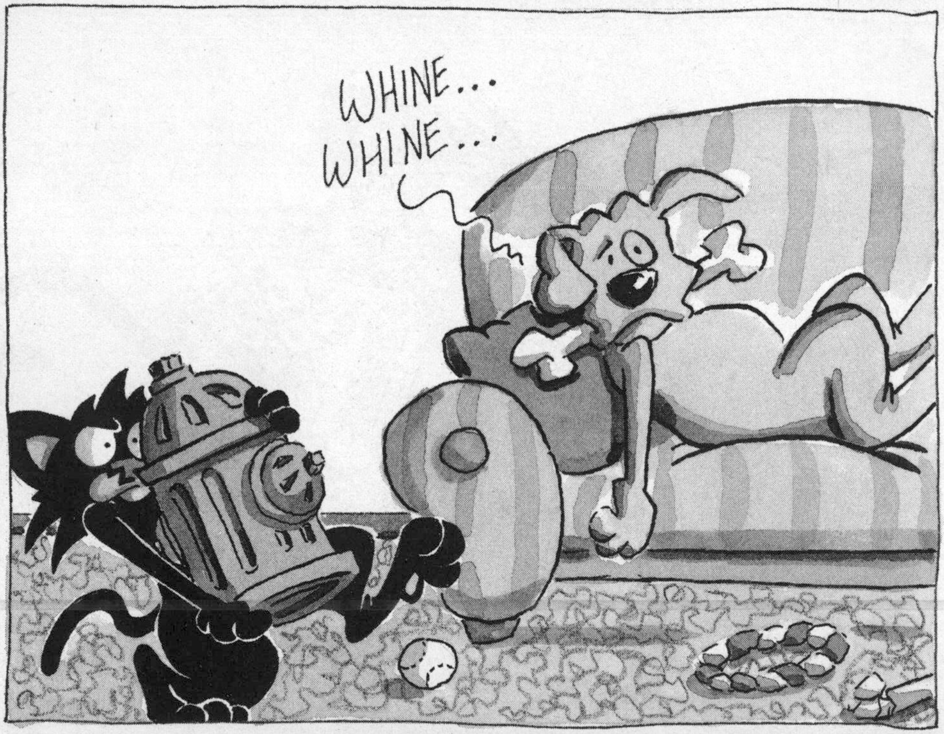
WHINE...
WHINE...

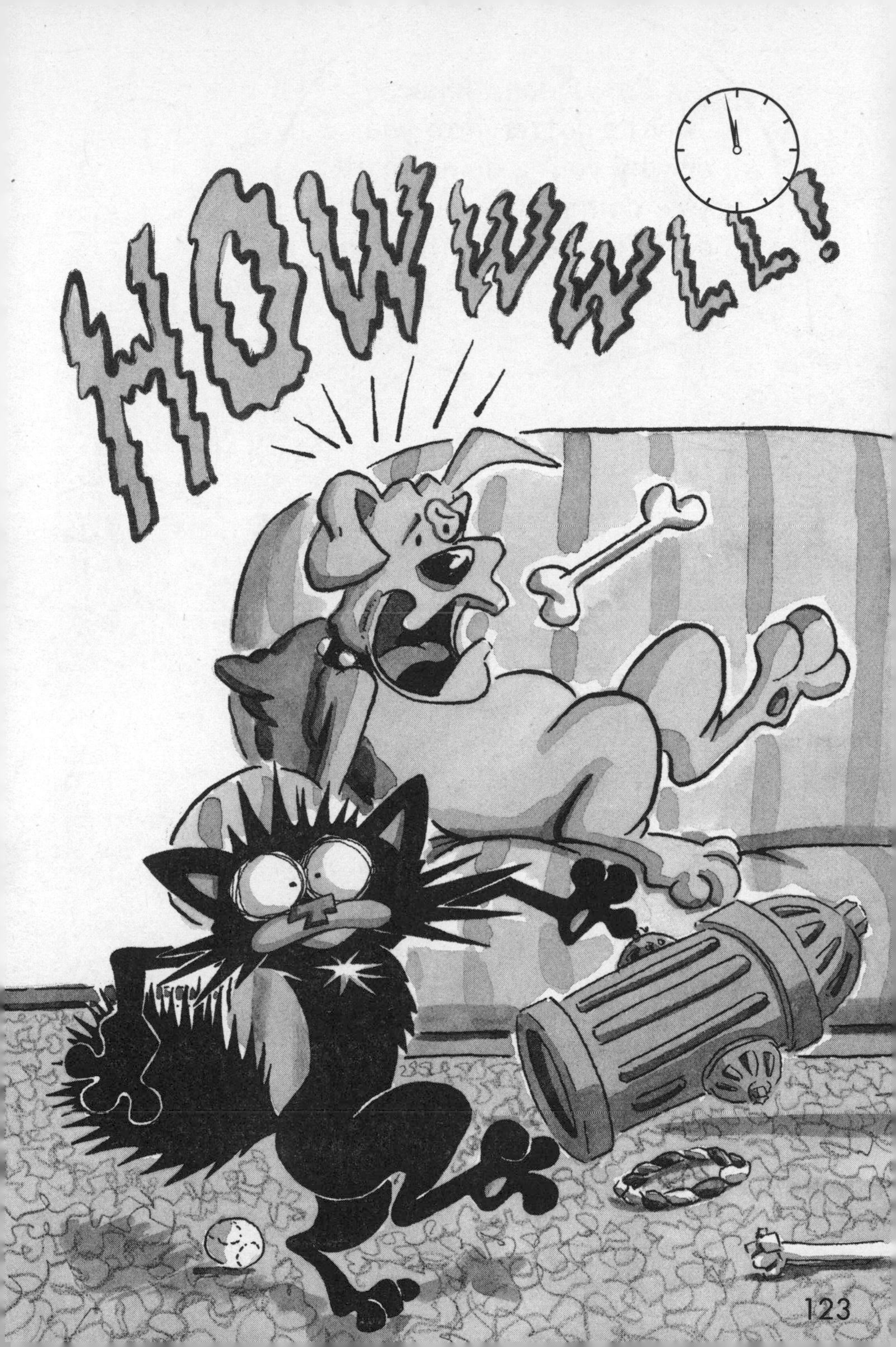
HOWWWLL!

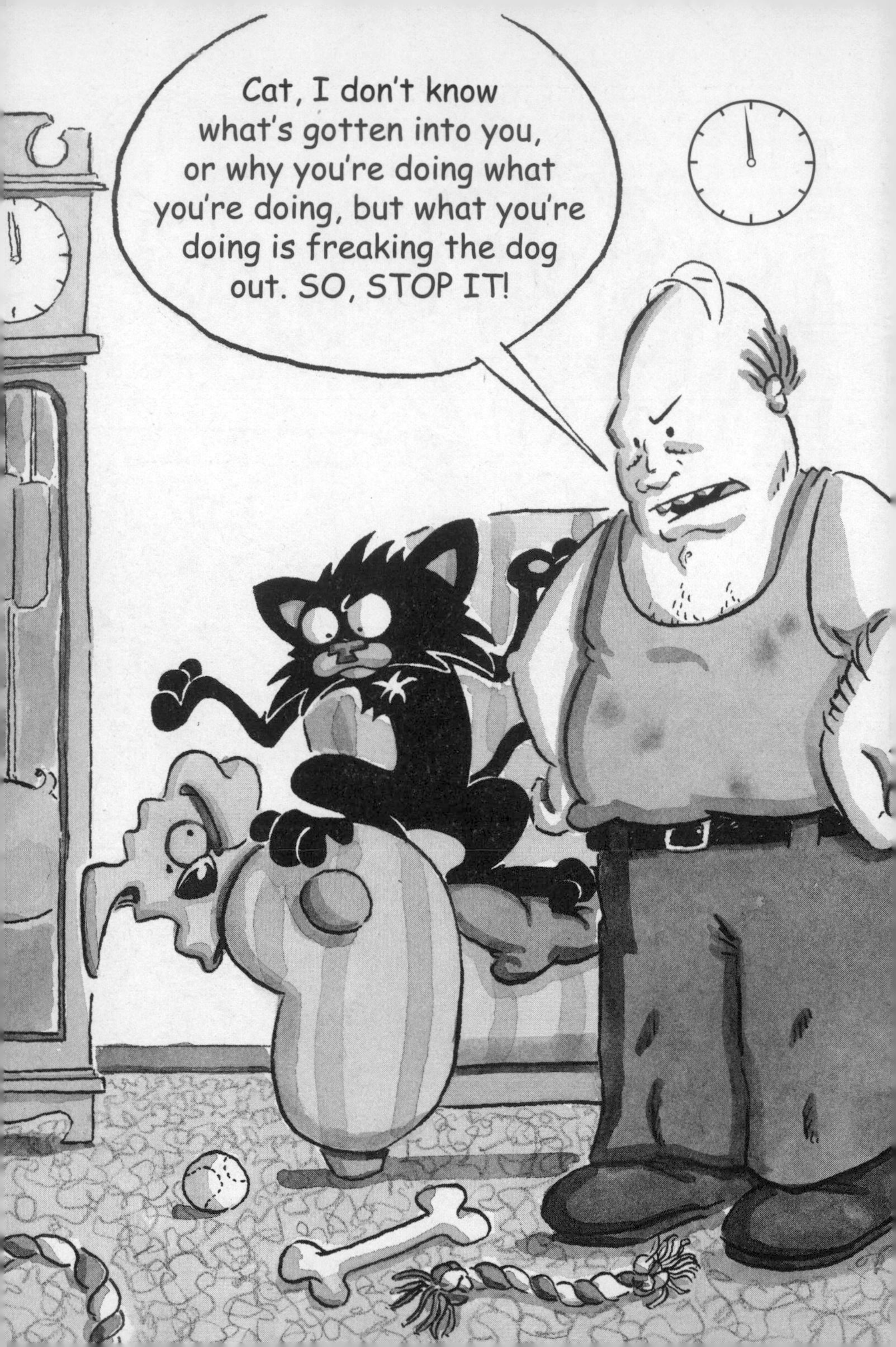
Cat, I don't know what's gotten into you, or why you're doing what you're doing, but what you're doing is freaking the dog out. SO, STOP IT!

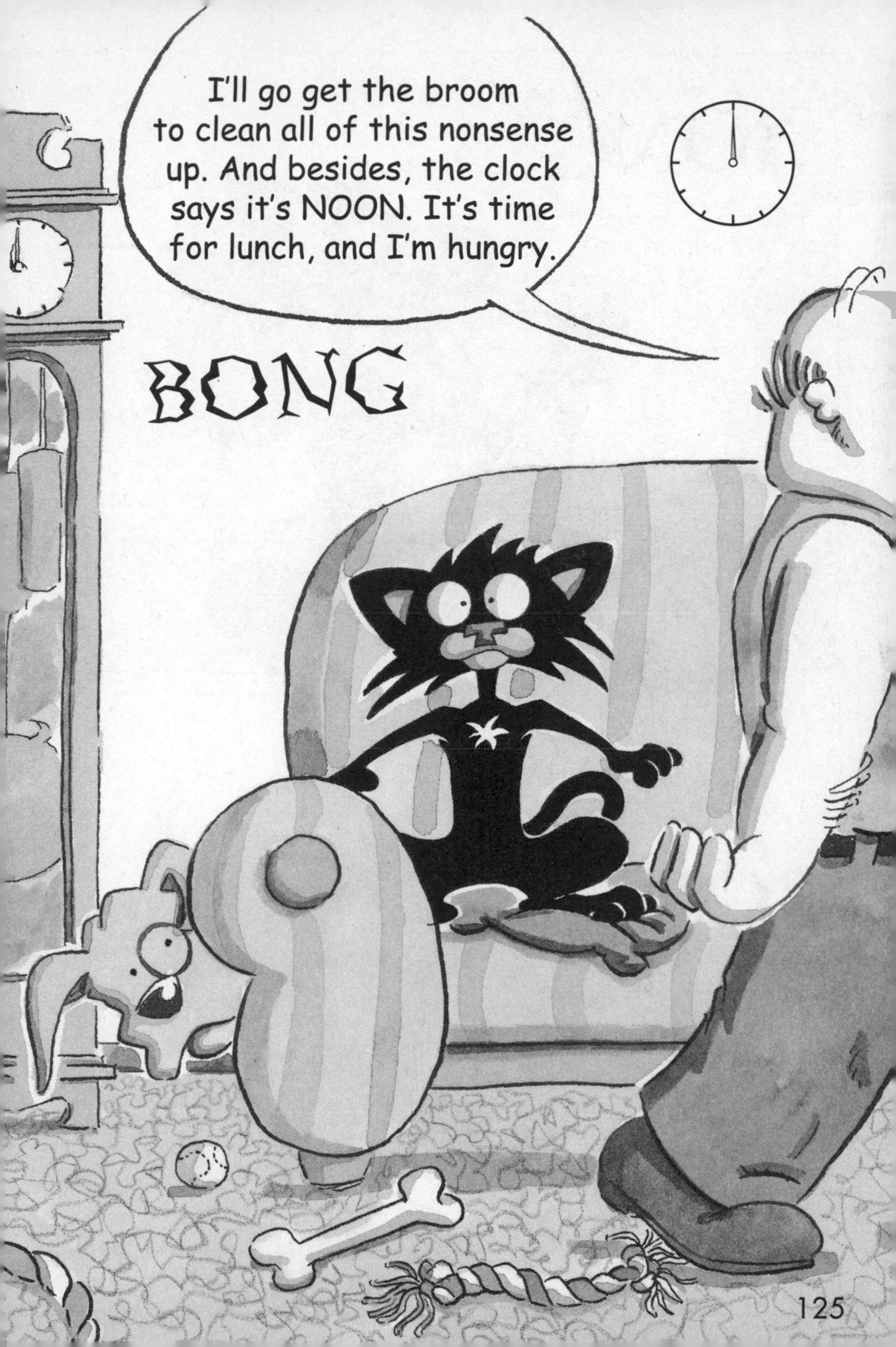
I'll go get the broom to clean all of this nonsense up. And besides, the clock says it's NOON. It's time for lunch, and I'm hungry.
BONG

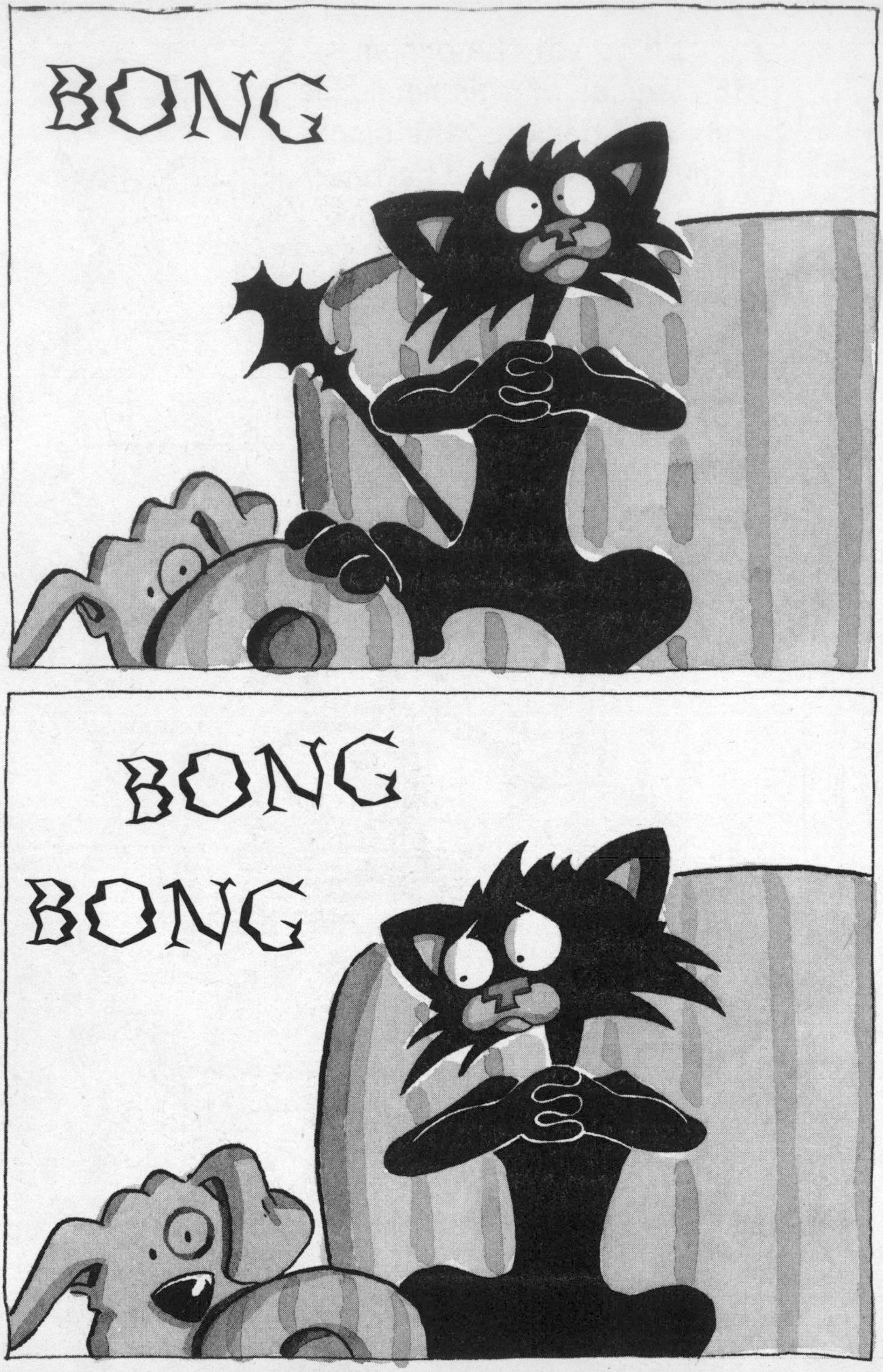
BONG
BONG
BONG

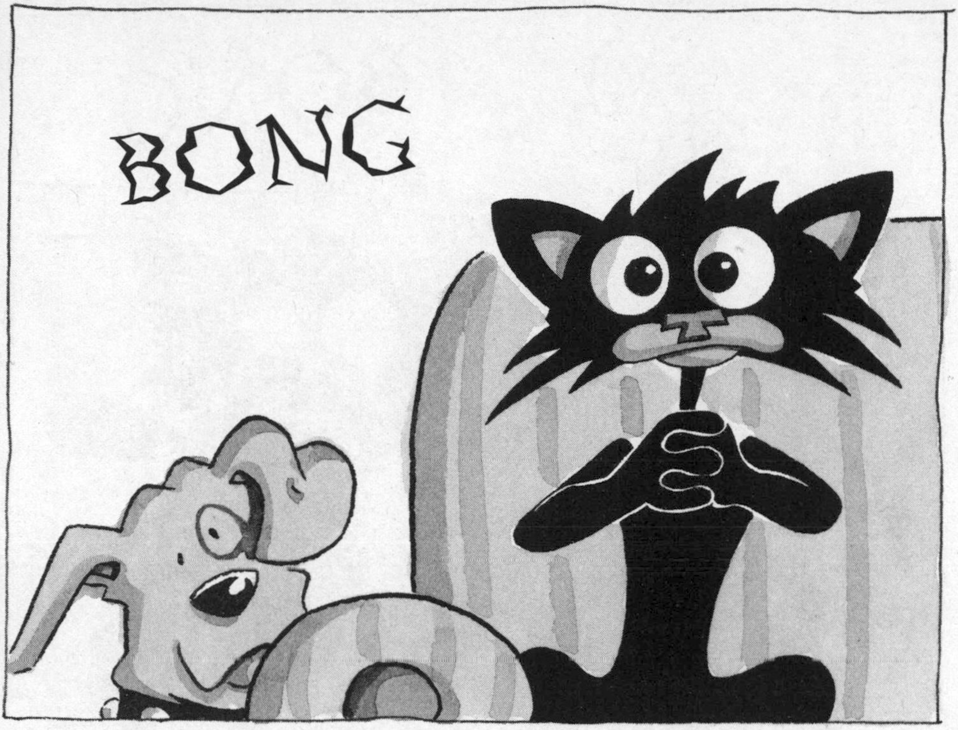
BONG

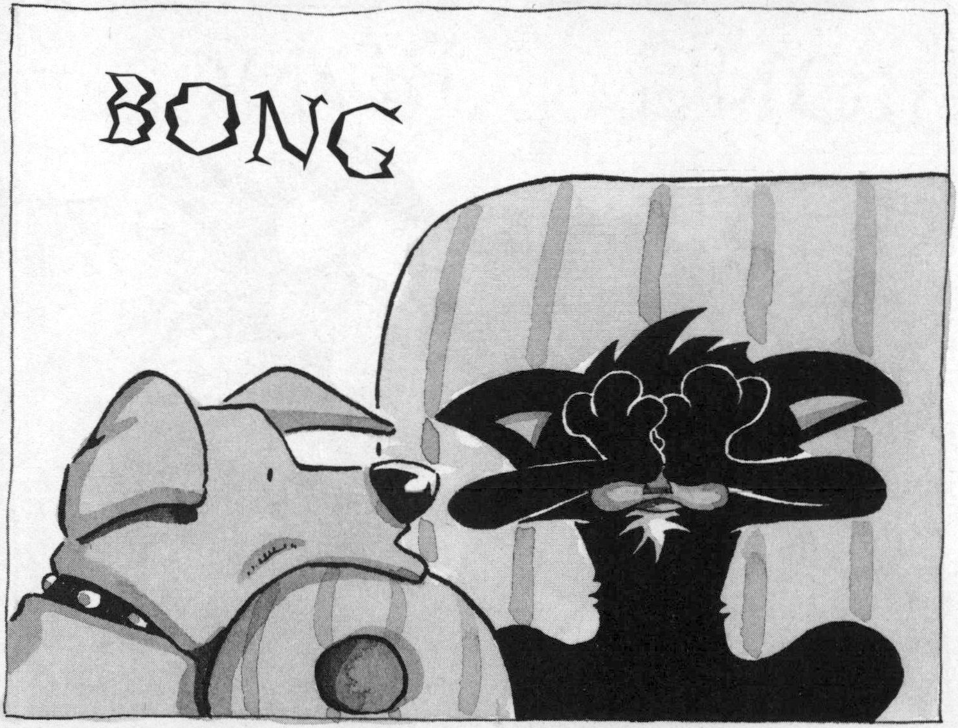
BONG

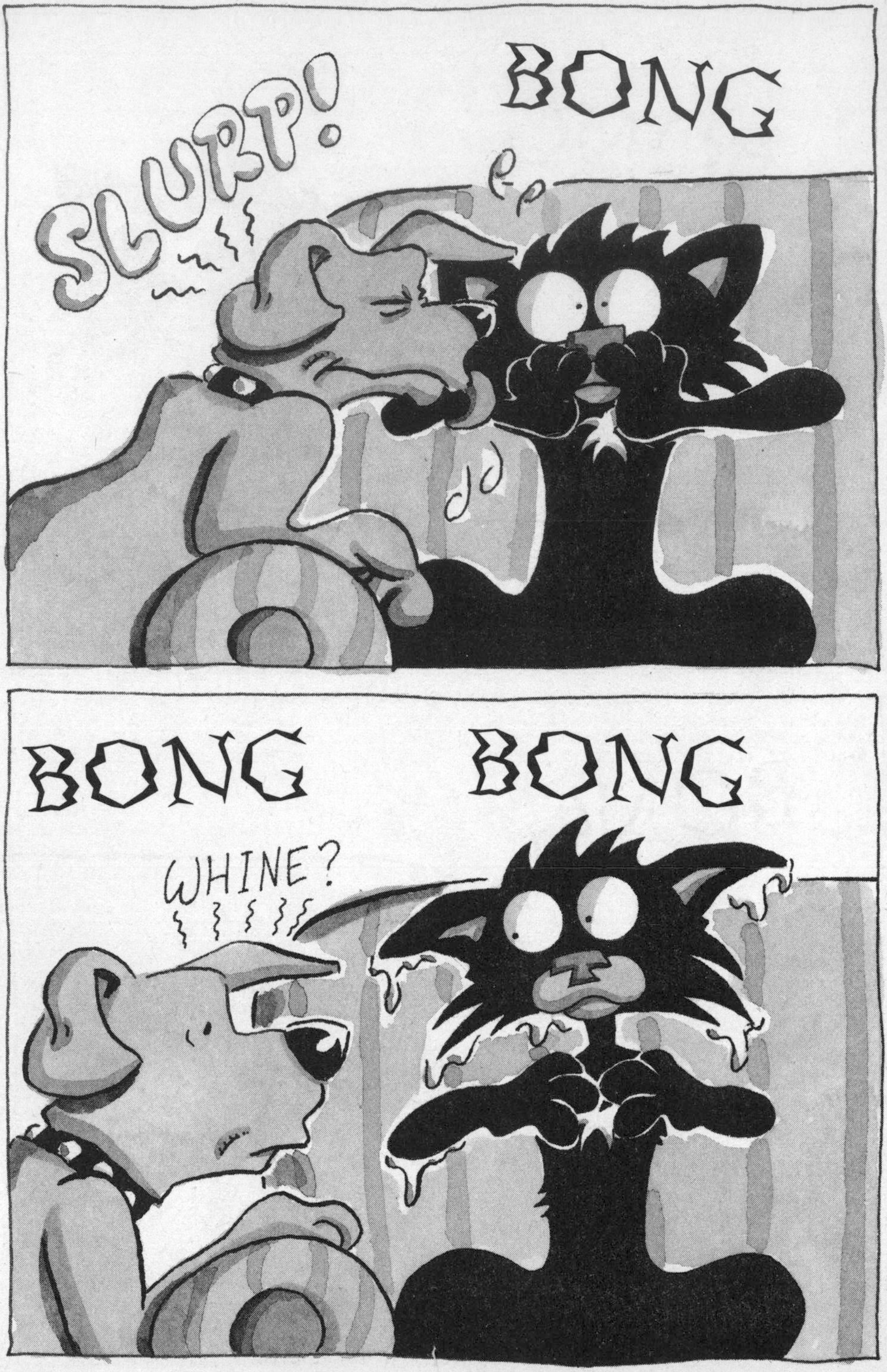
SLURP!
BONG
BONG
BONG
WHINE?

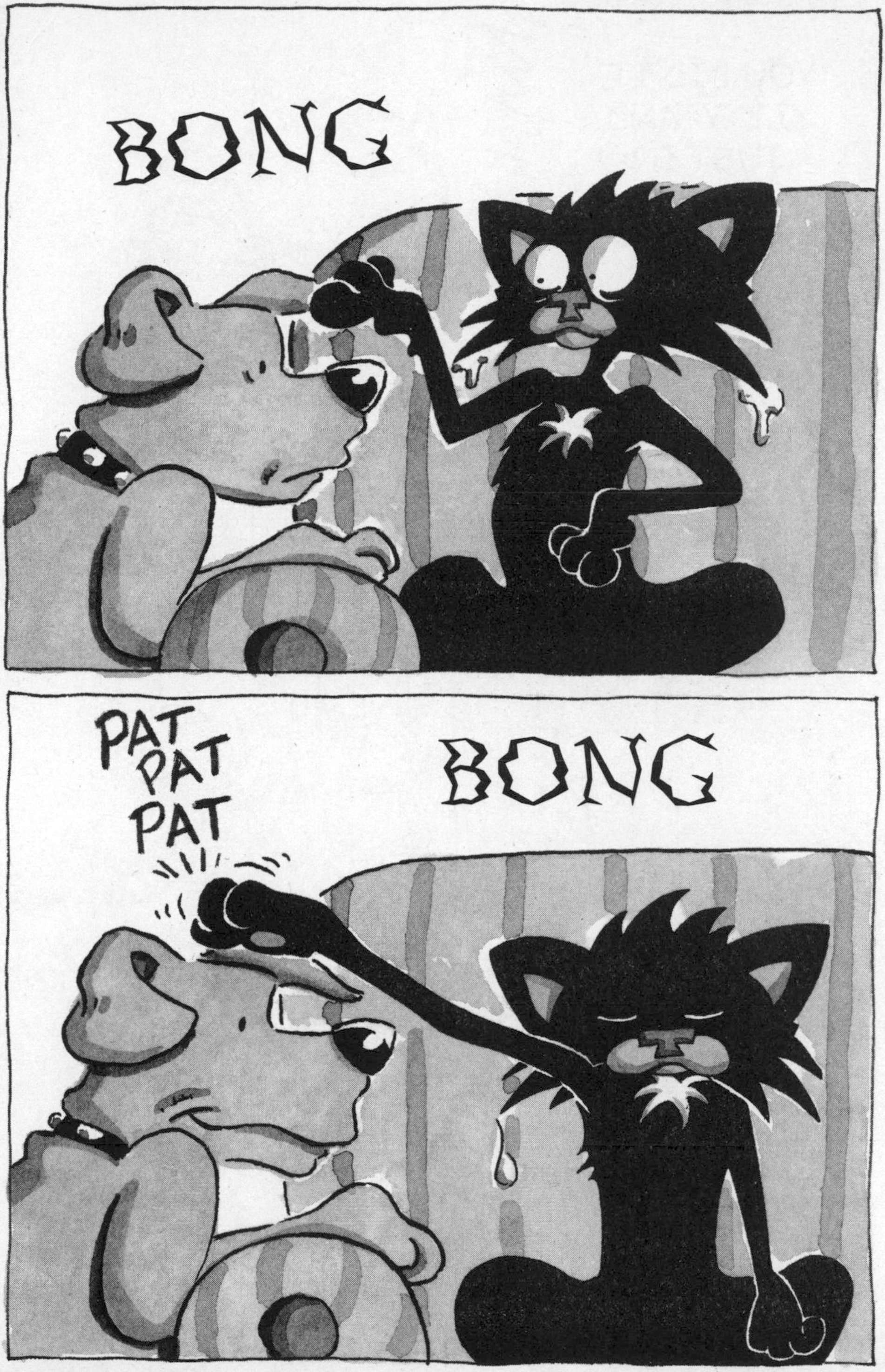
BONG
PAT PAT PAT
BONG

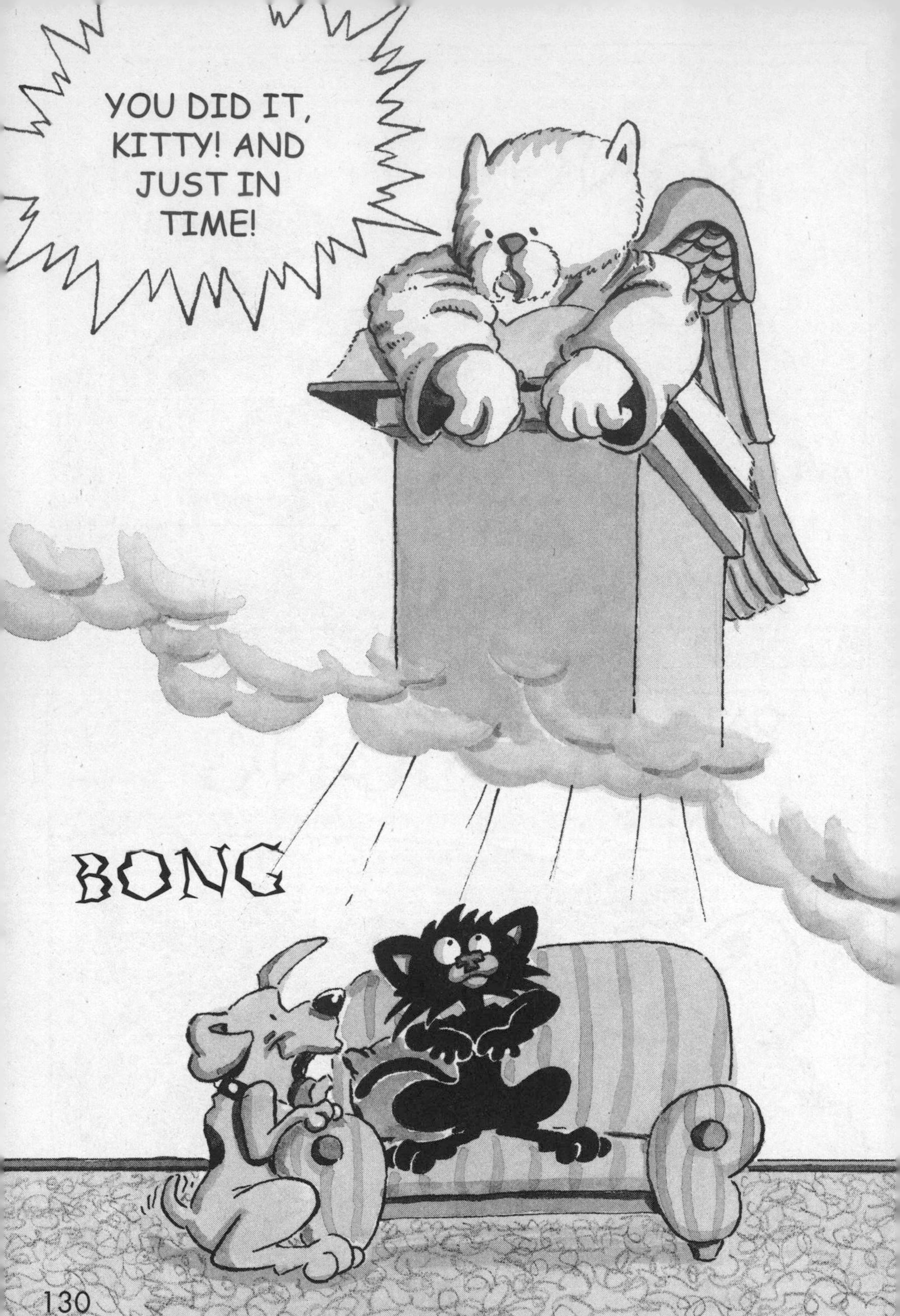
YOU DID IT, KITTY! AND JUST IN TIME!
BONG

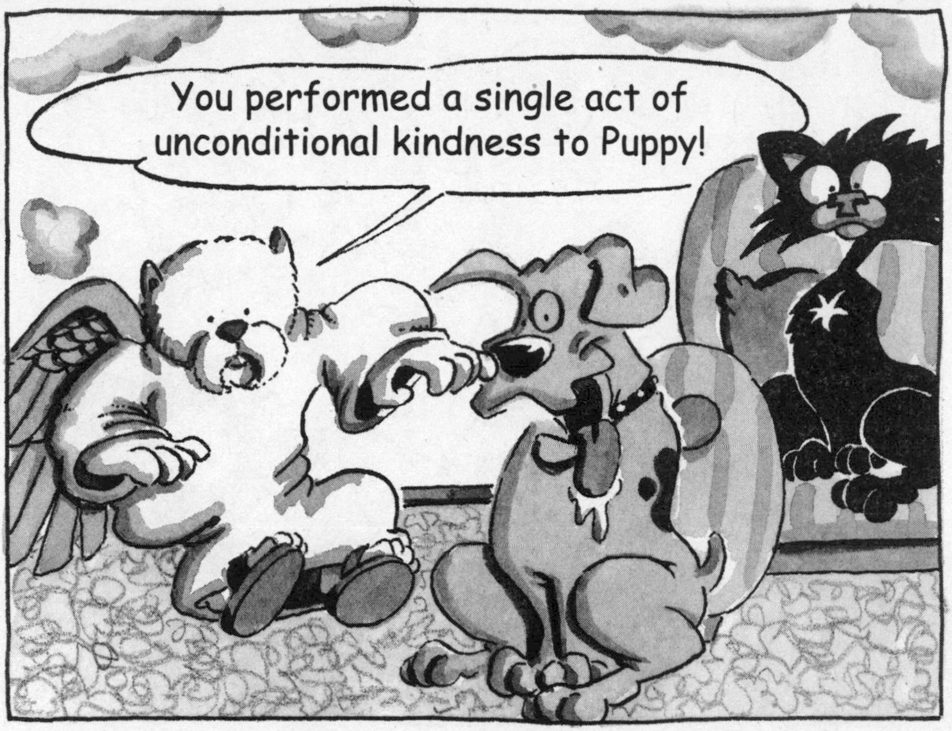
You performed a single act of unconditional kindness to Puppy!

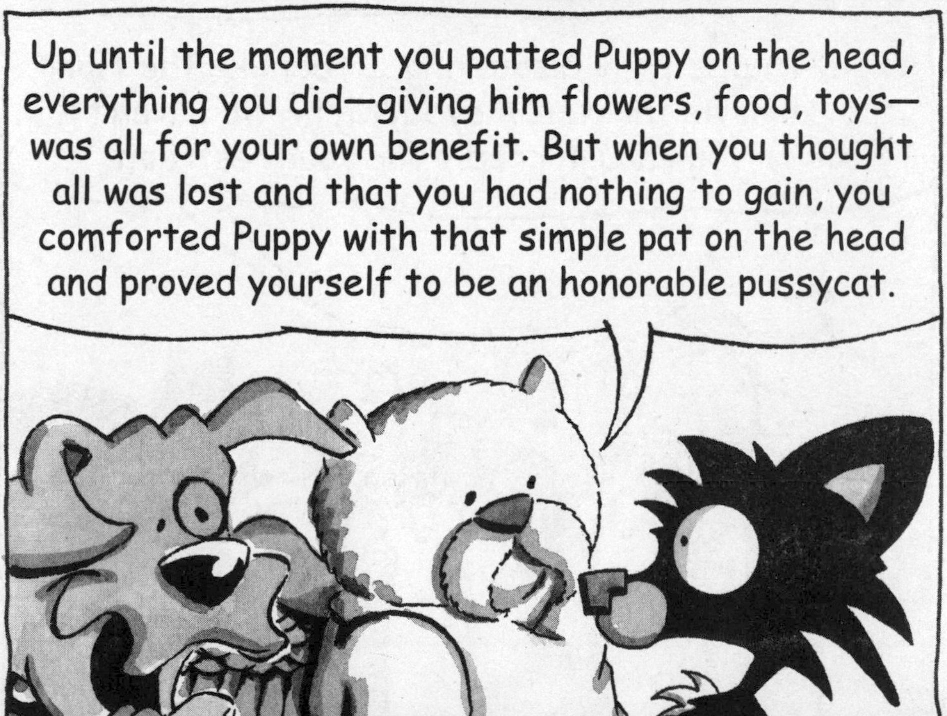
Up until the moment you patted Puppy on the head, everything you did—giving him flowers, food, toys—was all for your own benefit. But when you thought all was lost and that you had nothing to gain, you comforted Puppy with that simple pat on the head and proved yourself to be an honorable pussycat.

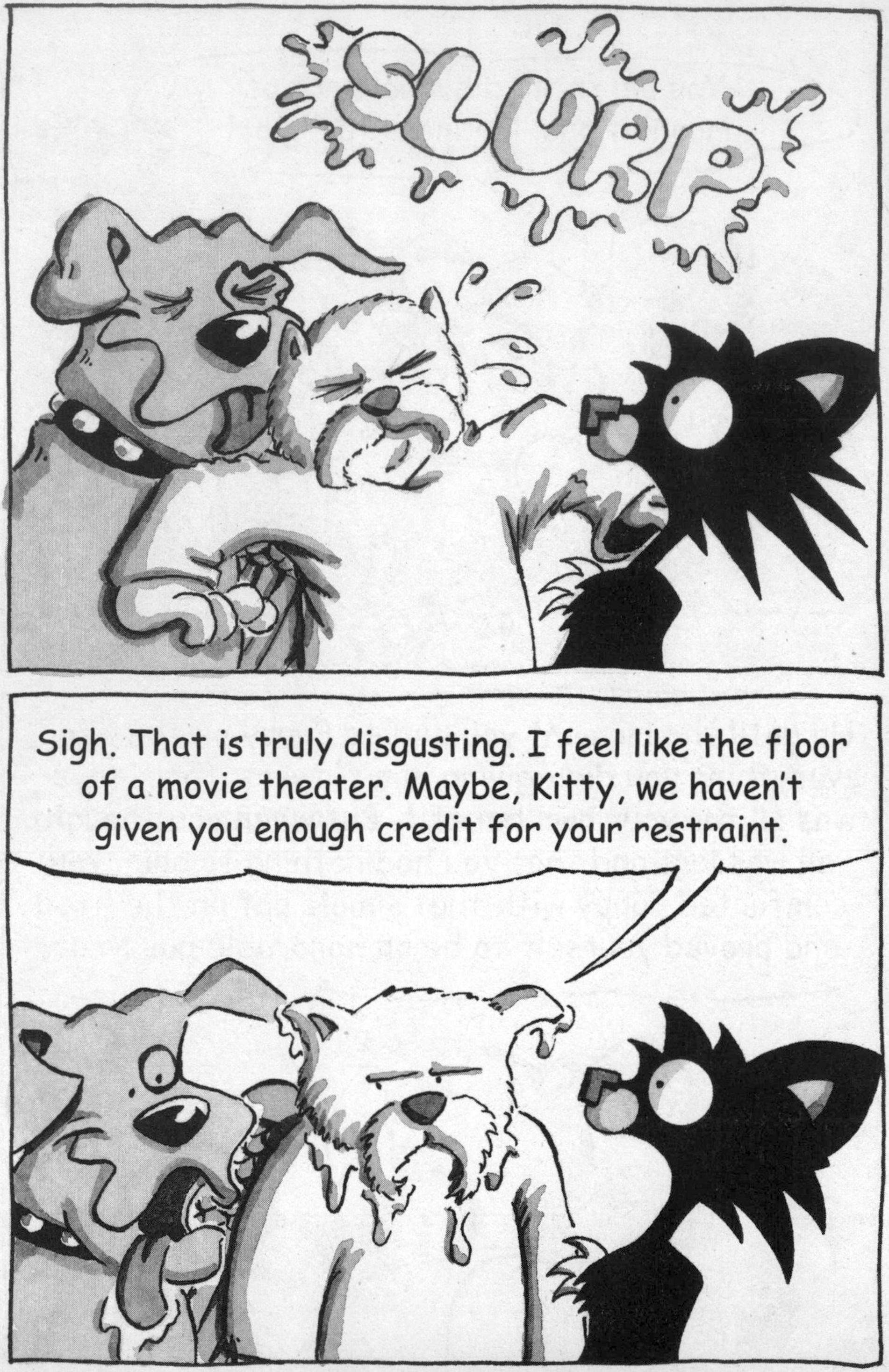
SLURP
Sigh. That is truly disgusting. I feel like the floor of a movie theater. Maybe, Kitty, we haven't given you enough credit for your restraint.

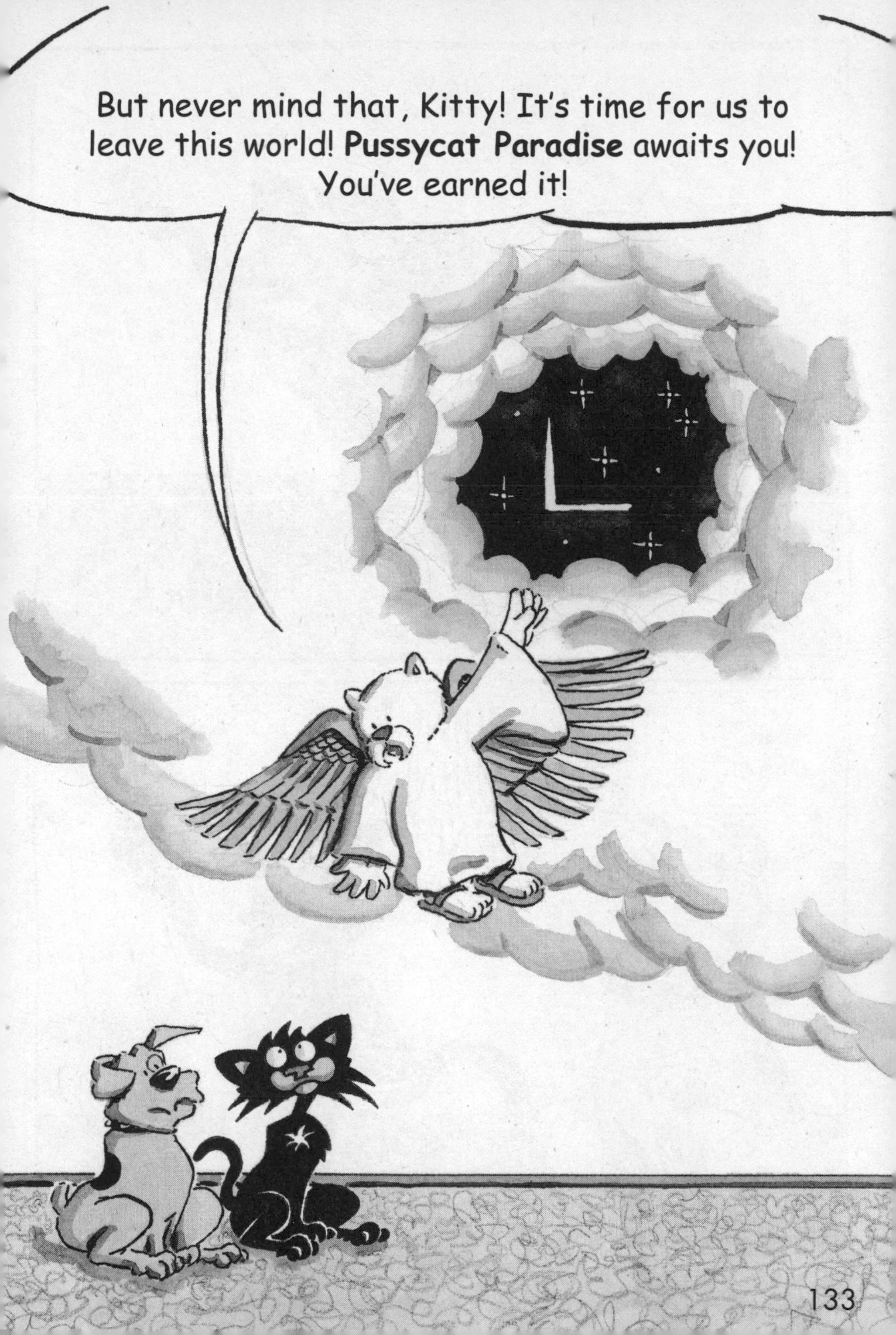
But never mind that, Kitty! It's time for us to leave this world! **Pussycat Paradise** awaits you! You've earned it!

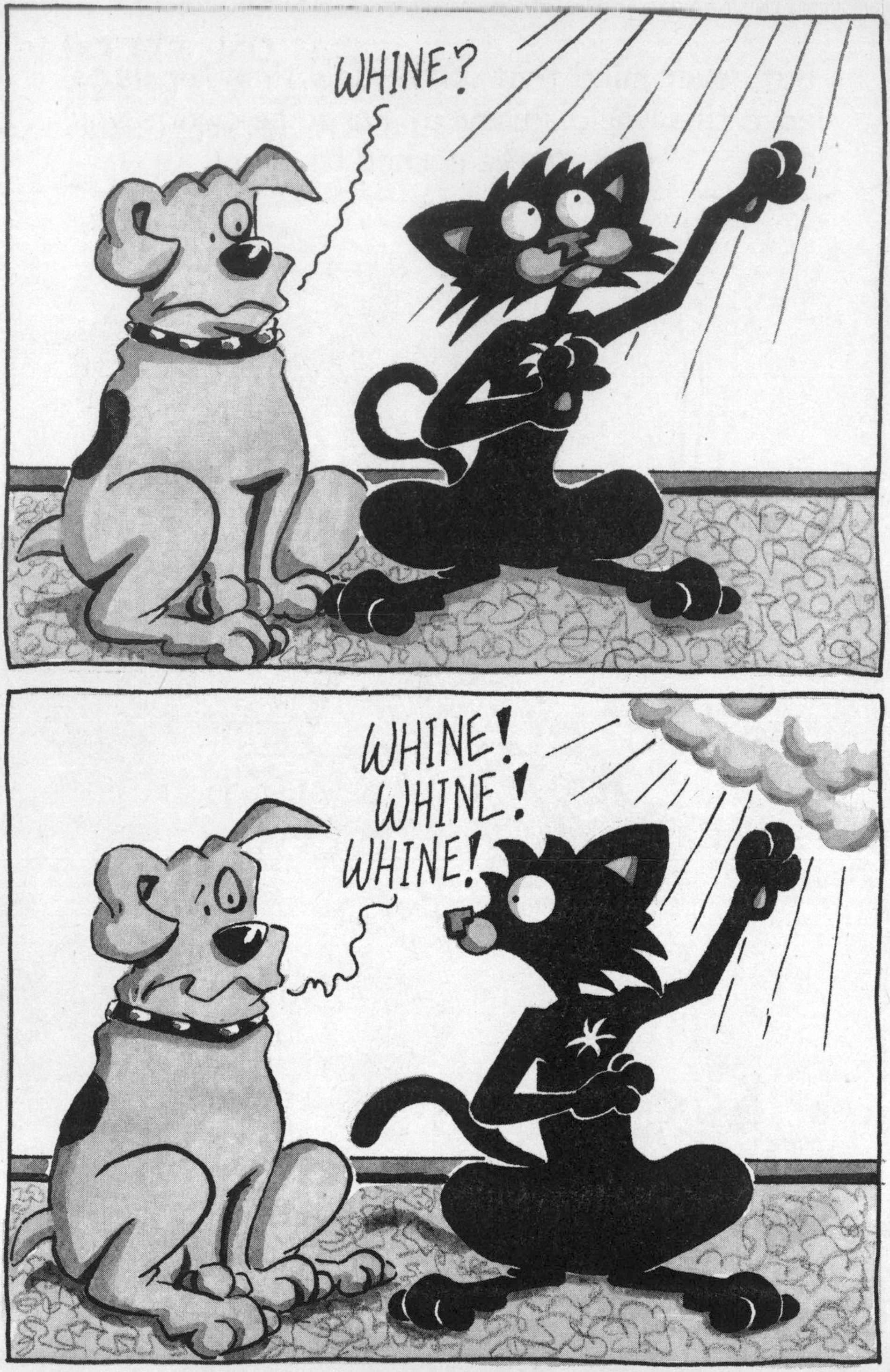
WHINE?
WHINE!
WHINE!
WHINE!

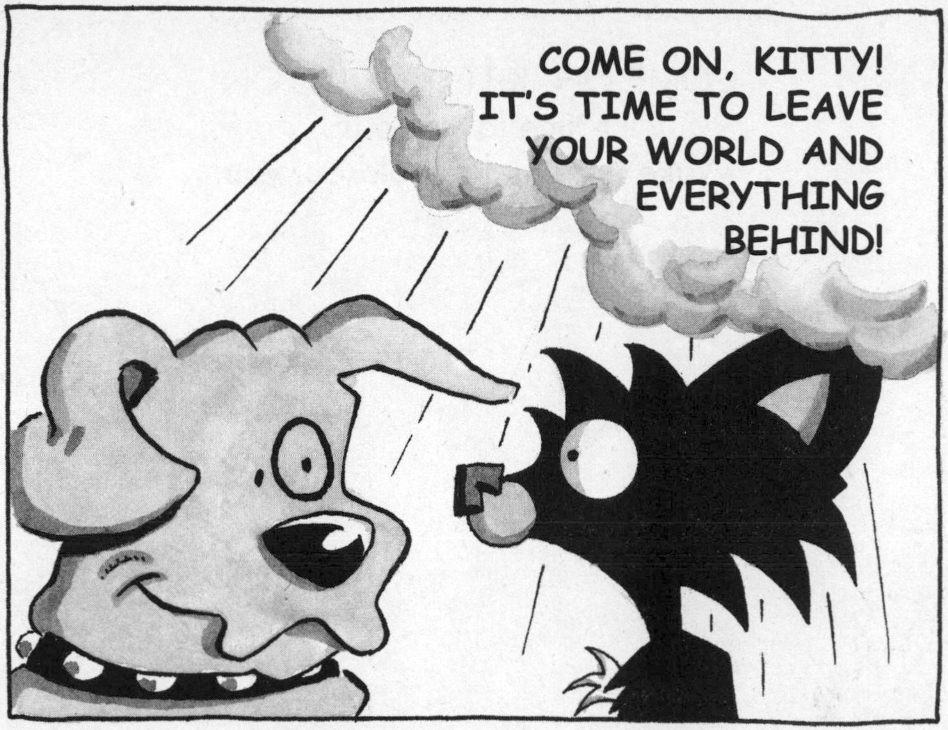
COME ON, KITTY! IT'S TIME TO LEAVE YOUR WORLD AND EVERYTHING BEHIND!

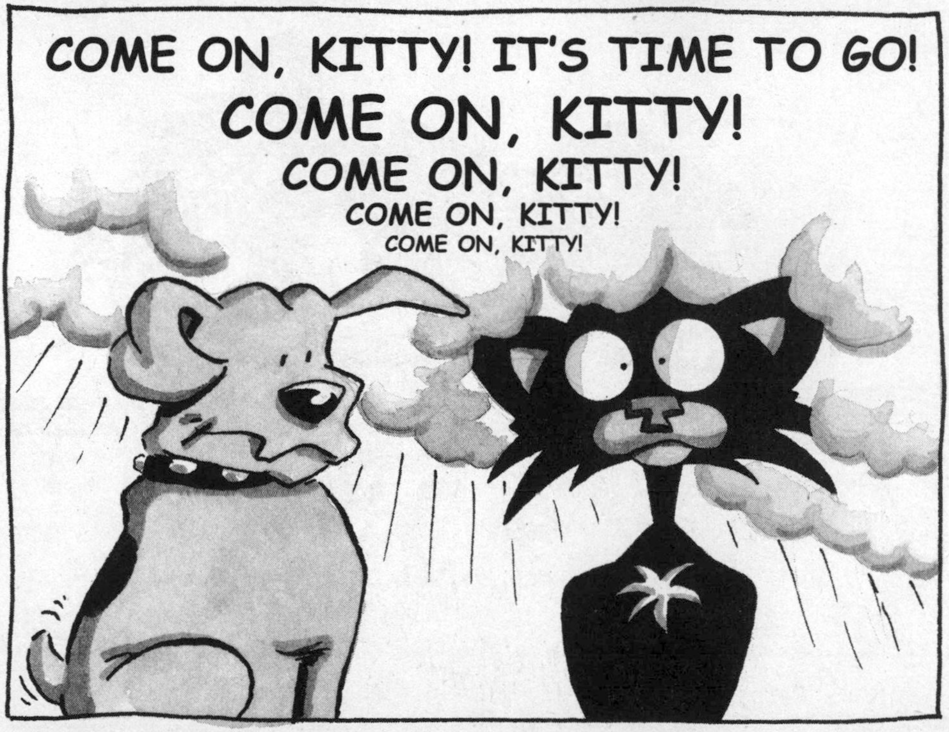
COME ON, KITTY! IT'S TIME TO GO!
COME ON, KITTY!
COME ON, KITTY!
COME ON, KITTY!
COME ON, KITTY!

COME ON, KITTY! COME ON!
It's time to wake up.
Wake up, you lazy old cat you.

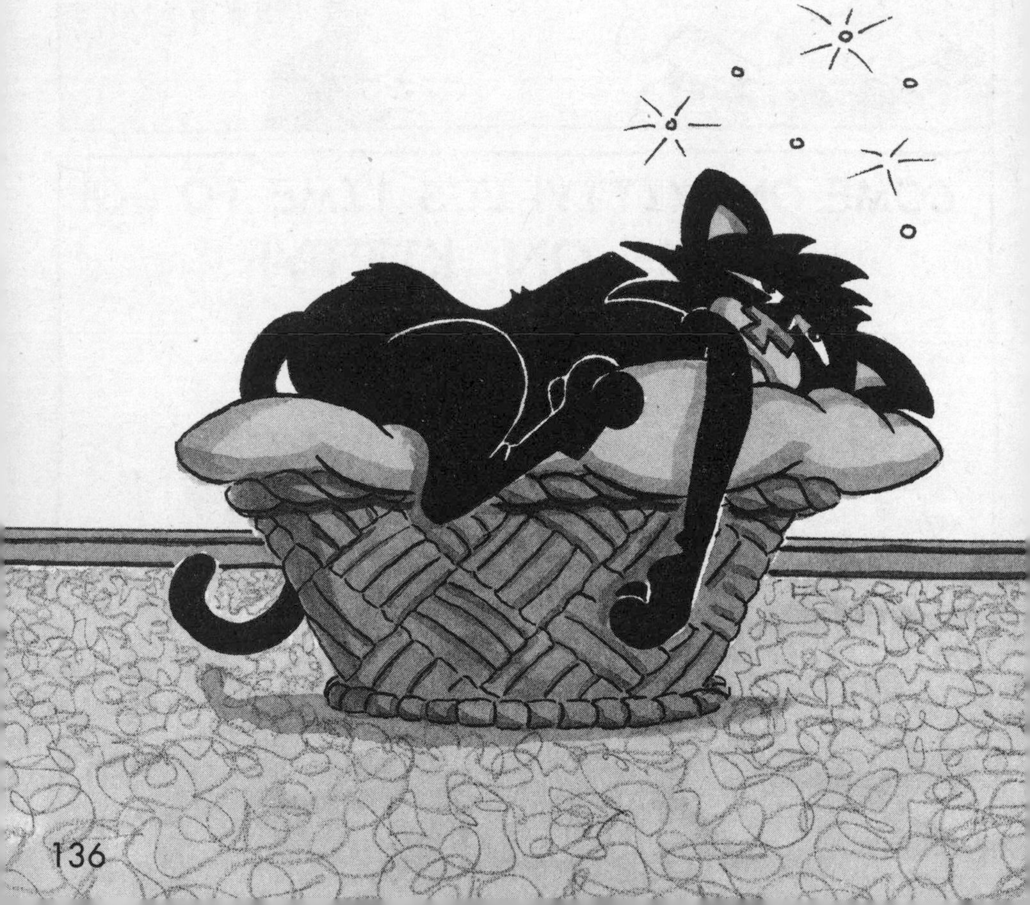

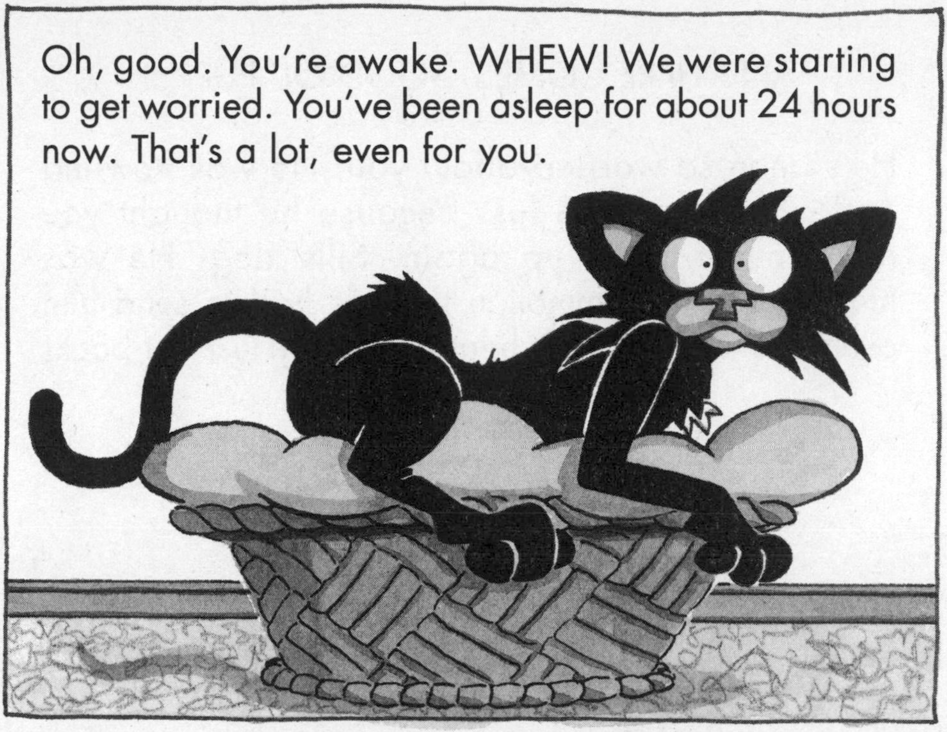
Oh, good. You're awake. WHEW! We were starting to get worried. You've been asleep for about 24 hours now. That's a lot, even for you.

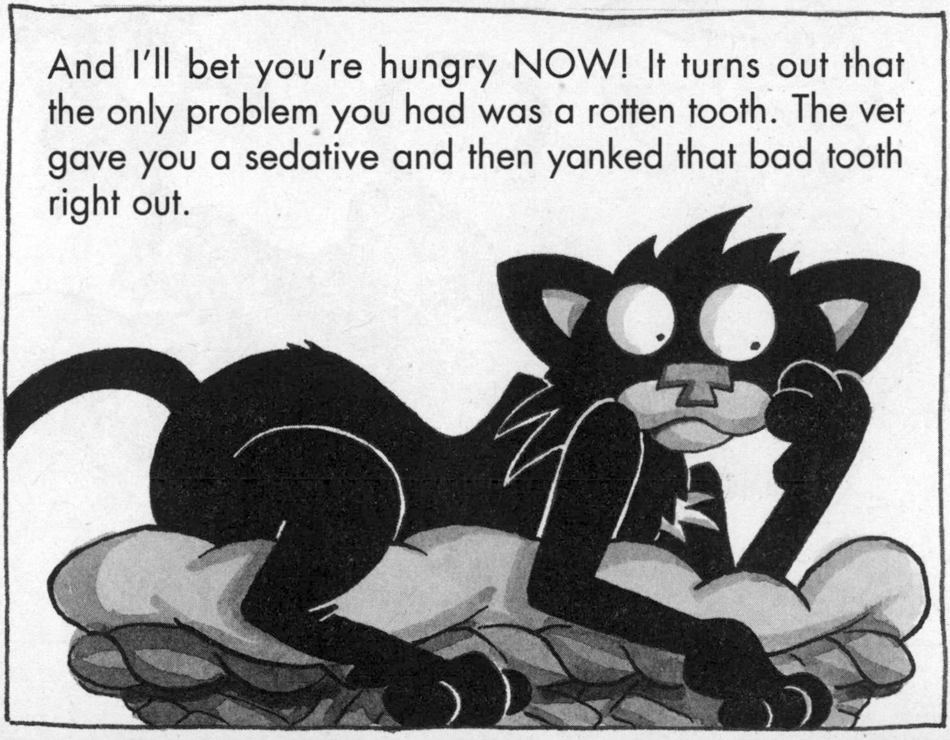
And I'll bet you're hungry NOW! It turns out that the only problem you had was a rotten tooth. The vet gave you a sedative and then yanked that bad tooth right out.

AND HERE COMES GOOD OL' PUPPY!

He's been so worried about you. He was howling and making a huge fuss because he thought you might never wake up again. Silly dog! He was making such a commotion that we had to send him over to Uncle Murray's house. He only just got back!

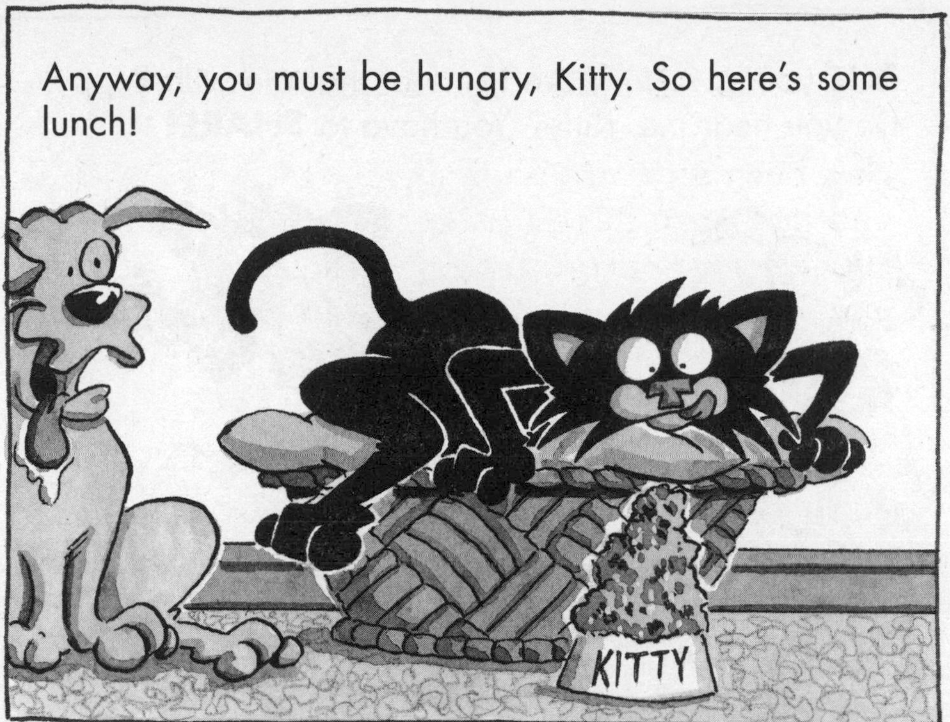
Anyway, you must be hungry, Kitty. So here's some lunch!
KITTY

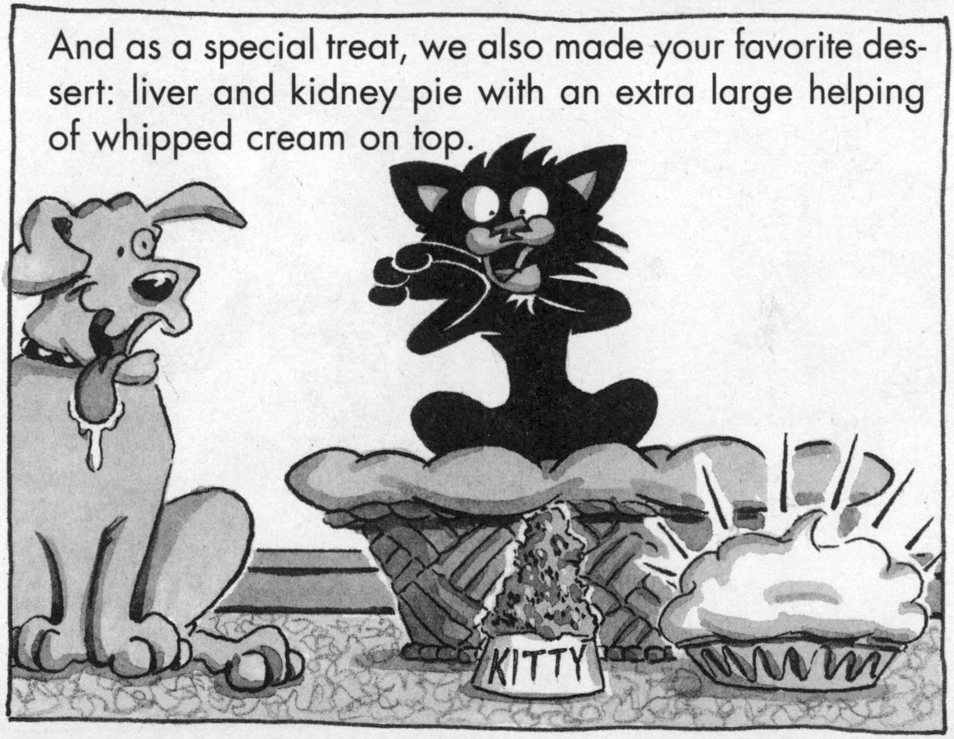
And as a special treat, we also made your favorite dessert: liver and kidney pie with an extra large helping of whipped cream on top.
KITTY

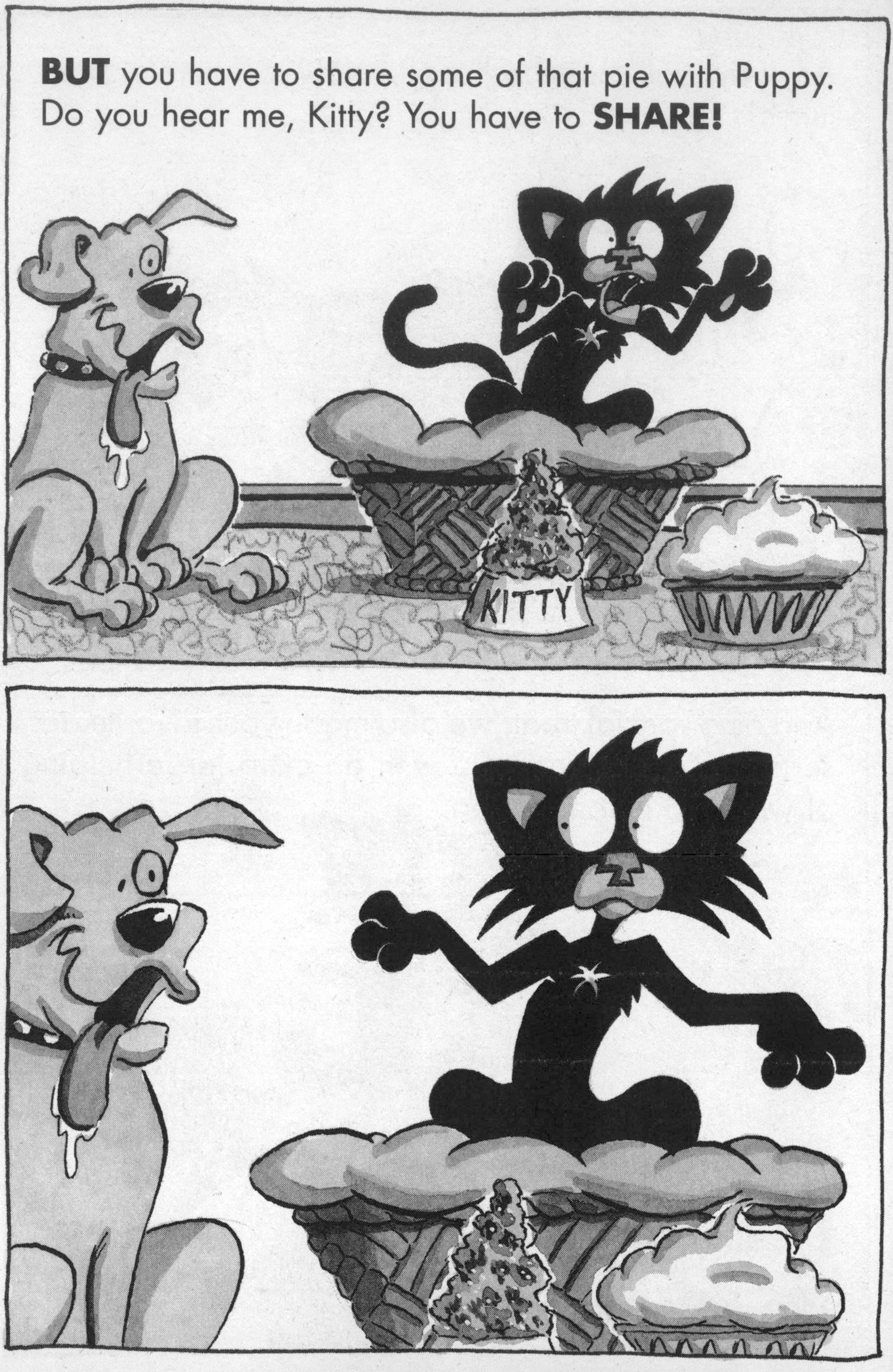
BUT you have to share some of that pie with Puppy.
Do you hear me, Kitty? You have to **SHARE!**
KITTY

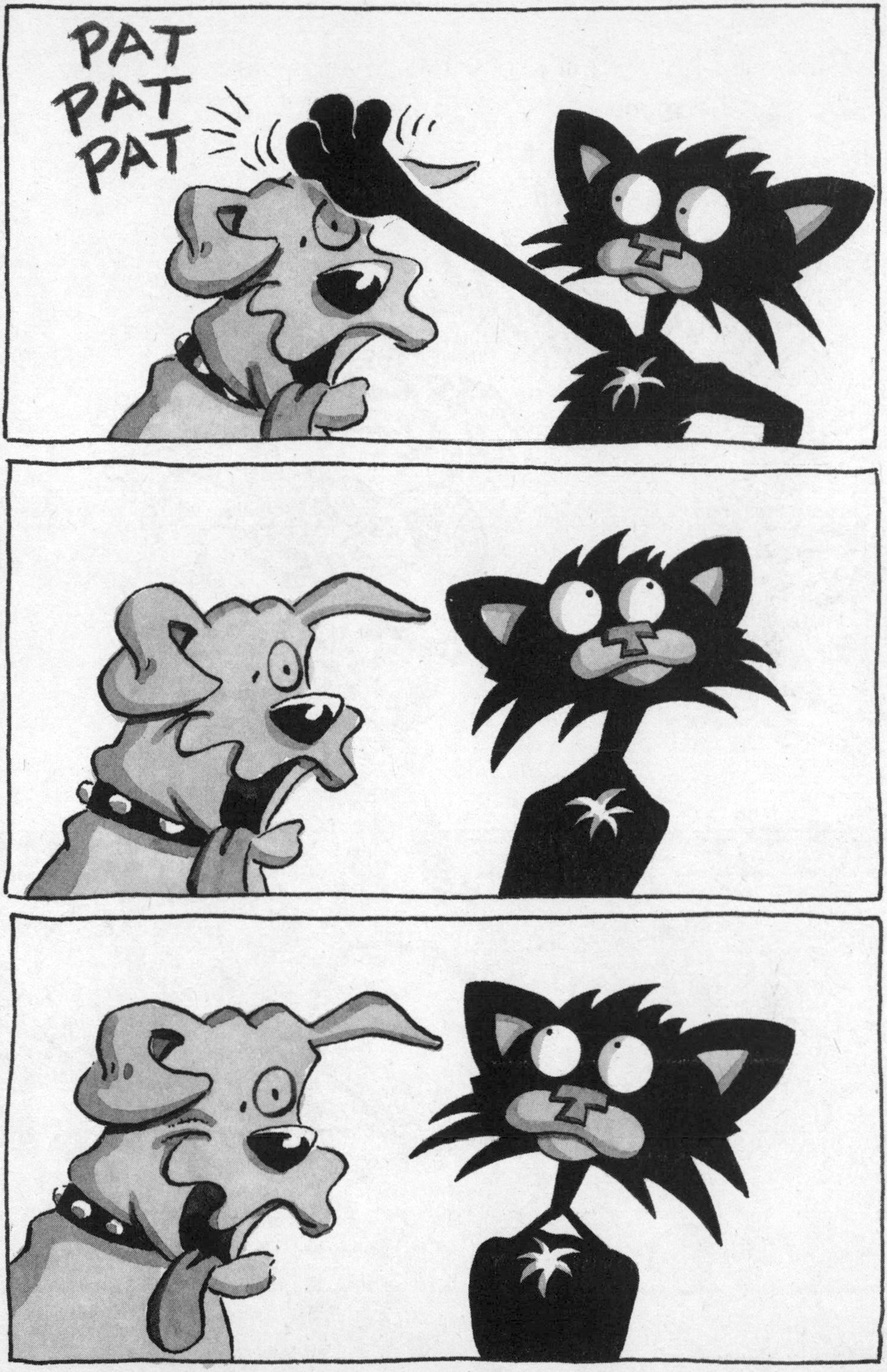
PAT
PAT
PAT

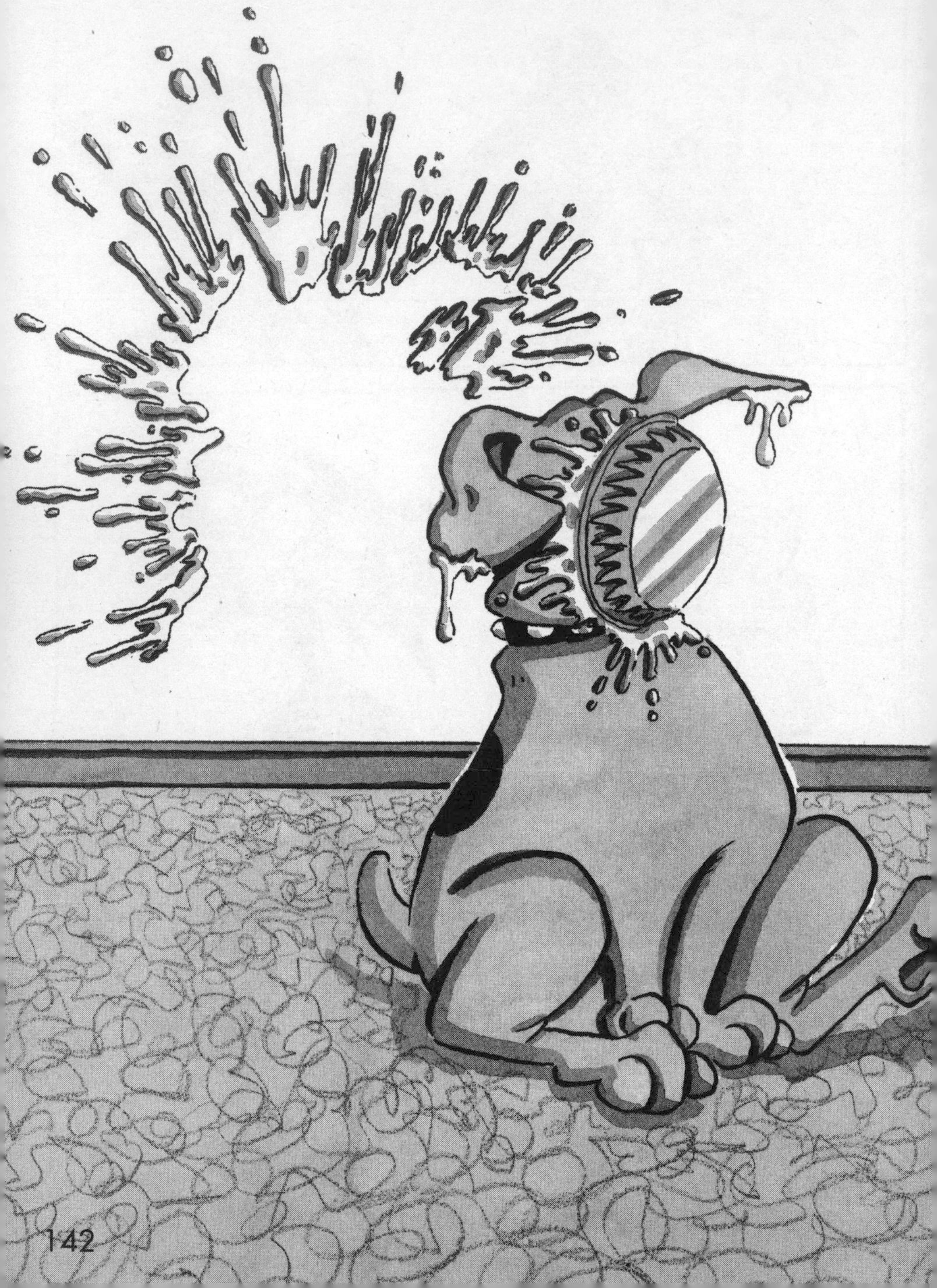

THE END

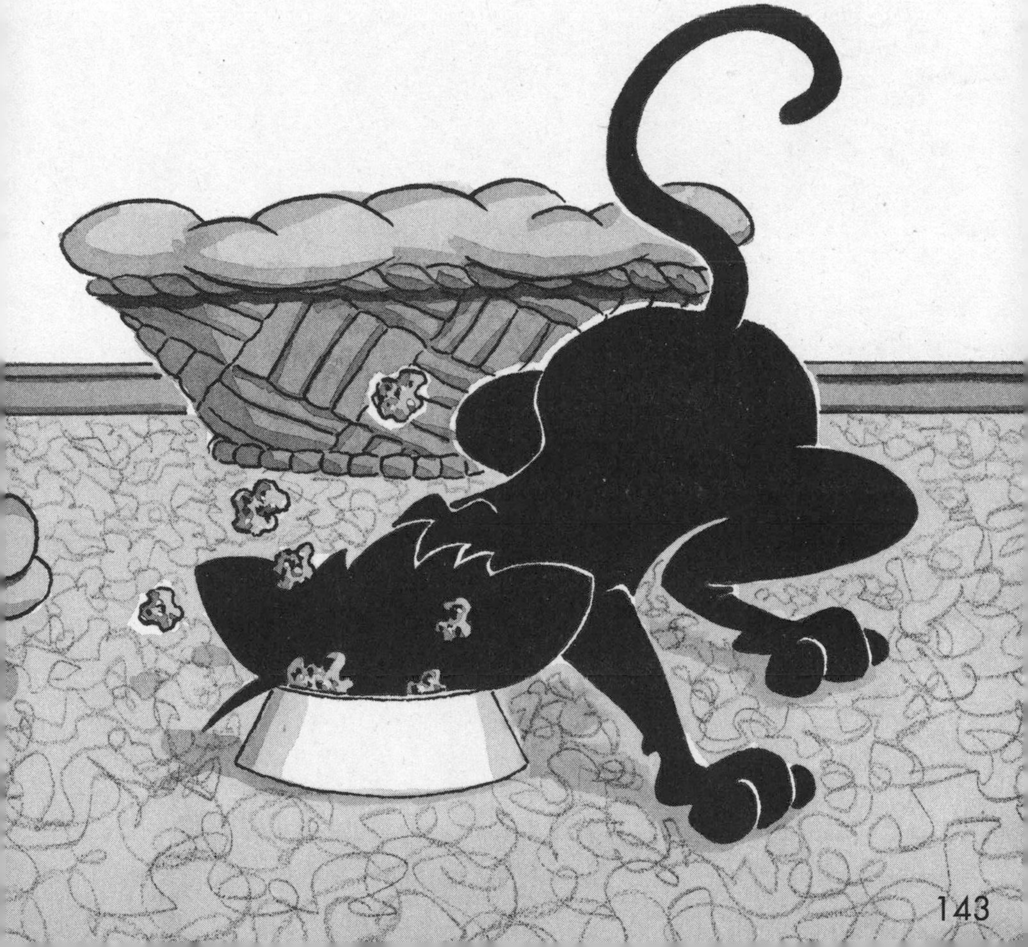

A CONVERSATION WITH NICK BRUEL

INTERVIEWED BY UNCLE MURRAY

Hi, Gang! Good ol' Uncle Murray here. You may know me as the star of books like *Bad Kitty School Daze*, *Bad Kitty vs Uncle Murray*, and now this one: *Bad Kitty Goes to the Vet*.

I thought it might be kind of fun to talk to the actual author of this book and find out what makes him tick.

UNCLE MURRAY: Hi there, Mr. Bruel!

NICK BRUEL: You can call me "Nick."

UNCLE MURRAY: That's swell. You can call me "Uncle Murray."

NICK: Well, I was going to anyway.

UNCLE MURRAY: So, I got a few questions about this book here. How did you get the idea to write this book *Bad Kitty Goes to the Vet*?

NICK: Well, it all started a couple of years ago when I had to take one of my actual cats to the vet. . . .

UNCLE MURRAY: WHOA! Hang on! You said "one of your cats." Does that mean you have more than ONE?

145

NICK: Well, yes. I have two.

[What follows is a long, uncomfortable pause as Uncle Murray stares at Nick Bruel for almost a full minute with a horrified expression on his face.]

UNCLE MURRAY: TWO goofy cats? Are you insane?

NICK: What? No. Why?

UNCLE MURRAY: ONE goofy cat is bad enough! But TWO?! What happened? Did you lose a bet?

NICK: No. Nothing like that. We just have two cats is all. Lots of people have more than one cat.

UNCLE MURRAY: [Mumbles to himself] Deranged maniacs, maybe. But not normal people.

NICK: Excuse me?

UNCLE MURRAY: Nothing. Nothing. Let's move on. You were saying that you had to take one of your goofy cats to the doctor?

NICK: That's right. She stopped eating one day. And you know cats; they LOVE their food.

UNCLE MURRAY: Boy, do they ever.

NICK: Just the day beforehand, Esme—that's her name—was eating just fine, but all of a sudden she stopped. Well, this really concerned me. I had no idea what the problem was. All I knew for certain was that there WAS a problem and that the solution lay in my taking her to the vet.

UNCLE MURRAY: Easy enough, right?

NICK: Well, no. Even though Esme clearly wasn't feeling well, she still put up a real battle before getting into her carrier. She's always hated that carrier. I managed to contain her inside my office, but I still had to chase her all over as she ducked under furniture and leaped over my desk and tried to hide inside my cabinet.

UNCLE MURRAY: See! That's what I'm talking about! All you're trying to do is take her to the doctor, and she's acting like you're going to feed her to the lions! Dogs don't do this! Dogs trust you and don't try to turn every little thing into the Battle of Gettysburg. Dogs don't . . .

NICK: Can I finish?

UNCLE MURRAY: Sorry. Sorry. Sometimes I get a little . . . Sorry. Go on.

NICK: So, anyway . . . Eventually, I managed to trap her inside my cabinet. I grabbed her as quickly as I could and took her to my vet, Dr. Reinemarie Willimann at Veterinary Care of Mt. Pleasant. When I saw how expertly she was able to handle my fierce little cat after I had so much trouble, I knew there was a story in this experience somewhere.

UNCLE MURRAY: Did Esme get better?

NICK: You ask that like you really seem to care, Uncle Murray.

UNCLE MURRAY: Hey, cats may drive me nutso, but I'm still an animal lover.

NICK: She did. She got better. And her problem was the exact same one Kitty has in this book.

UNCLE MURRAY: No way!

NICK: Way.

UNCLE MURRAY: And when did you decide that I should star in this book?

NICK: Well, I always try to find something for you to do in my stories, Uncle Murray. You've got a pretty fun personality to write about.

UNCLE MURRAY: Hey, you want to hear a great idea for the next book you should write?

NICK: Uh . . . sure.

UNCLE MURRAY: You should make a book about me fighting zombie vampires on another planet in the far future. I'll ride a giant pterodactyl named Philip who breathes fire . . . no, wait . . . he breathes powerful lasers that blind the werewolf pirates who kidnapped the princess! You should write that!

NICK: Well, I don't know. I think it's a terrific idea,

Uncle Murray. But it is YOUR idea. I think you should write that story yourself.

UNCLE MURRAY: Me?! Nah. I'm not a fancy author like you.

NICK: Why not? You came up with a terrific idea all by yourself. Why can't you write the story?

UNCLE MURRAY: Gosh. You really think so? You know what . . . I'll do it. I'm going to write that story. What have I got to lose? Nothing. That's what.

NICK: Plus, it'll be fun! It'll be hard work. But it will be fun, too. I should know.

UNCLE MURRAY: Gee, it's been great talking to you, Nick Bruel. I'm going to go write my story. You should probably get back to work making more books about that goofy cat. Let's do this again sometime.

NICK: I'm looking forward to it, Uncle Murray. Looking forward to it.

Bad Kitty's about to take the most important test of her life!

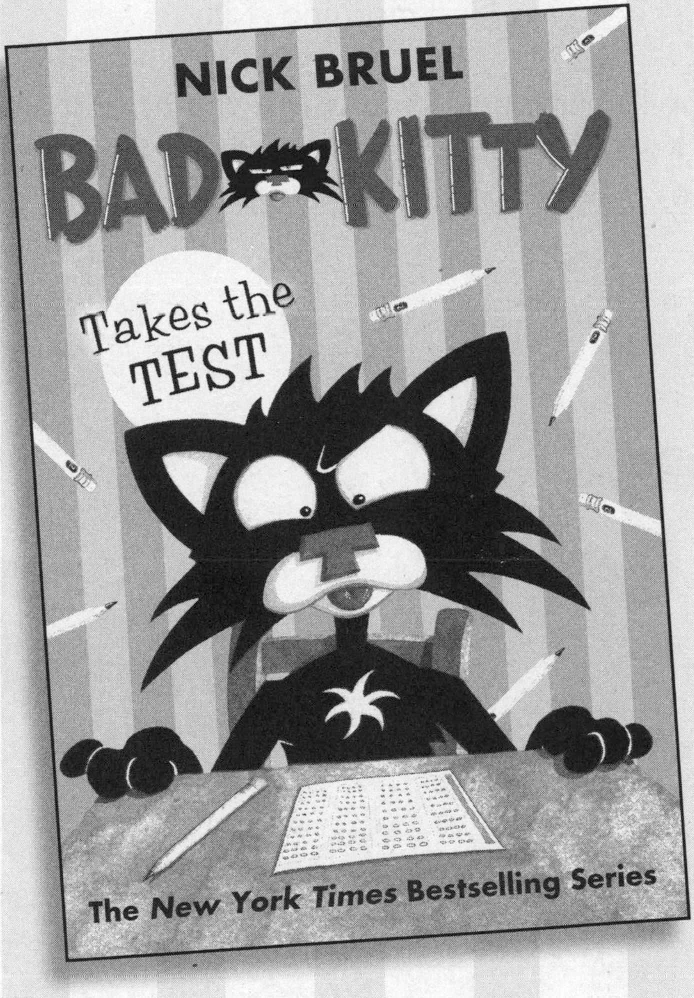
NICK BRUEL
BAD KITTY
Takes the TEST
The New York Times Bestselling Series

Keep reading for an excerpt.

Good morning, Kitty.

The mail's here, and it looks like you have a certified letter from the Society of Cat Aptitude Management. I've never heard of them. Have you?

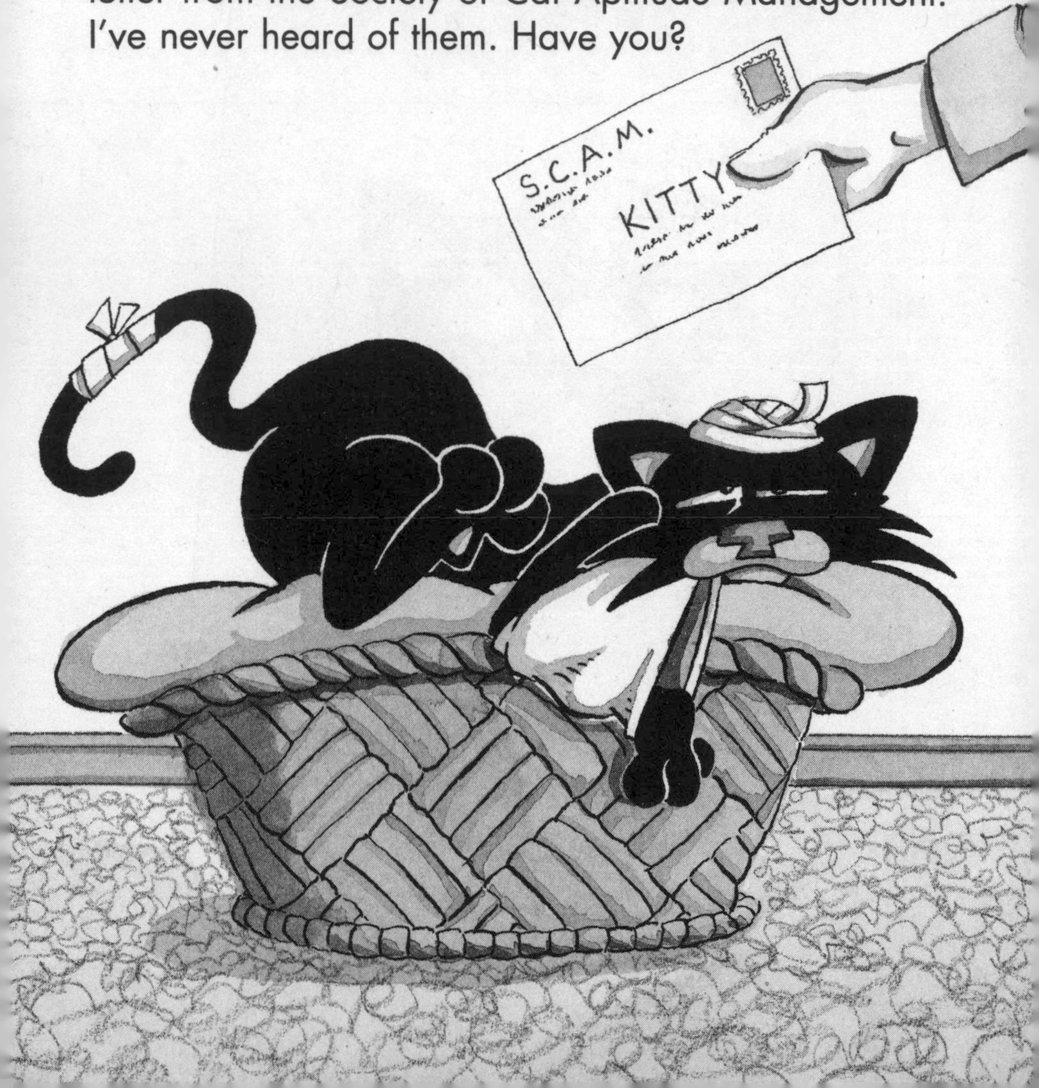
S.C.A.M.
KITTY

Uh-oh. This doesn't look good.

It looks like they know about your run-in with those birds yesterday. Apparently it's considered the most recent instance in a long line of "shameful un-catlike embarrassments." Others include the time you . . .

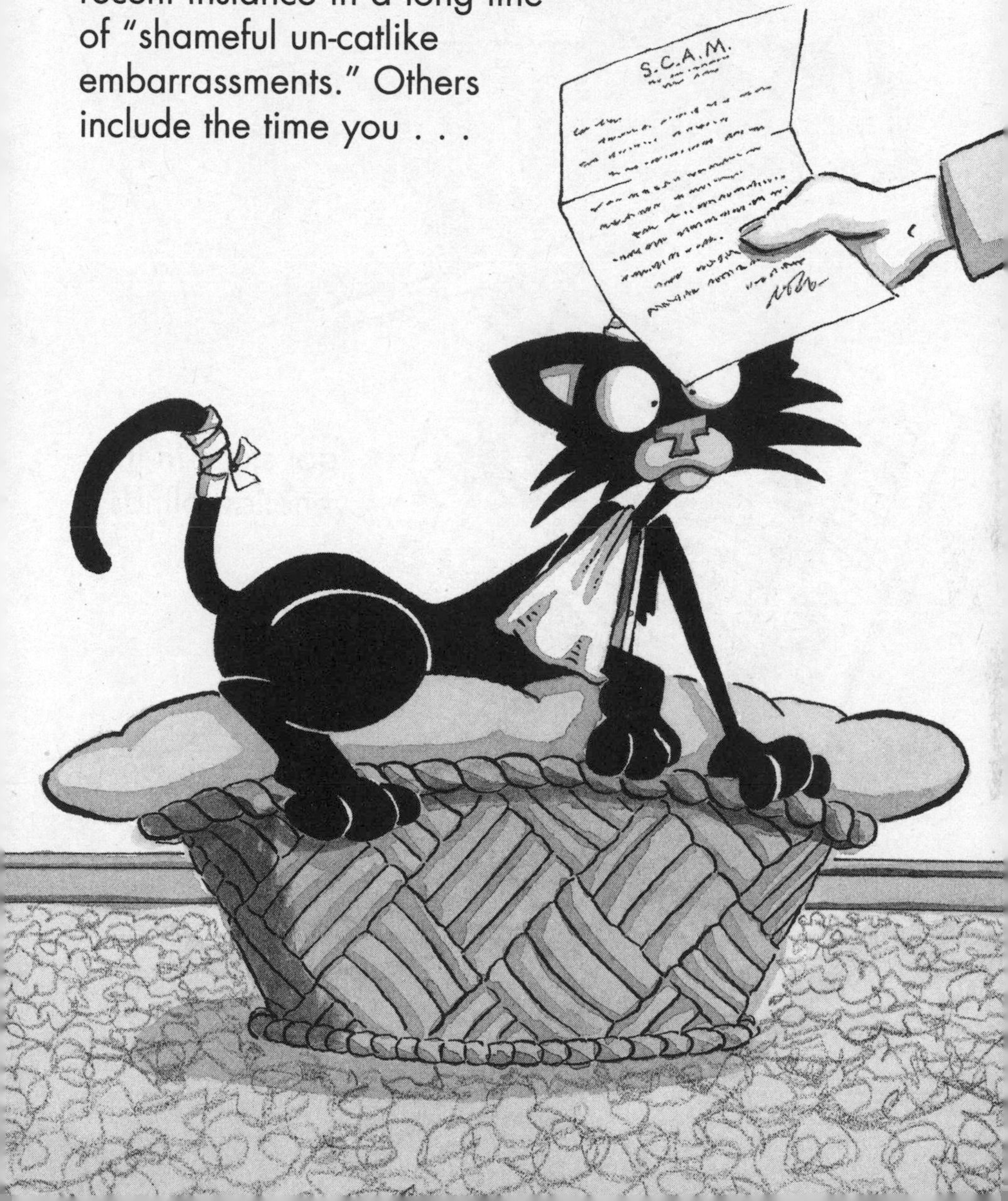
S.C.A.M.

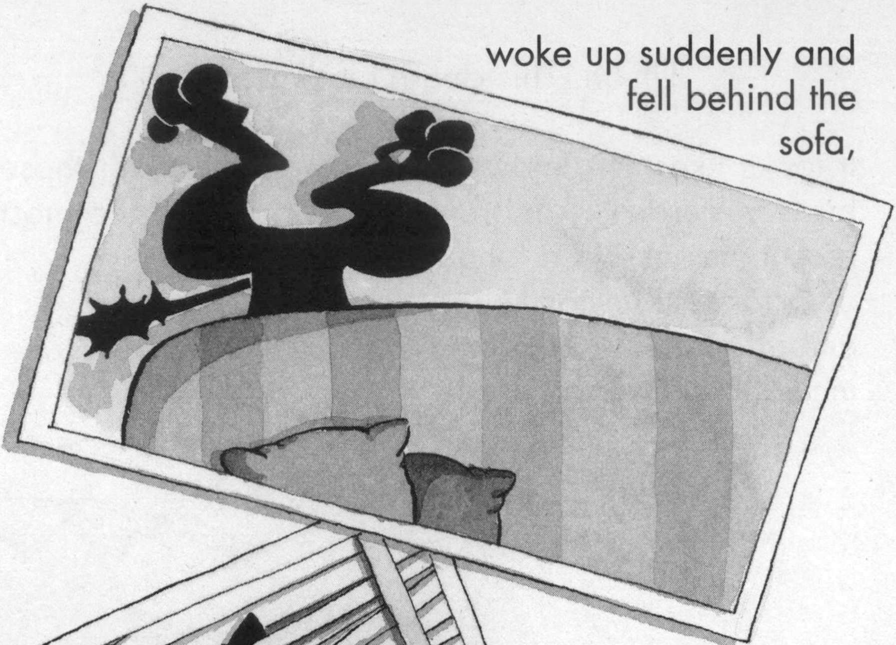

woke up suddenly and
fell behind the
sofa,

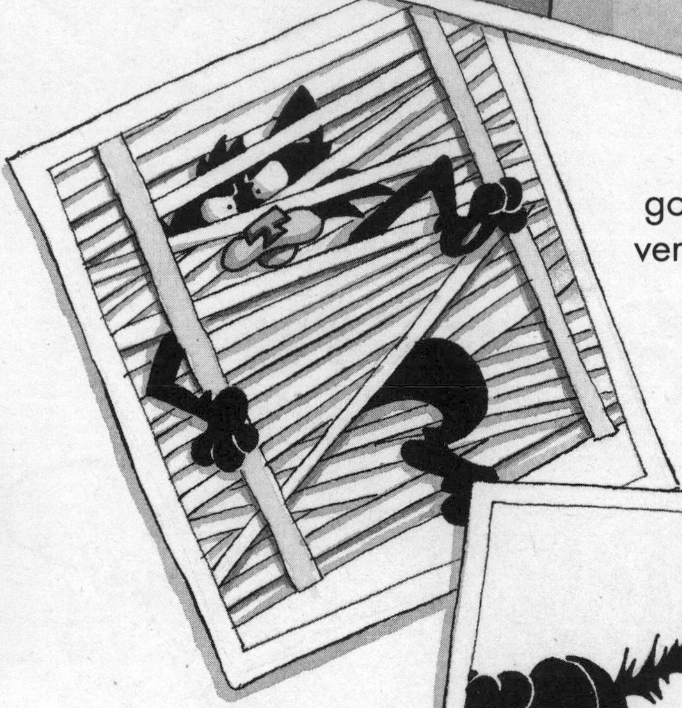

got stuck in the
venetian blinds,

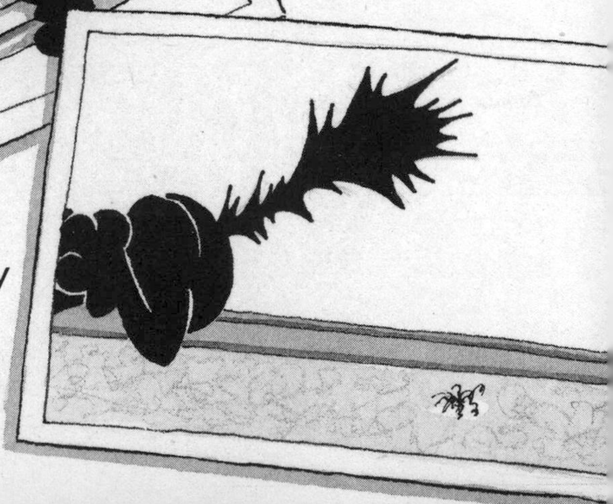

were frightened by
a spider, which
turned out to be
a ball of lint,

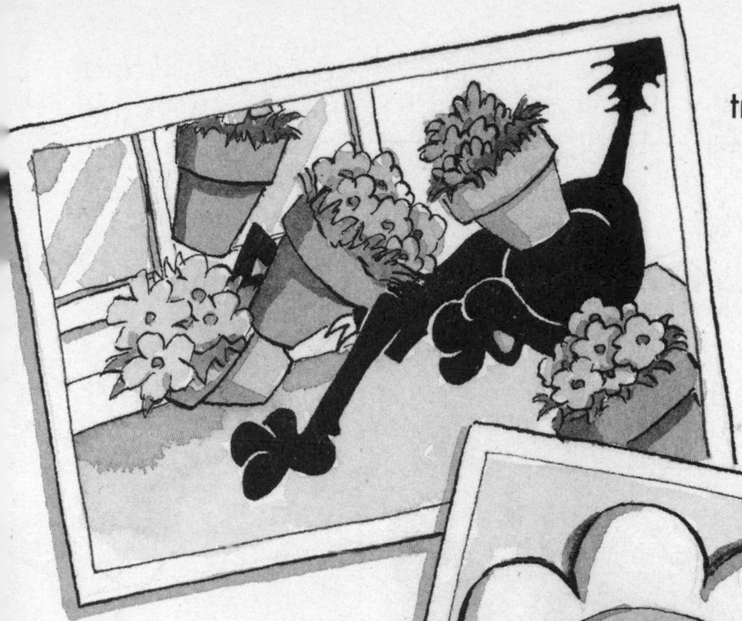

tried to jump
on the desk
but landed
in the
plants,

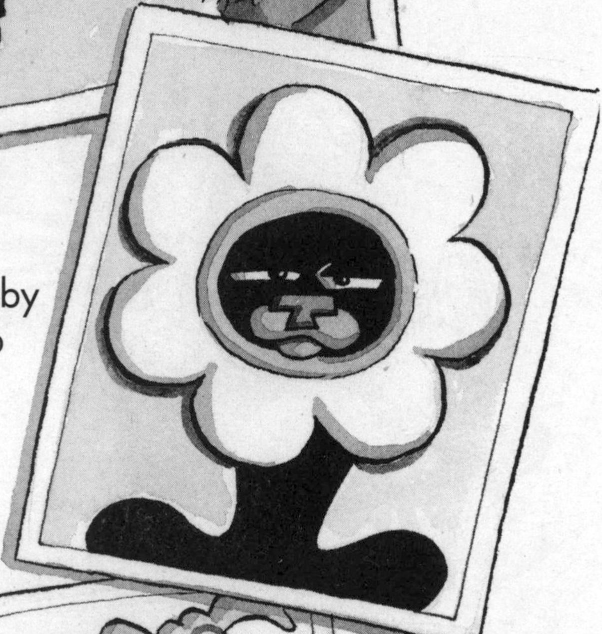

allowed the baby
to dress you up
for Halloween,

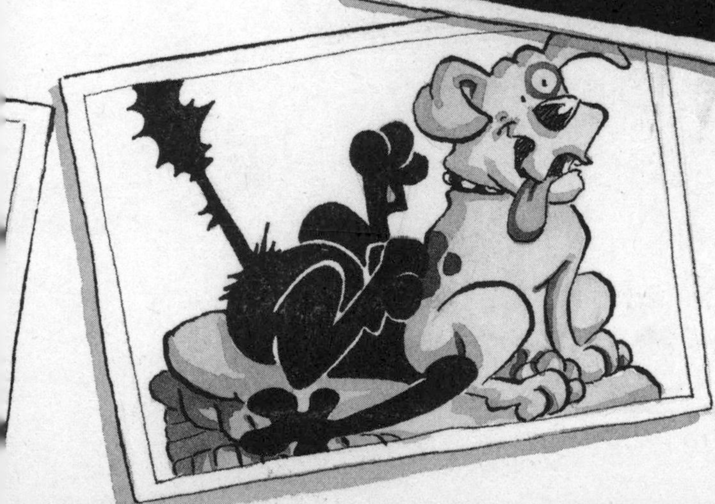

and let the
dog sit on
you while
you were
sleeping.

So apparently because of this recent string of embarrassing behavior, your cat license has been REVOKED.

I didn't even know there was such a thing.

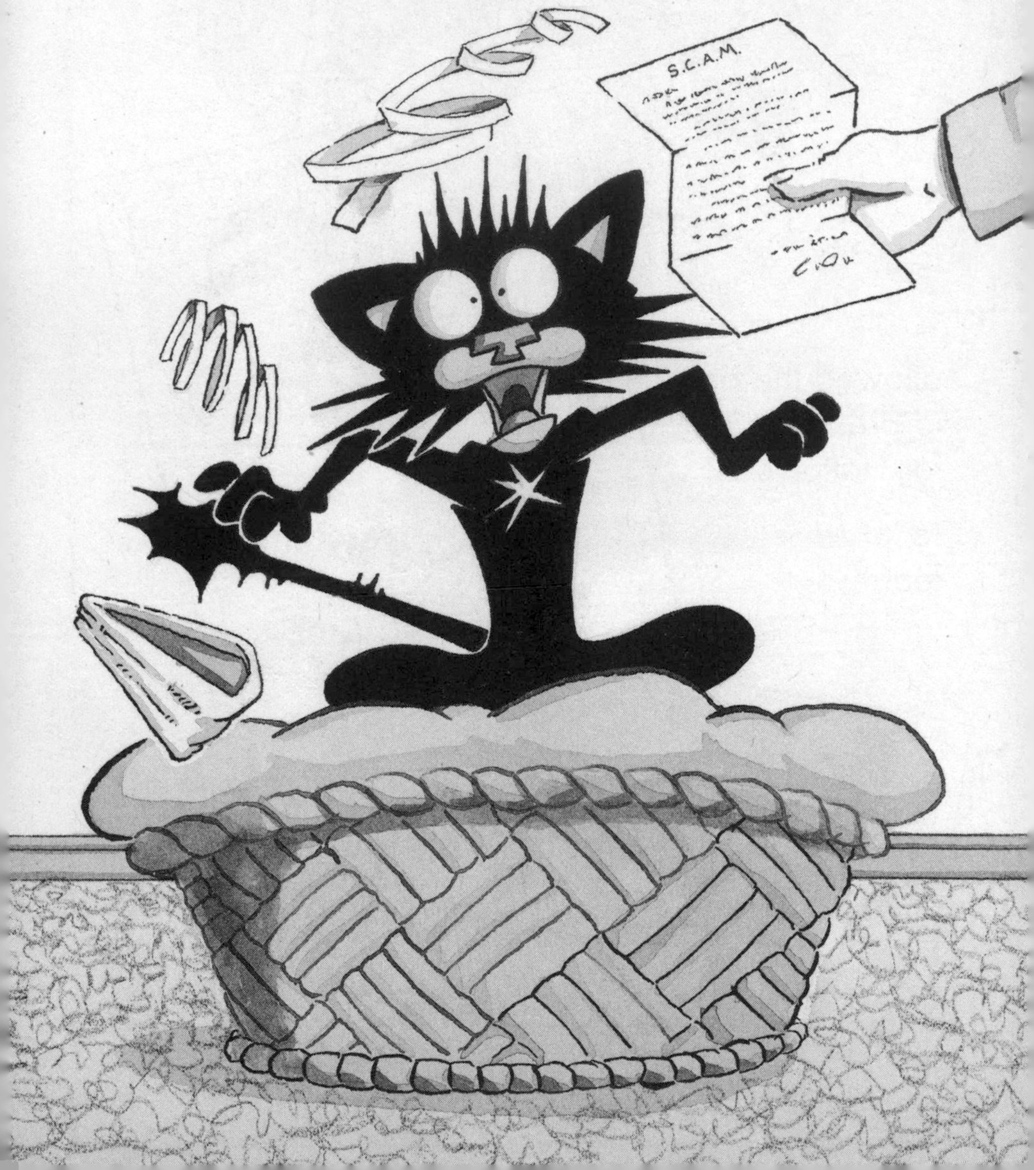
S.C.A.M.

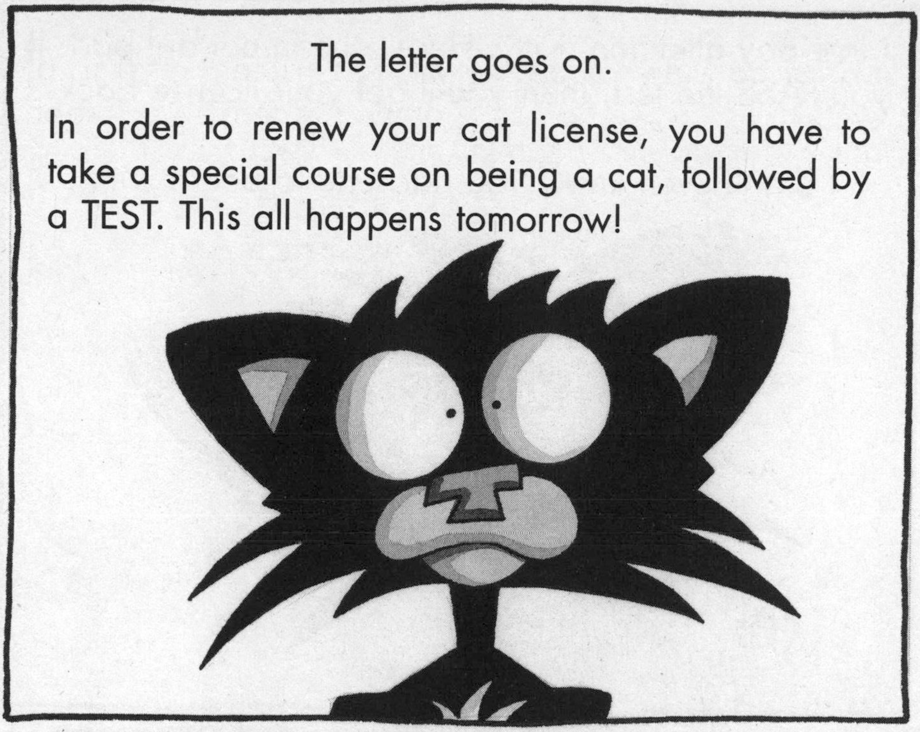
The letter goes on.
In order to renew your cat license, you have to take a special course on being a cat, followed by a TEST. This all happens tomorrow!

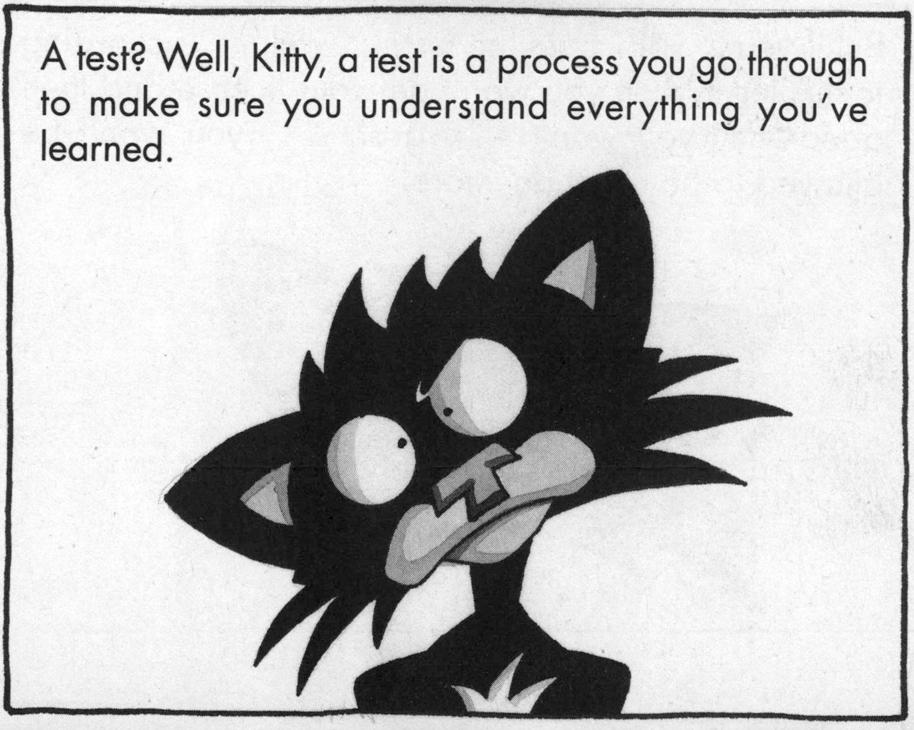
A test? Well, Kitty, a test is a process you go through to make sure you understand everything you've learned.

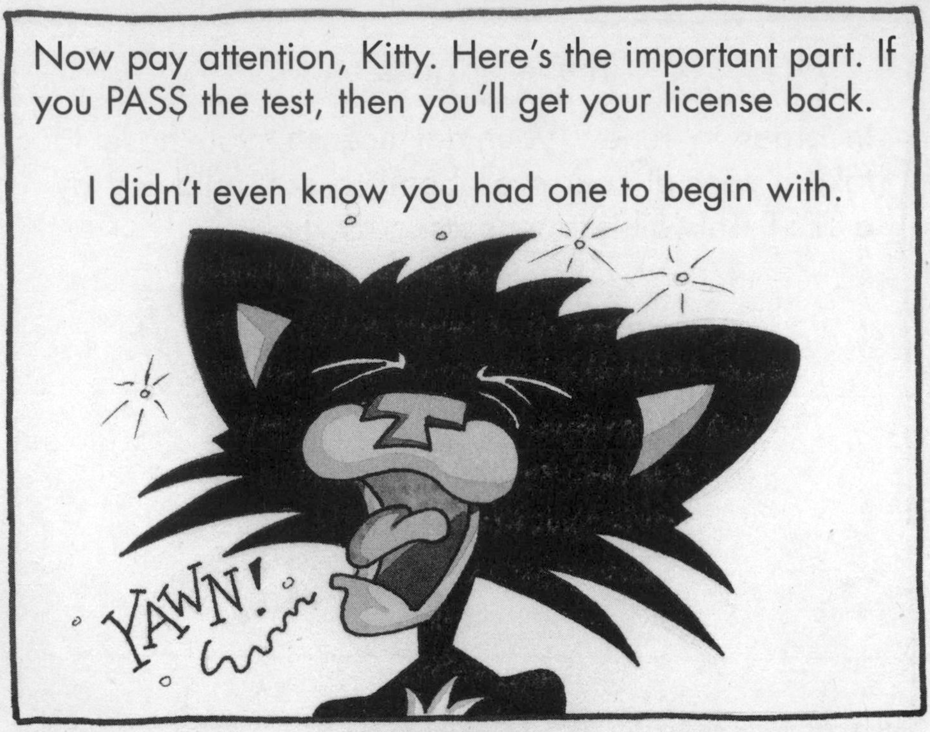
Now pay attention, Kitty. Here's the important part. If you PASS the test, then you'll get your license back.
I didn't even know you had one to begin with.
YAWN!

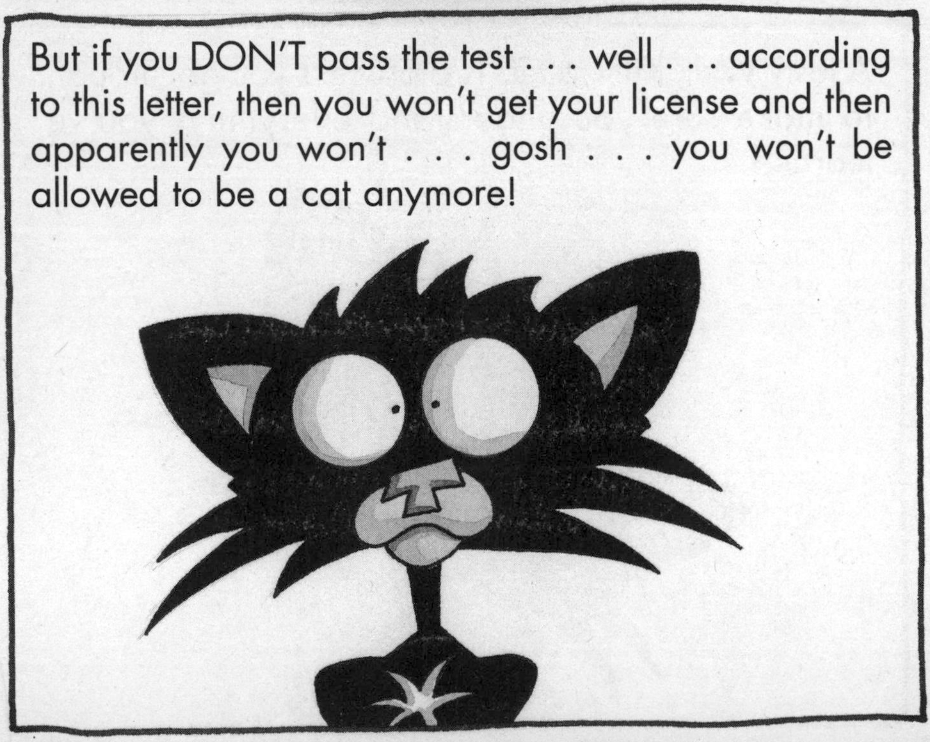
But if you DON'T pass the test . . . well . . . according to this letter, then you won't get your license and then apparently you won't . . . gosh . . . you won't be allowed to be a cat anymore!